FLAMES OF ATTRITION

THE UNREMEMBERED KING

BOOK TWO

VANESSA MACLAREN-WRAY

Published by Water Dragon Publishing
waterdragonpublishing.com

ISBN 978-1-959804-90-1 (Trade Paperback)

10 9 8 7 6 5 4 3 2 1

FIRST EDITION

For my dad, who served in Korea, Vietnam, and NATO
And for my Uncle Red, who served in France and Italy
And for my Uncle Bob, who served in the Pacific
You couldn't tell me your war stories, so I made one up for you.

FOREWORD

The Unremembered King is a two-volume story, and all the gratitude detailed in the Acknowledgments for the first volume applies equally to this one. The Morgan Hill Writers suffered through the first round of development, chapter by chapter. The East Bay Science Fiction and Fantasy Writers provided feedback to deepen the characters and realism of the story. Friends and family kept me sane, more or less. While I may not have taken everyone's advice, I'm indebted to everyone for their constructive criticisms and encouragement.

I owe much of the grounding for Corren's memoir to the hidden stories of my military-rooted family. So, I hereby digress into an essay on that topic.

My father and uncles—who saw combat of vastly different types—shared very little of the memories they had to live with, of the conflicts they endured. But they shared the surroundings to those events: their attitudes towards the country they served and the people they served alongside. So while the characters in this book are entirely fictional, these are the kind of service people they are meant to echo: patriotic (but for good reason) and skilled at war (because it's part of the job), but also egalitarian, caring, knowledgeable, funny, and complex. Flawed, in some aspects, but aren't we all? Damaged, probably, but not so you can easily see.

The way Corren tells his story—focusing on process, planning, and people—reflects the way I've received such stories. So that approach is also inevitably a product of my interpretations of hints, partial revelations, and a few accessible facts. Still, however unavoidable death and destruction may be, a war story isn't a celebration of blood and gore, it's about the people who stand for what's right against those whose ambitions create horrors, about the land and people who need defending.

My father, William G. MacLaren, Jr. (Major General, USAF) flew every military plane he could get his hands on, including spy planes, fighters, bombers, and Chipmunks. His uniform jacket proves, by the awards pinned to it, he had at least a dozen harrowing wartime stories he might have told. He kept in his office a seemingly humorous plaque, awarded by fellow pilots, that he could only have "won" by being shot down in wartime. I never heard that story, either.

However, the rest of his service was an open book. He shared stories of off-duty activities, such as meeting kids at the orphanage he raised funds for in Thailand or being teased by his comrades for spending his free time tinkering with reel-to-reel tape recorders. ("Doesn't everyone have two?") I leveraged those rare opportunities when I could watch his interactions with people under his command, in urgent and casual situations. I remember the honest respect between wing commander and airmen, attention to detail, and concern for his people's safety. He shared process knowledge, such as "The Three C's" (command, control, communication), the importance of trust, and the need to address security risks, whether due to individual vulnerabilities or system failings.

My uncles, John and Bob Logan, served in World War II on opposite sides of the world. Like their flame-haired sister Lorraine (my mother), they were dubbed "Red" by their friends, so it's good they weren't in the same service or the same theater. Might have been confusing. In later years, only John retained the nickname … and then, only with his relatives.

John E. Logan (Private, First Class, US Army) might have had some truly chilling stories to tell—he came home with a silver star (awarded for gallantry in action) and a purple heart. He would have said it wasn't anything special, that he didn't do anything anyone else wouldn't have done. (I read your commendation, Uncle Red. That's not what it says.) He was wounded, and returned to the field, because—he'd have said—why not? There was a war on. But he didn't tell those stories, and brushed off probing questions. He studied chemistry, invented a metal-plating process that he leveraged into a career, and settled into a life he chose for himself, far from those curious questions and close to the found-family he constructed for himself.

Robert L. Logan (Seaman, First Class, US Navy), dodged the whole awards business, so he could keep his war stories even more private. He'd rather talk about the time his big brother taught him how a kid could buy a bleachers ticket to see the Pirates in action and parley that into a down-front seat if you kept your eyes peeled for the ushers. He'd rather tell you about his kids—he raised six of them, shouldering the burden on his own when cancer took his wife far too soon. Or give you advice on quitting smoking. There was only one time I eked out of him a reminiscence about his time at sea. At first, he might have been describing a pleasure cruise, sailing the beautiful Pacific with friends. Suddenly, a flash of memory leaked out, an instant that transformed the sailor he'd just been chatting with into a casualty. They'd been talking, sharing photos and family news, and then … and then …

"Great guy," my uncle said. "He was a great guy." Seventy years later, he'd been plunged back into that moment. It might have just happened. You could see it in his eyes, hear it in his voice.

"Did I tell you about the time me and Red went to the game?"

"Yeah, Uncle Bob. But tell me again. I want to hear it again."

Vanessa MacLaren-Wray
June 6, 2023

FLAMES
OF
ATTRITION

PEOPLE OF JESKA

The people in my life, and what was up with them when the war started. You think you remember it all? Then skip it. Come back here at need.

· · ·

Essential people to know about, although most of these guys are dead:

Orkast: my true-father, armorer, shaman, explorer of thin patches and the worlds they lead to. Dead for years, since my first command.

Yutek of Jeska: twenty-first king of the Unified Districts of Jeska, my adoptive father. The condors are still picking at his bones. I miss him.

Yutek the Younger: son of Yutek, deceased. He did one good thing for Jeska: he dropped dead. I had nothing to do with it.

Tymon: foster-son of Yutek, my brother, senior member of Runners' House Jeskaryan. A few months ago, he suddenly retired, withdrew all his funds, and bought an apprenticeship with the shamans of Lakeside. Why? You tell me. Well, there was that incident where I caught him in bed with my wife.

Me: Corren, son of Orkast, adopted son of Yutek. Served at NeverSnows (don't ask), led the forces at Heart's Bend, survived a turn as Governor of Lakeside. Invested and soon to be installed as king, but only for the duration of the war, thanks to rumor-mongering traitors.

· · ·

I left family behind in Lakeside District when the runner arrived with the news Yutek had died. I'm trusting them to lie low, let the invaders pass by, stay safe. Keep in mind that hiding wouldn't be typical behavior for any one of these people.

Kul: one of the six men who've been with me since my first command. Fast and smart, strong as a bear, my right-hand man. He's supposed to be escorting my wife and son back to Jeskaryan, posing as my brother-in-law.

Heyliannin: the aforesaid wife, also called Ta-ma. Thin-patch traveler, Orkast's heir-designate, which makes her a shaman, technically. Almost married to Tymon, until she learned more about the ways of runners. Investigator of corruption in Lakeside. She's pregnant, but the two of us know it's Tymon's child, not mine.

Calestinise: my seniormost foster-son, trapper, lady's-maid, spy. He's a girl-looking boy, and don't you dare forget to call him by the right words.

•　　　•　　　•

Another clutch of the missing—my friends, longtime comrades-in-arms, and essential associates. I need these guys with me in Jeskaryan. Yesterday.

Case: our troop's expert on brews of all kinds, he had been leading an under-the-covers investigative party down the west side of the Great Lake. His crew should be on their way here now, if they got my message about Yutek's death.

Stevvin: my middle foster son, stableboy, humorist, spy, sports enthusiast. Drives me up the wall, that boy. He set out to carry the news to Case's crew, the day I left Southeast Township with Harad and Radeo.

Affram: my last foster son, stableboy, serious guy, gamer. Good left hook. Comes in handy when Stevvin gets to needling him.

Karthi and **Andus:** a matched set, part of my troop from the start. Married. Rarely apart since that one time I sent them off on separate scouting runs. They never let me hear the end of that. Karthi is older, quieter, less inclined to leap into a chaotic situation than Andus, who tends to dive in with both feet. Andus carries the added burden of his brother's memory. Keev fell at NeverSnows, our first engagement. Right now, Andus is coming up with ideas we'll need for the defense of Jeskaryan and Karthi is telling him what's wrong with those schemes.

Ganderrison: midwife to my wife, general medical practitioner. She's acting as the matriarch of Case's fake spy family.

•   •   •

The essential staff I have on-hand here in Jeskaryan:

Arnim: master interrogator, one of my original troop. I've just promoted him to commander and I've got a mission for him that he won't like and I don't want to send him on.

Dramin: our troop's medic ever since NeverSnows, he's taken on liaison duties to the Council of Elders during the current crisis. Raised in a medical family, he knows how to talk to the matriarchy.

Radeo: originally one of Ta-ma's bodyguards, great field cook. We posed as cousins all summer, and now he thinks he can tell me what to eat, when to rest. He's old enough to be my father and sometimes acts like it.

Harad: Radeo's partner. He's been acting as my head bodyguard since we got back from Lakeside, but I need his brain, not his sword-arm. He spent years working for my foster-father; that head of his has a lot of good ideas in it.

Magaran: seniormost officer in the guard, my mentor. He's managing outbound deployments to HandOverHand right now.

Errem: career captain, bodyguard to the king (that is, me). Haven't met him yet. Well, we were in under-guards together, but that was a long time ago.

Durse: career soldier, bodyguard; that is, one of the more-competent guys who'll be following me around for the next few days. The crimp in his nose is from one of those days in under-guards—the day Yutek-en ran his blade down my back.

·　　　·　　　·

Not to leave out the villains:

Fennic: Master Shaman of Jeska, schemer, back-dealer, liar. Typical shaman. Oh, ya, right. Traitor. He's hiding down in the Shamans' House, pretending he has no idea what's going on, when his organization's been funding the rising insurrection for years now.

Racac: Master Shaman of Lakeside. Traitor, sellout, conniver, child abuser, profiteer. Also, liar and thief. He's teamed up with the invading Southerners, including kidnapping Lakesider kids and turning them into fanatic soldiers.

Velisennin: leading manager of Southeast Township (home of Shamans' House, Lakeside), conniver, supporter of the insurrection. Certainly up to no good. Probably not in on the child-soldier scheme. Figure on her killing someone when she finds out.

·　　　·　　　·

People—and others—you'll hear references to and shouldn't feel you have to ask someone about:

Asdyel: thin-patch-hopping mantle creature, originally my father's; now belongs to my wife, but my brother has it in his hands. While the shamans have Tymon in their hands. Most people don't know the capes shamans wear are living beings.

Eldennian: the woman who should have been my wife, but refused me. Small-holding manager, event organizer. She's headed north, to keep our kid away from the war.

Deliasin: my daughter, with Eldennian, most beautiful child you ever saw or ever will.

Keev and **Shellon:** the men from our original troop who fell at NeverSnows. Keev was Andus' older brother.

Nandeen: merchant, manager's-husband, border observer, all-around good guy. He's safe down at South Point with his wife and enormous child.

Goram: Master Smith of Jeskaryan, old, old guy, good with puzzles, code-cracker. He's reading a book right about now. Not the kind of book you're thinking about. Or maybe it is.

PART I

BE PREPARED TO WAIT

1

ONE OF THE FIRST THINGS I DID when the kingship fell on me was sneak into town for a private confrontation with Fennic, Master Shaman of Jeska. The pompous bastard had little response to the clear evidence of his organization's financial misdealings, but enough to confirm his culpability in my mind. With the nation on the brink of war, dealing with the shamans' rotten connivance would have to be put off for a few days. My gut jabbed insistent reminders the thieves and liars were up to worse than redirecting funds, but what could I do? Until I could get my matriarchal bosses, the Council of Elders, to order a thorough investigation of a major guild, my hands were tied.

All the long way up the hill to the fortress, I had to fight the urge to march back down there with a dozen men and burn the Shamans' House down to its foundation. That would have put paid to the agreement I'd made with the elders, to serve as king until the war was over, and then step down. The rumors floating up from Lakeside, concocted by the shamans and their allies, the matriarchs of that restless district, had taken root in Jeskaryan.

The elders figured that if by chance I was right about the coming war, they'd need my skills. So I was useful. Temporarily.

Fine by me. There'd be time for my brother to get over his fantasy of becoming a shaman, and then Tymon could step into those boots. I'd always figured he'd make a better king than me. In peacetime, anyhow.

The next morning, Radeo dragged me out of the first decent sleep I'd had in days and demanded I eat a proper breakfast, as if we were still spying our way through the countryside and pretending to be cousins. I took my old spot at Yutek's table and picked at the meat and bread. The last time I'd sat in that place, my foster-father had been urging me to track down the corruption in Lakeside. I kept expecting him to walk in and demand to see the results of my labors.

Nothing was as it should be. Yutek dead. My wife, my closest friend, and the boy I was determined to make my foster-son hadn't made it out of Lakeside with me. I'd had to ride hard and fast when the news came. Heyliannin was pregnant—and a terrible rider in the best of times. Kul would keep her safe, but I couldn't help worrying about her. She wasn't the kind of woman to stop and think when a brilliant—to her mind—idea overtook her. Calestinise would have insisted on staying with her, even if we'd had an extra pony for him to ride. He took his job seriously, even if it was that of lady's maid to my other-world wife.

In Jeskaryan, my three closest retainers—Arnim, Harad, and Radeo—had fallen into place as my personal guards. Worse, here was Radeo, a senior captain, fetching my meals.

That wouldn't do.

I needed those men on bigger jobs.

As soon as I'd put away enough food to let Radeo believe I wouldn't starve that day, I told him to go fetch the other two in.

"But then there'll be no one at the door," he objected.

"Exactly. So go round up Yutek's bodyguards. Do they think they're on leave?"

He hesitated.

"What?"

"Arnim and Harad's been vetting them out, sir."

"Oh?"

"We had word some of 'em were not, shall we say, in line with your accession."

That was bad news. But not so bad it couldn't be fixed.

"Never mind," I decided. "Let's start scratch." I rummaged pen and ink and paper from Yutek's desk and made out a list of men I'd fought with enough to feel I could trust them. Not so much men I'd fought alongside. I chose ones I'd had disagreements with before, that we'd worked out one way or another. Men I knew. "These guys I've worked with since we were swinging wooden swords at each other in under-guards. Men who remember Yutek-en."

Radeo took the paper and turned it over in his hands. He squinted at it and his mouth turned down. "This isn't names, is it?"

He was right—it was descriptions, not names. Magaran would recognize them, that's what counted. He knew my trouble with names.

"Give the list to Magaran," I told him. *There's no excuse for a man at Radeo's level not to be able to read.* Except it was never required, was it, if you weren't training for a job in the bureaucracy, like me. "Tell him what I said. One or two may already be mustering out. Fetch them back if they're close enough."

He gave me a nod that was almost a bow and headed out. I heard Arnim's voice in the corridor and called him in. That would leave Harad cooling his heels outside the door, doing the job of a first-year guardsman. No, that wouldn't do at all.

I waved Arnim to sit opposite me, and he took Yutek's old spot with hardly a change of expression. Could always trust Arnim to stay focused on the task.

"So what do you think of the plan?" I asked him. He'd had plenty of opinions to share during last night's general staff meeting, but he wasn't the only voice in the room.

"I still think we need a three-tiered defensive line. If anything goes wrong at HandOverHand, they'll have a clear path to Jeskaryan. The fortress is defensible, but the town is weak."

"I agree."

"Really?" He stole a piece of bread off my plate. "Everyone was going along with Magaran last night. He was listing off companies and troops."

"Ya. I know. I wanted to see who listened to who."

"Eh?" He took a bite of bannock, and fastidiously brushed crumbs from his fingertips to a plate.

"Did you pay attention? Did you pick out the ones who were on your side?"

"Of course," he mumbled around the rest of the bread. "Caymer and Tamil. Aldred, maybe. He could go either way."

"You remember the stretch of the river that ducks through a series of low hills? A half-day's walk north of Lakeside City?"

"The Narrows. Locals say it floods every third year." Trust Arnim to have sat around listening to locals talk about river flooding.

"Right. I want you to set up your tertiary line there, at the Narrows. Take Caymer and Tamil, assemble a force." He nodded, his eyes glazing over in thought. I moved on to tactics. "This'll be a diversionary action, more than anything. I still think the main action will be further north. You'll need strike teams more than traditional troops. If you can cut down a fair quantity of their regulars, put the fear of battle into the hearts of the army of light, maybe what comes to HandOverHand will be manageable."

I waited to see how he'd be affected by mentioning the Lakesider kids the Southerners and their henchmen—the shamans—had stolen and indoctrinated. This wasn't a mission I wanted to put Harad on. He'd already had a bloody run-in with a mob of those mind-twisted youngsters.

Arnim's mind seemed to be on other worries. He grunted a laugh. "Almost manageable, you mean."

"No. I mean what I said." We both needed to believe this mission had purpose. "We're better organized now than we've ever been. Magaran's followed through on the plans we set in motion the past few years—the fast-action chain of command, the independent strike forces, the signaling system. Everyone's trained, even most of the reserves are up on the new structure."

He lifted one eyebrow, the elite's code for *you're having me on, right?*

I had to be honest. It made my gut feel like someone had stuck a knife about a hands-breadth from my navel. "It may be a diversion, but it'll probably be more dangerous than anything else we're looking at."

"You're sending us on a death-mission."

The knife in my gut twisted a few degrees. "It could be. That's why I'm authorizing strike teams. Use them as they've trained—harry and retreat, harry and retreat, get me?"

He nodded, his eyes narrowing as he thought on what I was planning. "Go on. There's more, isn't there?"

"Make sure the troopers know what to expect, that they've heard from Harad or Radeo. They have to be prepared to fight kids. Boys and girls. They can't be hesitating. Don't let them put down their lives because what's coming at them is the image of their little sister."

He frowned at his sticky fingers, then searched around for the hand-cloth I wouldn't have bothered with. "Sure I can't take a couple of Yutek's old bodyguards? I have a few names in mind." The last residue cleaned from his hands, he refolded the cloth.

"No," I told him.

Arnim gave me his best aristocratic eyebrow-lift, then opened his mouth to tell me about the dissenters.

"Send them to HandOverHand. Point them out to Magaran and be sure he knows who's who. Trust me, he'll assign them work they deserve." I stared at my plate, still with too much food on it. "I don't want to worry about you having the likes of them at your back."

He gave me that deceptive grin he'd use for interrogations. "I'd put 'em in front of me, Corren."

"I expect you to put 'em all in front of you, Arnim." He couldn't treat this as a game. "Be the commander I've made you, and stay alive. Promise me."

He settled his face to serious, but he didn't agree to that promise. "When do you want us there?"

"Day after tomorrow."

"You mean ..."

"Ya, I need you on the road before Radeo tells me it's lunchtime."

Between us, Arnim and I put together a few reasonable tactical choices for the Narrows. He'd have to work out the details in the field, depending on how the river was running right now, how many army of light kids showed up, and what kind of regular forces flowed in. The runners coming back from Lakeside had each noted non-Jeskans in the towns they passed through, more than I would have thought usual, and not enough of them traders or traveling entertainers. Arnim and I agreed those outliers were likely military—regular army, possibly scouts. The Southern alliance almost certainly had forces squirreled away in the hills, preparing to march northward, but they'd need regular resupply from the towns.

I sent him off with orders for whoever Magaran had put in charge of setting things up at HandOverHand. Arnim could draft from the forces already mustered there, to fill in the ranks of whatever troops he and Caymer and Tamil could get marching before midday.

Leaving Lakeside, I'd had the feeling the enemy was on the move already. I remembered the confident air of the officer we saw strutting around the Shamans' House in Frogtown, looking ready to start barking out orders. Or maybe it was the way the Lakeside Master Shaman narrowed his eyes at our demands, suspecting we were more than we claimed to be, that time we posed as a disgruntled family. Or maybe it was Tymon, sitting right there in the midst of them, the most unlikely apprentice shaman, his shaved head packed with Jeska's secrets. And mine.

2

ONCE ARNIM HEADED OFF to gather his troops, that left me alone with Harad, the most senior officer I'd co-opted from among my wife's personal guard. The old soldier abandoned the outer door in favor of a position where he could have his eyes on me directly. It didn't seem to ease his mind when Dramin knocked at the door leading up to the council chambers to let me know people were starting to drift in for that meeting I'd called for. My security-obsessed cousin would want me surrounded by guards when I headed up those stairs to meet a roomful of people who hated me. He wouldn't be satisfied with just himself and our medic, no matter how battle-hardened Dramin might be.

I hoped Radeo would get back soon, to be the reinforcements his partner looked for and the mood-lightener I needed. Once that council meeting was over and done with, we could move on to the real business of the day.

I wished we'd had time, on our dash back to Jeskaryan, to stop by the Lakeside Governor's House and advise Yutek's men, the ones I'd left to guard Heyliannin's treasure-trove of documentary proofs of corruption. They'd be on their own in what amounted to enemy territory. I said as much to Harad.

"Eh, Ennic and Tavor, they'll be fine," he opined, leaning against the wall by the window, his sharp eyes flicking from one door to the other, ignoring the view. "Don't be worrying about whatever you set them to. Ennic's a regular wolverine; you'll think he's all bluff but get him in a corner and he's no one you want to be stuck in a corner with, believe me. Tavor's more a badger; same kind of personality, but you'd swear he sees in the dark."

"You know them, then?"

"Ay, they were my seniors in the under-guard. And then, still, senior to me in Yutek's circle. I was always one step behind them." He let his eyes roam the room. "Look where that's got me."

Being sent off as guard to a low-class woman like Heyliannin would have seemed a demotion. "I see. You must have done something awful to get ordered down south."

"No, sir." His expression went still, cautious, as it did when we met over the campfire to plan our next moves in our spying tour of Lakeside. "I volunteered, sir. So did Radeo."

I tried not to show my surprise, but I was used to being myself with him, now. Like with my Six, the troopers I'd worked with all my career. "You're joking. You'd ask to leave the king's service and traipse around after some woman I pulled out of nowhere to take the wife-of-heir job?"

"No. I volunteered to serve the household of the future king, a man I'd been watching since he started thumping the daylights out of older boys in the practice yard. Sometimes with nothing but fists, as I recall."

That threw a new band of color over the past couple of months. The way he watched the Six and me, the little changes he made in the way he organized the Four around Heyliannin. On the road to Lakeside, and while we settled in at the Governor's House, I'd taken his quietness for dissatisfaction. He'd seemed to change over the long days on our tour together, but I could see it now: he'd been showing himself to me. We'd taken our fake-family roles and turned them into something resembling true-family.

"Well, Cousin," I said. "You jealous of Arnim for getting to run the first battle of this war?"

His brooding eyes flicked to the view then returned to me. "Truth be told, Uncle's-son-of-mine, no. I've had my fill of the army of light. I hope your man turns them back. I don't care what the enemy throws at us, so long as it's not our own kids."

"I'll drink to that," I declared, and took up the fruity concoction Radeo had brought. I tried to quaff the cupful, but it felt like swallowing a bowl of berries. I nearly choked on it.

"You all right, sir?" Harad's face had those long lines by his mouth, the ones that meant he was worried. I didn't need him fussing over me.

"I had a thought," I deflected. "How many kids we got in the under-guard these days?"

"Well … assuming not much has changed while we've been gone, around twenty in residence. Could be as many as a hundred that come for the sparring and physical training, kids from local families that turn up for classes."

I knew I wouldn't have to go too far along before Harad knew what I wanted.

"You want me to take charge of them," he said.

"Right."

"If it's not insubordinate, sir, what are you wanting me to do with them?"

I joined him by the window. The king's apartment had a long view northeasterly over the town. "I want you to keep those kids safe."

"Safe from what, exactly, sir?" He kept his eyes lowered, but I could tell he was watching me. The way he'd been watching me all those years?

"It's going to be close, Harad. It's my thinking that, at best, we'll nearly lose this war. There's going to be a moment when we're short-handed, and somebody, maybe me, is going to say, 'Hey, we have all these trained kids. Give 'em real swords instead of the practice tools, let them fly at the enemy. They're young, fast, eager to make their mark. Let them in. They'll go for it, won't they?'"

While I talked, the color slowly faded from his face. Suddenly, he tipped his head down and looked me in the eye. This close, the old man's gaze had the kind of intensity that made it tough to look away.

I caught him by the elbow. "I'm not having us go down that road, Harad. I won't send children to fight this war. Even if that's what our opponents are doing. Even if I'm the one thinking those boys would want to fight. I don't want drawn into that game. Hear me?"

He blinked, breaking his gaze. "Yes, sir. What can I do?"

"Take charge of the under-guard. Come up with a scheme, a reason, something to dovetail on the rest of what's going to be rolling out today." I took another glance outside, to check the time. "We could get the elders' approval at today's council meeting. Can you plan that fast? Whatever you come up with, I'll back you."

"Hmm. You're proposing strategic evacuation. How about we order the kids to escort the evac parties? We could arm them enough to fend off bandits, so the kids would buy into the idea. Tell the elders we can't spare soldiers for escort duty."

"Right. Let's do that. I leave it to you to get it organized. Today." I turned to assembling clothing that would remind the King's Council I was the man in charge, until we ended this crisis. Either way.

If we lost, I might well close out my tenure sliced up somewhere on the hillside below Jeskaryan. If we won, the Council of Elders would be giving me marching orders.

The formal wear hung stiff, as if I was coating myself in layers of bark.

I wished Heyliannin was there to make fun of me.

Calestinise should have been lounging in the corner, casting dark looks and rolling his eyes at every word I said.

Where are they? Shouldn't we at least have had word of them?

3

BEFORE WE GET TOO FAR into the war, you need a better understanding of what Jeska meant to us, why we would offer our lives to defend it.

You've had the geography lesson—our long, protected valley with the mountains framing croplands and wildlands, and our river flowing through the heart of it. I've taken you up and down the length of the land, from that infested Shamans' House in Frogtown to the river crossing at Tarak. Your feet should hurt, from imagining all that walking.

It's not the land, itself.

It's about seeing land properly.

In the countries south of Jeska, land is an object, like a sword or a sack of grain or a shop full of smithing tools. Or a wife. When Heyliannin came here, that was how she thought of land, so I suspect you think like them, the invaders who thought only of ownership. Whenever she got mad at me, she'd say, "I've got my little place up north. I can go there anytime. I don't need you."

You see how that sounds? Did she think she could walk away, abandon the land, fail to care for it, and expect to return and still be its keeper? If she'd been in Jeska proper, the local elders would have reassigned responsibility as soon as someone noticed she'd gone off without arranging for its care.

It's a little different up north, in terms of who makes decisions. Like in the outland valleys, it's families that take responsibility. Her "little place" would have been a small-keeping that had suffered somehow, where the farmer hadn't had any daughters, or lost her children to disaster, or had decided to move her family down into Jeska, where they'd have better prospects. Her neighbors would have been consulted, asked to keep an eye out for a responsible keeper, and the arrival of a skilled (if you want to dignify the profession) herbalist would have appealed to the community.

When Tymon talked Heyliannin into heading to Jeskaryan with him, he wouldn't have told her to go explain to the neighbors. He'd have expected her to know, just as he expected her to know a lot of things, such as how he couldn't possibly have married her.

There's more to keeping land than putting up a house and planting crops. You have to manage what grows—and doesn't—make sure nothing interferes with the creeks flowing through, hunt no more than is proper in a season, and keep track of the weather and the wildlife and the changes over time. It's women's work, all that, managing land. It's the most vital work, because if you keep the land right, you prosper. The soil grows the crops you need, the water flows clean, the wildlife stays plentiful.

Everyone knows this, with the kind of knowing that makes it near-impossible to understand people who don't know it. It's a knowledge that runs in your veins, natural as your attachment to your family.

Well, most people's attachment to their family.

My family attachments were odd by necessity, dictated by the needs of men—one who wanted to be a shaman and one who wanted to be a good king. It doesn't change the way I feel about my country.

Eldennian said it, that I'd cut off both my arms and run up and down the valley barefoot, if that would save Jeska.

She was right.

What does it matter if one man pours his blood into the soil, if the land is safe?

That's what we do, soldiers, we put our blood and flesh and bones into the land. The Great Ones, the condors, honor us for that. They come down to the fields where we've fallen, take up their share, and then soar up and down the length of Jeska, watching over those we've protected.

This is the job of the kings of Jeska, to protect this land. The elders called us to this duty long ago, to contend with bands of raiders from over the western range. Since then, we've united the districts of Jeska in one strong nation, each ready to defend the rest. We beg our share of resources from the elders, enough to equip and train and feed our soldiers. We enforce the law, and we're granted that right by the keepers of the land. When the kingship might change hands, we submit that choice to the elders, to be sure it won't fall into the grasp of one without the ability and heart it takes to defend this country—and its principles. Not even the king's own offspring is spared that judgment—that's why the king must have foster-sons, backups, just in case.

With coaching, Yutek's true-son might have passed muster, but he would have had to work hard at his lies. If he'd faltered after, if I'd had to kill Yutek-en for the treason he'd have ultimately done, the elders would have thanked me for it.

Tymon might have been a good choice for king, if he'd stayed in the household, trained for responsibility as I did. He had a way of connecting with people that could have done well, might have opened our borders to more trade. The Southerners could have been an issue, but he'd have had me, Magaran, the rest of us to take up arms, and I wouldn't have had to sign on to a job I never asked for.

If there's someone wants that job, that's how you know he shouldn't have it. That's a man who thinks like a Southerner, thinks you can own a country, take possession, defy the natural order of things. That's a traitor to the land. Remember the story of the unnamed chieftain who rode up into the Well and thought he could own it? He wanted to possess its wealth and instead created a ghost country, where no one but creatures from another world—and one brave boy—would venture.

And that brings me to the war, doesn't it?

The first battle, the fight at the Narrows—the history books won't tell this, but that anyone made it out of there, we owe to Calestinise.

4

W HILE I WAS PARADING up the stairs to the council chamber, my finery scraping at my calves and my extremely senior bodyguards flanking me, I couldn't shake the feeling that something had gone wrong with Heyliannin's escape from Lakeside. If the Southerners had already brought troops over the border, had my little family followed the lake road or the periphery? Could Kul have found himself fighting alone against a force of invaders? Did they choose to take cover, hiding out in a barn or smokehouse?

I had to trust to Kul's common sense and Heyliannin's caution. She'd proven herself a few times on that point, but she'd more often shown herself as impulsive and daring.

What I hadn't figured on was Calestinise—not his smarts or his courage, that was never a question in my mind. What I hadn't fixed on sufficiently was his anger, the fury at what had happened to him, those two days with the army of light, what he'd been made to do, what he'd seen others do. That bravery of his, that's what made it possible for him to go into that camp, stay long enough to gather the information we so desperately needed. His intelligence, that's what drove the rage in him, because he could see it, clear as I could, what those kids were destined for.

So while I was imagining the three of them hunkered down in an old, shabby outbuilding, waiting out the conflict, Calestinise was taking action.

I'm putting it in here, because it's the time for it. Keep in mind, though, I didn't know. We'd get pieces of it from runners who were still on the road at this time, but I wouldn't hear the full story until Heyliannin found her way back.

That morning, Calestinise and Heyliannin were easing their way through a busy crowd in the fishmarket of Reeds On Reeds, a town at the edge of Northeast Township. By this time, after days of working their way through each town on the Lake Road, they had a system. Calestinise turned out as he'd gone to the Shamans' House—bare-legged, bare-armed, his cuts and bruises showing yellow and green and purple and black. In a typical village, they'd not make it past one stall before one woman or another would remark on it or pull Heyliannin to one side and ask her did she need help from someone, was there trouble in her family, had they been set upon by bandits?

Calestinise dropped dribs and drabs of the story, letting the gossip spread the way fire spreads, flaring up on the most incendiary horrors. *Children of Lakeside are being stolen. The shamans have a secret camp where they beat children to death. That boy over there, he saw a Southerner set fire to a child.*

As per plan, Kul shouldered his way through the market and called Heyliannin and Calestinise back to the inn they'd picked out, making sure to let enough people hear where they could be found. Over the intervening hours, the gossip-fire would smolder its way through town.

At the top of my meeting, up in Jeskaryan, the Council of Elders took five minutes to make my temporary position official, which helped more than I'd expected. Still, it took past noon to finish the arguments between the Elders and the King's Council on who would be required to evacuate, who would be required to stay, and how many others could be permitted to leave. Harad got his permissions from the community and the king (now, officially, me) to delegate our young almost-soldiers as escorts to the most vulnerable parties being evacuated.

We had to deal with requests for release from essential personnel up and down the town, from armorers to food preparers. I couldn't let them go. There were harsh words said, to put it mildly. We couldn't run a garrison through a war without the town's support. We could move some people inside the fortress walls. Others had to stay in town. There was nothing for it. The workshops and armories were there. They always had been. No one had ever imagined an assault on Jeskaryan. Now it was all anybody could think about.

Three of the council members wanted to leave with the evac parties. What were they thinking? If the butchers and the bakers they represented were staying, then they were staying, too.

"You can stay with or without your heads!" I shouted, when it seemed that argument wasn't about to end. "Your choice." I reached over to Radeo, because he was closest, and drew his sword. I gave it a few quick swings, letting the nearest of the recalcitrant councilmen feel the rush of the air from its movement.

Everyone shut up. If Tymon had been there, he might have been shouting at me to stop it, but no one else would dare.

Radeo held out his hand, and I set the hilt of his sword where it belonged. The whisper of the blade sliding back into its sheath washed across the room like the sound of a pen scratching paper.

"So," I said. "Let's get the old and the infirm, and the kids and whatever adults are needed to care for them, safely out. Are we agreed?"

The murmurs became "Ay" and "Ya."

"You three." I picked three councilmen from among those who hadn't begged to leave. "Take charge of communicating to the people. Make sure nobody who should leave stays. Make sure everyone who shouldn't doesn't. And that they understand there's consequences for deserting—not least of which is the shame of abandoning their city to foreign raiders."

"Uh, yes, sir." That was Dineen. He was an accountant, like my wife, which made me somehow comfortable with the guy. We wouldn't need him managing money for this task, but he knew numbers don't lie.

Down in Lakeside, at that time, people were drifting into the public room of the inn Kul had told everyone about. He and

Calestinise and Heyliannin had already taken command of the most prominent table in the place, while the innkeeper was getting excited about seeing so much business coming into her place during the normally-slow time of day.

Once the room became full, while the innkeeper was scuttling around filling orders, Calestinise climbed up on top of the table. He'd be well into his talk before their host could even begin to object. He'd tell the whole story, from the moment those recruiters drew him in at an inn "like this one!" He began with how they helped him talk his parents into letting him go "camping! They said it was a fun camping trip!"

He described lining up and being lectured by the leader-like children, and what happened when someone wanted "to go home! All he wanted was to go home to his family and they killed him!" He showed his bruises and laid bare the horrors of the night, the fear that kept them from running, the hope that in the morning it would be all right. "Only, then, in the morning, you won't believe it!" And he cried, in front of everyone, our shy Calestinise who never wanted anybody looking at him. He pulled himself together, and those silent, stricken faces listened to the burning, and the drill-marching, and the strange man from south of Lakeside, and the shaman who ordered Calestinise executed.

Then Kul stood up, a bear in their midst, and shouted, "We'd have lost our boy, here, if I hadn't sent my cousins off to fetch him, because we had to leave, don't ya know, and they's vet'rans, my cousins, so they thought they'd chase them kids off, but they ain't kids no more, neighbors, they's soldiers, crazy soldiers, that'll fight worse than any proper guardsman."

That made it Heyliannin's turn. She called out, "Has anyone else here lost a child? Has someone gone missing and you thought they'd taken off to have an adventure or go visiting? We're here to tell you that's not true! Someone's stealing our kids and making them into monsters!"

Soon enough, people were standing in the crowd, shouting replies. "My kid!" or "My brother's son!" or "Did ya say girls? My niece went to meet a friend and didn't come home."

My wife and my foster-son and my old friend were making their own army, town by town. The mothers and fathers of Lakeside weren't in on any scheme of the district managers to take power from their neighbors to the north. It hadn't ever occurred to them shamans might do anything other than minister to the sick or conduct a funeral or dance around at a festival. These people were ready to follow a different kind of leader, an angry child backed by his mother and uncle, to find their missing children and bring them home.

5

THANKS TO THOSE self-centered councilors, I missed seeing Arnim off. He'd rounded up sixty or so troopers and bowmen, with the two captains he'd named, and they'd marched off towards HandOverHand before our meeting wrapped up. If I'd looked out the council room windows at the right time, I might have seen them go.

I made my new gang of bodyguards walk out to the fortress gate with me. The watchman there reported that Arnim's partial force had passed through a half-hour ago. They'd be at the bottom of the hill by now.

The useless excursion became a break-in exercise for the men tasked with tramping after me day and night. Magaran had made up a full troop of eight to cover the shifts—we had a running argument as to what constituted a proper troop size. Radeo stayed by my side that first day and lectured them on everything from what I was supposed to eat to how far to stand off from me in public spaces. Bodyguard duty has its unique requirements. Ideally, it's nothing but a lot of standing around waiting. Given that, it helped to have a crew with a sense of humor about it all.

As we retraced our steps back to the king's house, one of the guards took it on himself to make the usual declaration, " Your Majesty, it's proud we all are to serve you."

Another cleared his throat and added, "But we was wondering, sir, who's going to be protecting us from you?"

That remark generated a round of stifled laughter. There wasn't one of them I hadn't pounded over the head with a wooden sword or lit into with my fists when my own weapon flew out of my hand. I couldn't deal with them that way, not anymore. I put out my hand and clasped the jokester's arm when he lifted it in response. "That was a long time ago. We're grown-ups, now." I leaned in close and whispered to him, "You remember that over-the-shoulder move, from hand-to-hand class?" His forearm muscles went tense under my grip. I held for a second, then released him and stepped back. "Trust me, my wife will be back in town soon, and she'll be keeping me busy enough."

That got them laughing. Nothing beats a lie to make people feel at ease. No wonder the shamans are so good at it.

"Commanders' meeting," Radeo reminded me.

"Right." My head filled up again with the plans we'd worked on, with the new ideas that had come to me while boring people were droning during the morning council. I followed Radeo, and my new troop ranged themselves around me. They became invisible, from that moment, belonging to me but not a part of myself, like clothing. They were a weapon I could wield without having to think about it. They could never be like my Six. Useful, trusted, but not family.

•   •   •

"Sir—I mean, Your Majesty."

Radeo stopped short, and I nearly bumped into him. "What is it?" he said.

"Ah ..." The tall, broad-shouldered old man in his drab grey shirt and worn pants could have been a servant, but his rock-steady stance and calloused hands reeked of another type of skill. His eyes went from me to Radeo. "Commander Arnim said talk to no one but himself and the other one, and—"

"Arnim's on deployment. You can talk to me," I said. The symbol woven into the sleeve of his shirt held my eye—the hammer-and-tongs of a smith, with gold thread rimming it. I put a hand on Radeo's shoulder and stepped up beside him. "Tell me, Master Smith, what was it Arnim asked of you?"

The smith gave my fake cousin a skeptical look. "I've been dredging through the recipes in that book of his."

"What book? What recipes?" Radeo looked about to lose his temper.

I nudged his shoulder. "Seems it's a secret message, Cousin. You go ahead, get the meeting rolling. I'll be there shortly." We'd reached a junction in the corridors, and I gestured the smith towards my apartment. "This way, Master Smith. I have a few minutes for a private talk." The troopers weren't invisible to my guest, but they stopped outside the door, which seemed to ease his anxious mind. He carried a dark leather satchel, its long strap running across his chest, and kept one hand on it, as if he expected to be robbed at any moment.

I wasn't about to leave myself vulnerable, either. I stayed on my feet, paced to the window, and leaned beside it. "What's so important you couldn't share with my cousin?"

He wasn't listening to me. The old maker was busy wrestling the satchel strap over his head. The object he pulled out came wrapped in cloth, and its edges gleamed in the light from the window.

I should have known.

He held out Heyliannin's book, the one she'd brought through the thin-patch from the snake-man world. The weight of it settled into my hand. It occurred to me this was the first time I'd held the thing. It had the coolness of a beaten blade. "It's metal, isn't it?" I ran my fingers over the blue and gold design, trying to feel the texture beneath the surface.

"Yes, sir." His eyebrows twitched. "Metal and glass and something in between, resembles hardened wax, or the membrane in honeycomb, but much harder."

"So Arnim asked you to figure out what it's made of?"

"Oh, no, sir. To do that, we'd need to melt it down, watch what melts first and how. That kind of thing." He had a hunger in his eyes that said he wished he could do that.

"I see. No. Don't be destroying it. My wife would kill me."

"Why?" He frowned, disturbed. "Commander Dramin said it wasn't matriarchy business." Makers avoid conflict with the elders.

"It isn't, not the way you're imagining. The book belongs to my wife, Master Smith. We had to make all kinds of promises we wouldn't hurt the thing."

"Oh." His brow furrowed, and he cast wary looks around the room as though he expected a monster to jump from the shadows. "Your wife is one of the snake-people?"

The man had imagination, I grant you that. "No, no, she took it from the snake-men." Should I tell him my wife was technically a shaman? That she'd jumped through thin patches herself? Or that it was mostly my fault she'd gone to that world in the first place?

The smith put on a skeptical face. "That doesn't sound reasonable, Corren."

Since when does a commoner address a royal like a lazy apprentice?

When the commoner is a Master Smith and the king is a cast-off smith's son.

"It's a long story." One I knew too little of. What had she been doing with those weird creatures, in their alien world? Why did she go with them? "I don't have much time here. If you haven't noticed, we're getting all dressed up for a war."

"Yes. I mean, yes, sir, and that's what I've come about. I think at least one of these recipes could serve the war effort."

Finally, a hint of something useful. "You'd better back up and tell me what you're talking about, before I show you what I've learned I can do with those things my father used to make." My favorites hung on a wrought iron rack just within reach.

He didn't miss a beat. "And mighty fine weapons did Orkast fashion, young man. It was a great loss to the profession to see him put down his hammer." He lifted the book from my hand. "See here, young Corren, this book has more in it than those pages of accounts." Flipping the cover open, he expertly wakened the glowing page within. "Once we had those pages copied out by scribes, I was set the task of finding out what else is in here." He smiled into the glow, like a mother gazing into her child's eyes. "It's a wonderful thing, this, all you need is a few tricks, and there's plenty to find."

"So. Show me."

The only flat surface in the room was the low table. "May I, sir?"

I tipped my head, and he knelt on my favorite cushion to lay the book flat on the age-worn wood. I got down beside him, so the pictures would be right-side-up for both of us. He didn't even notice he'd stuck his king with sitting on the hard floor.

The surface was now decorated with a series of blobby shapes. I imagined them as snake-man heads, which maybe wasn't so far off, given the blobs had a variety of colors.

"See here," the smith said. He tapped one of the blobs, and the page transformed to one with tiny pictures I recognized as images from Heyliannin's ledger. "These are the ones your wife made, to send to the king, the ones we've been focused on." He did something to the page, and the colorful blobs returned. "Now, most of these are … I'd say, locked." He tapped one that swelled a little and glowed, but then settled back down. "These, I guess your wife has done something with, to keep us from opening them." His voice betrayed interest, not frustration. "I'm working on that. I have a few ideas."

"Move along. Ideas are for the future."

"Right, sir. Yes. A few she failed to protect. Or decided not to bother with." One blob opened to another set of tiny pictures. He tapped to bring to the surface a fairly accurate painting of a north-country scene with trees and flowers in it. "These seem to be art of some kind."

"I see that. Are we going to beat back the invaders with pretty pictures?"

"No, sir. Of course not, sir. But you seemed unfamiliar with the device …"

"Jump to the end of the story. You can teach me how it works later."

"Yes, sir." He returned to the blobby page and selected one in particular. It opened up to little pictures with words on them. "She wrote notes in these, sir, seems she was copying out information from somewhere else. Maybe somewhere in the locked-up part of the book. Her writing isn't too good. Her spelling is awful. The file-bin, she's named it Recipes."

"File-bin?"

"Eh, it's a shorthand, for a collection of certain items. Here, this one is for notes and the other one contains pictures."

"So, great. I had no idea she could cook. She hasn't set foot in a kitchen since I've known her."

He laughed, looked at my face, then closed his mouth and bobbed his head. "Sorry, sir." He tapped the screen. "They're not recipes for food, sir. There are a few herbal concoctions—I gather she worked as an herbalist at one time?"

"Yes, that's right."

"So, she has notes on those. Some of the notes seem to be in another language. But this one, sir, it's plain as day, if you disregard her spelling."

I pulled the thing closer and read the recipe's ingredients. "These are farming supplies. She managed a farm up north. Supposedly." Her village matriarchs might have been leaning on her to do more than peddle fake medicine.

"No, sir. It's a recipe that uses soil improvers, but then adds in a third substance, one that burns."

"So it's a recipe for firestarter."

"You might say so. It's a fire like I never saw before."

"Oh." Why do people hide the big news at the end? "You've made this recipe."

"Yes, sir. It produces a flame that burns fast and hot. Dangerous stuff. Like powdered lightning."

I stood up. "Radeo can take the commanders' meeting. Come on. You're going to show me this stuff at work. What's your name, Master Smith?"

"Goram, sir. Sorry, sir. One gets used to titles, Your Majesty."

Yes. That one I wouldn't have time to get used to.

6

F OR THE SECOND TIME that day, Radeo dragged me out of a dead
    sleep. After an hour of watching Master Smith Goram set fires, an
urgent conference with the councilors running the evacuation, a private
shouting match with Maledestine—an elder who still believed all the
lies about me the shamans had planted—and an evening strategy
session that went on far too long, I'd eaten … maybe … and collapsed
in that cold empty bed of Yutek's. He probably died in that bed.

I didn't care. I slept like a bear in winter.

"… back from Lakeside." The words broke through as I
realized I'd been ignoring an insistent rapping.

Moments later, Radeo and I were striding side-by-side down
the dark halls. My left boot kept flapping on the stones, because I
hadn't stopped to secure the straps. A driving tension I hadn't
recognized eased, and without the familiar gut-ache, I felt hungry.
I wanted to ask questions, but didn't want to spoil the moment.
Everything suddenly made sense. *They're late because they met up
with Case. They've been traveling together. They're safe. Calestinise,
Stevvin, Kul. Heyliannin.*

A door opened to the night air, and when the coolness hit my skin, I realized what my wife would see. I'd rolled out of bed in those night-clothes of mine, the ones she called *trash*.

I put out my arm. "Jacket."

Radeo rubbed his hands over his own jacket, still discolored from our weeks on the road. "Sir?"

"No, no, not you," I told him. I snapped my fingers at the nearest of my bodyguards. He was nearly short enough to not make it ridiculous. "Give me your jacket, buddy."

Radeo tightened his lips over his teeth as I wrapped that regular soldier's jacket over my threadbare outfit.

"You got something to say, Commander?"

He coughed. "Are you all right, sir?"

"I'm fine. Just didn't want to look bad in front of … you know, man!" I think I was probably grinning as I forged ahead of him, making the guards break into a trot to keep up.

The squeal of the gates being dragged shut followed us as we crossed the plaza to the stableyard. I picked up our pace, the oversized jacket flapping halfway to my knees.

Only one pony cart waited in the yard, leaning on its shafts, with a stableman leading the pony off, a couple of boys trailing after to keep the harness traces from dragging. Dim figures worked at the back of the cart, pulling baggage off the tray, sorting out the goods on the pavement, talking in low voices among themselves.

Not one of those shapes was big enough to be Kul.

I pulled up short, and my guard flowed around me. They were going to have to learn to pay attention. Yutek's guard never flapped around like that.

"Where's Kul?" I demanded. "Where are Calestinise and Heyliannin?"

I didn't need to hear it. My innards were already twisting knots in themselves again. It hurt so much, for a second I couldn't breathe. Kul himself might have had an arm crushed around my chest. My eyes burned, as if some of Goram's lightning powder had settled there.

Good thing it was dark.

I wheeled around.

Radeo put his hand on my arm, and I jerked away, my imagination sparking images of slashing a blade at him. It was too dark for him to read my expression. "Sir?" he asked. When I said nothing, he tried, "Your Majesty?"

My voice likely came out rough, not being able to breathe as I was. "Let them get settled. Debrief in an hour. Officers' briefing room, not council chambers. Got it?"

"Yes, sir."

"I want to hear from all of them, including the kids and the midwife. Got that?"

"Yessir."

"All right, then."

I left him standing there, watching me march through the shadows. My crowd of protectors swirled in my wake. They'd learn.

7

WITH AN HOUR TO KILL, I could eat a little real food, wash the fire out of my eyes, and dress properly. More or less. I still felt cold, so I kept the borrowed jacket.

Wore it straight through the war. Can't explain why. Felt right, that's all I can say.

Case and his crew didn't bring much new information. Mainly, they confirmed my worst suspicions. And left me too worried about Kul's crew to even ask. Our east-side party had a head start, at least a day's worth, given Stevvin had to jog halfway through South Point before he found Case.

The west-side group had caught hints of what Calestinise had encountered. They'd observed kids with odd jackets, matching outfits, and watched them approaching other kids. The recruiters never hit up Affram—he was small even for his age, and from what we'd seen, the recruiters targeted older kids, ones who wouldn't get the town in an uproar if they went missing. Kids in Lakeside generally seemed to have a lot of leeway from their elders. They were always cruising up and down the lakeshore, looking for odd jobs, hanging with friends, exploring. No one batted an eye if a fourteen-year-old disappeared for a month. They'd be back with stories, cash to share, a new recipe for turning frogs into food.

You'd never have pulled off such a scheme in the older districts, not even in the free-thinking city of Jeskaryan, where the furthest a stray kid might roam is from the kings' funeral ground to the river at the foot of the hill.

Once Case got the message, he had to decide between heading back along the east or west shoreline, and he settled on retracing their own route.

I wished they'd followed Kul, but I didn't say so. I'd have made the same choice, to avoid duplicating effort.

Another debate devolved on whether to follow up on a lead they'd found earlier that day, when Case sidled up to a border patrol troop and let them know who he was. A farmer at South Point had reported a concern—unverified—of a threat from the south. Case sent Karthi and Andus to reconnoiter.

Good move.

The warning had come from Nandeen, that manager's husband who'd invited me to visit, so long ago. Remember him? The one whose wife was out-to-here? He took them through his town on Jeska's southern border and up a rise where you could see a good distance.

"See the dark shadow out there?" he asked them. It might have been another lake, a small one. Possibly a field with a tall crop of hemp, deep, dark, ready to harvest.

Not the most popular crop down there. Not the time of year for harvest, either.

Karthi had the best eyes of anyone. "It's people. Men. An army."

"Ya, that it is, now that you tell me," Andus agreed.

"Turned up further off, a week or so ago," our volunteer spy reported. "Moved that close a few days ago. Been staying put. It's a lot of men, there, sirs. You best be telling the governor, quick as you can. I told a lieutenant on patrol with his troop, and he told me he couldn't do nothing about soldiers doing maneuvers in their own country."

"It's not maneuvers," Karthi judged. "And seems to me they're in Alcala's territory, not their own. So you did right. That troop met us on the road. It's why we're here."

Andus shook his hand, that way they have down in Lakeside of being friendly. "We'll get word to the governor fast as we can. He'll be grateful. Thank you."

Our informant wanted them to stay for dinner, meet the wife and the enormous child, but they had to move out. Of course, of course, he understood, he hoped they'd come back soon, his family would welcome them.

"And now I'm worried about him," Andus told me. "I keep thinking of the mercenaries we met at NeverSnows, and wondering what they'd do to a family like that. He's just a guy with a baby and a wife obsessed with managing her holdings properly."

They caught up with the pony-cart, and the group made good time, not stopping except for the necessaries. But they kept eyes open, and they reported seeing more of what Case called "suspicious activity" than they had on the outbound trek—people in noticeably non-Lakesider clothing, clusters of men who carried themselves more like soldiers than fishermen. There'd been a half-day delay when Ganderrison was asked for help with a difficult delivery, someone in that town having remembered her profession.

"Mighty unsettling, though," she told me. "That girl couldn't have been more than fifteen. What were her parents thinking, marrying her off at that age?" She'd said as much, in the scolding way that midwives are entitled to. The parents were aghast she'd thought them complicit.

No, no, they'd told her, the kid had gone off with new friends, the previous winter, to work a festival in South Point, and she'd come back alone, pregnant, and not talking. The poor kid had enough to cope with. They didn't press her on what happened.

New friends. Trips to interesting places. Boys and girls thrown together, under stress.

Could have been.

Could have been worse than that. In my mind's eye, I saw the little cabin Harad described, set apart from the kids' barracks, with a corrupt shaman and a Southern officer who'd joined forces to turn Lakeside kids into killers. In the long night, with senior kids shouting and recruits crying out, would anyone notice if a girl or two went missing for an hour or so?

I wished we were out on a boat, in the middle of the lake, so I could get rid of the meal I'd just eaten. Harad, sitting across the table from me, caught my eye. He looked about ready to vomit, too.

I slapped a hand on the table, to break us out of that train of thought.

"This ends, in the next few days. Focus, everyone. Do you have anything else to report?"

When they reached the northern edge of Northwest Township, they began hearing new chatter in the pubs and marketplaces. These stories began to sweep aside the ones about Evil Governor Corren.

Rumor had it someone was stealing children. Kids were being burned alive in the hills. Girls were being made to fight, boys beaten nearly to death. Families were gathering, sharing news of missing kids up and down the lakeshore. People were on the move, heading to Lakeside City. Something would happen. Nobody knew what that would be.

They ran into a cluster of travelers making their way to Lakeside City. Apparently, the families planned on joining a movement to take action against the faceless enemy. Case worked out a route home that would take his crew around the city, avoiding crowds. They traded in the pony and pushed the new one hard.

No, they'd seen no evidence of Southerners gathered at the Narrows.

Yes, they saw Arnim, briefly. He seemed busy when they passed through HandOverHand.

"Arnim's setting up a defensive action at the Narrows," I told Case. "I should have given him orders, in case he saw you. Never mind. How soon can you head south again?"

He sagged and scratched his head. "You want us to join Arnim?"

"No."

Karthi nudged Andus, who'd fallen asleep with his head on his arms. "Hey, new orders coming."

"What?" Andus looked like he needed a drink. "We just got here."

I slid the pitcher of water towards them. "Sorry, all we've got is water. And, ya, sorry to put you to work again, but there's no time." I waited while Andus poured for everyone, from Case down to little Affram. The kids seemed the least tired. They sat at the far end, playing a game with stones in a line on the table.

"Stevvin, Affram," I said. "You two get orders, too."

"Sure, Dad," Stevvin replied, not even pausing in the move he was making.

"Exactly," I said.

"What?" He'd been spending too much time with Andus and Karthi.

"Making it official," I told him. "Radeo's got forms for you to put your mark on. First thing tomorrow."

"Forms? What we gotta do that's legal stuff?" I hadn't gotten to know Affram, but the boy was sharp.

"I'm fostering you guys."

"Am I gonna have to call you Dad, too? I already have a father, sir." Affram had dark, serious eyes and his usual expression made him look vaguely angry. Just then, he was trying to fake a smile.

"Not a problem, kid. You get to keep him. It's a job. Like stableboy."

"Does it pay?" He had some nerve, that kid.

"Well, ya, but the pay goes to your family, get it?"

"Fine with me, then." He dropped the glare and the false smile and turned to Stevvin. "Whose move is it?"

Stevvin giggled. "Yours, *brother*."

They were like Tymon and me, back in the good days. Radeo gave me a nod. I knew I wouldn't have to say anything more on that topic.

Harad put us back on track.

"Case, everything you've said supports what His Majesty's been telling us. The Southerners are on the move, they've infiltrated Lakeside, and they'll be at the gates in no time."

Dramin, who'd done nothing through the whole debrief but sit and listen and watch, spoke up at last. "We're splitting up, guys. The king's plans have us spread through the forces. I've got the worst of it, dealing with the town and elders night and day. Arnim's got his cut-and-harry battle lined up. Someone's gotta take charge at HandOverHand. And someone needs to marshal the forces here. Who gets what job, sir?"

So he was finally going to let me talk.

I could tell Case was exhausted, but if we could end this meeting promptly, he'd get most of a night's sleep. "Case, HandOverHand has to fall to you. I need Magaran here, running strategy for Jeskaryan. He's been running deployments, and expects to be heading out to take charge. If you meet him on the road, send him home. You're the only one he'd take that order from."

"Hey, what about us?" Andus made a good show of being awake. "Why couldn't Magaran use me and Karthi?"

I sighed. It was awkward. "That action needs one commander. One."

"But—" He looked at Karthi and shut up.

"I'm giving you the home front. You'll have to plan on the fly. We won't have any idea what'll be coming at us until it gets here, and you know the town's not designed for defense. Two heads on that engagement, that's what I need." I thought about the lightning powder, about the notions Goram had for putting it to use. Those tools wouldn't be ready to send with Case.

Karthi gave me a long look. "What do you have in mind, sir? There's something you're not telling us."

Dramin stood up. "You're right, Karthi. But let it go. Trust me, it's a good thing." He looked over at me. "Sir? Sunup's coming faster than you think."

"Right. Everyone get some rest. Especially Case. You get tomorrow to recover, then I want you at HandOverHand. Got it?"

"Yessir." He blinked at me, the talk about fosterage and the words Harad and Dramin used for me had finally gotten through to him. "Your Majesty, I mean. Yutek's really gone, then?"

Yes, Yutek was dead, and I had his job. For the time being.

"Let's make him proud, why don't we?" was all I had to say.

As I was leaving, those two guards of Heyliannin's bowed to me. It was weird. I knew Harad and Radeo so well now, but these guys were still strangers.

"My wife will be back any day now. Wait for her."

They bowed again. Twice as weird.

I told Radeo to wake servants, to get my people whatever they might need. My new bodyguards kept me company, as I trudged up the long stairway, to return to my dead father's bed.

8

T HERE'S TIMES, usually in autumn, when the earth seems to be waiting for something. The weather becomes constant, steady, every single day the same as the previous one: warm but not hot, sun rolling through a cloudless sky, hardly any wind. You walk up and down the streets feeling like you're holding your breath, waiting for something. Not something pleasant. You're waiting for the ground to drop open at your feet and swallow you alive.

I told Heyliannin about it one night, sweating through the unremitting heat of that Lakeside summer.

She said, "Ya, we have that, where I went to *collidge*. We call it earthquake weather."

"Weather has nothing to do with earthquakes, wife of mine." I hadn't thought her people superstitious.

"Not just any quake. A big one. The kind that knocks down walls and sets cities on fire. You can feel it coming, a disaster too big to imagine."

There was something about the way she said that. It was more than a piece of shamanistic mysticism. It was about something that happened in her world. She wouldn't tell me. She wouldn't talk about what was on the other side of that thin patch she'd walked through. It was different from the shaman-type secrets, such as the way she somehow couldn't be direct about why she wanted that cape back so much. No, it was more that whenever she started to talk about her world, she'd stop, and go quiet, and it seemed to me she had a way of crying that didn't show on the outside.

One time, when she was more relaxed than usual, she forgot herself. "Even once I get the mantle back, I'm still stuck, Corren. I don't know where the thin patch is. We wandered around for so long, trying to find a safe way down the mountain, going in circles, turning back and looking for a way home to my people. Your dad, he spent how many years looking for thin patches?"

"My whole life, just about."

She sobbed out loud, one of the few times I heard her do that. "A whole lifetime."

I wanted to tell her, *A lifetime in Jeska could be a good life.* But I knew that wouldn't work. She let me hold her, without complaining about how I was doing it, and cried until she fell asleep. I was pretty sure, at the time, that she was wishing it was Tymon's arms around her. Now, I'm not so sure. Tymon would have had a different idea of how to spend the night, and it wouldn't have been doing nothing but lying in sweat-damp sheets listening to someone else cry.

The day Case arrived and most of the next were like that. Earthquake weather. Waiting for something. Something bad.

•   •   •

It didn't help that Heyliannin failed to turn up. Her guards—the two I'd never gotten to know, the ones who'd toured Lakeside with Case—came around complaining they needed real work. Their orders were "wait for my wife," while Harad and Radeo were doing council-level jobs for me.

I put down a piece of fruit I'd been trying to peel and told them to quit griping. "She'll be back, and she'll need protection, more than before. I'm not assigning just anybody. My guys here—" As I stood up, my day crew of bodyguards snapped to attention, which annoyed me even more. "These aren't the kind of guys who can work for that woman. It's an honor to serve her. Got it?"

The complainer I was closest to stepped back, his eyes wide. His partner stood his ground and put a hand to his sword-belt.

One of my guys wrapped a thick-fingered hand around my wrist, squeezed the way we're taught, and lifted the knife out of my numbed fingers. "Sir," he said, returning it to me, hilt-first. "Ya seemed to have forgot you were holding this."

I slipped the blade back where it belonged. "So I did. Serves you two right for whining at me during breakfast."

The pair of them edged out of the room and didn't bother me again. Radeo reported they'd claimed two more guys to put their number back up to four and got into some lively discussions with the staff about quarters for the kids. When the dust settled, I went round to see what they'd come up with. Staff have long memories. They'd put Stevvin and Affram in my old room, that tight space I'd shared with Tymon for so long. The boys didn't seem to mind. When I stuck my head in, they were laying out another of those pebble games of theirs.

"Where are they putting Calestinise?" I asked Radeo.

He frowned. "They might not have thought of that. I'll get them on it."

•　　　•　　　•

Case, Karthi, and Andus seemed to be lying low. If we'd been up in Koresh, I'd've figured them to have been taking in the hot springs. No such luxuries in Jeskaryan.

Then again, I was busy. Harad wanted a send-off for the under-guard, on their escort mission. He had them line up in the plaza like a company heading out to a battle. There were close to a hundred, all told.

I gave them the speech Harad asked for, telling them how important the job was, getting families safe, sending back intel by runner if they spotted anything odd out there in the countryside. Looking at those faces—some glowing with pride, others glowering with skepticism—gave me the cold shivers. Right now, somewhere south of us, kids this age—and younger—were lining up. The orders they were getting would get a lot of them killed. They'd be pumping their fists, shouting "Honor Truth!" until they couldn't think anymore.

I finished my speech and went to find Case. Found Karthi doing laundry behind the barracks. Case was off somewhere, he said, wasn't sure exactly where. He pulled a shirt out of the rinse tub and hung it up to drip on the stones. The badges from NeverSnows caught the sunlight. None of us talked about NeverSnows.

"Have any of you talked to Radeo or Harad since you got here?"

"No, not really, except for the debrief last night. You were there, sir." He hauled out a pair of pants, shook off the water. I would have told him to hand the job over to staff, but the badges proved what he was doing. It wasn't just laundry. He was gearing up.

"Make time, the three of you, before Case heads out. I don't care if you have to drag him out of her bed."

"What, sir?" Karthi looked honestly puzzled.

"If he's not in the fortress, man, he's down in the town. With whatshername."

"Oh. Right." He grinned a little. "We got used to treating him and Ganderrison as husband and wife."

"Ya, but he'll have been missing the real thing. They married, do you know?"

"Not sure, sir. None of my business."

I looked at the sun. Past noon. "I have an appointment with the Master Smith. And Dramin's bringing up other guildmasters for a meeting. I have to go."

"Not to worry, sir. I'll send a few troopers around in search of Captain Case—"

"You're all promoted to commander, now. Did you not pay attention last night?"

"Eh, Andus was worn out, and you know I don't care about rank. Sir." That grin of his flashed again.

"I'll tell Radeo and Harad you need their talk on the army of light."

"The army of . . .?" He stood there with water-wrinkled fingers, in his ragged worst clothes, this newly-minted commander, and closed his lips over the question. "Right. We'll get the word from Radeo and Harad."

I left him to his meditation and went to find Harad. He'd make sure not to let Case leave without a thorough briefing on that subject.

The men dogging my footsteps were beginning to get better at not letting me notice them.

•   •   •

The lightning powder had promise, but how to use the stuff? Once you started it burning, it went off in a flash. No time to hurl it against an enemy.

Goram must have been working all night. He wobbled on his feet like a trooper who'd had too much to drink.

"We've got ideas, sir, to run with a version of a wick, which could delay the lightning long enough to deliver it. But there's no time, no time. Commander Radeo says it may be only a matter of days."

Radeo, too, looked a sight, charcoal streaks up his arms and smudges on his face. "Any news, Your Majesty?"

"Not this morning. What have you been doing? We have council meetings this afternoon."

"They're short-handed, sir. And you know I can't pass up a good recipe." I hadn't seen that grin since before I sent him to follow Calestinise to that secret army of light camp in Lakeside.

"Let's deal with the shortages. Then the time." I surveyed the frenetic activity in the isolated courtyard we'd handed over to the smiths for their experiments. "First off, here on out, you're in charge of this business, Radeo. Get more manpower. Wash up and go down to the town with Goram. Any maker who's not an armorer, that Goram trusts, is hereby conscripted. Round up their apprentices, laborers to do the work you lay out. Quarter them here, in the fortress. No wandering in and out."

"Got it, sir."

"Second, this space isn't sufficient." I eyed the scorch marks on the edge of the nearest overhanging roof. "You're playing with fire here. I don't want the fortress burned from the inside." Karthi's uniform dripping in the sun gleamed in my mind. "Stone floors or sand, no roofs. Practice yard is big, and we're done practicing for now."

"Right. Good idea, sir."

"Of course it is." Where Radeo had left off working, a long wooden table held basins of various powders. "Is that all your supply?"

"That there's the working mixes," Goram indicated a row of sacks leaning against the wall. "We've plenty for today, but tomorrow we'll need more."

I stuck my thumbs in my sword belt, using the tightening to distract me from the way my gut reacted to the sight of a paltry six bags. "I'm adding an item to today's council meeting, top of the agenda. We're calling in all the supply. And I'll have runners out by mid-afternoon, to any town close enough to make deliveries in the next day or two. Give me a list. Exactly what you need."

Radeo lifted his charcoal-blackened hands. "But sir, this is a secret project."

"A secret agricultural project? Who's going to care? Listen, Radeo, no one in this world is going to recognize these ingredients as anything more than plant food. But I'll put it out that we're protecting the fertilizer supply from the invaders."

Goram, being a smith, picked out the key phrase. "In this world, sir? Does lightning powder come from the snake-men world? It's not something your wife invented?"

Radeo clapped him on the shoulder, then tried to brush off the mess he made on the smith's shirt. "She'd enjoy hearing you say that." To me, he added, "But what about the shamans? Wouldn't they know about these other worlds and their weapons, too?"

"I have it on good authority—from my first father and the Master Shaman himself—that as far as they know, there's no more than pretty landscapes and spirit stuff out there. Goram, if Heyliannin had that shaman's cape she wants, I'd send her to get more information on how to use the stuff. But that's wishful thinking, and the brotherhood of shamans, they're our enemies."

"Sir?" We'd kept out of the public news that part of the problem.

"Sorry, Master Smith," Radeo said. "It's sensitive information, as there are shamans right here in town. But you need to know, they've joined with the enemy."

"Oh, my." He didn't seem worried. I swear he was calculating how well a cape might burn if it came in contact with a flaming gout of lightning powder. Enemies dancing across the field of conflict, but with fuel wrapped around them, could be useful in battle.

I left them to their work.

•   •   •

I ran the day's council meeting as if I was conducting a training session for recruits. Be quick. Stay on point. Allow time for reasonable questions—but no time for arguments. Karthi and Andus showed up, as ordered, Karthi wearing his freshly-laundered battle dress. That helped focus everyone's attention on the tasks at hand.

We had one easily-fielded question from a councilor I didn't recognize—a tall, bony guy in clothing that made him look like a tradesman. "Sir? I mean—"

For a councilor who didn't dress like a toff, I waved off the waffling about titles. "*Sir* is fine. What's your question?" Dramin edged up behind me and muttered low, *new guy—speaks for Koresh.*

His accent spoke of a town on the northern border of that district. "You keep talkin' about Southerners, but I'm not understandin' who we're afraid of. Where I'm from, we'd call everyone here a southerner. Do you mean Lakeside's turned on us? After all we've done for that district?"

Sometimes we forget the basics, dealing with civilians. Harad stepped up. "If I may, sir?"

I gave him the nod.

"When we refer to Southerners, we're talking about an alliance—a partnership. At the core is what we call the Hashtek Empire." Harad kept the lecture moving by pacing along the edge of the dais. "Imagine what this country might be like if Jeska District held all the power, instead of sharing. Their nation's in constant upheaval, because the subjugated states—the ones without power—are always rising up, sometimes taking over."

"Seems to me," the new councilor said—though he softened his remark with a sly grin—"Jeska District has the power over everyone." Around him, some councilors chuckled and others huffed indignation.

"Be that as it may ..." Harad moved on to the countries that supported the Hashteks—their independent allies, joining in with an eye to sharing the spoils of victory. My mind drifted to Heyliannin and her games at identifying our enemy—she'd been so certain they were people out of her own world's legends—or history, I could never tell which.

"If they're not *azztaks*," she'd say, "then at least we don't have to worry about getting our hearts chopped out. Are they into *soh-shul meedya*? Are they *hahsh-dags*? Snarky boys posting rude messages on the birdsong? Maybe Hash is the name of a company, run by big-headed *tekbros* and the killing they want to do is in the … the … livestock? … market."

I glanced up to catch a few of the councilors with lowered brows and irritated frowns—I'd been smiling during Harad's serious, boring lecture. I drew back from memories of cheerful times, and their expressions smoothed to satisfaction as mine showed my current worries. I tapped Harad's shoulder, and he stopped in the middle of an explanation of trade among those fractious nations down south.

"I think everyone sees it now," I said. "We can expect this invasion to be a combined effort, which is why we speak of *Southerners*."

That should have settled it, but then an established councilor—one of those toffs favoring shiny, luxurious clothing—had the nerve to demand proof. "Where's our evidence these Southerners—the so-called Hashtek Empire and their allies?—are marching against us?"

My fingers twitched at the desire to throttle the guy, but instead, I put my hands behind my back and clenched them into fists. "We've eyewitness accounts, Councilor. Increasing presence in the towns, forces marshalled at the border days ago, traitors colluding with Southerners to abduct and conscript our own children."

His smooth, unscarred face went pale. "Children?"

He hadn't been paying attention.

Karthi spoke before either Harad or I could answer. "You must have missed a briefing, Councilman, sir. They've kidnapped hundreds, as many as a thousand, of Lakesider youths, and turned them into a fighting unit. One to put our soldiers off-balance."

Silent shock rippled through the room. *Good.* They needed to remember they weren't there to quibble over who had the most power in the council. They were there to defend Jeska, in whatever ways soft, inattentive civilians could contribute.

"Commander Karthi's right," I said. "They've done this to break down our defenses. But that's not going to happen. We know their plan."

Andus put in his contribution. "And we've plans of our own, sirs. You can be sure of that. We're not the same old-time fighting force they met at NeverSnows. When Arnim's troops strike them in the first battle, they'll not know what's happened to them. If they dare come to Jeskaryan, they'll never go home." He shot a glance to Karthi and gave a barely-perceptible nod.

Lifting their fists in unison, they shouted the battle-yell, "Hai-ya!"

The sound filled the empty, worried spaces in the council hall. I lifted my own fist, and shouted, "For Jeska!"

The movement spread through those gathered, from the councilors, to the staff, to representatives of the elders, to the invited managers whose expertise and support we needed.

Instead of retreating down the back stairs, to get straight to work on the mess of plans on the table in my apartment, I led my crew through the crowd. A few there stretched out their hands to me, and I reached past my bodyguard to slap palms. They called me by name, and it reminded me of floating above the crowd at my wedding, the fingers brushing mine, the voices crying, "Corren, Corren, Corren!"

9

M Y GUT HAD BEEN ACHING since our arrival in Jeskaryan. It got so bad, I made Dramin fetch one of those doctors in. She declared it was nothing but over-worry and I should eat better and avoid alcohol.

She was right. About the drink, that is. Outside the circle of my Six, I'd been taking in more than usual. I needed to pay attention to that.

How could worry make a man's gut ache? Then again, hadn't that always been the way, for me?

I took a plate of plain, healthful food up to the council chamber after the afternoon strategy meeting and ate there, alone, watching what I could of the evacuation from that high room. By 'I took,' I mean I ordered someone to fetch me a meal like Radeo would have handed me. By 'alone,' I mean there was the guy on the stairs to my apartment, the two outside the entry door, and the one standing on the far end of the windows, watching for anyone who might be watching me.

Those were the days.

A dark, broken line stretched out along the northeast road, the one we'd walked together with our cantankerous baggage ponies on those failed expeditions to rescue Orkast. The lowering sun stretched the shadows of wagons and ponies and people to a wide, irregular smudge. Eldennian, I was sure, would be at the vanguard of that army of refugees. I couldn't pretend I was watching her go; she'd be beyond the horizon by now. I had a suspicion she wouldn't stop at Koresh, that she'd move further than any of them, to keep our Delia safe. If there was anybody in Jeska I wasn't worried about, it was that broken family of mine.

My moment of solitude shattered at the creak of the main entry doors. *Need to get a workman in here, fix that.* In came the runner Heyliannin had held at knifepoint in our Frogtown rooms. His tidy, pulled-back hair had fought free of its Lakeside braidings, so it looked as though he'd come in from a windstorm. He brought with him a second runner, a skinny creature with her hair slashed off short, wearing those Lakesider clothes that showed most of her arms and legs. I couldn't miss the bruises there, despite the road dust. She looked young enough to have been recruited by the army of light; she even had that fixed gaze I imagined they would have.

I fended off any false starts by addressing the first runner. "I remember you, Runner, but I never had your name."

"No, sir," he said, his eyes jumping from one burly bodyguard to the next.

"So?" I prompted.

"Tar." He indicated his companion. "This is Melinateria. She went to Southwest Township."

She nodded. Her eyes didn't jump around like his. They stayed on me. "Sorry we're late. Tar had to wait for me." I didn't miss that she didn't call me 'sir.'

Magaran had told them to partner up on the return. My gut began to worry about the last batch of runners. They'd be walking right into whatever was happening at the Narrows.

I gave back the stare she was giving me. "So. Someone try to cram you into a grey shirt?" The colors that ran over her face then, I wished I could have interpreted it all. She might have been about to assassinate me or about to fall over in a dead faint.

I beckoned over the nearest guard. "Harad and Radeo need to talk to this woman." He reached to take her arm, and she flinched as if he'd swept a knife at her. I moved in, caught both her hands in mine, and leaned close. I knew my guards would be imagining blades flashing out of her fingers, poison under her nails.

"Listen, kid," I told her. "You can trust Harad and Radeo. They know. My own kid just about got killed. Tell them your story, all right?"

She nodded, still never moving her eyes off me. Her voice rasped in a whisper. "Governor, the things they said about you …"

"I know. You know they're lies, but they're still in your head, right?"

"Yessir."

The worst kind of poison, thoughts.

"Go with this guy." I edged my shoulder towards the guard I'd summoned. "He'll keep you *safe*, understand?" I let go of her hands and snagged the guard's elbow. "You now, hands off, get it?"

He scrunched his eyes in confusion and resistance, but backed off and gave her an awkward bow, gesturing to the door. "Ma'am? If you'll come with me, uh, please?" It'd be a while before he'd qualify as a courtier, but it wasn't too bad a show.

The first runner, Tar, gave her an encouraging smile. "I told you. He's not what they said. I'll see you later, at Runners' House."

"All right," she murmured, and she followed my guy out of the chamber.

I let the door close behind them before I hit Tar with the question I most wanted answered. "So, my wife?"

"Sir?"

Where were his brains? "Do you have news of my wife and my kid and our friend? Heyliannin. Calestinise. Kul. They're not back yet, which means they're sheltering somewhere. They should have sent you with that information."

His face went almost as pale as Heyliannin's. "Not sure you want to hear this, sir."

I had used up all my patience on the girl. "I'll decide that! Don't hold out on me!" My spit hit him in the face, I was so close.

"They're not doing either, sir."

"What do you mean?"

He had to wipe fresh spray off his cheeks. "They're neither hiding nor hurrying home, sir. They're—"

"They're what?"

"They're rabble-rousing, sir." He started talking fast, backing away at the same time, until he came up against the door. "They're going around the towns and taverns, telling what happened … Like what happened to Melinateria, too … And getting people riled up."

So, this was when I found out what they were up to, down there in Lakeside. They didn't have a plan. Or, to be more exact, the three of them each had their own plan. The messages they sent wouldn't have made sense to an outsider. Maybe they intended it that way.

Heyliannin's message had no information, only an order: "Don't let them get hold of my book."

The runner added to that, "She seemed very intent on that, sir. Never knew a woman so bothered about a book."

"Ya, well, that's her way." I wasn't about to explain to Tar that she didn't mean any kind of ordinary book.

Kul's words put my old friend right there in the room with me. "Sorry, Boss. They're right. Trust me."

I'd trusted that man with my life too many times to count. But what did he mean by 'They're right'?

It was Calestinise sent me a clue of an actual plan. "Hey, Dad. Save me some kindling."

He was doing more than riling up the people down there. Calestinise planned to fight.

When?

Where?

How?

I headed out, my bodyguards forming up around me, sweeping Tar into our wake. He could give us exact locations and dates. I needed to talk to Magaran, review the troop movements. We'd work it out more exactly, but my brain was putting the pieces together as we jogged down stairs and along those dark hallways.

Tomorrow.

The Narrows.

PART II

STRATEGIZE FOR AUTONOMOUS ACTION

10

T HERE WAS NOTHING I could do in the upcoming skirmish.
Rather, I'd already done everything I could do. We all had.

By now, Arnim would be in the low hills flanking the Narrows, positioning his strike forces. Case would have given him additional men, but the main battle had to be at HandOverHand, not the Narrows. There hadn't been time to set up a defensive line that far from the city. We'd have been caught unprepared.

Arnim's men would move fast, just as our old band of six had done. He'd have hand-picked trained teams for the kind of skill and ferocity this harry-and-dash would call for. They'd be mixed troops of four and six and eight, each fully-informed of the force's mission—and as little-informed as their commander of the numbers they went up against.

What we had to go on was a glimpse of the mustering in the south, my estimates of the size of the army of light, and Case's suspicion that significant numbers had been hiding in outlying regions of Lakeside, using the shamans' information network to communicate with the main force.

In our late-evening strategy meeting, Magaran allocated barely any time to what would be happening at the Narrows.

"Arnim headed out with a dozen archers, and I was hard-put to hand them over," he said. "But they'll do good damage if he can talk the shooters into staying up in the rocks. I doubt Case will have given him many more." He gave me a look I had trouble deciphering. "I held back on him, too, Corren. There's not that many archers at HandOverHand—we're outclassed there, no getting around it. You'll remember those enormous bows of theirs, from NeverSnows."

As if I could forget. "Your point?"

"We'll need them here, to lay down fire from the heights."

One of the younger officers stood from a bench at the back of the room. "Sir. Are you saying it's a given they'll reach Jeskaryan?"

Magaran looked to me. My turn.

"Ya, it's unavoidable." I paced as I spoke, trying to shake off my own worries. "They're a large force, well-provisioned, and with a secondary army of irregulars. Some of their weapons are better than ours. They've been training and planning for a long time. They're almost certain to break through at HandOverHand, and we have intelligence that their goal is the city, not the countryside. Worse, they have allies within Jeska, even here in the city. This place is their objective: it's a takeover, not a raid."

I paused and looked over the room. The older officers tipped their heads together, talking tactics. The younger ones shifted restlessly in their places, as if they wanted to jump up and go kill a few Hashteks right now.

I didn't blame them.

Radeo lifted his hand. "Shall we move on to the good news, sir?"

"Ya," Karthi called to him from the shadows. "Let's hear it."

The scheming oldsters silenced themselves and the youngsters sat still.

"Go ahead, Cousin," I told Radeo. "It's your project."

The promise of the lightning powder dispatched the air of gloom that had taken over the gathering. Radeo stepped lightly on the topic of how we'd deploy this new weapon, but supplies of fertilizer and charcoal had rumbled into the training yard in quantity already, and more would arrive the next day. Whatever tools the smiths fashioned to use the stuff, we'd have plenty.

The Southerners wouldn't know what they were walking into. I wondered how many of those in the room were beginning to realize that our whole battle plan had become a double-feint—first the Narrows, then HandOverHand—with the real action to be here, at the gates of Jeskaryan.

I hoped those invaders would be bringing along their pet shamans, and that they'd put them in the front of the ranks.

The meeting broke up in good humor. For me, it was a relief no one expected me to take part in the chit-chat afterwards. In my mind, a scant hundred men crept over the moonlit hills of the Narrows, readying themselves, while a woman, an almost-child, and a bear of a man trundled north in the vanguard of their own fragile army of angry parents.

The remnants of my circle gathered in my apartment. Karthi and Andus came in last, having been making their rounds. Despite the numbers we'd deployed at the old mustering-ground, the barracks were full, crammed with reservists who'd come in from the towns and those who normally quartered in the city. When the pair strolled through my door, dodging around the guards, Dramin was in the middle of his run-down on what he'd observed going on among the city managers, what the elders seemed to be up to. There were few surprises. None of the elders had evacuated, which I thought was a problem, but Dramin insisted was a Good Thing.

"If they'd left, that would be the end, sir," he insisted. "If the matriarchs leave, no one will stay. Look at it this way. The elders have faith in you."

"Right." From the window, Jeskaryan looked as it always did—calm, peaceful, ribbons of smoke rising from cooking fires and smithies. The plumes glowed white in the moonlight. I couldn't help looking towards the south, where our missing friends would be facing danger, while we waited for the war to come to us.

Radeo and Harad stood a little apart from the rest, conferring in low tones. It was odd, how I still thought of them as family, though the whole under-covers operation had been a sham. Were they as worried as I was?

"Who's for a dose of medicine?" Dramin said.

I turned from the window to find him holding out a full jug. Not fruit juice.

"Na," I said. "Not a good idea."

He raised his eyebrows. "Take the advice of your medic, sir."

"Oh, you're playing that move, eh?"

"I am. Get yourself one good night's sleep."

I ran my gaze over the faces in the room: waiting, worried, brows furrowed, eyes narrowed.

Radeo broke the stillness, reaching for the jug and pouring himself a dose. He passed the drink to Harad, who did the same. Karthi followed suit, and soon all six of us were standing in a circle, our cups brimming.

It seemed I was supposed to say something, but I couldn't think of anything.

"For Jeska," Harad murmured, lifting his cup.

All of us then, we said it back, our voices low as if we were deep behind enemy lines, where any sound might bring doom upon us. "For Jeska."

We drank without saying more. I swear Dramin gave me a magic vessel, a cup that contained as much as the container we'd started with. At least it was only cider. My head buzzed, but there was no aftertaste of rotten fruit.

One by one, Dramin first and Radeo last, they left me alone there, with guards and servants for company.

Radeo paused at the door. "They'll be fine, Cousin," he said. "Kul and Calestinise will bring her home safe."

I wish he'd been right.

11

A S WELL YOU KNOW, the next day, that whole long day, men and children fought and died along the banks of the Heart River. We could only guess. There'd be no new information until a runner made it out. And no one would be sending news until it could be more than 'it's begun.'

In the meantime, we had to think about ourselves, the tasks ahead of the city defenders. The matriarchs had authorized laborers to throw up a makeshift palisade where the roads entered the city. Other workers—many acting on their own initiative—filled in gaps, turning the homes and workshops on the periphery into portions of a wall that could slow the attack. We had complaints during the morning council, that freelancers were knocking down buildings to fill openings with rubble.

"Better to be alive to rebuild afterwards," I told the complainers. But I sent for a master-builder to supervise those projects. The makers were in high demand, what with weapons-making both traditional and new.

Everyone left in Jeskaryan was too busy to think about the fighting. It would come to us, soon enough. We had to be ready.

The smiths worked on their schemes to deploy the lightning powder. The commanders counted off organized troops and disorganized reservists. There were tough decisions. I wanted to send more support to Case, to shore up the defenses at HandOverHand, increase the odds they could hold the tide there.

Magaran contradicted me. "Case has what he needs, for the kind of battle we've planned. And there's no chance he's holding them, sir. You know that."

It was just the two of us, for a change, hiding out in my apartment, forming a unified plan before the day's meeting with the commanders.

I wished Dramin would turn up with another jug of something to take my mind off all of this. I did what Yutek used to do—shuffled papers around on that worktable of his, making little piles of things that might belong together, then rearranging them again.

Magaran hovered by the door, waiting, but patient.

I shoved the papers into a single pile. "I know," I said. "You're right. We have to stick with the plan. We're short-handed as it is, here."

"Indeed we are."

"What are the odds that last hidden defense force will come through?" I asked him. From the start, we'd planned for Case to regroup with whatever men survived that battle and turn them into a fresh strike force, to come at the enemy from behind, once they reached Jeskaryan. It was Case's idea to take those troops to the north gate, anticipating a back-door attack.

"Eh, it's Case. He'll be there. No guessing at how many, though."

"If he can gather a single troop, that'll do." I remembered patrolling the northern border, taking out gangs of ruffians that outnumbered us two to one, the joy in it, their inevitable shock and dismay.

"It better be more than one troop." He had no sense of romance, Magaran. All about the practical.

"Ya, ya." I stood and stretched. "We need enough to do what Arnim and his guys are doing right now."

"We hope."

"It's more than a hope. Magaran, I wish you could've seen Arnim in action. The man thinks and fights at the same time."

He clapped his hands together and rubbed them vigorously. "That's a good combination, indeed. Anything else we need to discuss, sir? Before the meeting?"

There were a million things I wanted to discuss. I wanted a thousand days of leisure to sit and talk all we wanted. If we made it through the next few days, maybe we would have that.

I shook my head. "We'd best be on it. I have meetings with the elders later, and I need to go see what the smiths are up to."

"Delegate, Corren. You've got to delegate. It's the whole basis of the autonomous forces. It's your own idea. Use it."

"I know. It doesn't mean we don't need a master plan." The little room was too small. I had a crazy impulse to jump out the window, clamber down the wall, and disappear. I closed my eyes until the notion passed. "I have to see it all, Magaran. I have to have everything in my head, so I can find the way through. Understand?" Tymon would have understood. For all that had happened between us, or maybe because of it, he knew how I had to be. Just as I knew he needed to be everyone's friend, he knew I needed to get things right.

Magaran nodded, though I couldn't tell if he was agreeing or humoring me. The guard opened the door for us. The guy had an odd quirk to his expression.

"What's so funny?"

"Nothing, sir." But his eyes dropped to my jacket and his lips twitched again.

I was wearing his jacket. From the other night. I brushed a hand down the sleeve. It fit. It felt right. When the elders looked at me, they wouldn't see a criminal trying to be king. They'd see a soldier trying to lead. I hoped.

"Ya, well, sorry, but I'm keeping it," I told him.

"You're more than welcome, sir." His expression suddenly seemed less mocking and more pleased. I hadn't counted on that. So if I wasn't impressing the elders, at least the men under me appreciated my choices.

"Then, well, thank you."

Magaran was already on the move, so I hurried after him. When I caught up, I asked, "Which one is that?"

He knew what I meant. "That's Errem, sir. Made captain last month."

Errem and his three companions flowed around us, the new captain taking the rear-guard position, where I couldn't see that smirk of his.

·   ·   ·

I couldn't be everywhere, and Magaran had the commanders used to his style, so I gave everyone a nice encouraging speech and left that meeting in his hands. If I'd been them, I'd've been glad to see me go. Took five bodies out of the room, at any rate.

I wanted to see how the weaponeers were faring. A haze of smoke hung over the training ground. The smell had a sharpness to it, not at all like woodsmoke, with an overlying sweetness. Hard to say if it was just my imagination, but it was invigorating, made me feel a little hopeful. Maybe we could pull this off, save our city and enough of our people to make it worthwhile.

I'd started down the steps to the practice yard when a flurry of sound burst into life behind me—a grunt, the snick of steel being drawn, thick percussions of blows, and a cut-off cry like an infant that had found what it wanted. Two of my escort grabbed me by the arms, and rushed us down to the field before I had a chance to turn around.

I shook them off, barely restraining the impulse to draw my own blade.

"What was that?" I demanded.

The pair of them edged back, hands raised. I didn't find it reassuring. One pointed to the stairs. My jacket-donor, Errem, reached the field level and hurried towards us. Well, towards his comrades. The three of them conferred rapidly.

"How many this time?"

"Four of 'em."

"Our side?"

"Mika has a nick. Not a concern."

I broke in on their private gathering. "Somebody better talk, or we're going back to training days and let's see who gets nicked!"

Errem had the decency to flush with embarrassment. "Nothing to worry about, sir. Just a couple of objectors."

"Objectors?"

The other two looked at the ground. One of them said, "We thought it best—"

His partner shushed him.

I gave Errem my best fake smile. "What, exactly, did the four—or eight—of you 'think best'?"

"There've been attempts, sir. We're doing our job, sir." He shuffled his feet like a fresh recruit on his first foray down to the training ground. The sand rasped under his boots.

I started to speak, but stopped myself. With one hand up, to keep anyone else from talking, I let myself gather up connected strands. A disturbance in the hallway outside my apartment, while I was in a meeting. My bodyguards thumping shoulders and signaling each other in their version of sign-talk. The way one or two of them would suddenly disappear, then reappear.

So they weren't visiting the privy or sharing jokes or escorting drunks away from my door.

I remembered the tone in Yutek's voice when he'd told me to take on more men. Yutek never didn't know what was going on around him.

What did I most need to know?

"Who's sending them?"

"Sending them?" Errem shrugged. "They don't talk much when we're done with 'em."

"Next time—" Here I was, talking about the next time somebody tried to assassinate me. I took a breath. "Keep 'em alive."

The one with the bloodstained boots lifted his head. "It's been getting worse, sir."

"Shh," said the other one I couldn't name. His boots looked clean, but dark brown streaks marked his trousers.

"No, I won't keep quiet. Four's the most we've seen. They're getting serious. Sir, it's best to put them down fast. There's no time for clever cutting."

Errem agreed. "Sir, it's your life we're protecting."

"That's where you've gone wrong," I said. "My life isn't important. It's Jeska that matters. They knock me out, Magaran and the rest of you can handle this war. Maybe one or two Jeskans would go that far to kill me—but anybody here knows I'm off the list in a few days. No, this is coming from outside. We have to find out who's sending these guys."

They didn't seem to have an answer for me. Errem licked his lips and looked over his shoulder to the fourth man, who stood at the foot of the stairs making signals that undoubtedly meant, *Hey, can you come help with these bodies?*

"This is an order," I said. "Tell your buddies. Keep at least one of these 'objectors' alive and conscious, for interrogation. Anything like this, anything going on that worries you, do not keep it from me. Got it?"

Nods and yessirs.

"Go, then, Errem. Clean up the mess."

He trotted off, his right sleeve flapping where an assailant's blade had torn the fabric. I ran my hand down the sleeve of my stolen jacket. *Who's trying to kill me? The shamans? The Southerners? That power-hungry Lakesider, Velisennin?*

I had to stay put at the practice yard for a while, then, with my personal guard down to the stained-clothing pair. Surrounded by lightning powder and with Radeo marching around giving orders, I felt safe. Given what the smiths were playing at, maybe I shouldn't have. Felt safe, that is.

Lightning powder goes up in a flash. Like … well, like lightning.

If you put it in a box, then set the box alight, what happens? For a while—nothing. You wonder if anything's ever going to happen, if the smiths came out there to set boxes on fire for no reason.

Then the flame gnaws through the box.

It touches the lightning powder. You can tell, because you get a whiff of that distinctive smoke.

For a few more seconds, the box continues to burn, like a vandal came by your shop with a torch, to distract you with a fire while he clears out your stock.

The flames lick up, orange and yellow, and smoke drifts lazy plumes of grey and white into the sky.

Then—

And you'd better have been warned to stay back—

In a flash of fire and shredded lumber, the box bursts apart. Flaming splinters shower into the sky and hurtle earthward—a hundred burning daggers.

They had injuries, from the first tries. Even a little box, if well-sealed, could hurl its vengeance the width of the yard. So we lost the services of a half-dozen otherwise-eager young apprentices and one skilled smith who wouldn't listen when the kids told him to get under cover. No deaths. Not yet.

Radeo assigned a pair of guardsmen as crowd marshals, to keep onlookers out and order participants to safety. Or else. Even a burly smith will listen to a guy with a sword.

"It's too unpredictable," the Master Smith complained to me, as we stood watching the apprentices clean up the yard after a test. "We don't have identical boxes, for one thing, so every trial is different. Some won't seal up, no matter how much mud you slather on the seams—edges aren't mated properly. As you know."

I nodded as if I knew. Doubtless he'd forgotten I never learned my father's trade. I did wonder, "Why does it matter if it seals?"

"To bind up the fire, of course!" The things smiths expect everyone to know.

"Binding fire? Sounds like shaman business."

He laughed and made a move as if to pat my shoulder, but then caught the look in the nearest bodyguard's eye. "Ha, yes, sir, that it might. You can bind up heat in a thing if you feed it fire from the outside and don't give the fire a way to get out."

Radeo wandered over and listened to us with that wry look of his. "Here, sir, remember on the trail that night, when Calestinise burned himself?"

I cast my mind back. "Ya, what idiot thing was he doing, there? Not a cook by any means, that boy." He set a pot on the fire, left it to get to boiling, then somehow got himself scalded when he came back—much later—and tossed in a bunch of chia seeds. The next thing we knew he was yelling and jumping around and the pot was upside-down in the fire.

"When you heat water to make it boil but keep a lid on it, it does what the Master Smith said, binds up the fire. It gets loose when you throw something in, like Calestinise did. It'll boil dangerously hard." He rubbed his chin. "How does water do that, though, Master Smith? I've always wondered."

"Let's get this war done, young man, then we can talk about an apprenticeship for ya."

That was the point, wasn't it? Getting this war done, and us being on the winning side. I waved a hand at the mess. "The boxes are terrifying, sure. But we can't be carrying out a mysterious box and setting fire to it right in front of our enemies. For one thing, they wouldn't give the carriers a chance to start the fire, and for another, they'd probably stop the fire, wouldn't they? And then they'd look in the box. It would be delivering them a gift of lightning powder."

The Master Smith looked stricken. He'd been expecting praise for what he'd accomplished, and here we were talking strategy, instead. The things soldiers expect people to know.

"He's right," Radeo said. "Can't we make something that works this way, but in a small package, that we can throw at them? Like a water skin full of the stuff?"

"Ya," I said. "Or something even smaller, that you could attach to an arrow." I looked up at Radeo. "Imagine it, Cousin, an arrow misses, seemingly, sticks into a wagon. Then—pow!—fire and noise like they've never seen!"

The smith was already conjuring ideas up in his head. I could tell by the way his gaze went off into the distance. He might have been any man dreaming of a lost companion.

I checked the shadows. "I've got a meeting with the elders. Radeo—"

"Sir?"

"Be sure I'm first to hear if any news at all comes in."

"Of course."

"Good." My paltry bodyguard wasn't too comfortable with my insisting on taking off right then, but I had no choice. You don't insult the elders if you want to keep your job.

Errem and the other guy caught up, and their general nervous attitude abated, so I could let them disappear from my attention again.

I wondered how many would-be assassins the night crew had taken down, then put those thoughts out of my head.

•　　•　　•

That evening, after the last of the meetings, the six of us—me and Harad and Radeo, Dramin and Karthi and Andus—made an excursion to the edge of the town's fortifications, supposedly to inspect conditions there. We climbed to the top floor of the tallest building bordering the closed-off road. Whatever family lived there had taken their leave, gone with the evacuation. A neighbor opened the door for us.

Tomorrow, we'd begin placing defenders here. Archers, mostly. I wondered whether we'd have arrows equipped with lightning powder by then.

We leaned out the windows where we hoped to rain down fire on our enemies soon. The countryside lay below us, calm and dim as the sun set behind us.

"There!" Andus pointed south.

"Ya, I see it," Karthi said. "Boss, they've lit fires."

Could we see that far?

I squinted. Was I imagining a ribbon of shadow oozing up from the south, picked out for us by the lowering sun?

"Smoke, yes, I see it," Radeo confirmed.

We thumped each other's shoulders and tried to feel hopeful. We couldn't know how well the battle had gone; but we knew enough men had survived to burn our fallen enemies.

I strained my eyes against the dimming light. In my mind, I could see them clearly—the advancing forces moving towards HandOverHand, where Case waited to test an untried battle plan with far too few soldiers.

12

TYMON USED TO TELL ME stories of night runs. Even in peacetime, there's always someone who thinks their message is so urgent it's worth spending a premium to get the word delivered. Never one to turn down a commission—unless there was an opportunity to go interfere with the work of a certain guardsman—Tymon would snap up those jobs.

"There's nothing to match a night run," he told me. "The road's your own, nothing but the slap of your own feet hitting the dirt, shadows so deep you can imagine wading through lakes."

He knew every road and path the length and breadth of Jeska—where the footing might be chancy in moonlight, the spots bandits tended to linger, good places to pause for a drink and a meal. Often enough, a free meal.

As I'd reminded Yutek so often, people liked Tymon.

I'd commissioned two runners to travel with Arnim's force. The first one came in before dawn. He must have been on the move since the start of that engagement. How he managed to miss all the ground-dog holes between Jeskaryan and the Narrows, that was the mystery.

I'd taken to sleeping in better clothes, so all I needed to do was pull on my borrowed jacket when the tapping at the entry to my bedchamber roused me out of the fitful doze I'd settled for.

The night-shift guards were men I hadn't seen much of since training days. I kept getting their names and faces mixed up in my head. The one who'd woken me had a distinctive irregularity to his nose. Was it me who did that break?

"Be sure the runner gets food and water first," I told him. "There's time. Is anybody rounding up the commanders?"

I got my *yessir*, but he just stood there, looking at his feet.

"What's the problem?"

"Er … We're short a man—Errem says you wanted one of 'em held. So we're missing Durse—he's down with the one we caught."

I focused on the middle statement. "One what?"

He coughed and rubbed his chin. "Objector. Errem said—"

"Got it." If they'd had a visit from an assassin, the guards wouldn't be letting me roam around unprotected. "Let's go there, then. To wherever Durse has this man—"

"Woman. Sir. Young thing. Practically a kid, if you ask me."

At that point, I wanted to talk to that girl more than the runner. "Fine. Let's find someone on the way to get the message out that we'll have a briefing with Arnim's runner in a half-hour." I ducked past him and yanked the door open for myself. The pair outside fell into formation, and I moved on down the corridor as if I knew where I was going. Their glances and unintended movements were enough to guide me. They'd commandeered a small room with one door and no windows.

Before letting them open the door, I pulled back my hair and tied it tight. Then I took them a few paces back down the corridor for a pre-interview conference.

"Listen," I ordered. "No sirs, no titles, I'm another one of you guys, coming to relieve Durse. Got it?"

"Sir, you're not saying to leave you alone—"

"I want information, and she won't know what I look like. And who's in charge here? Me or you?"

"Err …"

"You guys will be right outside. I'm no fool—if I need help, I'll shout out."

Before they could assemble any more arguments, I pulled that door open myself and marched in. Durse—I recognized him, now, one of my sparring partners from way back in the under-guard—jumped to his feet. I gave him the sign we'd used back then, for when we'd play certain stunts on Magaran.

It worked. Instead of shouting out "Sir!" or worse, he stood up and yawned.

I yawned back at him. "My turn, buddy. Good luck getting some sleep."

He edged out, eyes full of questions.

I shut the door behind him and took his place in the lone chair.

Our prisoner owned a patch of floor in one corner.

She didn't have the army of light uniform. That would have made her conspicuous in Jeskaryan. But she had the attitude—her eyes blazed at me. I rocked in the chair and shifted my gaze from her glare to the door and back again.

"Give it a minute," I said, as if answering a question from her.

My guy was right—she couldn't have been older than Calestinise. Might have been younger, even. She didn't have her hair braided up Lakeside-style, but you could tell it had been that way recently, by the curly waves in it.

After my minute was up, I went to the door and eased it open a little. Durse stood guard to the right; another guard had posted himself to the left. Neither could be seen by our prisoner. I left the door open a crack.

"Good," I announced. "They've gone off to bow and scrape over His Royal High-and-Mighty-ness."

Her eyes fixed on the sliver of open space I'd made.

Instead of resuming the chair, I slid down next to her and drew my long-knife.

That got her attention.

My cue to begin.

"Who do I blame for this cock-up?" I growled, keeping my voice low and secretive. "You were supposed to be here tomorrow night. It's my off-night today. I'm here now because they're a man down. Thanks to you."

She made a confused noise. Might have been words, but that didn't matter.

"You didn't think they'd send you without inside help, did you? The man's guarded like he's some kind of valuable merchandise."

"But—"

"Never mind. We need to get you safely out, so you can report back."

"I—"

"They'll need to send someone else, though. You're a known face, now."

"If I come back a failure, they'll think I'm a spy."

I looked her in the eyes. That always makes people think you're being truthful. "It's not your fault you got bad orders." She had wide, deep, friendly eyes. Could have been any kid you might meet across a table in the market.

Then again, she'd come here to murder me.

I had to remind myself of that. The army of light had turned this kid. I couldn't let myself forget, start thinking of her the way I thought about my boys.

I flipped my knife end-over-end, enjoying the flash and flicker as it spun in the air. The moment I caught it, I turned it on her—that is, on the bindings my men had done on her arms and legs.

She jumped to her feet nearly as fast as I did. Before she could make a dash for the door, I took hold of her arm.

"Wait. I know a back way out. No one will see you go. Do you know the town well enough?"

She nodded, but I could feel uncertainty in the tension of her arm muscles.

I raised my voice enough to be sure my guys could hear me. "Listen. You'll come out of the fortress south of a workshop with a bear's-paw for a sign—he does leatherwork. Good stuff if you can afford it."

She tugged her arm free and rubbed where my fingers had left a red mark.

"Sorry. Once you're safe down, spot that sign, then hang a right and work your way downhill. Once you reach the market, you can find your own way. Am I right?"

Her nod had sureness to it, now.

"Hang on, let me check again." This time, only Durse stood at guard. He tipped his head towards the hallway, where his partner had sped to arrive first at the landmark I'd named. With a quick salute in honor of my scheme, he ducked around the corner, out of sight.

I held up a warning hand to the young assassin. "Give it a minute. I think I saw someone heading down the corridor. Best be safe."

After I'd counted off two minutes, I gestured to my new comrade-in-arms. "Come on."

She edged up close, her fingers twitching at the empty scabbard at her hip. "What about you?"

"I'll be fine. Don't you worry about me."

A shadow of fresh suspicion crossed her face.

I deployed my secret weapon. "Honor Truth."

That secret phrase transformed her tension to relief. She even smiled, shy as a girl meeting her boyfriend's parents. I should have felt something, sending this kid back, to be treated the way Calestinise had said they treated their soldiers. I gave her an honorable mission in service to Jeska. It should have been enough.

Confidence restored, she followed me out the door and around to the empty kitchen. The light in there was dim, with the fire banked, so that gave me an excuse to take my time. Even so, we soon reached the hatch in the far corner, the one that opened to the drain, where pots could be dumped and hot water sent down to flush the grease and tallow. For a moment, I was a boy again, leading my brother on our daring escape, to bring Tymon out of this house and to his new family—the one he'd abandoned in Lakeside, to take up a shaman's life.

"Look here," I told her. "It's not clean, but it takes you clear out of here, and fast. Don't imagine you can clamber back up this way. There's a couple of stretches it goes nearly vertical. You'll kill yourself if you try that."

"But—"

"No buts. Listen, there's not much time. You need to get back, tell them tonight's a bust, and get someone else assigned for tomorrow night. I'll be on door duty, as planned. Got it?"

"Yes. Got it." She looked like she might be about to cry. "Thank you."

"It's what we do for each other." I gave her a hand as she clambered up into that passageway. Sitting there, that scrawny kid seemed to fill the channel. We were such a pair of skinny nothings back then, too, me and Tymon. Who knew I'd ever come back to this spot?

"You want me to slide down?"

"Ya. It's exciting, in a way. But keep quiet. Don't scream, even for fun."

"I won't."

"Hurry, get your report in." I gave her a push, a little one, to get her started. Her braid-curled hair flew out behind her as she dropped into the race.

13

WITH LUCK, THEY'D ONLY SENT the one assassin that night. Durse had trouble staying invisible, he was so anxious as my sole bodyguard, following me along the dim walkways until we arrived—late—for the latest runner's debriefing.

Magaran hadn't wasted time waiting for me, which I appreciated. This runner would have no more than the bare minimum of information to share: how long ago he'd left, how far the enemy had advanced at that time, and how many special-forces troops Arnim had at his hand. I didn't need to hear it first-hand.

The commanders were already discussing timelines and troop movements by the time I walked in. They were waiting for me to hear the news and deliver my orders. I knew they'd have already developed firm opinions, so planned not to be too contradictory. No commander wants to hear orders they disagree with, even if the orders are right.

The runner had been fourteen hours on the march, on foot. From the look of him, he hadn't taken many rest stops. I wondered why Arnim hadn't thrown him onto a pony, get the information to us faster.

"They needed the pack animals, sir, to move gear between positions," he explained. Oddly knowledgeable, this runner.

"You had a stint in the Guard," I guessed.

"Yessir." He shrugged bony shoulders. "Didn't have the constitution for it."

I could see that—he was one of those skeletal-type runners, the type that can go for hours, as he'd done that day. Never fast, but steady and reliable. I did some arithmetic in my head.

"So. We'd guessed the attack would come at dawn, yesterday. But it was later than that, wasn't it?"

"Yessir. Their vanguard turned up shortly past noon. Commander Arnim held off any moves until the main body of the force was in the Narrows."

"As planned. So how many? I know you've told it already. I'll have my own questions."

"By the commander's count, close on two thousand." Nobody in the room flinched—it was more than we'd hoped for, but they'd already heard this.

"Was that all of 'em? Or is two thousand the number in the Narrows?"

"A scout from the southern reach came in with a report there was several hundred more queued up behind that bunch." This time, chairs scraped behind me and voices stilled.

"Did Arnim give you any details for us? Officers? Archers? Any animals?"

"Eh, sir, the commander was right busy. I watched and listened, while I was waiting."

"And what did you spy out?" I didn't have to wonder who had been clever enough to choose a retired trooper as the runner for this task. Arnim always knew his men's histories.

"Let's see." He closed his eyes, likely to think more clearly with those grim military faces staring at him. "At the vanguard, they had a rank of men on ponies—oversized animals if you ask me. Might have been scary to see, if they came up at you afoot. Behind them was a mob of undersized soldiers. They went along together in tight rows and columns like they was doing a festival dance. There was a lot of 'em. If the commander's count was true, must have been five or six hundred."

"Army of light," Harad broke in. "They drilled them on marching."

"Right," Radeo agreed. "But I'd've guessed at double the number, given the recruitment we've heard about. Were there more of those, further back in the ranks?"

Our informant shrugged. "Not that I saw, sir. Behind the little soldiers, regular-sized ones. About one in twenty wore colorful headgear—fluffy, poked up high, used feathers, I think. The commander said those would be officers—lieutenants, captains, higher-ups even fancier."

I moved him past guessing at rank levels. "How many?"

"There was two bunches of about the same size as what Commander Harad called the army of light. In between: archers, sir. They had bows big enough you could see them plain even from up high where I was."

Magaran grunted. "Told you. I hope Arnim took down as many of those as he could. Those bows throw a distance we couldn't believe, first time we saw them used."

I didn't need his I-told-you-so. "We've got lightning powder to surprise them with, this time." I returned to the runner. "So, to summarize: a threatening-looking vanguard on giant ponies, six hundred maniac kids—"

"Kids, sir?"

"You wouldn't know, would you? Ya, the army of light, they're youngsters."

He subsided, eyes wide in disbelief.

"Then another five hundred or so regulars, a band of archers—how many would you say?"

"Close on a hundred."

Bad news. I felt agreement with Magaran coming on. "So archers to throw above the ten or twelve hundred ahead of them, then another six hundred regulars. And behind them, we're not sure, but another rank of six hundred or so, possibly including more archers or more scary ponies. Have I got that right?"

He nodded. "Yessir."

In total then, we had more Southern regulars and fewer army of light than anticipated. I wasn't sure if that was better or worse. For myself, I'd rather have these numbers, but that was because I could too easily imagine facing one of those kids and having to decide to kill him—or her. That moment of decision could be deadly.

"Now then. What was Arnim deploying, and how?"

"It was confusing, sir. He sent out men before even one of the enemy arrived. They went one troop at a time, some to the southern end, others to the northern end, all scattered up and down, and on both sides of the Narrows. They were hiding up draws and in clumps of rocks, like … mountain lions stalking deer, not soldiers getting ready for a battle, sir."

"Don't let that bother you. We've got new styles you missed out on learning. How many troops did he have on hand? Or how many men, total? Modern troops, you may have seen, they're more variable than they used to be."

"I wondered about that, sir." He gave himself another moment of thought. "I told the master commander sir, that there was two hundred men—but what I was counting was troops, about twenty in all. I was forgetting how small those troops were. I'd say the complement wasn't over a hundred twenty, all told, counting officers."

"We call them strike forces," I told him. "They're different from our old troops."

"Still, sir. Is that right? We sent a single company to take on an army?"

I put a hand on his shoulder. Even though he'd left the service early, he'd have developed that sense we all have, that we're one in the Guard, that we're brothers. "They volunteered, to make a strike that will cut down that mob enough for our main force at HandOverHand to have half a chance to give the city an edge at the end of this. Understand?"

I got a nod from him, but I could see the thoughts running through his head. He'd be worried about his fellow runner, wouldn't he?

I was, too. There was no guarantee we'd get the post-battle report.

I was worried about all of them. Even the kids in the army of light. After all, they were Jeskans, and I'd sent some of my best men to kill as many of them as they could.

If the harrying at the Narrows started yesterday noon, the Southerners would reach HandOverHand today. Would Case be ready for them? In my mind, they advanced like a spring flood, inexorable, thirsty, unpredictable. The mustering-ground, the traditional gathering place for generations of Jeskan soldiers, waited for them, with our defenders dispersed over that landscape, not formed up to meet them, companies ordered to act without orders, led by senior commanders and called-up reservists. Leaders men could trust with the strike-and-retreat forms.

We'd lose men to confusion, to misdirection, to error.

We had no choice.

We were outnumbered. When you can't match the enemy at their own game, you have to make new rules.

I felt certain, now, that I'd left Case short-handed. Why had I let Magaran talk me out of sending reinforcements yesterday? That was the crucial battle. We could have spared one more company.

And now it was too late.

Arnim's runner looked the way I felt: drained, as if I had a mortal wound no one dared to mention. The floor should be sticky with blood. I put a hand to my abdomen, where I ought to have the usual pains, but for once, nothing.

The room went dim, shadows ringed my vision. "Hey," I complained. They shouldn't be dousing the lights yet.

"Boss? You all right?"

Karthi's voice pulled my attention away from the exhausted runner and back to the commanders.

At this point, they were mostly under-officers: captains, even a pimply-faced lieutenant shifting from one foot to another as he leaned against the back wall. Maybe Magaran had been right, that we couldn't have spared more.

The troop movements sliced through my brain. No, I'd been right. Magaran had been wrong.

My throat burned, as if I'd been chewing peppers on a dare, me and Tymon and the other boys competing for survival. The fire flowed up the back of my neck and around my head, spiking into my temples. At the same time, a web of ache spiraled downwards, flinging barbed strands to bite into my shoulders before tearing into my chest, clamping around my heart like wires fresh-drawn from the forge.

The officers watched me, expectant, like boys waiting for an assignment from their tutor. Maybe an assignment they didn't want, but one that would send them out of the classroom for another day.

I couldn't speak. I gave them a grunt and a cough and waved them at the door.

Someone led the runner out. I didn't see who.

I gasped in air and choked it out again.

Radeo had me by the elbow. "Cousin?" he said. Then, to someone else, spoken low and close, "Get a doctor."

14

T HERE WERE FOUR of us left in the briefing room. No, five.
I never remember to count myself.

Harad and Radeo fussed at me, made me sit in a chair and when that didn't help, told me to lie down on the floor. I refused. Karthi dragged over an extra chair and convinced me to put my feet up on it. He and Andus knew how far they could push me.

Where was Dramin? He'd missed the meeting.

He was spending so much time in town, with the elders and town officials, you might have thought he'd retired and gone into politics.

Maybe he had. Or maybe he would. Day after tomorrow.

What would I do, afterwards? Go run Calestinese's old trap line?

I leaned back and watched shadows on the ceiling while I thought about that. Too late to take up smithing, not that I ever wanted to. I could find that job I'd dreamed of as a child, pulling drinks for travelers at a crossroads inn. Who would hire me, after the elders were done with my reputation?

The midwife turned up first. She'd been coming back in after doing a delivery.

I rambled at her while she poked at my throat and listened to my chest.

Imagine. Someone produced a baby in the middle of this.

Tymon and I had a baby out there, his child, my foster-child. What would become of it, when I abdicated? Were there rules? Would we go live in the Runners' House, together?

No, Heyliannin wouldn't like that.

Besides, Tymon would be a shaman. Shamans don't have families.

"No sense worrying over a baby until it's arriving," the midwife said.

I must have been breathing easier, given I was talking so much.

"Right," she agreed. "It comes on a person like that, sometimes, when there's too much for one to cope with. You've got all these friends here, Governor—"

I laughed.

"That's better," she said.

She was packing up her kit by the time the first of the doctors skidded into the room, awash in professional concern. The midwife caught her colleague by the wrist and turned her around. "Nothing for you here. He was worrying over his pregnant wife."

Worried? No, I wasn't worried. By now, Heyliannin and Kul and Calestinise should have finished their rabble-rousing. They'd either be hiding out somewhere or sheltering at the Governor's House in Lakeside City. I'd've guessed the first—except that my wife would be anxious about those financial records. She'd insist they stay close by, so she could sneak in and out, confer with the men we'd left behind.

Maybe my after-the-war job would be assistant accountant, helping her ferret out the rest of the corruption hidden in those records.

The worry started up the moment the midwife spoke, became a warning drone at the back of my mind. It buzzed during a hurried breakfast while Karthi and Andus laid out a new scheme they were working on, then during the morning's chaotic mess of a council meeting. Three of the five elders attended, each with her own complaints about wall-building or soldiers occupying perimeter houses. Neither of the two that liked me a little accompanied them. Those two would be busy getting things done. I'd allotted an hour for the meeting—the elders dragged it out nearly two hours. The whole time, I was thinking, *what is she doing? Where are they? Kul should have got them home yesterday, the day before.* Calestinise's message twisted in my brain: *save me some kindling.* Would Kul let him get into the fighting? The boy had no weapons training, only his anger.

Because the meeting ran long, I had no time to visit the weapons workshop our practice yard had become. I had to make do with a summary from Radeo. He strode alongside me as I headed back to the garrison, to discuss the plans Karthi and Andus had been working on.

"Using lightning powder on arrows isn't practical," Radeo reported. "The quantity has to be too small. Besides, we can do as well or better by coating the arrows with pitch and lighting them on fire."

"Like boys throwing flame sticks for sport? Hardly impressive."

"Given arrow flight time, the slow burn with pitch is an advantage. Slow to start and hard to put out, that's the power of the stuff. I've been organizing a work crew to assemble pitch arrows."

That made disappointing sense. You couldn't overlook the ferocious speed that lighting powder burned. I remembered lazy afternoons down by the river, dipping sticks in pitch, lighting them, and competing to see who could hurl one the furthest across the water. One time, Tymon got one clear to a little grass-covered island—it started a fire.

My brain itched. "What if …" I mused.

"What if what?"

I let my thoughts form up as we clattered down the steps and out to the courtyard. I needed to check in with the commanders—and captains—on the progress of force placements. The elders might be annoyed now, but they'd be much more annoyed if we let Southerners walk into our city.

When the idea finally came together, I stopped so fast, I nearly fell over my own feet. There was Radeo, grabbing at my elbow again. Did he think I was on the verge of collapse?

Well, maybe I was.

"Listen." I shook my arm free. "What if we coat the arrow shaft with lightning powder—not all the way along, but, say over the half at the business end. Then—add an overlay of pitch. While the arrow's in flight, the pitch burns—dramatic enough, but not unexpected. But when any part of the flame reaches the powder—the arrow flies apart, flinging splinters, like the boxes."

Radeo caught the idea immediately. "I say we pack the pitch with metal shavings, waste scraps. The lightning powder will fling that stuff, hot metal as well as splintered wood."

"You've an evil mind, Cousin, to think of such things."

He gestured the bodyguards closer. "You guys are on your own with the boss," he told them. "I've got to get this idea in front of the Master Smith." He gave me a look. "You know he's going to tell me you should have gone for smithing."

"Tell him I've plans for after the war and they don't involve anything more complicated than pouring drinks."

My day-guard were enthusiastic over the exploding-arrow idea. I had the impression they were wishing they could have a turn raining those things down on Southerners.

I had about decided to give up on having invisible bodyguards, when I remembered.

"Where'd that assassin end up?"

Errem put on his confused, apologetic face. "Ah … night guard didn't report?'

"You guys know perfectly well shift change hit in the middle of a debriefing." A debriefing that ended in me being … ill. Whatever that was, these guys wouldn't want to show they'd noticed anything.

"Ya, ya."

"Well?" If I'd had breakfast or anything like a decent sleep, I might have done more than glare at him.

"It was as you thought, sir. She went straight to the Shamans' House." His tone told me I shouldn't be angry, given my suspicions had been confirmed.

"I'd hoped to be wrong about that, trooper." Hearing this earlier, after the debrief, would have been unsettling. *The shamans are trying to kill me. Not Southerners. Not managers. My own true-father's friends are out to get me.*

Now, though, I was too busy to worry. And my non-invisible guard had fended off the assassins perfectly so far. "Keep me alive through tomorrow, guys, that's all I ask."

"Uh, yessir."

As you see, they did that.

15

I NEVER DID make it down to the workshops that day. Harad intercepted me on the way to that meeting I'd promised Andus and Karthi, and he wasn't happy.

"Don't listen to those boys, sir," he insisted.

My mind went to the kids playing at stone-counters in my old room. "What do you mean? I haven't seen Stevvin and Affram since yesterday."

"No, no. I meant Karthi and Andus. They're full of a scheme that's going to get them killed."

I hadn't given Harad much attention lately. He'd gone red-eyed and wrinkly. How had that happened? I shook my brains back into order. I kept forgetting that Harad and Radeo were so much older— if none of this had happened, they'd be giving me orders, and I'd be honored to obey them. To them, we were all boys playing at war.

I looked him in the eye, trying the trick I'd played on the girl assassin in the chill of the scullery that morning. "I'll take your advice, Harad. But I'll hear their idea out. Give us credit, commander, we're not kids."

"Sorry, sir. But—"

"I mean it. I'll hear them. And then I'll hear you."

He bobbed his head, but his eyes still crinkled with worry. "Yessir."

Their scheme—to put the notion as briefly as possible—was to replicate Arnim's action at the Narrows with a gauntlet of strike-force attack troops spread out along the line of approach between HandOverHand and Jeskaryan. There wasn't a convenient natural channel with hills and gullies, but there were streams that became dry routes in summer, stretches of country left to the wild, with good stands of chapparal that could conceal half an army if one had enough men for that.

"We'll be harriers, Boss," Karthi explained. "We'll work the way wolves do, hunting game."

"I don't know much about wolves," I admitted. "Can't you be bears?"

"No," Andus chuckled. "Bears hunt, but not in a coordinated way. A wolf pack will spread out along a herd's line of travel, then run relays, diving in, making them run, confusing the prey until it's clear which are the weak ones, the ones they can take down."

"Right." Karthi had a map tacked up on the wall of the briefing room. "Look, sir. If you can spare us even a dozen troops—"

"Except...you don't want a dozen, do you?" Once he'd started outlining the plan, the conclusion was clear. "You want a hundred men, at least. A company."

Karthi shrugged. "It would be better. But we can make do."

I studied the map, where he'd sketched in positions. "If you're going to do a thing, best do it right. If you're not effective, you're wasting lives." I gave him a hard look. "Jeskan lives."

He flushed. "Right, sir. Well, yes, when we worked it out, our best guess was roughly a company, in strike-force groupings, about sixteen troops."

Andus stepped up and tapped a finger along the line of markers. "See, here, each would be positioned to make it possible to join up with the next troop, once the enemy force has passed each position."

"The survivors, you mean."

They didn't have much to say to that. Like Arnim's venture at the Narrows, this would be a mission most would not return from.

Harad took his opening. "My point, exactly."

I gave him a measured look and held up a hand to fend him off. "I'm not sure it is, Commander. This is a desperate time. The men have been training hard. Independent units work well—"

"Theoretically. We haven't yet had word back from Arnim."

"You're wrong there. We've been fighting in this style since day one, Harad—me and my Six. Magaran ran exercises, while you and I were roaming the wilds of Lakeside. Time and again, the new forces outmatched the old-style ones. Under changing conditions, troops reorganized *themselves*, Harad. It's a tested approach."

"Under exercise conditions. And they haven't seen the army of light." He leaned close to me, lowered his voice. "It's these boys of yours here I'm speaking of. They've no idea, and, besides—"

I caught him by the elbow, much as Radeo had done to me twice already today. I pulled him straight out to the hallway, past Karthi's and Andus's surprised faces, dodging my confused bodyguard.

I put my face up into Harad's. "What's your problem, *Cousin*? Are you that troubled by your one encounter with those kids?"

He sagged against the wall. "No, no. Well, yes, of course I'm troubled." He held up a hand against whatever I might say to that, and brought his voice down to a whisper. "You know what the risks are. You know what the casualties will be. So you're going to lose one of those boys—maybe both of 'em. And the risk is higher if you send them together. You got that, right? That they both want to go, each to command one side of the harry?"

I had to agree.

"And what do you think that means for the men under them? To have their commander constantly thinking of the man on the other side, worrying about him?"

"I—"

He used a sharper line. "You're worrying about Heyliannin. And the others. Right now. Aren't you?"

"Well …"

"And it affects you, doesn't it, Cousin? I watched your attention drift, during the briefing, in council, minutes ago, as Andus and Karthi were showing off their plan."

"So?"

"Are you sold on that plan?"

I nodded. "It's a good idea, Harad. I don't know why we didn't think of it before. We've been treating the approach to Jeskaryan as a free passage for the enemy."

"Send me instead."

"What?"

"Don't send them both. Keep one here. Then the other will focus. Maybe even survive."

"You're volunteering?"

He blinked down at me. "Are you surprised?"

I was. I admit it. I'd been treating him as a man ready to retire, one who'd met his match. "No," I told him. "Which one will you partner with, then?"

"Andus is younger, right?"

"Ya."

"Then keep him back here. Send Karthi. The other way round, something happens, he won't forgive himself."

At the far end of the hallway, a commotion approached. Something else I'd have to do something about, no doubt. I needed to decide on this matter first. It would take time to get those men into position, time we were nearly out of. I dragged Harad back into the room. Karthi and Andus stood close to each other, ready to argue against Harad's objections.

"Take ponies," I ordered. "Get your men out to those positions as quickly as possible. You can use riders to communicate, shift forces quickly, and send runners back with word early in the action. Karthi, you command the north rank, Harad, take the south. Andus, sorry, I need you here. Harad's senior. He's seen more action than any of us."

The voices down the hall got louder.

"Time's up. Get a move on. Andus, I need a plan for the main gate defense. By mid-afternoon. Get on it." I left them like that, three men with different ideas, having to cope with orders they didn't like. They'd manage.

●　　　●　　　●

The voices down the hall were my foster-sons, running ahead of a cluster of guardsmen who probably didn't know whose kids those were.

"Dad!" Stevvin shouted. "Mom's here!"

It took a second to process the Lakesider slang. I broke into a run, ignoring the heat of the day, ignoring my bodyguards sweating alongside me.

The boys led us back up to the government buildings, the king's house. Halfway down the hallway to my apartment, we caught up to a cluster of people I recognized.

Doctors. The one who'd told me Yutek was dying turned and blocked my way.

"We need to talk, sir," she said. Beyond her, a bedraggled woman with limp brown hair dangling down her back staggered along between two more of those women in their dull brown tunics.

"No, we don't." I countered. "Out of my way." I didn't raise my voice, but my guards tightened formation around me.

The young doctor ignored them. "She's had a rough time. You need to hear about it without putting her under stress."

I thought about drawing my knife and ending the self-righteous know-it-all right then. It wouldn't be polite. Or legal, though at the time it was still the case that, if the king does something, that *makes* it legal.

Then again, did we want to legalize killing doctors? The matriarchy wouldn't like that.

What could they do, though? Fire me? They'd already done that, as of tomorrow night. Assuming I was still alive then.

On balance, it seemed sensible to begin by listening. She met my gaze unblinking.

"Talk fast," I told her.

"She's exhausted, dehydrated, has a few minor injuries, from falls."

"Falls?"

"She came in riding a pony. My understanding is she's not—"

"—no, not that good a rider. Why was she riding?"

"We don't know, sir. The important thing—"

"What about the others?"

"Others, sir?"

"Kul, Calestinise. Big man, youngster—not a kid, not an adult, either."

She shook her head. "She was alone, sir."

I looked over her shoulder as the doctor gang hauled Heyliannin through the door and disappeared. "None of that is a reason to keep me from my wife."

"One more thing, sir." Her eyes were dilated. Why? What was she scared of?

Me, probably. "What?"

"I understand she was pregnant, sir." She moved one hand as if she might have been about to touch me, but Errem twitched and she turned the gesture into a brush at her own hair.

Then I heard what she'd said. *"Was*? As in, *isn't* now?"

"I'm sorry, sir." With that she whirled away, getting out of my reach before my bones could unfreeze themselves. "We'll send for you very soon, sir, once she's settled."

They locked me out of my apartment. Left me standing in the hallway with a bunch of ignorant soldiers. Radeo and Harad, the ones who knew about the baby, were busy, on my own orders. Who could I talk to? What did it mean, when a woman had been pregnant and then wasn't anymore? Regular people would know about that kind of thing. It never happened to Eldennian, so how could I know?

I snapped my fingers under Errem's nose.

"Sir?" he said.

"One of you go fetch Ganderrison."

That got me a vacant stare.

"The midwife. The woman who came to the briefing room this morning."

Shrugs of reluctance to leave me short-guarded.

"Now. Or else."

Errem sent one of the other guys. That was good. I liked having at least one guy nearby that I knew by name more than rank.

Where could I wait for these doctors to decide I could see my wife?

I settled on the council chambers. I could use the back stairs, get down to my apartment fast. I was about to go break down that door myself, when Dramin turned up.

He opened with, "I've got news."

"I know. Go down there and make those doctors talk. They've locked me out and all I know is Heyliannin isn't pregnant anymore.

What does that mean? She can't have had a baby already, right?" Even I knew that would be impossible.

Dramin watched my face. He had a way of seeing what I was thinking. "Ya, Boss. A lot of the time, babies get started and then … stop. It's called a miscarriage."

"Makes it sound like a mistake."

"It's nobody's fault, sir. It happens."

"Why? Is it dangerous? For the mother, I mean."

He shrugged. "Mostly, no one knows. It's not usually dangerous, no."

"So, it's normal? Women are fine with that? They don't care? They just go start a new one?"

He gave me that long, patient look. "Of course they care. And they're never fine with it. But, yes, usually, eventually, they will try again."

"She won't." I'd said too much, but he spared me the questions that would be rattling around in his head, ones I couldn't answer. Heyliannin wanted that baby because it was Tymon's, but now Tymon had gone into the shaman business. Shamans *abstain*, as they call it.

Why? It makes no sense. They claim the mantles don't work otherwise. Given the mantles were living creatures, it made even less sense. But rules are rules, and shamans are maniacal about their rules.

The silence between us got thick enough to sit on.

He seemed anxious, kept looking behind, to the door.

I made a guess. "That wasn't your news."

The medic dropped away, and the soldier came to the fore. I felt better already.

Dramin, on the other hand, seemed anxious. "We have a group of … asylum seekers, they're calling themselves."

Why was he being so vague? "This is no safe refuge. We've evacuated everyone at risk to the northern districts already." I began to question how well that had been done. There weren't any towns along the march we expected the Southern army to take, but people in the foothills might have panicked. "Send them home. What town are they from?"

He had a quick answer for that one, "Frogtown."

The map of Jeska District swam in my vision. "No such … Wait. Lakesiders? Ahead of the battle force?"

"More than Lakesiders. Shamans. My guess is they headed north the day after you did, maybe the morning after that."

A noise beyond the dais dragged my attention away from shamans begging for help in the middle of a war they'd arranged.

"Sir?" One of the doctors stood at the top of the stairs to my apartment.

"What?" I probably sounded annoyed. Her mouth set in a tight line, the kind that usually meant somebody was thinking bad thoughts about me.

"Not what, but who. Your *wife*, sir."

I wasn't sure if my gut was predicting bad news or worse news. "Tell me." Best to find out quickly.

"She's resting comfortably. I advise leaving her undisturbed overnight."

Dramin said it, not me: "She has information we need. Now."

The doctor laced her fingers and held them in front of her chest, as if preparing to fend off a knife to the heart. Or preventing herself from throttling one or both of us. "We're agreed that's highly unlikely, sir. From what she's said, she left the party the day before yesterday. The battle you're concerned about was yesterday, correct?"

I didn't want her to be right. But if that were true, Heyliannin wouldn't have intel we needed right away. But … "Did she say where our kid is—Calestinise? And Kul?"

Dramin tapped me on the shoulder. "Sir. She's in good care. We have a situation."

My head swung from him to the doctor and back. Heyliannin was back, but on her own, and I wouldn't hear her story until after tomorrow's battle. If ever. But Dramin was right. I had a job to do, as much as the doctor.

I gave her what I intended to be a respectful nod. Then I tried to forget her, the way I forgot the four men hanging around ready to fend off assassins.

Dramin started for the door.

"Where are these shamans now?" I demanded.

He looked over his shoulder as Errem pulled the door open.

Voices and the clatter of boots on boards filled the high space above the stairs.

"They're here," Dramin said.

16

A BAND OF REBEL SHAMANS invading the council chambers? My bodyguards looked like they might all drop dead of attack heart right there. I waved them back towards the dais and jumped up to my usual spot beside Yutek's chair. Once in motion, the four men settled down and arranged themselves into an unbreachable wall.

A cluster of councilors led the way, so we had a little time to sort our thoughts.

With the current councilors came Kerrin, the one I'd fired, the one I'd always hated. He pushed his way past the rest and dared to move right in front of Errem.

"Don't believe them," Kerrin called over those hulking shoulders. "They're traitors, Corren! They've been conspiring with the Hashteks!"

I looked him in the eyes. There was a complicated story there, one that Arnim could have extracted with a few words in the right order. Yutek had kept Kerrin around, despite the obvious overspending. The man wasn't holed up in the Shamans' House, home of the assassin corps. Had he had a change of heart? Had he always been playing both sides? Or was he Yutek's man all along?

"I know what they've been up to," I said. "Your verifying it has value." I tapped Errem on the shoulder. "Escort the former councilor to Commander Radeo."

"Boss?" Even I could hear the *What? Now? With traitors at the door?* in his tone.

"We're good. Dramin's here. This guy's got intel we need yesterday."

This time, Kerrin left without being dragged. There was a lightness to his step I'd never seen before. *Another story I'll never hear.*

The remaining councilors formed a second phalanx between me and the asylum-seekers. Even Dineen, that scrawny little accountant, had a fierce look in his eye. Or maybe Heyliannin had taught me accountants can be fierce. Those civilians turned in place as neatly as a bunch of second-year guardsmen, to face the new arrivals.

At first, it looked like four shamans, but they'd formed into rows, like an oversized troop of the army of light. Twenty all told. I'm not good at faces, you know that, but I recognized two of them.

In the back row, a dark bundle of mantle clutched in his arms: my brother.

In the front, his shiny braided hair tied to hang down one side and his mantle swirling from his shoulders like the live thing I knew it to be: Racac, Master Shaman of Lakeside.

He took one look at me and proved himself a master of recognizing people. "You!" he blurted out. "The idiot with the lawsuit!"

I let him stew for a few long seconds. "Ya," I allowed. "Your minions assaulted my son. We have witnesses. I presume you've come with a settlement offer? My wife will be pleased." I gave him my best regal wave. "She'll get back to you with a counter-offer." Then I took a step sideways and—for the first time—sat in the king's chair. Just to be sure he knew for certain.

He stood with his jaw clenched. I could almost hear his teeth grinding.

"Good-bye, then." I repeated the wave. Through a gap in the bodies, I caught a glimpse of Dramin waiting with his back to the door. He grinned. This was our kind of game. He clicked the latch and began to pull on the door, at the right speed to get the hinges creaking.

"That's not why we're here!" Racac announced.

"Oh?" I made my voice lazy and drew my knife.

He took a step backwards. As if I couldn't throw a knife that far. "We seek asylum. For ourselves and our prentices."

"Oh, really?" Easing to my feet, I made a show of counting them off, while silently signaling to Tymon, *all right?*

He struck me as anxious, shifting on his feet the way he never did, but his return sign came, *all right.*

Time to stop playing the bumpkin.

I sheathed my knife. "You can't stay here, shaman."

"But—" He stepped forward again, and the nearest guard moved to block him. I waited for Racac to return to his position.

"You shamans—" I indicated the first row, the fully-qualified men. "We'll put you on a wagon within the hour, with a guide to take you off north."

"But our Jeskaryan brothers have invited—"

"I've no time to build a fire for you, not now. We'll hunt you down later. Mark my words."

His face went dark. So he'd got my message.

"Your prentices, we'll have them checked out by senior personnel. It's possible a few may have family or other obligations here. The rest will follow you shortly."

I can't say where this plan was coming from, but I didn't want these new shamans in town, colluding with the ones I already had to deal with.

"You can use us, Your Majesty," he blithered. "You'll need shamans to combat the invaders. You know there's an invasion, do you not?"

I laughed. Dramin roared. We kept it up until the councilors got the hint and joined in. Dineen had a musical laugh that reminded me of Heyliannin's. Moment by moment, Racac's fury grew.

Before he could turn that anger into words, I struck first. "Shamans are useless in battle. I've seen action, old man. I'll not have your flappy capes interfering with my archers or distracting my foot soldiers. Besides … aren't you worried the poor mantles might get … *injured*?" I leaned towards him with that last, and lowered my voice as if sharing a secret others wouldn't know.

His face went from deep brown to pale in an instant.

Aha. I'm right. Now they know I know.

By that time, Errem was back, a column of fresh troopers with him. Looked to be enough to match the shamans man for man. Dramin corralled a guardsman with lieutenant's insignia and sent him to me.

"Lieutenant."

"Sir." He saluted instead of bowing. I wanted to promote him on the spot.

"These men here, the ones wearing capes. Escort them to the quartermaster's office, and have transport arranged for them. To … let's say Koresh—"

Racac kept interrupting, but we talked over him easily.

"Yes, sir," the young officer replied. "Koresh it is. Can I commandeer a guide?"

"Choose a trooper. Make it two, to be safe. These men are to be *cawnvicks.*" I'd had an inspiration, from one of those arguments with Heyliannin.

"Sir?"

"Deliver them to the garrison at Koresh. Have them confined to barracks. Got that?"

"Oh. Like recruits on report?"

"Ya, only more so. See that all exits are secured."

The lieutenant took on a thoughtful expression, probably imagining ways to turn a barracks into what my wife called a *jayle.* Thoughts didn't impede his actions. In one motion, he turned, grabbed Racac by one elbow, spun him around, and caught the other elbow from behind. The traitor was marched out with all the dignity of a boy caught stealing in the market. Racac proved he knew most of the same curses my friends and I had used back in the day.

We had a few minutes of seeming chaos, as Dramin dispatched soldiers to collect the rest of the shamans. The prentices shuffled off to the side, clutching their mantles, exchanging anxious words. Once their masters had been dispatched, we brought in the rest of the guardsmen Errem had rounded up and paired them off. Dramin quietly placed himself in charge of that one prentice I knew so personally.

I kept to my fancy chair and spun ideas in silence until I hit one that might work.

"Listen!" I ordered, taking to my feet and moving past the protection of my bodyguard. I'd been watching those young prentices—and Tymon. None of them were assassins. Whatever else Racac had planned, it seemed he was ensuring his new trainees were relatively out of reach of whoever might be down in Lakeside right now.

All those shaven heads turned my way.

"You are hereby released from your contracts."

A dozen mouths gaped and flapped, but nobody said anything.

"Your apprenticeships are now officially terminated."

One of them gasped and collapsed. His accompanying soldier dropped to his knees and felt for a pulse. "He's just fainted, sir."

One of the other shamans-in-training came up with words. "You can't do that! All we have is in the House. None of us has any resources. And Dolan there doesn't even have a family to go home to!"

"We'll be confiscating the coffers of Lakeside's House." I was talking off the top of my head, but everything made perfect sense. "They've committed gross misuse of funds, not to mention treason. You'll be reimbursed." It might be a while. Certainly, they'd have to wait until the war resolved itself. "Once you're processed, go to your families. Tell your matriarchs what's happened, that there's compensation due. You there—what's your name?"

"Ansill. Sir." He'd gone pale. Did he think I was about to send him off with Racac's gang of conspirators?

"Take charge of Dolan, there, if he's got nowhere to go."

He nodded, and the color started to come back into his face.

"Councilors."

The clot of them had retreated to the far corner during the dragging-out operation. They oozed back to the front row.

"Sir?" Dineen ventured. Caldrim looked as though he might compete with Dolan in the fainting event.

"See that word gets to the elders about this situation, would you?"

They nodded as one unit. Dineen fumbled at a salute.

"You're excused. See you at this evening's meeting?"

They bowed and smiled and oozed out of the room.

"Errem."

He gave me that now-familiar look that said, *What inappropriate orders am I getting now?*

"You're in charge of these prentices."

He rolled his eyes.

"We're short-handed, and the bad guys are on their way to Koresh. Get these men's particulars, *introduce* them to Radeo—you know where he is, so wait for him to finish—and cut these guys loose. Got it?"

He scrunched his eyes. Had he caught that I wanted Radeo to vet them out, first? That this was a task he was being *trusted* with? In a low voice, he asked, "If Commander Radeo has other orders?"

"Obey those orders."

"Ah. I see. Yessir." He started through the crowd, giving the ex-apprentices a friendly come-along wave.

They began to follow. The fainter, Dolan, staggered to his feet.

"Wait," I said.

They froze in place, ready to be sent off to jayle.

"You don't need the mantles. Leave them." I gestured to the wall under the windows. "Spread 'em out over there. Give them room. You know. In case they don't get along."

A few of them flinched at that comment. So, they knew. How far along were they in training? Radeo would get that out of them. I guessed we'd be packing off two or three in Racac's direction.

Tymon began to shuffle along with the rest of them, but Dramin held him back. I stepped down from my kingly position and lifted the mantle from him. I swear, it stirred in my arms.

"There's someone who needs this guy. She'll be grateful you were able to rescue it."

He choked on words. One of them might have been, "Sorry."

"A lot's happened, brother." I lifted the vaguely squirmy mass of fur. "I'm right, aren't I? It's Asdyel I've got here."

He nodded. The one skill the shamans seemed to have taught Tymon: silence.

I handed the mantle to Dramin. "The doctors will probably let you in. Get this to Heyliannin. No matter what."

He took it, but acted like the thing was going to attack him. I remembered Fennic's joke, that one time in my office. *It's not going to bite you.* I guessed the things were dangerous, if you didn't know how to handle them. If they had teeth, where did they hide? Or did they have stingers or venom? I had an impulse to spread it out, interrogate it, but now was not the time.

Tymon had perked up at my wife's name, but he tried not to let me see. We stood together, watching Dramin disappear down the stairs. We listened as the door clacked open, then closed.

Get him thinking of his own situation. "Where will you go?" I asked him.

"I don't know. Shamans' House?"

I waved off that idea. Worse than bad. "The runners will take you. You're done with your project, go home. Come back tomorrow. Yes, she's sick, but she'll be all right."

"No, no, I can't go there." I could barely hear him. Was there a complication, because he'd officially resigned?

I thought for a minute. He could stay here, in the king's house. But how would that be for him, remembering the bad times? "Listen. Eldennian's gone with the evacuation. Go to her house. Lock up tight. Stay safe. There's a war on, you understand that, don't you?"

A nod. Serious eyes. When did he get wrinkles there?

"Afterwards …" I wasn't sure how to put this to him. I didn't want to be direct. He wouldn't understand, and something told me he'd been through more than I guessed, pretending to become a shaman. "I've got a commission for you."

"I'm not a runner anymore."

"Do it this once, for me."

He blinked at me. "Go on."

"Go to the Council of Elders, to Adestinian."

"All right." He waited for the message.

"Tell her this: Corren's done as agreed."

A trace of professional flair lit in his eyes. "Just that? I'll give you a free pass. The House won't send an invoice."

"Then I want you to introduce yourself. She'll have a job for you, once this is over."

He scoffed. "A government job? Me, a bureaucrat?"

"Sorry. It's the best I can do right now."

He looked at the floor and rubbed his stubbly head. "You don't owe me any favors, Corren."

"Maybe not. Maybe not." I debated telling him about the baby. What good would it do, to make him that sad? Would it make me feel less alone?

Dramin emerged from the back stairs. He didn't say anything, but gave me the sign that said he'd done what I asked.

"Can you walk Tymon down to my old place? To Eldennian's house? He's going to hole up there for a while."

"Sure you don't want him to chat with Radeo, first, Boss?" He brushed at his jacket as if clearing it of mantle fur and dodged around the bundles laid out across the floor. I wondered if his medical sensibilities had clued him in to their nature. Under cover of his other moves, he was throwing signs at me, urging me to send my brother off to be interrogated.

What good would that do? Tymon had been through enough. "We've had a chat, ourselves. He just needs a place to go."

Dramin gave Tymon a smile, but it didn't seem to cheer either of them.

Dramin would be planning how to critique my choices—or to conduct his own interrogation. Tymon would be wishing he could go where that mantle had gone—where not even I was allowed to be.

My troop's medic took my vague-eyed brother by the arm and led him to the door. "Let's take a detour down by the kitchens and get you supplied." Neither of them looked back.

I half-expected my bodyguards to have vanished with the rest of them. But, no, we were alone, the four of us, with those mantles lined up like an army of little monsters on the far side of the room.

"Let's go check out the new weapons," I told the guys.

We shut the door tight behind us.

17

O N OUR WAY DOWN to the practice yard, we met Harad and Karthi, each carrying a bundle of odd-looking arrows.

"Magaran's given us a few of his archers," Harad said. "We'll post them with the lead-off harrier teams. Look for a runner from us with a report on how these perform in the field."

He put one of the arrows in my hand. With its coat of pitch, it looked burnt, and it felt overweighted, off-balance.

"Do they fly?"

Karthi made a wavering gesture with one hand. "More erratic than we'd like. We'll have to count on the surprise factor. For the city's defense, showering from above, they should be effective enough. Aim won't matter so much."

With a nod to me, Harad nudged Karthi's shoulder. "No time, lad. We need to be on the move. Now." With a start, I recognized they were both fully kitted-out, ready for battle.

Karthi flashed a grin at being called 'lad' and retrieved the arrow Harad had given me. "Andus is waiting for you in the briefing room."

"Right." I'd nearly forgotten. "Good luck, you two. Use those troops wisely."

"Ya, Boss. You got it."

They were gone before I could think to tell them to be careful.

Wouldn't have changed anything. But it should have been said.

That one arrow might be the closest I'd come to inspecting the new weaponry. I sighed and headed for the briefing I'd demanded from Andus. I couldn't find fault with his program. He'd consulted Magaran—I could tell, by noting a few of the old commander's favorite designs being incorporated. Likely others of the senior command had given their critique. A younger brother, used to taking advantage of his elders' experience, Andus was never shy about seeking advice.

His plan leveraged the vantage points created by turning buildings into walls and blocking off streets. He had protocols for retreat when the blockades would be breached. Jeskaryan's twisting back alleys made for useful routes. He hoped to pull most of the survivors behind the fortress wall, while the rest could make their way to the northern perimeter of the city.

When I didn't have much to say on his plan, Andus moved straight on to my job. "What about the civilians, Boss?"

"That's for this afternoon's council meeting." It would be a contentious gathering, and my last council meeting. I hoped I'd make it through without killing somebody. Certain citizens had announced they'd not move from their homes or workshops. Others made noises about tearing a gap in the makeshift northern gate and making a run for it. The elders were more concerned about whatever the invaders might do to the lands they passed over than about the fates of the people standing in the way. I couldn't expect anybody to be focused on the needs of the moment, the hazards of the day. "If I can get half the remaining populace safe behind the walls, I'll count myself a success," was the most optimistic statement I could make.

"Have you eaten?"

I couldn't remember. "Probably not."

"Magaran's got tables laid out in front of the barracks. The cooks have been loading them up. Let's stop by, get our share."

"Sounds good."

"You can give the men one of your speeches." He began to roll up his plans, glancing up at me with a grin that reminded me of weeks on patrol.

"What kind of speech should I deliver?" I considered the times I'd tried to do that. "One where I forget what I was planning to say? Or one where I drop my dinner plate in the fire?"

He laughed.

Errem looked shocked.

"I could do both," I suggested.

Andus clapped me on the shoulder. "No need, Boss, no need. Or maybe you'll think of something even more inspiring."

He'd undersold the feast Magaran had arranged. No one would be heading hungry to battle tomorrow. We piled our plates high and found a bench off to one side. I waved my bodyguards over to grab what they could. Andus ate fast, talking most of the time. He had great hopes for the scheme he and Karthi had cooked up.

People kept wandering by. They'd ask Andus a question, or drop a bow in my direction. I had my mouth full most of the time, so I didn't say much. Anybody bowed, I'd throw them a salute as if they were my superior officer, instead of the other way around.

They seemed to like that. At one point, I had a steady stream of young recruits strolling by, faking surprise at seeing me, bowing ... and waiting to get a salute from their commander in chief. Some laughed at the incongruity of it; others seemed ... touched. Either way, it was better than a speech.

"See?" Andus said. "I knew you'd think of something."

Errem put himself right behind me and muttered, "Nearly time, sir."

I stuffed one last hunk of bannock into my mouth and mumbled, "I know."

Across from us, men who'd be fighting and dying for Jeska tomorrow competed to grab the best slices of meat, and punched each other in the shoulder, and laughed at jokes I couldn't hear. I wanted to give them a speech, like one of the old kings. Did those guys really do that? Or did the historians make up the speeches afterwards?

We delivered our plates to the cleanup crew. As we began to cross the assembly yard, to head back uphill, men began to gather around us. They didn't say anything. They didn't bow or salute at me. They wanted to be close, for their own reasons.

I didn't know what to do, but I couldn't do nothing.

At the edge of the yard, I stepped up on the brick edging and turned around.

"Forget about me," I told them. "Think of yourselves, and why you're here. Think of the land that supports us and the people who care for it. Think of your families, your friends, and those you've never met but swore to protect." I raised my fist and said the words like I was speaking to each of them, as individuals. "For Jeska."

The murmur rolled across the square, with fists raised and hands forming salutes. "For Jeska."

Andus and I went our separate ways, to our separate tasks.

For Jeska.

18

T HE AFTERNOON COUNCIL MEETING started badly and got worse.

In the first place, those mantles were still lying there, two rows of four and one of three, spreading halfway across the dais from the windows. Except the orderly grid had become a skewed array. The mantles in sunlight lay fully spread out; the rest were clumped bundles of fur.

Wait. The count was four and three and three.

Had one of the creatures crawled off somewhere?

I kept expecting to spot it lurking under Yutek's chair or slithering from the shadows in the far corner.

The councilors gave the herd of mantles a healthy, respectful distance, as if councilors always stood on the left half of the room.

The elders, with their retinue of key matriarchs and town officials, paid no heed to the shamans' quiescent minions and spread themselves out in the remaining space.

An observer might have thought we planned it that way.

I'd roped Dramin into the meeting, to handle the agenda, try to keep the attendees in line. Though he didn't have Arnim's smooth manners, he had a physician's commanding tones.

"If everyone could settle," he announced. "We've a lot to manage and very little time."

One of the townsmen pushed himself in front of the rest. "The military has no right to keep us here. We demand the north gate be opened."

Councilor Caldrim stood close enough to touch the man's shoulder. "Hold fast, friend," he said. "It's too late for that now. Have you not listened to the news?"

At the word *news*, the doors thudded open, and a runner staggered past the guards and into the hall.

"I've word from the Narrows," he announced. "A message for the king."

Everyone in the room turned and stared at him: elders swirled their long robes and swung their staffs as they moved, councilors caught each other's elbows and muttered in one another's ears, townsfolk shuffled out of the way of matriarchs. The runner, streaked in sweat and road dust, swayed on his feet. Everyone forgot the mantles.

"I'm here," I called out, stepping down from my place and forging a way through the crowd. My bodyguards helped with that.

He looked nearly as bad as the first runner Arnim had sent. No, worse. He had that staring look men get, the first time they've seen battle. "King Corren?" he asked.

"That's me," I admitted. "Let's get you out of this crowd." If I'd been Kul, I'd've lifted the skinny, worn-out guy and carried him out. Being me, I gestured to my guards to lend him an arm or two. "Errem," I said. "Let's set up a debrief in the kitchen somewhere. Let's not make him walk any further than that."

"How about the storeroom, the one we used before?"

"Good enough."

Behind me, a staff thundered on the floor. "Let's have this message," Adestinian demanded.

I let the men lead off and faced her on my own. "This message is for me, Elder Adestinian."

"It's news that affects all of us, I warrant."

I shrugged. "Possibly. I'll not keep to myself information that you need. But I'll not break a runner's commission, ma'am."

Trapped by the law, she glared at me. "There are matters at hand in this council, that must be attended to."

I gestured to Dramin, who still stood on the dais. "The commander here will take note of your recommendations and requirements, ma'am. He'll make sure I'm informed of any discussions I miss. And I trust those here to conduct themselves with respect for each other. I'll return shortly."

Before anybody—especially Dramin—could object, I hurried after my guards and the runner.

•   •   •

"Captain Tallan says—"

"Who's Tallan?" I interrupted. "This message is supposed to be from Commander Arnim."

The runner clutched the cup he'd been handed and drank half the water in it. "Captain Tallan says ..." He waited for me to interrupt him again.

I knew better than to repeat my error. Hadn't I delivered my own brother into that profession, to have him lecture me about protocols and rules every time we met?

He drained the cup and set it on the table in front of him. "The surviving force has split. The uninjured have formed a troop together and are marching to HandOverHand, as reinforcements. The injured men are camped at—" and here he rattled off the detailed markers that would enable others to locate them. After we were done with our own battle.

I made him repeat that information twice, while writing it out myself. The next generation of soldiers needed to be literate. That's something I'd have to tell my successor.

Most likely, Tymon would let me stay in the Guard.

"Anything else?" I expected a fragment of sarcasm, a touch of that upper-class attitude, something to remind me the real source of the message was Arnim.

The runner shook his head. Someone refilled his cup and he drank silently. Even I noticed the way his hand trembled, and the rapid blinking, as if he had dust in his eyes.

I pushed harder. "No personal message for me from Commander Arnim?"

He choked, began coughing, and I moved around and thumped his back, as I'd done so often for Tymon. Once the coughing eased, he sipped the water, then put the cup down and pushed it away.

I judged it time to move on. "Now then, let's get any other facts you have. You understand? It's more than the message you've been given, Runner, it's all you can remember. Can you manage that? Do you need to rest first?"

"I'm all right," he said.

He didn't look all right. But we were in the middle of a war. None of us were all right.

"So let's get the numbers, as best as you can. How many men went ahead to HandOverHand?"

"Just the one troop, sir. They were ten, but only one was experienced, so they decided they'd be a single troop. They built a fire for the enemy fallen, sir, but they didn't have time to burn them all. They had to go. Some of the injured, they were working at the fires, best they could, when I left."

I leaned back and tried to feel my way through the fog that descended around me. "Ten? Ten individual men?"

"Yes, sir."

"And the surviving injured?"

"Nine, sir. Though, from what I saw, I'd expect it's eight by now." He looked like he might either vomit or cry. Well, a scullery is relatively easy to clean.

"We'll get a medic to them, soon as we can," I vowed. Seemed a good time for an empty promise that wouldn't hurt anybody. We'd known it would be a losing battle. Arnim had called it a suicide mission. The first runner had told us the odds.

Still.

Hearing the toll hurt. We'd lost over eight tenths of the force we'd deployed, and sidelined half the survivors.

"Is there an estimate of casualties on their side?"

"Close on three hundred, I think. Tallan was telling the others, at the camp in the hills, 'We took them down three to one, you can be proud.'" He choked again, even though he wasn't drinking anymore.

They'd cut down as much as a tenth of the invaders. I calculated that Tallan might have been exaggerating, to cheer the others, but there was no doubt the tactic had worked.

What it cost, that was the thing twisting my guts into knots and pushing tears out of the runner's eyes.

"So. I won't keep you much longer, Runner."

He nodded.

"Where is Commander Arnim, then? With the troop that went north?"

He shook his head.

"But Tallan is the one who sent you."

"Yes, sir."

A hand on my shoulder forced me to look up. That hulking bodyguard of mine had tears running down his face, enough to match the runner's. "Boss," he said.

"What, Errem?"

"Would you let me ask a question?"

I frowned at him. "Why?" Was he angling for a promotion already?

"Cuz' you're not getting it, sir."

"Not getting what?"

Errem moved around the table, crouched down next to the runner, and put that thick hand of his on one trembling shoulder. "I'm right, aren't I?" he asked.

The man nodded.

"You want me to say it for ya?"

Another nod.

Errem turned to me. "The commander's one of those lost, sir."

"Lost," I repeated.

"Yes, sir. He's gone."

I looked him in the eyes. I needed to say the word to make it real. "You mean, he's dead."

"Yes, sir."

The runner started up to his feet, though he leaned on the table. "There was a troop got surrounded, sir, by those strange fighters, the short ones. They fought like madmen, sir, you never saw anything like them. Even from up the hill where I was, you could tell. Where they got those fighters, sir, I can't imagine."

From a dark hollow somewhere in my chest, a laugh leapt out. "You can't imagine! No, you can't."

Errem and the runner both, they looked at me like I'd gone mad myself.

"Army of light," I told them. "They got those fighters from us, from Jeska." *And they killed him.*

"I didn't know," the runner said. "I'm sorry, sir."

I didn't want to hear it, but I needed to know. "Tell me. A troop was surrounded. And Arnim went in, didn't he?" *I told him, stay back, be a commander.* The light in the room began to dim, shadows sliding in, leaving me peering down a tunnel, framing Errem and the runner in darkness.

"He did. Not alone, sir. They were a proper troop drove in to cut those others free. But—"

"But they didn't make it out." I knew the shadows in my vision weren't real, but they crept into my body, numbed my hands.

"Some did, sir. Not the commander. It was those fighters, sir. They're the demons the shamans teach us about."

I wanted to laugh again, but I didn't want to be scaring them. "No," I said. "They're demons the shamans made." I wished I had the freedom to march down to the Shamans' House, right then and there. I'd cut down those scheming monsters like the demons they were, burn their foul corpses, and scatter the ashes to the four winds.

I stood up. The chair I'd been using tipped over with a crash. "You know the place."

"Sir?" The runner looked at me with wide eyes. I'd scared him, after all.

"Where Arnim fell. You saw, didn't you? You know the spot."

He swallowed and bit his lip. "Yes, sir."

"Give me the markers." I pulled the sheet of paper over into the patch of table that I could still see, and scrawled down the notes he gave me. I couldn't go there. Not now. But I could go to my father.

I turned and fumbled for the door, through a darkness no one else could see. I sensed my bodyguards forming up around me. "Sir?" one of them said.

"I'm going up the hill," I told them. "This may be my last chance to visit Yutek."

When I stumbled over my own feet in the doorway, I figured it wouldn't hurt to ask for help. "Errem. You'll need to lead the way."

•   •   •

At our approach, a pair of buzzards flapped lazily upwards, catching the hot air rising along the slope. I found myself a rough boulder to perch on, a stone not far from a mostly-disconnected ribcage. The old man's bones had held up well to the disease that had eaten away at his insides. As I sat there, the hot afternoon wind cleared the darkness from my vision, reminded me why we were working so hard.

The kings' funeral ground, a patch of hillside hardly anyone visits, has one of the best views of old Jeskaryan. The fortress squares up close to the slope, leaving no room for an enemy to sneak in that way, and from that vantage point, I could pick out the king's house, the barracks, the training ground, the stables, even the low thatched building that had been used as a dormitory for us fosters back in the day. The town spread out around the fortress: workshops, markets, homes, gardens. At the edge of the town we'd put up our palisade: a flimsy barricade, another delaying tactic.

Beyond, the land fell away to the great valley, the river a strand of silver cutting through the heart of Jeska. Further off, in the blue distance, a low band of shadows marked the mountains that were anything but low once you got that far. I imagined I could see the crown of snow that lived through the summer on the highest peaks.

This was Jeska, the land we protected, the watersheds and forests, the fisheries and hunting grounds, the wildlands and farms that gave us life. It was my duty to defend it, step by step, winnowing those invading forces with delaying tactics and diversions. Whatever it took, I'd do this job Yutek had laid out for me.

Arnim's sacrifice, and that of the eighty who fell beside him, were only the first. While I argued with elders and interrogated runners, safe in Jeskaryan, Case and his forces were taking their turn. Tomorrow, Harad and Karthi would whittle away at the remainder until the invaders fell on the flimsy barricades defended by Andus's troops.

They'd reach the fortress last. I still had hope our strategy and tactics and partly-developed weaponry would be enough.

19

BY THE TIME we got down off the hill, the afternoon meeting had closed out. We were crossing the central plaza, nearly to the king's house, when I spotted the cluster of colorful fabric that marked the elders. I broke into a run, chasing down those venerables like a child running after a grandmother in the market.

"Adestinian!" I called out. She turned, and the rest followed suit. A stern bunch of grandmas, they were.

The chief elder looked down on me with less of a frown than the others. "Well?" she asked. "Your second handled the meeting, as promised. We have business to attend to, young man."

I caught my breath. "The runner's news—"

"Bad news, was it?" Her frown became something else, not friendly, but almost maternal … as if she was showing more patience than I'd known she had.

I realized what she saw—the borrowed jacket, the grass-stained trousers, the dirt on my hands and likely my face as well. "Yes. We lost most of the force deployed on that first engagement. And the commander as well." I couldn't voice his name. Not yet.

"But they achieved their task. They slowed the invaders, reduced their number."

"From what your second said this afternoon, the enemy force is larger than anticipated."

"Yes, and we've sent out a second company to winnow them further, before they can reach Jeskaryan from HandOverHand."

She pursed her lips. What did she not want to say?

The woman next to her, the marginally younger one, rapped her staff on the pavement and barked, "They'll die as well, won't they? We'll all die. What use is any of this?"

Adestinian's staff whipped out, caught Maledestine's, and tripped it free, to fall with a clatter to the stones. "What use?" she cried. "What use? What use are you?"

Her face contorting, Maledestine bent and snatched up her staff.

I thought for an instant they'd have at it right there, two old women battering each other with sticks.

"Elders!" I interrupted. "It's all of use. If we tear at them enough, we'll hold them here. They won't take Jeskaryan. We'll protect this land, as we've sworn to do, and we'll send the remnants home in such a state they'll never dare try again."

It was Maledestine heard the undercurrent. She paused with her stick clutched in both hands. "You've a secret you've not told us."

I couldn't hesitate. "Yes. We've a new weapon, one they haven't seen. One we've never used, though, Elder. We can't be sure—"

Adestinian caught my shoulder and leaned close. "Surprise them, Corren," she ordered. "Destroy them with terror at the unknown, the mysterious. Be like the shamans, deal with them as if you wield magic."

As if? So she knew their lie. But me? Be like a shaman? Still, I liked the sound of *Destroy them with terror*. "Yes, ma'am," I said. "We'll do that."

She released me, and her companions formed up behind her. I watched them as they moved off. They'd given me hope. How had they done that?

"Sir?"

I broke free of those thoughts. "What is it?"

My guards had a man in tow: thin, nondescript, sweaty. He looked me up and down, and his lips moved silently. *Short, big nose, dresses like a ragpicker.* His wry half-smile reminded me of …

My bones went cold. Those were Case's words. He always dressed sharp. And he'd seen me in my current uniform— borrowed jacket, road-worn trousers. "You've come from HandOverHand. From Case."

The mutterer straightened up, pushed the hair off his face. To the guard gripping his arm, he said. "That's him? That one?"

I waved off my men, and let the runner rub his arm and stare at me again for a few seconds. "Yes," I said. "That's me. Short. Big nose." I straightened my jacket and stole a glance at Errem, who managed not to smirk this time. "Ragpicker clothes. Corren of Jeska."

The runner flushed.

"Don't get worked up. I'm king until tomorrow night, that's all. Let's have your news." To Errem, I said. "Briefing room. Send someone to fetch Andus, any other senior officers."

20

IN THE END, we had a small group to listen to Case's runner, what with most of our forces already deploying themselves, readying for the next day. I snagged a couple of scribes to sit in, take notes, and then go around to the forward positions with any changes in orders. Andus arrived late and sat scribbling notes alongside the scribes, glancing out the door frequently as the shadows out there began to lengthen.

This being a start-of-battle report, the hesitant reporter hadn't brought dire news. We could imagine the worst ourselves, knowing this whole day men had been working the rough ground of HandOverHand, drawing the enemy in, then hurling themselves into battle in fierce tight masses of blades, too scattered for the notorious Hashtek archers to target, too fast-moving to fight in the old man-to-man way of battle.

The runner hadn't seen any of it unfolding; he'd been sent out shortly after dawn. Even so, Case had numbers to report, from troops he'd set out along the southward road, as scouts. A small party of men dodging through the hills moves faster than the best-organized army, especially if that army is slowed by the short legs of child soldiers. The fact came as part of the report: "You may have an hour or two extra, as their so-called army of light can't keep pace."

We'd laid out the details of the engagement to allow for battle continuing after sunset. During that strategy session, I'd earned quickly-hidden smiles and eye-rolls for proposing the idea; now, the officers kept patting each other on the shoulder and commenting as to how we'd given our men an edge by planning ahead. In my head, though, the numbers came down to a conclusion before nightfall. Case's count of the Southern forces nearly matched Arnim's—or rather Tallan's—minus the three hundred or so felled at the Narrows.

I say, nearly matched. The count came up short by at least two hundred, and I knew where to look for them. I had no illusions that the shamans would have kept the layout of Jeskaryan secret from their allies. The enemy would try to surprise us with a rear action from the north. If not, the Empire's generals weren't the military masterminds the textbooks claimed. They'd almost certainly peeled off a secondary force, in the night, heading due north, to take up that position. I hoped Case didn't forget about them, in the fervor of the moment. It had always been part of the plan for Case to pull back at some point, and bring his remainders to the defense of that gate our townsmen thought so safe.

"Don't count on the second runner," was Case's last word. "They've their own scouts and spies roaming wide of the march."

I looked out the door of the briefing room and measured the shadows on the stones in the courtyard. By my reckoning, the battle would be winding up soon. If that second runner made it past the Southerners, he might arrive by midnight. We could hope the invaders would take a nice long rest, have a relaxing meal, care for their injured.

Not likely.

I told my officers to be prepared for fighting at the gates by tomorrow. The mad children and their masters would take rest from time to time, but no more than they needed to march again. They'd be enlivened by the thrill of battle, the joy of their apparent victory.

We'd teach them a different lesson, once they reached Harad and Karthi. The unnatural fire of lightning powder would rain down on them from invisible attackers. Would they question the teachings of the shamans?

Possibly.

All I needed from the harriers was a road full of bodies, a reduction in the force that would fall on my city. Fear and terror would be a bonus, but I wouldn't count on it, given the army of light was trained on terror.

The runner ran dry of news. I ran dry of dire predictions. The officers and the two young scribes fell into silence.

"Listen," I told them.

They looked towards me as if I'd thought of a new, perfect strategy. Instead, I told them about my visit to Yutek, about my vision of the fortress and the city and the land of Jeska from that vantage point. I told them Jeskaryan crouched on this hill like an angry bear, gnashing her teeth, ready to tear the limbs from anyone foolish enough to challenge her.

"When you look out on that army," I said, "think of them as the hunter in the old story, the one who chases a young bear up a tree, and then says, far too late … who'll finish the yarn?"

Grins spread through the room. One of the scribes giggled as he transcribed.

"Anyone? You, there." I pointed at the laughing scribe.

He put down his pen and stood, transforming from serious worker to performer, peering upward into imaginary branches. "I wonder," he began, then paused, held a hand to his brow against the invisible sun's glare, and gazed out with comically widened eyes to each corner of the room. "Where's the mother bear?"

I nudged Errem's shoulder, and we moved out as the rumble of laughter filled the room we'd been planning our deaths in.

I walked in a fog, calculating and recalculating the odds. Would the larger formations we'd worked out for Case's maneuvers at HandOverHand be as effective as the strike forces' slash-and-dash approach? The shape of the land at the old mustering-ground—wide spaces interspersed with low hills and tall scrub—demanded an alternate approach. On top of that, the Southerners would arrive already schooled on our strikers; we needed to keep them off-balance. The factor in common—autonomy by unit deployed—carried over well enough. Magaran had let Case make off with enough senior officers to manage those multi-troop units, men who'd be trusted by those under them, who could inspire courage in the face of the overwhelming opposition. There had to be trust in the methods, enough confidence in their training, if we were to have any hope of success.

Even then, we knew success did not come down to winning that battle. Success meant creating a chance for Jeskaryan—and Jeska as we knew it—to survive.

I began to think it would be best if Case's second runner didn't make it to the city. I wanted him hiding in a safe spot somewhere, losing his commission, but not bringing confirmation that my calculations were correct. Case might make it out of there with a half-dozen troops, maybe as many as fifty men, but I gauged he'd bring fewer than thirty to take on whatever the enemy threw at our north gate.

As for the rest of those brave soldiers who'd followed him out to that dry valley? I didn't count on seeing many of them back home. I hoped for it, but it was a narrow thread of hope.

One of my guys caught me by the arm in time to keep me from walking straight over someone.

I stepped back, gesturing apologetically. "Sorry. Didn't see you there."

"Your Majesty."

I blinked, cleared my vision.

The long, dark brown tunic marked her a doctor, and it was in that moment I finally understood their uniforms' color—the shade of dried blood. "I'm fine," I snapped. Had someone called in the medics after that last interview, when I'd run off to the funeral ground?

She frowned and jerked her eyebrows. Was she annoyed or hiding amusement? You can never tell with medical people; they're so used to lying about how someone is doing. "I'm not here for you, sir."

"What, then?" I wanted to sound annoyed, but instead betrayed my own tiredness.

Her tone softened. "It's your wife, sir."

A slice of clarity cut through the haze of numbers and patterns in my head. "What is it? She's worse? Don't tell me—"

"She's much better, sir. Very much better."

"Oh." One layer of shadow lifted.

She looked expectant. I was supposed to say something else.

"Good." Would that be enough to make her get out of my way?

"You may see her now." She beamed benevolence at me.

It seemed a year since I'd been shouting about her colleagues keeping me away. But, now? The fog closed in. I had to be sure men were positioned along the palisade, at each of the defensive points in the fortress wall, provisioned for a long night and a longer day to follow. I needed to hear reports from Karthi's units, from the townsmen and managers orchestrating the retreat of civilians.

I didn't have time for Heyliannin, any more than I had time for myself.

"Later," I told the doctor. "Tell her, will you? I'll be there, but later."

She pursed her lips at me, but didn't voice her disapproval.

I stepped to one side and moved past her before she could come up with anything to make me regret what I couldn't change.

•   •   •

I'd imagined conducting the campaign from the council chambers, watching events from the tall windows, marshalling crews of runners and aides in the comfort of that wide sunlight-filled space.

Practicality had overruled the idea early in our planning. We couldn't spare the time for runners to dash up and down the stairs and navigate the maze of the king's house. We settled on a little-used old building that had had many lives. Originally a barracks, it served as storerooms for a few decades, but in Yutek's time it became a sort of barracks again, a dormitory for the foster-sons he'd purchased. We lived there together, sleeping, studying, training. Fighting.

I've just realized we were six at the start, like my Six.

Not every foster is suited to the job, and some of the boys thought themselves worthy for no good reason. The ambitious ones did their worst to force Tymon or me out of that house. I taught them a few hard lessons. Others left the job, unable to cope with the tutors, repelled by the king's true-son, or reclaimed by their families. Tymon and I, we had nowhere else to go.

The long, narrow, thatch-roofed house had the right amount of space, the right degree of anonymity. If invaders breached the fortress gate, they'd head straight for the king's house—and find nobody there worth ransoming. I'd already arranged for my odd little family to move out of there during the night, to a secure position near the elders. Thanks to the doctors—and the mantle—I could stop worrying about whether my wife would be able to travel.

The refurbished dormitory had no windows and two doors— the tidy, unassuming door I'd entered by as a child and a concealed rear exit that appeared to be part of the wall. Then, the place had felt more like a prison than a house, but the utilitarian furnishings had been removed long ago. When I arrived after my encounter with the doctors, I found staff and guardsmen working together to set up tables, organized by task. A vaguely-familiar man grinned and snapped an amateurish salute as I passed.

"I'll never forget how you took Dawat to the floor here that first day," he said. "Blood everywhere. We shoulda known you'd overtake us all, Corren." He flushed and bobbed his head in an awkward bow. "Uh, s-sir."

The faint stutter snagged a name out of distant memory. "Fentin?"

His grin broadened. "Thought you'd f-forgotten me, sir. Or was pretending to."

Fentin had washed out early. I never knew why. Might have been me. My fist seemed to recall burying itself in that wide nose, and, sure enough, you could see the irregularity where my knuckles had found something to break. "Should be me hoping you'd forgotten certain things," I said. "It was a rough time."

"Na, sir, my own fault for siding with Dawat and them. Tymon, now, he had the smarts."

"Ya, ya, that's true enough." If only it had been an ordinary day. We might have worked out old differences. I might have learned more about what drove those other boys back then.

But it was my place to be laying out battle plans and contingencies and his to be setting up tables. I left him to his work and returned to my own.

My guys pressed in with their own ideas of arranging the room. They wanted my position to be close enough to the back door that they could drag me to safety if our position came under attack. I didn't have the energy to argue with them, but took the chair they gave me and propped my feet on the table. Aides scurried around laying out maps and diagrams retrieved from the briefing room. Scribes slipped in with their pens and pads, claiming a table along the far wall but also spreading a mat under the table so they could take turns resting.

Clever guys, scribes. I had a flash of unease, recognizing that all but one of the pen-wranglers we'd brought in for this duty were kids. The elders had kept the senior scribes for themselves. Well, if there could be one safe place for kids in this fortress, for kids who had to be part of the war, it would be here in this room with my guards.

Andus rolled through, gave me his report. He left out the details I couldn't help with, but made it clear he was ready, his men were ready, they had their newfangled weapons stockpiled, ready to let fly.

"I can tell ya, Boss, some of these guys have outpaced me on this. We're posting everyone early, right, so they figured they'd be there a good long while, but most of 'em are on upper floors, lots of steps down to any privies. So they hauled jars up there ..." He waggled his eyebrows, waiting for me to get the point.

I wrinkled my nose. "They better not kick any of those jars over, or I'll have householders out for my neck when this is all over."

So then we had a roomful of grown men laughing about piss jars, while the young scribes huddled over their pads and rolled their eyes at us.

They reminded me of Calestinise.

Andus gave me his casual salute, readying to leave, but something stopped him. "Hey, Boss. What's wrong?"

"Nothing." Heyliannin losing Tymon's baby. Stevvin and Affram playing games while we planned deaths. Calestinise standing on a table, raising his own army. "Family, Andus, that's all. Nothing to concern you." He hadn't been with us, wouldn't have known what that boy had been through, wouldn't know how I felt about it.

"Right then. I'm for a few hours' rest, Boss. Suggest you do the same."

"Sure, sure," I said. I leaned back and closed my eyes for a minute, to have a go at puzzling out what could have happened to the kid, to Kul.

After the news about Arnim, maybe I didn't want to know.

A sharp noise startled me, and I thought I was falling, then my chair settled back on all four legs and my eyes jerked open to the glare of lamps up and down the tables. I missed sitting on the floor in my old office. I missed sleeping on the floor.

"Sir." It was one of my guys, but not Errem. Right. They'd changed shifts.

"Ya, Durse."

"We have things in order, sir."

I creaked to my feet, wondered when I'd gotten so old. A thought oozed through my exhaustion. *Heyliannin knows about Kul and Calestinise.* "I've an appointment with my wife, and then I think I have a meeting with my bed."

"Right, sir." Durse still hadn't got the sense of my version of humor. I missed Arnim's ready wit. My gut ached, so at least that was like old times.

"Shouldn't be a long meeting. You be sure I'm on my feet by dawn." I headed for the door, trying not to weave on my feet. It felt like being drunk, without the benefits.

"Dawn. Right, sir." He sounded skeptical.

"I'm serious. First light, I'm up, armed, and we're back here, at the ready."

"Yessir."

Sometimes you have to repeat yourself to get the message across.

21

HEYLIANNIN SAT at Yutek's place, a steaming concoction in a wide bowl on the low table in front of her. Despite the warmth of the evening, she wore the mantle. Its browns and blacks shimmered in the candlelight. So did her eyes, in almost the same shade of brown.

I took my old place, where Arnim had sat two days' previous. "So the doctor wasn't lying."

"Oh?" She sipped her medicine and her brow furrowed.

"They could have been trying to keep me away by telling me not to worry." She couldn't know what it had been like for the rest of us. For me.

She tipped her head to one side, like Tymon used to do. We might have been sparring at word-games. "No, you probably couldn't tell what they meant."

"It didn't seem likely you'd recover so fast." Less than a day ago, they'd implied she was at death's door. "Were they mistaken about your illness? Or what?"

She ran a hand down the fur draped over her shoulder. "This is what."

The old memory, that time Orkast used his mantle to cure the fever that should have killed me, wormed its way to the surface of my mind. I shivered, recalling the rasp of that voice in my ear.

"Or who," I said.

She sat back, blinking. Had she not figured out that I knew? Was I that good at keeping secrets?

The guards in the room stopped being invisible. I twisted my neck to get my eyes on Durse, who'd posted himself at the door, his partner hovering in the shadows of the stairway to the council chamber. "You guys step outside," I ordered.

His brow wrinkled, and the frown that was his normal expression deepened.

"I need time with my wife. Go help the outside crew beat off assassins."

He gestured to the second guard, growled a *yessir*, and exited, closing the door without a sound. We waited another minute for the other man's footsteps on the stairs to end with the thump of the council-room door.

The nap in my chair at our makeshift command center hadn't done much for me. I rubbed my eyes. *I don't have time for this.*

That left it to her to ask. "Have you known all this time?"

What she meant by *all this time*, that was unclear. "I'd forgotten, but I remembered, the day in my office." I'd called Arnim to help , using his cleverness to wrest truths from her. "You said its name, Asdyel. That's the name Orkast used for it. That's how I knew he meant for you to have it."

"Why?"

"You wouldn't know the name any other way. At least, that's the way I saw it." What had been going on, that day I tried to interrogate her? Why hadn't we talked it through?

Oh. Yes. That was the day I found out Yutek was dying but that I could marry Eldennian. The day my daughter's mother refused me, and my brother's fake wife volunteered for the job, because she was mad at Tymon for being himself. So, not a good time for discussing shaman secrets.

She seemed lost in her own memories. "Your guy. Arnim. He was so shocked, that you told him to take me to the shamans." I imagined my old friend whittling away at the mystery on the way down to the Shamans' House. Did she give him any answers then?

If not, he'd never know, now.

My gut made a good try at convincing me I'd caught Yutek's illness, to stop me thinking about Arnim. I turned the interrogation back to my side. "Here's one thing I need to know, right now. Are these creatures slaves to the shamans or the other way around?"

"A good question," she delayed. She rubbed the back of her neck and muttered to herself. Or maybe she was muttering to the ... *thing* ... draped over her shoulders. "It was meant to be mutual, helping each other. Asdyel and his kind, they're able to see what you call thin patches, but they're weak in this world; they can't get around on their own." She closed her eyes and sighed in sympathy. The expression gave her an eerie beauty, reminded me she, too, missed her true home. "In their own world, they fly free and connect with others only to communicate."

We could have gone on to talk about those other worlds. She'd given me hints, clues. This would make four worlds: hers, mine, the snake-men's, and the mantles'. Were there more? I didn't have all night, though. Another time, another time. "You said it's *meant* to be a partnership. So it's not that way?"

"Maybe for a few, but I get the feeling most wanderers are under control of the shamans." She shrugged. "It's complicated. Asdyel says the contented ones have been infected with the human need for power."

"It's a disease, all right," I agreed. "Wanderers?"

"That's my word for them. They got lost somehow, among the worlds. They're looking for a way home. They haven't found it yet, he says."

"He says? So it's a him?"

She shook her head. "I don't think so. They don't have, what's the word? Gender. It's a flaw of mine, to presume. I still sometimes say *she* for Calestinise."

She'd opened that door. I had to go through it.

"Where is he, then?"

Her eyes went vague and she ran her fingers through the fur on her lap.

I needed to bring her thoughts back. "Enough about your furry friend. Where's Calestinise? And Kul? You rode in alone, carrying news like a runner, but you never got debriefed. What were you doing all that time in Lakeside? I know you weren't lying low, staying out of trouble." I smacked my hand on the table. Rings of ripples formed in the bowl in front of her, rushed to form a splash at the center, then faded to jagged, glittering waves. "We had a runner report in. You three were out rabble-rousing, not keeping safe. I need details. What went wrong?"

She clutched the mantle tight around her body, exactly as a shaman would. As Fennic had done the other day, when I'd confronted him in his stronghold. Her eyes crinkled, and I thought she might cry, but instead her face went still. The whites of her eyes were stained red. Maybe she'd already cried enough.

She couldn't say it, so I had to. "They're lost, aren't they?"

She nodded, and a sob whimpered in her throat.

I reached across the table for the bowl. I needed something to wash away the taste in my mouth. Whatever was in that mixture flowed warm and sweet over my tongue. The smell of fresh berries filled my head, put me out in the wilds, my Six around me, safe, strong, ready for anything. I wanted to drink it all, but it dawned on me she might need some, to answer my questions, so I put down the bowl and pushed it back towards her.

"Tell me," I said. "Tell me all of it."

Word by word, I got from her the details of what my family had been doing down in Lakeside—the ruffling of community feathers at the town markets, the gatherings in the pubs, the rounding-up of mothers and fathers and cousins and uncles. They'd made a regular business of it, moving on each day, staying ahead of the incoming Southern forces.

"Calestinise was amazing," she said. "He'd jump up on the table and start into his speech, and the room would go silent. Everyone listened—cranky old grannies, fishermen, mothers, shopkeepers. Even the kids quieted down. By the time he finished, we'd have another cadre of angry, determined people ready to fan out across the township, round up more followers."

"Did you have a plan?"

"Not at first. I think we imagined the families would head out to those camps, break them up, and bring their kids home."

"But it was too late for that." Off to the side of the table, a covered tray tugged at my attention. Under the cover: bread, smoked meat, sliced fruit that had gone brown around the edges. "You should eat," I told her. "If you're really better."

"That's yours," she said. "Your older … cousin … came looking for you. Radeo. Said he'd send something, that you wouldn't have eaten."

I'd been in motion all afternoon. Radeo and I hadn't crossed paths. Andus had his fire-arrows in hand, so issues with the new armaments must have been resolved. I grinned at her. "He's been having a fine time with your lightning powder recipe."

"My what?"

I didn't want to get into that. "Go on. What's important is what happened in Lakeside." But I started in on the food as she talked. Let her think Radeo was cooking up one of her herbal remedies.

She returned to the rabble-rousing. "You're right, that it was too late to break up the camps. On the third day, we had a company of fathers and uncles catch up to us. They'd gone to that camp we knew about, and it had been emptied. Kul said that meant the army of light was on the march."

"He was right."

"So, then we needed a plan. There were too many people getting involved. Kul said to keep it simple, so that's what Calestinise did."

"You put the kid in charge?"

She shrugged, and the mantle echoed her move. "The enemy made it a children's war. Made sense to let him take the lead. Besides." She stopped, losing herself in memory, and a stray tear leaked from one eye and rolled down beside her nose. "You should have seen him, Corren. You'd have been so proud. The way he talked to them, raised up their courage, their need-to-do-right. I'm sure there's a word for that?"

"Righteousness."

"Yes. That. He built a righteous army from those wronged families and their friends. Kul did organizing, behind the scenes.

He'd pick one man from each town to lead a cadre. Once we crossed a township line, he pulled the leaders aside and had them choose one of the women to be a matriarch over them. Those women made themselves a council, and they'd have me to their meetings. By the time we hit Lakeside City, each township group had a commander, too, chosen by the council. Not by me. I sat in their meetings and listened."

Kul had made strike forces from the town representatives, created a governing council, and established fighting units under commanders selected by the matriarchs but under Calestinise's direction. All while marching through territory the enemy considered their own.

"What happened in L-City?"

"I wanted to go into town, but Kul said no, wait. And he was right again. People came out from the city, to meet us. More than we'd have gathered ourselves. They'd come from the far side of the lake, following rumors."

"Case and his crew met some of them."

Her eyes widened. "They're back? Stevvin's all right, then?"

She wouldn't have had that news. "Ya. He's fine. Both of the boys are well. We're fostering them, officially." I waited for her smile. "Go on."

The quirky tension in her shoulders seemed to lighten. "With the east-siders, our numbers close to doubled. We called a stop, and camped down by the river. Remember, during the turtle festival? The people camping outside town?"

"I remember the guys behind us on the road, whining about how they'd have to bed down among the mosquitoes."

"Don't remind me. The bugs were bad. People built big smoky fires, but it didn't help much."

I remembered that day in the pub: Calestinise, with that sly grin of his, demanding to go camping with his new friends—a trip we thought would involve a few days of tapping into local rumors. "So, it started and ended with a camp-out."

That gave her pause, but then she caught my drift and went on. "Calestinise and Kul had a conference with the women's council, and then went off with their commanders and captains." Trust Kul to ensure protocol was followed. "I walked around the camp for a while, listening to what people were saying. Everyone had arrived riled up, but they calmed down as the evening went on. Later, I saw Kul going around with the captains, giving orders, I guess."

She went silent.

I pulled off a hunk of bread and offered it to her.

She shook her head.

"What is it? Did the Southern army arrive in the night?"

At the look of dismay on her face, a terrible image filled my mind: tall Hashteks bending their huge bows, raining spikes down on those innocent civilians-turned-fighters, swordsmen charging out of the night, blades glimmering in the firelight ...

She seemed to catch a glimpse of what I was imagining and leaned across the table to take my hand, ignoring the crumbs and grease on my fingers. "No, no, nothing like that. No." She looked down, so I couldn't see her eyes, but her fingernails dug into my palm, she was holding so tight. Her voice dropped to nearly nothing. "While they were out making battle plans ... I lost the baby."

It felt like a needle coated with lighting powder had lodged in my chest. How could it hurt this much, when I already knew? I needed to be Dramin, a cool observer, not myself. "How did it happen?"

She shook her head, and her hair slid down around her face. I couldn't even see if she was crying again. "I don't know. That was the scariest part. Everything was fine. Then, suddenly, there was blood. I was terrified. Someone ran for a midwife, who told me I'd be all right, that I could try again, that it happens to everybody." She looked up, and sure enough, she'd found more tears to cry.

"You can do that, you know." It was the one thing I could offer. "After this is over. Did they tell you? I've been fired. As of the end of the war."

"So?"

"I won't be king. Which means you can set me aside. Any normal woman would. Go back to Tymon. He's left Runners' House."

I wished I had Arnim there, to read the expression on her face. With the tears still running for her lost child, she seemed sad, but it was more than that. Her fingers in mine quivered, and her nails cut deeper. "I wouldn't do that, Corren. Not now, not since ... that day."

She meant that day I'd flung my brother's blood in her face.

She looked down at our linked hands and released me, puzzled at the flecks of red on her fingertips. "I thought long and hard on it, staring into the dark, mourning a child I'll never know. I hadn't seen it before, Corren. Tymon wants people, needs their approval, the way most people want to own things."

"The way shamans crave power," I said.

"Yes, yes, like that. It's what feeds his soul." Her hands slipped away to hide under the mantle's protection. "And he wants what you have, more than anything."

"He wants the kingship? He can have it." What would the elders do when I stepped down? Tymon was a recognized foster-son, raised in Yutek's house.

"No, that's not what I mean. He wants your friends, your family, your confidence, your strength." Her words came clear, powerful. They'd have convinced anybody else.

I knew better. "No, he doesn't. He wants his freedom. And he has his own family, the runners, who take care of him in ways I never could. All I've ever done is fight for him. And Tymon hates fighting." Had I ever told her which of my scars came from defending my brother?

"Maybe he wants both. The freedom and the family. That's why he's the way he is."

Pieces of what she might have been saying filtered through. "After all this time, you're telling me the way he is isn't what you want?"

Something in her expression spoke of other scars, the kind you can't see. She'd never told me her whole story, either. "He thought he could *own* me, Corren. Remember those lectures you gave me about owning the land? I'm not anyone's property. Not yours. Not his."

The knife in my gut twisted at the idea. "You're not my property."

She rested her hands on the little table, as if to steady herself, while the fruit turned even more brown and the tears dried on her cheeks. "I know."

22

I COULDN'T THINK of anything to say after that exchange. Did Heyliannin mean she wanted me, or that she didn't want Tymon? Were both true? Or neither? And was this any time to be having such a conversation—or was it the best time? Any—or all three—of us might die in the course of the next day.

Heyliannin stood up, the mantle shifting itself to hang smoothly, and she walked around to my side of the table. I brushed the food and traces of blood from my hands and made to stand, but before I could, she knelt beside me and spread the edge of the mantle over my shoulders.

I flinched at the touch, half-expecting to hear the creature's eerie voice at my ear, but it kept quiet.

"I haven't finished what you asked me to tell," she said.

We'd drifted far from Kul and Calestinise. The knife in my gut hadn't forgotten. "I don't think I want to hear it."

Her arm came around my waist and she pulled me closer, her warmth a presence I needed in that moment. "If you don't, you'll imagine it worse."

I couldn't look at her. I pressed my hands on my thighs and made myself still. "Go ahead."

"I came down sick the day after the miscarriage. The midwife said that happens sometimes. It worried Kul. He unhitched the pony from the cart and made me ride, to go faster."

"I bet you argued about that." In my head, I could hear her complaining about leaving supplies behind, fussing about someone stealing the abandoned pony-cart.

"He didn't give me a chance." I could hear the affection in her voice. "He picked me up like a child, shoved me aboard, and told the pony to behave. Calestinise fumed at him and fussed at me— back in his lady's-maid job. Then we crossed the river—"

I recalled last spring, crossing that swirling brown flood over the narrow bridge. "How long did it take, with so many people?"

"It's summer, Corren. Most people waded across. The pony wanted to stand in the middle of the stream and drink. Kul had to slap its rear to get it going again."

"So, not much time at all, then."

"No, but when we got to the top of the rise, we could see them."

"The Hashteks?" My heart tried to attack me. I pretended nothing was happening, waited for her to go on.

"No—it was the kids. The army of light, Calestinise called them. They were waiting for the real army. It was unbelievable, Corren, the number of them. Kul called out orders, and the men spread out, closing the kids off."

"Wait—were they armed?" I imagined the warm-hearted parents of Lakeside opening their arms to their lost ones, but meeting the kind of violence the campsite kids had delivered.

"Well, with what farmers and fishers might have. Axes, poles, pocket knives. And nets. Fishing—"

I didn't need that list. "No, no, the kids. How were they armed?" I'd yet to get a clear picture of what weaponry they'd been issued, and when. Had they been waiting for their weapons, or were they ready to fight?

"They had—" She choked back a sob and went on. "They had what you guys have. Great big knives. The older ones had swords. A lot of them had what looked like fighting, um, poles?" Vocabulary still tripped her up sometimes.

"Staffs? For walking on rough ground?" I knew that would be wrong, but I needed a better description from her.

"No. Nothing like that. These had knives on one end."

"Ah. Those are *spears*. How far could they throw them?"

"No, no. I know what a spear is. These were bigger, heavier. They wouldn't be good for throwing, even for an adult. The kids held these things, braced them against the ground, sometimes jabbed with them."

"I … we don't have a term for that. I wish I'd known about them earlier." Our guardsmen couldn't count on having a greater reach, but we could come up with a counter, given time. We'd trained our men to adapt, so I could hope they'd manage. But those untrained citizens. What would they have done? "I take it you mean the kids fought. They didn't run to their mamas?"

"Yes. It was terrible, Corren." Her voice had gone thick again and her arm tightened around me. She was probably crying.

I couldn't change that, but I could help her focus. "Then what happened? Surely the families had to turn away."

"A few did. But others went in, to shout for their children by name, to wrestle a knife away from the nearest kid and pull him free. Or her. Parents staggered back with horrible gashes, but still came with kids dragging their heels, screaming. The fishermen had the most success in the end, with their nets. They'd haul in two or three at a time, bring them over to the waiting families, and go back for more."

I imagined how fishers might have worked the mass, like handling a school of fish: wait for a disruption to loosen the edges of the mob, sweep the stragglers off their feet, and make away with their haul. "Ya, a good fisherman, that would be the trick."

"But then the kids tightened up their formation, started acting soldierly, obeying commands from someone, though we couldn't see who."

"Ya, they should have had someone in charge, a shaman or a Southern officer. Remember the one at Calestinise's camp?" And the one we'd seen at the Lakeside Shamans' House.

"That's so, but it took time to figure that out. They'd stayed hidden in the crowd. But Calestinise spotted them setting up a command post at a better vantage point. One of Kul's captains proposed sending a group that way, but Calestinise stopped them, claiming he had a plan." She sucked in a long breath.

I had a feeling I wouldn't have approved that plan. "Go on."

"First, he took aside one of the recently-retrieved kids and demanded his uniform shirt. Once he had it on, Cal could have been one of the army of light seniors, with that sword he had."

My gut clenched. "What was he doing with a sword?"

"Kul gave it to him. For protection."

An untrained swordsman is a hazard to himself and everyone around him. I'd had that lesson drummed into me from first days in under-guards. How could she not know such a basic principle? *I'll have words with Kul on that.* The thought calmed me. He'd have given Cal training, wouldn't he? Kul knew those lessons better than I did.

Heyliannin was still talking. Something about Cal talking to the Lakesider parents. "Then he told the captain, 'Wait here,' and took off running. The captain wasn't taking orders from a kid, though, so right away, he sent a group of men after him. But Calestinise had a head start, and they fell further behind as he dodged through the field, working his way around the main force of the kids. He'd been practicing with Kul. He thought he knew what he was doing."

I knew where the story was headed, but I didn't want to rush her. "Where was Kul?"

"He'd been leading a group of townsfolk to retrieve kids. When they came back, I told him where Calestinise had gone. Right then, a family who'd been delayed crossing the river came running, screaming a warning."

I visualized the territory. "The Southern regulars, right? At the river?"

"Yes. Kul told the families to run south and west, away from the oncoming force. He raced around the clusters of rescuers, telling everyone, 'Take the kids we've saved and go!' He kept looking over his shoulder, tracking Calestinise, I think. I can't say for sure; I'd lost sight of our boy in all the movement.

"And I was so sick, Corren." It was hard to believe, looking at her now. Why hadn't the shamans found a way to use mantles this way? Then again, I knew shamans who seemed far too energetic for their age. Racac, for one, that slimy Lakeside child abuser.

She leaned on me awkwardly, shifting from kneeling to sitting. The mantle slid and slithered on my back, and I tried to imagine it wasn't alive. "Sorry. Kul took my pony's reins and dragged the hairy thing in the direction of the retreat. 'Go,' he told me. 'We'll catch up. Don't worry if you fall off, this one will wait for you.' Then he smacked the animal's butt so hard it jumped into a trot. I thought I would fall off right away, but once the pony felt safe from Kul, it went back to a walk.

"I think he meant for me to follow the Lakesiders, who were doing what he said: heading for safety on the west side of the lake. They'd retrieved a bunch of kids by then; they had a lot to deal with." Her fingers clutched at nothing, remembering holding onto Friendly Pony's mane, no doubt.

"Why didn't you follow the crowd?" I figured I knew the answer, but I had a notion it would be better for her to talk through it herself.

"The stupid pony had decided to go home. It wouldn't turn, no matter what I did. Nobody saw that I was off course." She forced a harsh laugh; and I caught myself smiling. She must have looked ridiculous, a non-rider arguing with an experienced, determined pony.

Awkward in the moment, I patted her knee. "Ponies can be tough-minded. That one especially."

"I gave up and let it do what it wanted, so I could watch what was happening. I saw one good thing. And then a lot of bad things."

"Good thing, first." I figured that might be easier on her.

She leaned into me, almost relaxed. "When the Lakesiders began their retreat, a lot of the kids took off after them. As if they'd recognized their chance, once they weren't having to fight against it. They ran like demons were after them."

"He did it," I said. "Calestinise cut a hole in their army of light. You won't have heard this—Arnim's report had fewer of them on the march than we expected." I almost turned to look at her, but I didn't dare. The bad news was still coming. "Cal may have saved us, Heyliannin. Those few hundred, that made a difference you can't measure."

Her arm around my waist tightened, then released. "That's good to hear." She took a breath, thick and wet, like a woman trying not to drown. "As the pony made the turn onto the north road, I spotted Calestinise and, well behind him, those angry dads, heading for the cluster of commanders on the hill. Kul was still plowing through the mob, swinging that sword of his like a scythe. The kids who dodged away swirled in behind him in waves."

"Did you see them fall?" She knew who I meant. I didn't need to say their names.

"No," she admitted. "The pony took me behind a rise in the land. I lost sight of them. But there were hundreds and hundreds of men coming up from the river. They had weird hats on and they marched as if they could never get tired.

"I wanted to go back, but the pony wanted away from that place. All I could do was hold on. When I fell off, it would stop. My fever must have been rising the whole time. I kept thinking I heard Calestinise or Kul yelling at me to *hurry, get the word home*, and I'd kick the pony to make it go faster. Then I'd fall off and stare at the sky, wondering where I was. The pony would rub its nose in my face until I got back on."

"Ya, that's Friendly Pony for you. He doesn't like being left alone." It might have happened in another universe, when Friendly stuck his nose in my face to wake me from the snake-man's stunning-device. That was the day Heyliannin disappeared through a thin patch with those monsters, leaving her mantle behind.

"I could hardly believe it, when I saw Jeskaryan on the horizon." She stopped for a minute, took long, slow breaths.

The pause let me breathe as well. My mind wandered to the day she'd returned with Tymon. My obsession with her connection to my father's death. Her crazy idea to take the place Eldennian refused, to be my wife … was it more than a scheme to get the mantle back? Our motives were so muddled, but things had worked out. Hadn't they?

And her latest return … was that only yesterday?

What could I talk about, to bring her to the present, with me, now? *The kids.* "You shoulda heard Stevvin yelling, 'Mom's back!' We're fostering them. Did I tell you yet?"

The mantle slipped off my shoulder, and the cooling air made me shiver. She slid it back into place. I was almost used to it by then … but still glad it stayed still and said nothing.

"While the doctors were poking and prodding and pouring horrible drinks into me, I kept asking, did Kul come, did Calestinise catch up? I'm sure they thought it was the fever. They talked in strange, whispery, panicked voices. I think they were running out of things to try. If you hadn't sent me Asdyel, the infection might have killed me."

My arms went around her body—no raging fever, no shivers. She might have settled into my arms after a long run … or a practice session. "They wouldn't let me see you," I said. "It was worse than when Yutek was dying. I wasn't even sure they'd let Dramin in."

"I'm fine, Corren. " She leaned back, and I loosened my hold. With first one small hand, then the other, she wiped my face dry. "You're exhausted," she said.

I was too tired to make up lies. "It's been a long, terrible day, and tomorrow will be worse."

"Don't think that. Tomorrow will be better. And the day after that, and the day after."

She stood, shook the cape smooth, then pulled me to my feet.

"How can I make that happen, Heyliannin? I've only ever tried to do the right thing, and here we are." My mind filled with images of the desperate rescue, the oncoming army, the furious, terrified families.

"For now, I think you need to get some sleep." Did she remember that time I snapped at her, *Do you think you can comfort me?* Who else could, if not Heyliannin?

"How? My head is full of stuff. I can't stop thinking about everything."

"Well, let's start by getting you out of that jacket. You'll want it tomorrow, right?" She helped me peel off Errem's jacket and hung it over a piece of furniture. She gestured at the rest of my outfit. "And how many days straight have you been wearing this shit?"

"Enough that Case's runner recognized me, because he'd been told to look for a ragpicker."

She kept her face still, ran her eyes over me and lifted her eyebrows in silent agreement with Case. I tried not to calculate the odds he'd died that afternoon, against the chance he was on his way to our north gate, to reinforce those defenses. She opened a trunk and pulled out clean trousers and a uniform shirt I'd forgotten I had, then spread them next to the jacket.

"See? You're all set now, for the morning. Let's get you out of this dirty laundry."

I didn't want to dump dirty clothes in the sitting room, so I headed for the bedchamber. She tucked an arm in the curve of my elbow, kept me from staggering.

It was a bad parody of our wedding night. I couldn't manage to get my pants off by myself. She didn't laugh as she helped me, but she wore that sneaky smile I knew too well, as I sat on the bed in nothing but a shirt, and let her work the laces on it free. I clasped her arm and gave it a tug, but hadn't the energy to swing her off her feet. She yielded to the pull anyway, stepped right up close, my legs dangling off the bed to either side of her.

"You remember your lessons?" she murmured.

"Why?" I asked. "You planning to renew our vows?" I reached for her, but recoiled when my hand brushed the mantle.

She looked startled. "What's the matter?"

I held up two fingers. "Two against one. Not fair."

She put her hand behind her head, rubbed at her neck, and sighed. It might have been my imagination, or a hallucination from exhaustion, but I swear I saw it. A furred head with a diamond-shaped skull, bright daggers of teeth lining a long, pointed jaw, lifted from the cape at her shoulders. It sucked in a long, long tongue, making a sound like a man draining the last drop from a flask. It had bright pinpricks of eyes, glittering jewels that regarded me with amusement. If you could put emotion into a brief glance from a creature of another world.

Heyliannin shrugged the mantle free of her shoulders and cradled it in her arms. "Asdyel can rest out in the sitting room," she said. "He's had a tough day, too."

"So long as he can't see through walls," I said. I flopped down on the bed and closed my eyes for a second while I waited for her to come back.

Suddenly, I was sitting up, breathing hard, as if I'd just run up to Yutek's grounds, my vision full of Calestinise lifting a sword against a troop of grey-shirted Southerners, Kul screaming from behind him, drowned in a wave of wild-eyed youths. Heyliannin's arms held me tight, kept me from flailing at shadows.

"It was a dream," she said. "Only a dream."

It didn't feel like a dream. It felt like a memory, her memory in my head. "Are they all going to die? Calestinise and Kul and Arnim? Karthi and Harad and Case? That's what Maledestine said, that we'll all die, that it's no use, no use."

She released her hold, let me balance on my own, even nudged my shoulder as if checking to be sure I wouldn't topple over. "Whoever that woman is, what do you care what she thinks?"

"She's an elder, Heyliannin. She's my boss. Well, one of them."

She rolled her eyes. Calestinise could have been her true-son, they were so alike. "Is giving up ever the right thing, Corren?"

"It never occurred to me, before, but maybe I was wrong." Maybe, sometimes, giving up *was* the right thing.

She leaned back and let her eyes rove over the now-familiar territory. "All those scars you have, Corren. Do you regret them?"

"No. Of course not." It was all for Jeska, always. Except for the marks Yutek-en had made. No—especially those, considering.

"Because you've promised to protect Jeska." Her eyes bored into mine. I couldn't look away. Couldn't not answer her.

"Yes."

"And you won't go back on a promise."

"No."

"Well, then."

That left me nearly awake, almost myself again. She'd shed whatever it was she'd been wearing under the mantle. I'd fallen asleep without even thinking of pulling on night clothes.

What had I been thinking of?

Oh, yes.

She slipped close, and the smell of her washed over us: sage and manzanita berries, hot under the sun, ready to press into cider. Her fingers traced the length of the scar on my back, waking me the rest of the way.

Yes, I remembered my lessons.

PART III

DEPLOY TACTICS TO SUIT ACTION IN THE FIELD

23

AN INSISTENT KNOCKING at the doorframe tunneled through the dreamless nothing I'd fallen into. I disentangled myself from Heyliannin and barged out to the dim sitting room.

Durse was soldier enough to show no reaction to a naked commander barking out questions while pulling on clothes.

"What's going on?"

"We got a runner in."

"Case?"

He shook his head. "Commander Karthi."

"When?"

"Not ten minutes ago, sir."

"Has Andus been called in?"

"Yessir."

"Briefing room?"

"Well, sir, no, we're quartering civilians in that sector. Command center, the Master Commander said."

"Why isn't Magaran in bed? He's needed tomorrow." I was talking without thinking. Of course Magaran would be awake, with news coming in.

Durse answered the question I hadn't asked. "He said to leave you be as long as we could."

My fingers seemed to have forgotten how to do lacing. *The last day. It's beginning.*

"What's going on?" Heyliannin stood in the doorway, wearing nothing but that short Lakesider dress she'd arrived in, the doorway curtain draped over her shoulder.

Durse started to speak, but I cut him off. "News from the front, nothing to worry about. But we're clearing the king's house, it's too exposed. Durse, has anyone notified my wife's guards?"

He looked flummoxed. "Er—"

I turned back to my wife. "Pack what you'll need for a day or two. Your guys are here, two of the Four and a pair of replacements." I paused at her silent stare. "I've claimed Harad and Radeo for other duties. The team should be moving Stevvin and Affram by now. Be ready for them."

"All right." I'd expected questions; she was always questioning everything.

Where should I send her? To civilian quarters? To the elders?

"What's the matter?" she asked.

"Nothing. I'm thinking. Tell me, do you know any *practical* herbal treatment? Or was it all a fake?"

"It was sort of a fake at first." She tugged at the skimpy skirt, as if suddenly realizing we weren't alone in the room. "I learned. The book helped."

"The book?"

"You know." She pretended to flip open a snake-man book and scribbled in the air.

"Oh. Well, then. Radeo has that. Tell your Four to take you down to the training field, where he's been working. Then join the medics for today. They'll need all the help they can get."

Her face went still, serious. She abandoned the doorway, ignored Durse, and moved in front of me.

I could have dodged her, but I waited. "Is there a problem? We need everyone. Wear the cape. It'll give you authority."

"Do you think so?" she said. "Doctors don't seem to trust shamans any more than you do." As she spoke, she brushed my fingers away from my shirt and fastened the lacings for me.

It dawned on me, at last, that to all intents and purposes, my wife really was a shaman. "I confiscated a bunch of mantles yesterday. Should I send them with you? Can you use them?"

She shook her head. "It's one to one, Corren. They're not tools."

I pulled on the jacket and let her tug it straight. Her brow creased, and she ran a finger over the badges that marked it. I coughed. "It's a loaner."

Across the room, Durse seemed to be trying not to sneeze.

My wife ignored the muffled snort, stood on tiptoe, and pressed her mouth against mine. One of her weirder habits—warm and friendly-seeming but disgusting at the same time. I wondered if I'd ever get used to it. "Good-bye, Corren," she said.

"See you later," I said, and followed Durse.

•　　　•　　　•

The command center seemed too quiet, after the commotion of setting up. Two kid scribes snuffled in their sleep, trying to share the mat they'd put down under their table and the blanket only one had thought to bring. The older scribe snored outright, leaning back in his chair, feet on the table.

Karthi's runner sat at the narrow edge of the commander in chief's table—the one with my stamps for verifying orders, copies of Andus's deployment plans—the accoutrements of command. A tall, lean woman with years of experience showing in the lines on her face, she nursed a thick mug of something hot and sweet-smelling. She hadn't run as far as the guys from the Narrows, but she'd run in the dark. Even if she went in for night runs, relished them as Tymon did, she'd have had to wait until moonrise and then go all-out. I was doing the math in my head as I moved to my place and motioned to the others to take their seats.

At the scraping of chairs and muttered *yessirs*, the senior scribe thumped awake, yawned, and sharpened his pen. He raised an eyebrow at me—*you want this on the record, sir?*—and I gave him a nod. From this moment, we'd need to get everything down, if we wanted to learn anything from this day.

"It's not looking so good, Boss," the runner recited. She carried Karthi's manner of speaking surprisingly well, put his voice in the room with us.

I allowed for Karthi's natural skepticism to make the news sound worse than it was, but the runner wouldn't know his way. Ripples chased each other over the surface of her drink.

"Don't worry," I said. "Proceed."

She put her mug down and cleared her throat. "HandOverHand ended at sunset, earlier than expected. We've got Southerners on the move here. We intercepted a volunteer runner—"

The runner added, in her normal voice, "He means a regular trooper, sir, not a proper runner."

I glanced to the scribe, to be sure he'd caught the detail.

The runner caught the look and started again. "We intercepted a volunteer runner, who told us losses at the mustering ground were hard to calculate, given the scattered battle plan, but high, very high." Her face scrunched tight, as if she was about to cry, but she went on with Karthi's words. "The volunteer told us the commander was *missing*. He couldn't say it outright. You know Case, Boss. He'd be here or he'd send word. He wouldn't leave his troopers." Tears overflowed. "We lost him, Boss. Didn't think it was possible. Sorry to send this news. Ya need to know. Impacts strategy."

Karthi was right. Would any of Case's captains step up to lead our surprise reinforcements to the north gate? Would their training hold?

The runner wiped her face. It occurred to me the tears weren't her own, but Karthi's. Even so, I figured she needed comforting. "Take a minute, Runner. There's time yet."

"Thank you, sir." She sniffed and took a swig from her mug. "He gave me numbers and positions. Shall I do those next?"

"Sure." I ignored the scribe's pen-scratching and scribbled notes for myself. Writing the information down helped fix it in my mind, slipped it into place among the calculations churning in my head. As the information flowed, it focused my mind on what I needed in the moment, to resolve the strategic implications. The work held thoughts of my friend at bay. Those that trickled in, I pushed back with, *it's not yet certain.*

The volunteer runner'd done a surprisingly good job of gathering status information, estimating losses, citing positions. If he survived the next day, that trooper'd deserve a promotion. I was right about Karthi's pessimism oozing into his tactical report. Yes, the losses were great, but in line with what I'd anticipated.

It's part of the job. A cold truth the moment you step into an officer's boots. You dispatch men to battle, and no matter how well you've trained them, even if they aren't outnumbered, you know you're sending too many to the condors. I didn't have time to cry for them. Not yet.

"There's one more thing, sir."

I looked up from my notes. "Yes?"

She went back to Karthi's voice. "I think Kul may be there. The trooper described the officer who'd sent him. Not Case."

Given the primary message, it couldn't have been Case. But why Kul?

I may have stopped breathing, because my next question came in a gasp. "Was he sure?"

There must have been something in my voice, in my face. She seemed calm, but I could see the ripples in her drink trembling again. Her words came in a hoarse whisper, her own assessment. "No, sir, he said it wasn't certain, but I was there, when the trooper told him. Commander Karthi seemed better after that."

"I understand." I was relying on her judgment of the moment. If you can't draw on other people's interpretations of events, you'll never get anywhere. She'd said nothing of Calestinise. I didn't ask.

Andus spoke up. "If Karthi guessed it might almost be true, then I'm ready to rely on it, Boss." How had he felt, hearing Karthi's words from this stranger, with no way to ask after him but knowing him in pain?

I drew lines between numbers in my notes, let my pen make a few estimates for me. Then I ran my eyes over the quiet group sitting around that table. Radeo's fingers twitched, ready to get out of there, back to work. Andus leaned with both elbows on the table, listening. A junior officer whose name I couldn't recall flinched at my gaze. Magaran sat chewing a rough edge on his thumbnail, as if this were any other day, as if I were Yutek making plans for a late summer military exercise.

"We'll hope you're right, Andus, that Kul's taken charge of the remainders," I said. "But you'd best shift more men to the north gate, just in case." I had new orders for the rest of them, and we got someone to lead our messenger off to wherever they'd quartered the runners.

For a little while, then, it was just me, and my invisible guards, and the scribe. The old man finished his notes, propped up his feet again, and went back to sleep.

24

WITH PLANS IN MOTION, we had nothing to do for a while. I made my bodyguards let me out of that closed-in room for a pre-dawn tour of my domain. What little I could get to. Still on the alert for assassins, the guys wouldn't let me out the fortress gate.

"We'll have to quit worrying about that soon, boys," I complained. "The elders insisted on space for the shamans in the evacuation. They're going to walk those traitors right in."

"Yessir." The way Durse bobbed his head annoyed me. I threw him a salute, to get his mind back where it belonged. He stood straight, saluted back, and the slap of palm to shoulder restored our balance.

"That's better." I straightened my borrowed uniform jacket. "So *after* the shamans and their assassins move in, we'll take a stroll down to the market."

Errem would have rolled his eyes, but Durse kept his gambler's face still. I had half a mind to demand an early shift change, but the day crew needed their rest.

The main plaza had become a campground for evacuees. As first light began to soften the sky, it turned into an impromptu market. Even on the flat pavement, a winding path imitated the one on the hillside below, weaving among tents and canopies, tables and produce carts. Dogs tumbled across the path, yapping, threatening to trip us up. Merchants called out as we passed, "Here, lads, don't go away hungry!" and tossed fruit, buns, dried meat. To them we were five more soldiers mustering for their defense. For those few minutes, I soaked in the life of my city, let go of the years, and stepped out with the energy I'd had when my Six and I patrolled the border together.

At the king's house, the staff were hard at work shifting the last few irreplaceables out of the building, under the quartermaster's watchful eye. Documents, sensitive records, artwork, and valuables were destined for a deep corner of the storerooms, where a team of masons waited to conceal their existence. Should Jeskaryan fall, we'd be back for those treasures one day.

I found the major domo and asked him what he'd done with the capes we'd left in the council chamber.

"Capes, sir?"

"Shamans' mantles."

"Oh. Those. We boxed them up, sir. After the last meeting. The elders complained about the mess. Should I send the crates down to the shamans? I heard they moved their household into the fortress." He bobbed on his toes, eager to get on with his work, probably calculating how much delay this extra crate-hauling would pose.

"Where did you put those boxes?"

"Lower storeroom, sir." Where they kept seasonal items, less-used furnishings.

"Fine. Leave them." It wouldn't do to have the fact mislaid, though. Fennic kept Asdyel in a crate for, what, a year? They were living things, those mantles, so they must be able to hibernate. Like bears. "Find a runner, send him to the command post, have that information recorded. Note that those boxes should be unloaded within the year, if not sooner."

His eyebrows rose, then fell. "We'll do that." Then he bowed at me. "Your Majesty."

"You had to call me that, didn't you?" How long had the two of us known each other? Nearly thirty years? The muscles in his face twitched. I gave him a get-along wave.

The military quarters had been turned over to the elders to allocate as they saw fit among managers and townsfolk. I avoided the senior-officer quarters, home of our briefing room. Durse told me the elders had set up their council-room there, and the last thing I needed was more demands from my bosses.

We ducked through my old barracks, greeting those who were awake and walking softly to avoid those who weren't. In my former office, we surprised an old couple enjoying themselves over the current captain's cider supply. They were deep enough in to beg us to join them, but Durse gently fended off the invitation. Muffled sounds caught my attention from the cubbyhole of a room where Tymon had interrupted Eldennian and me, when I was a green lieutenant. I lifted the edge of the drape enough to verify it wasn't a gang of murderous spies. Judging by the clothing strewn in front of the doorway, the couple would be busy for a while yet. At least they wouldn't have a runner barging in and asking to join the party.

The practice yard remained a beehive of activity. Assembling fire-arrows, makers and their apprentices toiled over kettles of steaming pitch. I found Radeo bent over a worktable, with lanterns guttering to either side of him, sawing the caps off pegs.

"What's going on here?" I demanded. "All the materiel should have been distributed by now."

Setting down the handsaw, he brushed hair out of his eyes. "Good morning, Cousin!" He grinned like a boy, his wrinkles decorated with sawdust and grit. "Working on a new idea. Hold them off until the afternoon, and we'll have something new to … throw at them." He chuckled. What was so funny?

I moved closer and picked up one of the pegs, turning it over in my hand. Leather cords dangled from it. "Hey. You're playing with toss-ups. Why sports equipment? We're well past settling this with a friendly game."

He retrieved the peg from me and summoned an apprentice. "Hey, Malak, get a finished one for me." The kid ran off and returned moments later with what seemed to be an ordinary toss-up. Stevvin left dozens of the things scattered behind us on our tour of eastern Lakeside. The two pegs were linked by leather strips, so they could be flung across a field, snagged by an opponent's stick, and flung back. Or thrown over a wall. Or into an enemy force. The surface was sticky—like the fire-arrows, it was coated in pitch. Radeo twisted the knobby end of one peg and pulled it free, revealing a hollow drilled into the center. A hollow packed full of lightning powder. "See?"

"Ya. But do they work? And how many have you got?" In a city the size of Jeskaryan, in peacetime it might have been easy to round up a barrel of toss-ups, but the game was considered a kids' pastime. We'd packed most of the kids off in the evacuations.

Radeo shrugged off my skepticism. "Enough to make for a nasty surprise, when they think they're used to the fire-arrows."

"You got throw sticks, too?" I wouldn't have expected the people camping in the plaza to have brought toys with them, at least not toys that needed a lot of space to play in.

"Some. We'll make do." He gestured to a carpenter working a few tables down. "Making a few extra sticks, when there's a break in other demands."

"Other demands?"

"We're still stockpiling arrows. There'll be calls for resupply, once things get started." He peered up at the sky. "Hadn't realized it was getting light already."

"So what are you calling these things? Fire-toss-ups?"

"Na, I liked Heyliannin's idea. She called them *boms*, but I think we'll use *fire-boms*. Matches fire-arrows, but doesn't make you think it's a toy."

"Heyliannin was here?"

"Ya. She came for the book." He waved me closer. "Your wife's not too happy about all this, Cousin."

"Why not?"

"She had a lot of words I couldn't follow, sir. Expect a rant from her on the subject. Or plan to stay out of her way." So now I had to worry about a matriarch yelling at me in a foreign language while I tried to defend my city. And here I thought we'd settled things between us. Radeo seemed to be following my thoughts. "She didn't arrive angry, but she left that way. I gather she hadn't expected us to find this recipe, that it was a secret we shouldn't have."

"I don't see why not."

He laughed softly. "Don't tell her, but the smiths extracted more ideas from it. Didn't seem to involve more weapons, but we can assume she'd be mad about those secrets, too. The Master Smith said he had a good time figuring out how to, as he put it, break in." He waved his hands at the look on my face. "Nothing's broken. It's a metaphor."

So at least she wasn't going to cut out anybody's heart today. Wouldn't have mattered. Arnim didn't need to worry about her threat anymore.

"Boss? What's wrong?"

I shook off the mood before it could overtake me. "Nothing. Everything. Thinking about Arnim, and Case, all the men we have out on the lines today." I sniffed and summoned an expression I meant to be a smile. "You make your fire-boms. Have them ready before the Southerners break through the palisade."

"Yessir."

He was back at work before I started to turn around. The man should have been a smith, with a family at home to cook for. He didn't even have his sword-belt on. "Radeo."

"Yessir."

"Get yourself geared up. And I'll send you a few men. You may need to defend this place before the day is out."

His shoulders squared up. "Ya, yes, sir. We'll be ready."

25

I'D PLANNED TO STOP by the infirmary, upgraded to a hospital to serve the doctors and such we'd enlisted from the city and its environs. With all the guardsmen on assignment, nobody needed the rest of the space in that building, anyhow. After Radeo's warning to avoid Heyliannin, I figured it best to presume the medics could manage their own arrangements and wouldn't benefit from my crew tramping through their territory. They'd keep my wife busy, once things got started, so that was all that mattered.

Unless...

Right. Unless she decided to take her complaints directly to me. By the time she'd forged through the plaza, located the command center, made her Four push past the posted guards, and found me gone, she'd worked up a good temper.

I'd barely concluded my good-will tour of the stables, where staff had turned a harness room into a command center for Runners' House and had found similar spaces for other guilds' leaders. Keep in mind, I hadn't directed this. My order had been no more specific than *provide useful space for the guilds.* Clearly, the principle of autonomous action applied beyond the military.

The tour consisted of entering a feed room or a repurposed foaling stall, admiring what they'd done with makeshift accommodations, and receiving cheerful thanks in return. I'd expected complaints, so the stable visit had lifted my mood considerably. One tends to forget the practical nature of those who sign up for the service guilds. They're not in it to get rich.

I was exchanging thank-yous with the newly-elevated head of the Food Sharers, who make it their mission to be sure no one goes hungry in our well-provisioned district, when my wife marched up. Her guards hovered behind her, their expressions a mixture of anxiety and confusion.

"There you are!" she announced. "You can't hide from me, Corren!"

"I'm hardly hiding," I told her. To the earnest Sharer beside me, I said, "Apologies, ma'am. My wife has need of me. Thank you for your good works."

She tipped her head. "No, thank you, Your Majesty." I swear I caught an understanding smile on her face as she slipped away. Maybe charity workers have special insights on turmoil inside a family.

Heyliannin had the grace to look a little embarrassed. "Sorry. But it's important." She waved something at me: flat, shiny, book-sized.

"Oh, no. Was it damaged? Radeo should have told me." I reached for the snake-man book, my fingers eager to detect the problem, find a solution.

She pulled her hand back, clutching the book to her chest. "No. It's fine. It's what you're doing with it—you've got to stop!"

"We can't talk about this here." I reached for her free hand and pulled her along, moving us out of the stableyard and around to the nearby command center. The long room had already filled. Everyone assigned to command operations for the day had shown up on schedule. All eyes turned to us, but I fended them off with an impromptu order. "Command conference in fifteen." Then I ducked back outside and led my angry wife down the alley between that building and the next.

She stayed quiet through all that. Whatever bothered her, then, it had to be something important.

"Now, what's wrong?" I reached for a deflection. "Did the Master Smith change your passcodes?"

"My— what? What do you know about passcodes?"

"You can't hand a device to a smith and not expect him to figure it out, Ta-ma."

She ran her hands over the book cover, and her shoulders slumped. "So much for the *priyyam drectiff.*"

"I don't know what that is." Sometimes, saying that line would get her to explain.

"The *guwun* powder," she said. "You weren't supposed to get that. It's too advanced for you."

"You mean lightning powder? It was right there with your headache remedies and all." She needed to know I hadn't *ordered* any prying into secrets. Though I knew the smiths had collected more than she'd have expected.

"You shouldn't have … Listen, Corren, using that stuff, it's going to make changes, big changes that you're not ready for. If you put it out there, start using it in battle, everyone will know, everyone will want it. You can't use it once, then put it away."

I let her ramble on about the nebulous hazards of unleashing lightning powder on an unsuspecting world. You'd think we'd discovered a poison that would kill everybody or a magic spell that would set the world on fire. When she seemed to be running out of breath, I poked a hole in the notion she could stop this. "It's already happened, Heyliannin. It's being used, right now, in the field."

"What? Where? How?" She looked to the top of the fortress wall. Did she expect to see fire hurtling into the sky?

"Not here—on the road. Karthi and Harad have been harrying the Southerners all night during their approach to Jeskaryan, using arrows treated with lightning powder. You're asking me not to use it—well, it's too late for that. You can't stuff a rattlesnake back into its hole."

She shuddered. Heyliannin wasn't much on proverbs, but she had a city-dweller's abhorrence of snakes. "Arrows? With guwun powder?"

"They burst apart on landing, cause damage even if they strike nothing, kill instantly if they hit someone. We think. Haven't had a report back yet."

"That's awful!" In the dim morning light, the shock in her eyes became tears starting up. "It'll be horrible, Corren. Imagine it!"

"War is horrible, Heyliannin. A man dies because a blade slices through him, or an arrow strikes his heart, or a bolt of lightning-like fire tears him apart. It's all terrible."

"You really don't care, do you?" Sure enough, rivulets ran down her cheeks, making silvery streaks on her soft skin.

What did she take me for? "Of course I care. I care about my people, about my city, and this stuff—your lightning powder—it may be the edge that lets us save our place, our people." How could she not see it? Who was she trying to protect? "Are you worried about the army of light? The Lakesider kids?"

"No. Well, yes, but— It's the big picture, Corren. What about the next war? What will you do when the enemy has guwun powder too? And the war after that?"

"We'll cross that river when we reach it, Heyliannin. As your people did, I imagine."

"And you know how scrood-up my people are."

I did. But— "We'll do better."

"That's what they all say." Her mouth twisted, and she crossed her arms. The mantle over her shoulders shadowed her movements. "Radeo's down there building boms right now. He's not even waiting for the next war to escalate things."

I could see this argument running out a day, a year, a generation. What could I do, there and then, to reassure her enough that I could get back to work? She hated her home world, but she missed it, too, scrood-up or not. One of these days, she'd go back there. Maybe soon, now she had that cape of hers back. I half-expected Asdyel to chime in with a hissing argument of its own. So it took daring on my part to pull her close, wrap my arms around the two of them—Ta-ma and Asdyel—and pat them on the back as soothingly as I could manage. "We'll do our best. I can't promise more than that. But know this, you may have saved the best part of my world, by giving us lightning powder. Thank you."

She trembled under my embrace. It could have been sorrow, or fury, or regret. Probably all three. I didn't wait for her to pull away, but released her quickly and turned to leave before she could say anything else. My guys fell into formation and we left her bodyguards to see her safely to her work for the day.

Soon, she'd understand what I meant. When the injured began to come into the hospital, she'd be ready to fling those fire-boms herself.

26

C IVILIANS HAVE AMUSING IDEAS about how a war is run. Do you think the king takes up his own sword and runs around a tidy, rectangular battlefield, shouting speeches and handing out orders? Does that make any sense when the battle is spread around the perimeter of a city, through its twisting streets, then along the walls and gates of its inner fortress? How will the campaign fare if the king gets unlucky at one of those exposure points? If something changes, how can he know, how will he organize the response?

Success in a complex engagement demands excellence in three areas: command, control, and communication. Command isn't a series of orders; it's knowledge of the field, with an organization capable of mastering the situation. Control is exercised at every level, down to the individual trooper. Communication ties everything together.

Listen. If you want the king's view of a war, it's a view from a closed room, behind layers and layers of protection. I was locked in our command center from before sunrise until after nightfall.

We got our information as fast as possible, knowing every time it came a little too late. Every moment of the day was a test; one way or the other I'd prove my worth—or lack of it.

As a captain, I'd sold my commanders on a new way to organize the Guard. We'd retrained everyone, from the kids in the under-guard to the grizzled old guys who answered the mustering call to reserves. I'd learned from experience that autonomous action is what you need from troops in the field. They need to know the battle plan, because when conditions change—and they *always* change—it's the men in the field who have to make the necessary judgment calls, pivot to a new set of tactics, keep the press on against the enemy or form a judicious retreat.

Field commanders are closer to the action, not only to guide their troops but also to observe what the autonomous units have decided to do. Vision is faster than any runner. That enables the field commander to redirect maneuvers at his scale of the action.

Likewise, the commander in chief relies on the field commanders to manage their forces and communicate up the chain of command anything that might affect the overarching strategy. Major enemy actions. Observed new tactics and attempted responses. With that information flowing, central command manages the whole of the engagement from one point, with constant adjustments to strategy and tactics, recommended troop movements, direct orders when necessary. You have to rely on your field commanders, and the troops under them, to act in the moment in response to what's on the field. You have to be flexible, change your plans to match their reality. It's all about time.

Here's a story from Heyliannin's world. She claimed they built small, obedient creatures—mechanical dogs—that they fill up with commands and hurl far, far away, to places in the sky as distant as the Great Wanderer. Not sure I believe it, but according to her, that body is so far away, if you shine a light at it, it'll take an hour for the beam to get there. So if the roving creature sends a message on a light beam, asking a question, you don't get its message for an hour and it can't get any orders for another hour. It has to be autonomous, doesn't it? It has to be able to answer most of its own questions, or something's going to kill it out there. Right?

I know, nothing's really that far away, but it's a good metaphor for real life. It takes too long for runners to come and go from the battlefield. Sometimes their messages don't get through at all. We have to plan everything in advance—a primary strategy, specific tactics, alternatives, responses to anticipated enemy actions, on and on. If anything unanticipated comes up, we're sunk—unless our forces have their own smarts, their own ability to pivot and make a new plan. I sent Arnim to the Narrows before Case came in with his report on forces massing south of the border, because I'd had reports from earlier runners, so I made a guess at potential troop movements. I knew how much time it would take for Arnim's unit to travel from Jeskaryan and set up at the Narrows. As it turned out, we were barely in time.

At each point in our deployment, we acted on improved information, but we also had to rely on the capabilities of those we'd deployed already. They were as best-prepared as possible *at the time.*

On this day, this final day, time remained our critical factor. Our new system gave us the ability to operate as if communication time didn't matter. That was a bigger edge to us than the new weapons Heyliannin was so worried about. The attackers would be using old methods. Even if they'd recognized we were trying something new, they wouldn't be able to adopt our key tactic—autonomy—because it takes years to retrain your forces. And they didn't have time for that.

27

T HE DOOR OF THE COMMAND CENTER closing behind me sounded like a boulder dropping to block a canyon. My entire body focused on finding a way out—when my mind knew perfectly well about the door on the opposite side … the one Tymon and I had sneaked out of so many times as kids.

Luckily, Errem came in right behind me, then left the door open for the rest of his day-shift crew. The flow of air from outside cooled my nerves, let me concentrate.

Durse and Errem began arguing about whether I needed my entire troop of bodyguards. "You guys best go get a couple of hours," Errem told Durse and the others.

"We're fine," Durse insisted. "We've been doing nothing here. You're not cutting us out, buddy."

I drank in the sweet morning air for a few more seconds, then broke up their party. "I'll need you all soon enough. Night shift stays through the command conference, then I want you out of here, Durse."

Durse looked smug. Errem grunted and shut the door again. The closed-in feeling wasn't so bad, the second time.

Absent any new information, the command conference went quickly. A few of the younger officers had questions they should have asked earlier, but what mattered was that they asked, didn't guess. That was why they'd been promoted, how they'd earned command positions. Older officers—Magaran's contemporaries—covered most of the replies, and offered to follow up with the juniors later.

Magaran took his time, reviewed a few issues he'd run into, from a need for more ladders along the wall to my failure to order up breakfast for us. "That's on you. An army marches on its stomach; you know that. Sir." From his glare, I might have been a raw recruit who'd failed to scrub a latrine properly.

I'd started an angry response, when I caught the gleam in his eye. I shifted to one side to see around him. *Ah.* The narrow table pushed up against the far wall looked barely sturdy enough to hold up the provisions spread across it.

He jabbed a thumb over his shoulder. "Good thing one of us is on the alert, wouldn't you say?"

My stomach rumbled, and that put an end to the conference. No one made a move, so I dragged my feet over that way and loaded a plate. Andus had been pacing the whole time, but he stopped for a minute to scarf a few rolls. He stabbed questioning looks at me until I released him to see to his troop placements. Durse's crew followed—after stuffing their pockets with snacks.

No sooner had they left than the door swung open and a runner scurried in.

This one wasn't from either Karthi or Harad. Instead, he'd been sent by the elders, declaring the city evacuation complete. A thought struck me. "Say, Runner, you know my brother?"

"Sir?"

"Tymon. Good-looking guy. Long legs."

His face brightened. "Of course, sir. Everyone knows Tymon."

"If you haven't got a follow-on assignment, I need someone to run down and make sure he's followed the evac order." I tried to make light of the situation, but getting my brother safe would ease a serious itch at the back of my mind. "He's been away, may not know what's going on. I can tell you where to find him. It's right in town, near the market."

He held up both hands. "Not necessary, sir. He's here. And besides, the elders have me booked for the day."

"Tymon's in the fortress? With the runners?"

He shuffled his feet, eager to get on with his next assignment. "No, sir. I saw him come in with the shamans."

"The shamans?"

"That was the last House in, sir."

I didn't know how to interpret that. Had Tymon joined the Jeskaryan shamans, or did he happen to enter when they did, as a latecomer? Neither made sense—going to Fennic's crew or figuring out on his own to leave Eldennian's house. Either way, he was safe for now. As safe as any of us. "Very well. Thank you."

His feet twitched again.

"Dismissed!"

That set the pattern for the day: the narrow door opening, news delivered, questions asked, orders given, the door closing. All the while, scribes noted each stage of each encounter, the discussions we had in between visitors, the times one of us stood up, went to that door, and called for a runner because we'd thought of new orders to send out—orders that would generate different news. Better news, we hoped. We worked steadily, fueled more by hope than by the slowly-dwindling pile of provisions on that table.

Hope has a chaotic pattern; it's clouds flowing over the mountains, bringing unforeseeable weather. It comes in steadily for a while, then slowly builds towers against the sky. Far above, unseen forces tear at its upper levels. Should you become used to hope, it turns fragile, dissipates—at first gradually, then collapsing at dizzying speed. When you least expect, it reverses course, recovers, piles brilliance high … impossibly high.

Until it shreds to nothing, like fog in the wind.

28

WE ANTICIPATED the southerner forces would strike the city at dawn, so the perimeter posts had orders to report at that time, but all we got was a flurry of "nothing happening" messages from the posts on the palisade. I sent those runners straight back with orders to report in as soon as any action began.

Either the enemy had other plans, or our harriers had slowed their progress. Either way, having more time to prepare never hurts.

I sent a runner down to the practice field, to tell Radeo he had an additional window to relay fire-arrows to the perimeter. A report came in of a commotion at the fortress gate, but that turned out to be a collection of townsfolk who'd changed their minds about staying to guard their homes and workshops.

Nothing better than the light of day to wake up a person's common sense.

An hour after dawn, a few runners came in from the palisade with questions, most of which I could defer to Magaran. One pocket of defenders reported they'd been delivered fire-arrows, but hadn't had the training.

Using those arrows had more dangers than might be obvious. First off, the archers needed to break their routine—aim, pause, release. When you've nocked a rod of burning pitch, none of that applies—you point in the general direction of your target and let fly. I sent that runner straight to Radeo, to get an instructor out, and I gave him Adestinian's words to share with those bowmen: *Destroy them with terror.*

By afternoon, Radeo's second terror weapon would be ready to hurl from the fortress walls. The delay—whatever the cause—served us an advantage.

Around mid-morning, more-serious news began to trickle in.

A runner we assumed to have come from Harad or Karthi turned out to be something else entirely—a messenger from Kul.

He didn't try to match Kul's northern accent, but I could hear my friend's tones in the cadence of his words. "Boss, troopers at HandOverHand tell me you'd a plan to send our survivors north. I've a half-dozen troops here. Most're missing a few troopers. We got about fifty men, total. Look fer us. We'll make the north gate in time. Got guys here what know this territory."

The runner paused and drank from a mug one of my guys put into his hand. "Thank you."

He set the cup down and went on with the narrative, though his words slowed to match Kul's mood. "The HandOverHand engagement was a rout, Boss. I hope you planned for that. Took out two of them for every one of us, but they'd the numbers for it. No time to set the fires. After we beat 'em, you gotta send crews out, clean the land." I could hear the echoes of Kul's farm-based matriarchs—*get that poison out of our soil.*

"You got numbers? Locations?" I cut in.

The runner avoided my gaze, rubbed his nose. "Sorry, no. Not my kind of job, sir. But we were an hour north of Kellish when he sent me. He seemed in a hurry."

"I know Kellish," someone said. One of the juniors. I told him to mark the map.

"I didn't get numbers, but he told me to say …" This time, the guy narrowed his eyes, to better recite, meaning this message he couldn't risk paraphrasing. "Ya need to know, Calestinise is with the army of light. Set us up to make an attack on their leadership, led the charge, then turned and fought me off. I had to yield, Boss. I couldn't be killin' the boy, could I?' The runner paused, his eyes flicking to my face, probably seeing an unpleasant expression.

The pain in my chest rivaled the usual gut-ache. I focused on one point: Calestinise joined the army of light. "That better not be all you got."

"No, sir. Then he said, 'Had my suspicions, but the primary force was marchin' up right then. Sent the Lakesider fam'lies off west. Got to a safe position, kept an eye on the boy."

"Wait—" I interrupted him. I needed a moment to visualize. Calestinise making a scene … he had a plan. Become a spy, as he'd done on our tour?

The runner used that moment to take another drink, but kept his gaze on me, until I gave him the nod to go on.

The cup clanked on the table, and he took up Kul's words again. It was as if Kul heard my thoughts—from a distance, hours ago. "'Ya, his plan was to get on the inside. Since, he's been sneaking off small parties of kids. Seems he finds potential deserters, leads 'em outta the line of march. So ya need ta send teams to collect those youngsters, after. They'll be scattered along the road, from the Narrows to yer front gate."

The runner added, "Sorry, sir. I might have missed some of that. An army made of light? A woman and a boy? Rescuing children? I did my best, but I'm no military runner. I must have got some of that wrong."

I saw it then—what my team would have noticed right away—he lacked the ribbon at his shoulder that marked a battlefield reporter.

"Sounds accurate enough," Magaran replied, and went on, for my benefit. "You're not the runner we dispatched for this commission."

The runner sipped at his water, probably wishing it was cider. "The commander caught me on the road, on another commission. This one sounded important, so I left off." He sent an appealing glance towards Magaran. "If someone could validate that, with the House, might save me a penalty?"

I leaned back in my chair and gestured to the scribe on duty, one of the boys this time. He held up his pen, called out, "Yes, sir, I can take care of that," and began to scribble something out.

Being told to find his way to the stables made the man frown as he collected his affidavit.

"Bring it here," I told him.

He approached awkwardly, as if I might be about to take that from him, leave him unpaid for a service job and then penalized for a civilian one. I pulled the paper from his hand, made sure the scribe had noted down what Kul had promised to pay, and slapped my stamp on the thing. "There you go," I told him. "Makes it a king's command." Assuming the treasury survived the day, he'd be well paid.

The runner thanked everybody as he made his way out. He might not be able to read the words, but the numbers were clear enough.

We added an item to the plans, to send out search parties for troops of kids hiding in the hills and to allocate fire crews for HandOverHand. I sent an appeal to the city leadership, for civilian volunteers as searchers. Those kids would likely hide from men in uniform.

I wanted Kul in that room with me, to align what Heyliannin had seen with the information he'd sent with the runner. I closed my eyes, recalled the landforms in that area, imagined the chaotic movements, my wife's limited point of view, the way Kul had sent her off.

What she'd seen: Calestinise running towards the enemy leadership, a group of parents plunging after him. Further off: Kul, fighting his way through the mob of kids, striking fear into them, teaching them what it meant to face a real soldier.

What Heyliannin imagined: our boy falling on those enemies, but too soon, with Kul not yet at his side, the ill-prepared parents fighting their way through youngsters chanting *Honor Truth*, while the surge of an army of mad children flowed behind Kul, carried him down by sheer force of numbers.

What Kul told me: our boy had another of his schemes. He hadn't bought into the notion the kids would run to their mamas and papas. He knew what the army of light did to them, to their minds. Those kids needed a stronger lesson—an example of what it meant to break free. It would take someone on the inside to make a real difference.

Calestinise knew the system. All he needed was a uniform and a reason to get close to the leaders. With Kul at his back, he'd be chased into their willing hands, with the bear-man an obvious threat to their command and to their ill-gotten soldiers. Calestinise would block the path of that monstrous warrior, and make a show of offering his life to protect the Southern leaders. He'd beat off the attacker, saving their cowardly skins. Then, he'd be a hero, a paragon of loyalty, of *honoring truth*. Over the long weary march, through the deadly battles to follow, he'd winnow out the unfaithful, the frightened, and he'd bring to his side those who'd seen Kul in action and had enough imagination to see their carrion future.

Kul sounded confident that Calestinise had survived the battles so far. I couldn't be reassured. That boy reminded me so much of Heyliannin—as if she was his true-mother—inspired to leap into action as soon as he had an idea. He'd get himself killed.

The thought haunted me. *Maybe he's already fallen.*

How many of those kids fell to Arnim's forces? To Case's? *More of them than us*, Kul's runner reported. When would the boy break off his rescue effort? Before or after the fire-boms flew? He'd work to free those kids until the very last. If he survived, I'd have to quit calling him a boy.

29

T HOUGH THE ENEMY hadn't reached the city, the arrival of Kul's runner marked the beginning of the day's action. Next came a runner from Harad's side of the harrying line. He reported the Southern force had paused for a rest an hour out from HandOverHand. Once the column of invaders had settled, he'd set up his archers to fire—but had to call a halt. A scout reported something strange: a small party of fighters creeping off from the group. Spies? Deserters? Had the battle at the mustering ground broken them already?

Harad followed the scout through the brush and caught up with them. Kids from the army of light. Their leader? Calestinise.

"He wouldn't come back with me," the runner narrated. "I'd've had to draw blade on him, and I don't think even that would have done it." It was a good rendition. The man even caught the roughness in Harad's tone. "They didn't turn him to their side at that camp, but they brought out his own kind of madness. Nothing I said got through to him. All I could do was hold off our attack, that time. He brought out a few more before the camp got on the march again. We'll have to take action, at our next checkpoint. Nothing for it, Cousin. We've a job to do."

The runner gave me a curious look. I guessed he was trying to gauge any family resemblance between the tall, handsome old soldier and his scrawny, buzzard-faced king.

We got observations and location markers, then sent him to recuperate. I imagined Calestinise in his place, giving me the half-lidded stare that said I didn't understand him, never would, but that he understood me well enough.

At least somebody did.

The door snicked open before my thoughts could go too far down that road—Durse and his slightly-rested crew bringing my bodyguard up to full muster for the duration. We may as well have let the door stand open the rest of the day. News kept flowing in from scouts, some direct, some relayed by runners.

Enemy scouts spotted along the road to HandOverHand.

A force approaching the north gate—couldn't be told yet if it was our men or theirs.

A fire on the east wall—a team of archers testing their equipment dropped a torch on the wooden walkway. I expected Andus had words for them, once they'd doused the flames. I ordered up carpenters to make repairs.

That meant fewer carpenters manufacturing weaponry.

Fighting broke out in the makeshift market area—somebody thought somebody else was taking up too much space. I sent a troop to break it up, ordered all the alcohol sequestered for the duration. No penalties, no repercussions, no making matters worse, I ordered. Get any injured to the hospital fast, before there are real casualties to deal with. Well and good, but that troop could have been deploying materiel to the perimeter instead of policing the plaza.

The elders kept sending runners with useless advice, requests that were really orders, status reports that we didn't need. Each had to be answered. Yes, ma'am, we understand, we'll watch the north gate as well as the main road from the south. Of course, ma'am, we'll send staff with additional furniture for you. Thank you ma'am, we're relieved to hear the briefing room is satisfactory to you. Please do keep us advised.

The back of my neck itched every time I thought of those traitorous shamans being sheltered with our good people. Finally, I had to ask where they'd been quartered.

Errem rolled his shoulders, slapped out a salute, and bowed. "You're aware, sir, of the need to combine certain materials, from the stables and elsewhere? Before applying to the soil in the gardens?"

"I'm aware of every square foot of this place, Errem. I've lived here since I was six."

He cleared his throat. "Well, sir, we had the gardeners clear out that space. It went well enough. They said it was well-composted."

I gave him a steady look, measured the likelihood he'd start laughing.

"You put them in the waste treatment facility?"

"Ya. Only space available." He clamped his jaw tight. "Sorry, sir. I know how important the shamans are to you."

I tried to match his expression. "Indeed. Well, seems you did your best."

He quickly found something important to do on the far side of the room. The guard he left behind stood to attention. When I burst out laughing, that poor guy looked confused, checked his uniform for missing badges, worn patches.

We might have talked, I might finally have settled that other guy's name in my head.

But another clutch of runners rolled in.

The latest report showed the "force" at the north gate to be an angry group of families from a nearby farm settlement. They wanted compensation. Strange-looking soldiers had marched into their village, taken provisions and tools, broken equipment, and generally behaved badly.

The north-gate crew sent them straight to the elders' compound for explanations, reassurance, and legal advice. Not much use suing an invading army, but who knows? If we lost, maybe that would be their best recourse.

The good news was, if the Southerners were taking time for a rest stop in an undefended village, then Kul's band of Jeskans had a fair chance of catching up and treating them to another round of what Heyliannin called *gawrella* warfare.

A runner from Karthi's side, but not from Karthi himself, came in with a report on the fire-arrows. Suffice to say, they worked. First, you might get a normal strike: no fire, but one soldier down in the ordinary way. Second, a functional fire-arrow might miss, leaving the opponents complacent for a few seconds—until the mockery of an arrow, with its sad, guttering flame, became a demon spewing splinters of fire into any flesh in the vicinity, sparking flames on any wood or cloth gear nearby. Third—and here, Heyliannin's objections echoed in my mind—a well-struck arrow would, on bursting, tear into the target, driving burning shards through his body, hurling gobs of flesh into the faces of his companions.

Or her companions.

Remember, the army of light didn't shirk at conscripting girls.

Relentless, tears streaming down her face, the runner detailed the results from each of a dozen successful strikes. That was, after all, a key element of Karthi's mission—to test the new weaponry. No one in the room was unaffected—perhaps the scribes had the least to deal with, tasked with writing so quickly they couldn't have time to think on what they were hearing. One of the juniors plugged his ears after the third recitation and leaned over the map in front of him, as if trying to memorize each curve and annotation. The other two seemed to be bearing up well, but then one suddenly stood and scrambled behind chairs to get to the back door. At the sounds he made out there, the other followed him soon enough.

The old guys gave each other looks and went out to help them recover. One of them, a bit deaf I think, could be heard easily from inside: "Don't blame yourself, lad. We've all stood where you are, no shame in it. It's a good runner paints the picture that clear, puts you on the field."

The runner broke off at that, rubbed her face dry. "Sorry, sir. Didn't realize."

"Not a problem," Magaran said. "It's better to know. They have to learn it. Go on."

She reported that several of Karthi's men had thrown down their bows and walked away. "Don't put 'em down as deserters," the sender urged. "They couldn't help it." His voice wavered—he might well have been one of those leaning towards desertion after what they'd seen, what they'd done. "Tell the defenders: don't aim. Fire at nothing. Drop the sticks in the dirt."

I asked the runner if she'd watched the tests herself? What were her thoughts? She avoided my gaze. "True, Your Majesty, it's an awful sight. But we're at war, aren't we? They'll do worse to our people, if we give them half a chance. There's so many of them, sir. You won't believe how many they are, marching on Jeskaryan." Her cheeks were dry, but flushed; I could hear my thoughts in her head. "Don't give them quarter, sir. They won't go easy on us."

We got her count, her locations. She hadn't noticed anyone that matched my description of Calestinise. Despite her horror at the size of the invading army, the count raised my spirits a fraction. She'd verified the previous numbers with an estimate taken in daylight, and, if anything, the force marching towards us was less than I'd feared, not greater.

30

T HE NEWS FROM Karthi's harriers would be the last report from forces outside the city, because the enemy struck our south gate right about the time we'd sent that last runner to report to her House. Despite the young officer's plea to change plans, go easy with the lightning-powder arrows, I agreed with his runner, and gave no new orders to the archers posted in the buildings overlooking the road.

I hoped they wouldn't set too many accidental fires.

Given the intensity of our defense, it wasn't surprising to hear that the Southerners quickly reorganized to place the army of light where they'd take the brunt of the damage. We'd already set orders for the archers to shift their flights further back, as soon as that move happened. We knew the kids weren't the leadership, and we needed that terror to fall where it could change orders. Our bows couldn't let fly as far as the Hashtek ones, but firing from the top of our makeshift wall, at three and four stories above the ground, our bowmen could lob fire well back from the front lines.

Magaran had the idea to pull a troop's-worth of men from other duties and put them on fire control, first on the perimeter line, then to the fortress wall, after the pullback. I authorized it before he finished explaining.

Word came in that Andus had started the outer-defense retreat. While we'd placed troops outside the palisade, to present as a defensive force, they weren't intended to do much more than hold off the attack while we measured our opponents. If all went as planned, those hundred or so defenders would flee the vicinity of the gate, seemingly in desperate retreat, to vanish into dive-holes dug under the palisade. They'd soon emerge to re-join the defense from within. Andus had created at least a dozen of those short tunnels, so that a given troop would see their own guys through and then trigger a collapse.

We had a few reports of enemies attempting to follow. What damage did they expect to do, slithering one at a time through a tunnel, to find themselves facing a fully-armed troop on home territory? Then again, maybe it was kids who thought that would be a good idea. They'd have been crushed in the tunnel collapses. I wrote out an order that the tunnels weren't to be dug out—let anyone who paid that price have their burial. Worse than burning, some might say, but the dead don't care about much and I didn't want to risk my people having to dig up mangled children. Besides, the farmers and fishers of Lakeside mostly put their dead into the earth, one way or another.

Radeo sent fresh shipments of fire-arrows to the front lines and reported that he'd have a stockpile of fire-boms ready to deploy, but we only had enough for one try. I decided to save them for the fortress-wall defense.

•　　　•　　　•

There was one way the Southerners could cross the boundary set by the palisade.

They would have to burn it down.

Ironic, considering our archers fought back their fire crews with volleys of fire-arrows. The smiths had forecast the invaders would come with devices to hurl flaming torches over the makeshift wall. I had no such concerns. At every report, that army had shown itself to be marching far faster than any force hampered by equipment larger than a bow.

Next time—if we let there be a next time—those Hashtek bows would be hurling fire-arrows back at us. Sure, then, we'd burn fast. For now, what they hurled were ordinary burning sticks, easily extinguished, merely a distraction.

They might have hoped to build larger tools, once they occupied the roads and locked us into our own city. Such a laugh. The western hills have trees, but nothing worth building with. Generations of Jeskan lumber and watershed managers had negotiated those forests down to cyclically replanted timber meant for land maintenance and light furniture, yielding small trees not suited for construction. In a burst of optimism, the day of the evacuation, I'd sent a runner north with orders for scrap wood—for the bonfires.

My commanders were prepared for the city to burn. No doubt the elders knew that part of the plan. They're old, not dim-witted. But when runners started arriving with news the palisade gates were burning, ripples of dismay flowed through the people quartering in the plaza. Everyone could see the plumes rising from the western edge of the city. They knew how quickly it would spread beyond the heaps of obstacles we'd used to close off the streets. My door guards had to hold back regular citizens trying to tell me their city was on fire.

Our city.

I sent one of the kid scribes out to sit and take reports from the citizenry. One of them might have noticed something we needed to know. If not, then at least they'd be heard. They'd stop clamoring at the door for attention. I set one of the senior officers to manage that process and scan those reports—an older man would be better able to sort serious concerns and calm any hysterics. They mostly matched what our local runners were bringing in—though it was a citizen who reported the first significant fire within the city. The runner verifying that report had the added information that enemy troops had broken through the southeast palisade gate. Andus would be signaling his men at the north gate to pull back, get to safety. Those on the southeasterly rim would be in motion already, autonomous units responding to their own knowledge that the city boundary had been breached.

Reports poured in thick and fast. I let Magaran's team and the juniors winnow them, so only the most crucial hit my desk. Even so, I had no time to breathe, only to think, to shout orders at a shock-eyed runner, hand him a stamped paper he couldn't read.

I know, how could I shout if I couldn't breathe?

I don't know. I don't know.

My young friend Andus had concocted an outlandish method to get his troopers into the fortress once the gates were sealed. He made use of the drainage, the sluice I'd sent my assassin down two nights previous, the escape route I'd used for my brother so long ago. Andus had set up ropes and winches, so men could walk right up that impossible slope, helped by workmen at the top, winding the cordage along. The smiths were keen on the idea, naturally. I wished I could run over there, watch the scheme in action.

But I had no breath for wishes.

Once the Southerners entered the city, they wasted no time destroying it. Did the Jeskans they'd allied with—the shamans, the Lakeside managers—expect that? Did they anticipate their friends would lay waste to the prize itself?

In my darkest moments, I expected them to level the city to the sandstone it stood on. On the other hand, they needed to bring their own army in, so they couldn't make the place an inferno. Not until they'd taken our refuge, the core of the unified districts—the fortress of Jeskaryan. More practical than I might have hoped, the enemy leaders dispatched small parties from the main force, to set fires where they wanted them, and hunt down any stray Jeskans they stumbled across.

If the strays were lucky, Andus's troopers would scoop them up first. Otherwise, they'd have to lie low and hope to be missed.

Runners and lesser messengers kept colliding in the doorway, exchanging words, raising the level of anger in the room more than suited a command center. Magaran stole Durse from me, sent him to the doorway to settle those conflicts before they could interfere. That smoothed the flow of information, but did nothing to ease the intensity of our situation. Sure enough, fires were sweeping through neighborhoods, threatening the workshops—and the rope-route into the fortress. I ordered more workmen for Andus to speed that process, double up on rope pullers. I stood at my table, instead of sitting, so I could lean over it, the better to hear what was being reported to me, with others reporting to Magaran and the others or arguing with Durse.

At one point, Durse left his new post and dragged towards me a terrified-looking citizen, a stableman by the smell of green-grass hay and dry manure that clung to him. Magaran intercepted them, shook his head at Durse, and pulled the citizen off to one side to take his report in private. Did the man have a family member trapped outside the fortress? It would be bad news, then. Magaran had orders for Durse, that took him out for a while. I noticed that Errem stepped over to the Master Commander's table to ask what was up. I'd never figured out which of them considered himself troop leader—Durse or Errem.

Suddenly, Errem was missing as well. Magaran was overstepping his bounds. I'd have words for him.

Later.

Moments—or a half-dozen decisions later—Dramin turned up, Errem slipping in behind him.

"What are you doing here?" I challenged the medic. "You're supposed to be keeping the elders happy and ordering doctors around in your spare time."

"Doctors don't take orders. They give them." He dragged an abandoned chair opposite me and sat. He'd gone serious. Probably the elders' constant complaints about me had gotten on his nerves. To match him, I settled back into my chair.

In that instant, another runner appeared at my desk, so I had to take that report. From the look on Dramin's face, it seemed his issue was more than Maledestine beating people with her staff. Anyone meeting him for the first time would think he'd never smiled in his life, the frown lines cut so deep.

I waved the next man off to Magaran. "Make it quick, Dramin. You see how it is."

"It's Andus, Boss," he said.

"Ya, ya, Andus is doing a great job out there."

"No, Corren. That's not it." He looked down at his hands, as if he was trying to remember which one he fought best with.

Behind him, Errem said, "Tell him straight, Commander."

"Corren … Boss … Andus fell off the wall."

"He what?"

"He was running on the wall-walk, tending to his troops. Put a foot down on a slick patch, went over the safe-rail." The look on his face reminded me of Heyliannin talking about her lost child. "Wasn't anything anyone could do."

A realization flung me to my feet. Maybe not any*one* could help, but maybe some *thing* could. "Get Heyliannin. That cape of hers, it fixed her. Make her fix him, too."

Dramin eased to his feet, something glittering in his eyes. "I'll find her for ya, Boss." His feet moved slowly, but his strides were long; he was out the door before I could say more.

Magaran pushed back from his desk, waved off a runner, and said, "I'll get out there, cover for Andus."

I waved him back. "No. I need you here in command." I cast my eye over the junior officers in the room, who'd learned how to relay the right information to me and take care of the less-catastrophic things themselves. The older men … I respected their experience, but couldn't see them running up and down stairs and along the wall-walk. "Errem!"

"Yessir? You want me to fetch Commander Radeo?"

"No. You've been at all the conferences, and you've stood with us here. Get yourself out there and take that command."

"Me?" He managed to look offended. "I've a necessary job here, sir!"

"No, you don't," I told him. "I don't need an extra bodyguard, I need someone who can take charge. Like you did with Dramin. You've a necessary job out there. Go do it."

He slapped out a good salute, but his eyes still rebelled against abandoning me to a roomful of soldiers and seven bodyguards. He'd begun to turn away, but came back and leaned over the desk with an uncharacteristically solemn look in his eyes.

"They don't get it, sir, that they need to talk direct. F'rinstance … sir? That last runner from Commander Karthi couldn't tell ya."

My fingers curled around the papers they rested on, crumpling edges. "What *didn't* she tell us? She told enough blood and gore to keep a man from eating ever again." Her description of an enemy soldier torn apart by a fire-arrow still filled my vision.

"Ya heard plain and clear it wasn't the commander sent her, right?"

"Of course." I'd've recognized Karthi's voice, whether a man or a woman delivered it.

Errem tapped on the table, enough to recover my attention. "It's the commander sends the runner, sir." He waited for me to piece together … something … then gave up and went on. "It means they'd already lost him."

I lifted my eyes from the table to Errem's face. The familiar smirk was missing. He watched me unblinking, like a famished hawk. For a moment, we were back in the scullery, talking to Arnim's runner, who'd been unable to answer when I kept asking, *where's Arnim?*

Errem inhaled slowly, exhaled, rubbed his hands together. "They're afraid to tell you, sir. The harriers' commander musta been seriously wounded or killed. Otherwise, it'd be Karthi sending the message." He swallowed and added, "Likewise, they're afraid to tell you direct about Commander Andus. He fell off the top of the wall, sir. Onto the pavement. The fall woulda killed him."

My mind pushed back, against all of it. We'd sent Karthi with the harriers so he wouldn't worry about Andus. None of this could be true.

But Errem's grim face, the sheen of moisture in his eyes, told it plain. The man was incapable of lying.

First Arnim, then Case, now Karthi and Andus both. Calestinise had set himself up to die by friendly fire. Kul had taken a tiny party of men to face a superior force on non-defensible ground. That left Dramin, alone of the Six. I wanted to run after him, surround him with bodyguards.

Maledestine's words crowded out Adestinian's. *We're all going to die.*

Errem must have been reading my lips. "No, Your Majesty. We're all going to fight until we win this, and if we prevail it's thanks to you, sir. There's no one else could have done it."

He spun on his heel and swept out of the room, moving like the commander I'd made of him.

Durse, now. Durse looked a little annoyed.

31

S TORIES LEAD YOU to expect the wrong things. In a story, this
is the point where the cowardly king finally emerges from his
refuge, great sword in hand, and hews down the enemy.

Or is it this one? The tragic king, broken in spirit, mopes his
way to where his friend lies dying and weeps over him until he's
wailing above a corpse.

Maybe both?

How about neither?

Play back in your mind the words Errem threw at me: *If we
prevail…*

If isn't a word for gamblers, it's a word that reminds us there's
work to be done. If we are smart enough, if we listen to each other,
if we take action when it's necessary and conserve resources
when we need to … *then* we *might* prevail.

The king's job isn't to lead a charge but to lead the force
entire. The king is the people's tool, their instrument. He's not free
to cry over his lost comrades—no matter that his insides have

turned to fractured clay. He's not meant to wrap himself in glory—though his bones ache with the need to take up arms.

In my case, the ache burned like a fever. My sword slipped from its scabbard with a familiar hiss, but it was not my time to put it to work. I laid the blade across the table in front of me, as a reminder of what we'd embarked on together. Then I unsheathed my favorite knife—the one my true-father had brought me from another world … Ta-ma's world? Or yet another one? I set it close to hand, where I could see the stylized etchings on it, the symbols in an alien language, a reminder of the secret advantages we'd brought to this battle.

Then I took my place, accepted my duty in that closed-in room: to take in the bad news, see what it meant for the campaign, provide the resources my forces needed, and stay out of their way.

• • •

I wasn't sure I'd use the fire-boms until I gave the order.

After we'd heard what the fire-arrows could do, the fire-boms generated a lot of dissension in command. Everyone talked around me, over me, behind my back, any time a spare moment presented itself. I tried to stay out of it, to let them work out the issues without me.

The youngsters were mostly for it—the junior officers and the kid scribes. So were one or two of my guard—who weren't supposed to have opinions—to judge from their faces when the topic flew around the room. Had they forgotten the descriptions that sent two officer-grade soldiers out to vomit in the alley?

The arguments came down to a mixture of anger and excitement.

"Did you hear what they did to those kids, to make them fight on the wrong side? We'll make them sorry!" Did they forget the fire-boms would fall on the army of light, without discriminating?

"Imagine it! They see an ordinary toss-up fly across the battlefield. Someone laughs, makes a joke about starting a game. Then—pow! They're destroyed before they even know they're surprised!" Those lightning-packed toys weren't going to kill that many soldiers. They were weapons of terror. If no one's left to be surprised, then who is there to be terrified?

The older men—Magaran's remnants of his own original troop, summoned out of retirement—cautioned against deployment, either because they had philosophical objections or because they lacked confidence in the tool.

"It's dishonorable, turns battle into trickery, when it should be a proper match, man to man!" I remembered how my seniors had objected to the new, tricky scheme of autonomous units and distributed command. Once proven, does a trick become a tactic?

"We can't rely on new technology. Sure, if we've run out of options, then give them a try." How quickly did they think we could deploy a new weapon, if we waited until the last minute?

Durse let in a runner from the practice yard, with news from Radeo. He reported an inventory of a hundred or so boms, with more being manufactured. I scrawled a written order, stamped it, and ordered the runner, "Tell the commander it's time. Get those things on the wall. Then find Errem—the new commander—tell him he can let fly with those things the moment he sees a good opportunity."

"Yessir."

A silence spread from my desk, across the room from table to table, so quickly you could hear the runner's footsteps as he turned at the door and vanished. I looked around at them all, the promoters, the naysayers. I wasn't going to call them on either set of errors.

"New topic?" I said. "I have one. Who should the elders lay the kingship on tomorrow?"

•　　　•　　　•

I'd never witnessed an engagement like the one we were in the middle of: a fortified position holding off a greater force. Our tutors had us read written accounts of battles far to the south, where our enemies came from, where they built bigger, battled harder. There are tried-and-true strategies for taking down a fortress. Most of them start with leaving the fortress alone, starving the defenders out.

We had a lull, early after the taking of the city, when I wondered if that was what we'd face.

My gut told me otherwise.

There was something about this whole venture that felt rushed. We might never know what drove that troubled empire to ally with our rebels and decide this was the time to take our country from us. If history is any guide, other forces were at play, dangers of their own. They could be losing a long-running fight with someone even further south, and needed a new territory for themselves. If Heyliannin was right, that there are lands beyond the great ocean—and that there's a second great ocean to the east—they might have needed our resources to fend off invaders. In her world, seafaring conquerors had overrun whole continents, swept away civilizations great and small, consumed forests and rivers, drained lakes and filled valleys. Entire populations of wild game, fishes, even plants were wiped out of existence forever.

If that were the case, I thought, our neighbors should have sent ambassadors, not an army.

I'd have joined with them to fight off such incursions. If there's anything a Jeskan understands, it's the need to protect the land.

·　　　·　　　·

Reports from the wall came in steadily, with few surprises other than the oddity of hearing Errem's words from a runner. "I'll be holding off on the fire-boms until twilight, sir. More impact, seeing as you want the enemy frightened. And ya don't need good light to aim those things." He'd sorted out a few soldiers who'd played toss-up competitively as kids. They set up a stretch along the southwest wall as a run-up line, and hurled a few trials deep into the forces gathered precisely beyond arrow-shot. With a run and a flick of the stick, they sent the boms out so fast, no one even noticed their flight, perhaps mistook them for birds. Errem reported commotion in the Southern ranks, as fire burst unexpectedly, seemingly from nowhere. He spared us specifics, so I didn't need to imagine a kid leaning down to pick up a smoldering toss-up . . .

If he was out there, I hoped Calestinise could make use of any terror raised in those young hearts and drag a few more of them—and himself—down a winding alley to safety. And that he'd stay there until it was over.

·　　　·　　　·

The weak point in any wall is the gate. Which is why it's heavily defended. But there's only so much you can do.

Our gate consisted of two massive wooden doors, the out-swinging gate on the outer wall, the in-swinging one on the inner side. Both were metal-reinforced heart-wood, built from lumber dragged down the mountains from groves of trees that stand through fire, almost like magic. Almost, I said. The magic that smiths make of good strong wood, with metal bracing.

As the sun began to set, I sent out an order to clear the plaza. I didn't care where they put the people.

"In my bed chamber, for all I care," I snapped at the one who dared question me. "Get those citizens out of the way of what's coming!"

Why we hadn't made that part of the plan, that was an error we had to share.

Once the enemy broke through the gate, the plaza would become a battlefield, in the heart of the fortress. The families and merchants who'd tossed breakfast snacks to us that morning—they'd be on the front lines, with nothing to defend themselves with but bread and fruit.

•   •   •

At dusk, everything changed.

Outside the gates, the mass of soldiers surged forward, ducks in a pond for my defenders to send back to the earth one at a time, using old-fashioned unsurprising arrows. One column came holding boards overhead, protecting something.

No mystery.

They'd torn timbers from one of our houses and fashioned a battering ram. It would take time, and casualties, but eventually, they'd break that old door. And the inner one. The sound resonated through the fortress like a strange, erratic drumbeat. From somewhere within our walls, somebody started a counter beat. Drummers gathered on the practice field, and started up one of the old traditional songs. We couldn't hear it directly, in command, but runners coming and going told us how it kept their spirits up, that people hiding in kitchens and storerooms were singing to that beat.

Errem had chosen well, to unleash his fire-boms as the light faded. People in the plaza could see the flaming orbs sailing high, as if the sun had fragmented, sending these whirling points of fire to destroy our enemies for us. Errem's guys invented more than one game to torment the enemy. For one, he used his best throwers to pound again and again at a single point, close to where he'd judged the leadership had huddled. The throwers would pause a little longer after each throw, to let the Southern soldiers wonder if another might fall. It would have seemed as though an invisible demon hovered in the smoky haze, spitting burning stones down on them. For another game, he had his less-skilled guys let loose a volley all at once, and accompany their throws with a weird cacophony of howling screams.

"It sounds like mad ghosts!" a runner told me. "You'd think everyone's angriest dead matriarch had returned to eat their souls for dinner!"

I didn't know if the Southerners had such superstitions, but the Lakesiders did. Living alongside the water, where wisps of fog rise out of nothing, seems to make people susceptible to imagining ghosts. So there was another reminder to Calestinise, if he was out there, or to anybody who'd listen to him, that it was time to run away.

"It works," the runner reported. "It's dark, I know, but there's buildings on fire, sir. You can see them running away, the cowards."

I wondered if he'd call them cowards if he'd seen someone hit by one of those random throws. In that kind of crowd, it couldn't be avoided. There would be missing fingers, shredded feet, holes burned into limbs and torsos. We were making more ghosts out there than anyone wanted to imagine.

32

WHEN THE NOISE of the battering ram stopped, the sound of nothing reverberated like thunder.

Then came screams, shouts, the clash of steel on steel.

The gates were open.

While our forces were fending off the attack on the outside, somebody on the inside had made their move. Sheltered by the shadows of nightfall, someone—or some ones—slipped the bars on the inner gate, crept into the cool darkness of the space between, and lifted off the bars on the outer gate. There's five bars of well-aged wood. They'd have needed a party of four.

The traitors needed to do no more than open it a crack.

The attackers could take a hint.

In minutes, the fighting moved inside the fortress walls. Our troops flooded out to meet them, in the way the old men said they preferred, man to man, blade against blade.

"Close the door," Magaran ordered the guard at the entry. "Tell messengers to come round back—and only if it's urgent."

Durse let one runner through, relayed the message to the next one, then sealed the door tight.

Errem surprised me, then. He'd held back a substantial fraction of his supply. During the clearing of the plaza, Radeo'd sent out all his resupply materiel. By now, the practice yard would be hosting a crowd of displaced citizenry. When Errem got his last load of boms, he clustered his men in a tight group, just above the gate, and instead of throwing the fire-boms, they dropped them on top of the people flowing through the gate to join the attack. Must have been close to fifty boms, detonating at once. It would have matched the force of the exploding boxes, from the early experiments—deadly to anyone too close. Errem had posted a troop on the ground, somewhere out of sight, and the moment the blast struck, they ran to close the gates again, shoving corpses and screaming injured out of their way.

Then he sent most of his troops down off the wall, to form a phalanx guarding the exit. Whoever had entered our fortress wouldn't be getting out again. What remained on the wall were archers, now with fire-arrows, and they dealt damage as far as they could. The Hashtek archers had left off firing, now that their own were inside. They hadn't been that effective anyway, not in the tight alleys of Jeskaryan, downhill from the fortress.

We got that one report from Errem.

Then nothing.

•　　•　　•

Magaran paced. He made it seem like he was snacking, by picking up one or another thing from the food table. He didn't eat much, though, mainly handed food off to others. His old troopers let him be, as mine would have done for me.

A cinching across my chest suggested I had another attack heart coming on, so I put myself in my chair with my feet up on the table. Remembering how to breathe, that was the difficult part.

I don't think anybody noticed.

Suddenly, Durse pushed himself away from the door he was guarding. "I can't stand this," he announced, then jumped on top of the junior officers' table, scattering papers. He jumped again, caught hold of a cross-beam, and hoisted himself into the rafters. There, he became a shadow shifting from beam to beam overhead. New sounds filtered from above, as if he'd opened a window up there.

Right. Thatched roof. Somehow, neither side had managed to set it on fire.

Clambering down, Durse was less graceful. He may have cracked a board in the table, landing.

"Fighting's still going, sir," he reported. "There's action over by the king's house. Can't tell what. I bet they're thinking that's an important target."

Everybody laughed. The shamans wouldn't have guessed I'd run this war from a shuttered dormitory.

"Errem's guys are holding their own at the gate." He paused. "There's safe passage down the alley. We could make it to the hospital, if you think that's a good move."

I wanted to see for myself. More than that—I wanted to take hold of a weapon and get into the melee. I flicked my knife where it lay on the table, watched the light flicker on its edges as it spun.

"That could be a disastrous move," I said. "If we abandon this post, where will the intel flow? We're here for the duration. Unless they breach that door." Heads turned to the entry, but the door didn't seem to have an opinion.

"Right." Magaran bit into the plum he had in his hand, made a face, and swallowed. "Also, we'd make the hospital a target."

"However." I had my eyes on the kid scribes, one of whom was scribbling down everything we said, his pen scrabbling in scratchy bursts, like insects in the walls. "Durse, I want you to escort the kids down there. And anyone else who feels a need to move out of here."

"Sir—" He had a look about him like Errem had, a couple of hours back. "I'll be delegating this one. Fallon here—he grew up in Runner's House." He gestured to one of the other guys—the tall, thin one with a bend to his nose that reminded me of under-guard days. "Bring us a situation report. The hospital will be buzzing with news. Get every scrap of intel you can gather. Casualties. Shortages. Who's coming in—including civilians. More than how the doctors are holding up."

I hesitated, but needed to say it, even if it demoted me to worried husband for a few seconds. "And check on my wife. Dramin's been gone too long."

Durse's chosen alternate snapped out a salute. "Yessir."

Evidently, my lectures on autonomous action and independent thinking had found another landing place.

The kid insisted on finishing his transcription, then handed the pen to the old guy. "See you soon, father," he said.

None of the adults left. Magaran's oldsters turned their backs against any suggestion they'd retreat and set to inventorying their weaponry. I had the feeling one of the junior officers wanted to follow Fallon and the kids. Instead, he spent an inordinate amount of time sorting out the papers on his table. It reminded me of Yutek, using paperwork to push back against the sickness that was killing him.

I scrounged a sharpening stone from Magaran's kit bag and worked on my blade edges. To each his own.

My remaining bodyguards shifted positions in the room, as if any arrangement could be more effective than watching the doors. Magaran distributed snacks. I put him down as a potential employee at the inn I was imagining working at someday. Would Heyliannin go for that? She could leave the scut-work to me, manage the accounts the way she liked 'em.

Durse's alternate, Fallon, still hadn't returned when a tentative rap at the back door stopped our anxious messing-around. The nearest guard admitted a runner with singed hair, a bloody, rough-wrapped gash running the length of her arm. I'd have sent her straight to the medics, except that she had a report from the north gate.

I don't remember the name of the officer she was speaking for, but Andus would have been proud at the way he put not only the facts but also a sense of the action into his message. "We got a hundred or so Southerners turn up outside the gate. They thought they'd scare us with arrows fired over the palisade. Idiots! Did they think we'd left anyone at risk?" The defenders let them waste arrows for little while, then their top bowmen delivered a selection of well-placed fire-arrows. Screaming ensued.

Meanwhile, at the rear of the attacking force, they observed a series of "scuffles," the runner relayed. "Bursts of action. At first, we thought their soldiers were getting into fights with each other. Except you could see they'd left bodies behind. More than what our fire-arrows could have put down. When everything settled, they'd begin a fresh volley, but then another scuffle would start up."

Had something broken their command structure? My mind leapt to Calestinise, but the report didn't mention—"Were there kids in the attacking force? Did you see?"

She swayed on her feet. "Children?" The soft splat of blood hitting the floor filled in the silence. Magaran signaled one of his guys, who brought her a chair. She settled into it with a long sigh. The old soldier slid his hand under her elbow, gentle as if she was his own granddaughter, and lifted her arm to rest it on the table. I could tell he wanted to do more, but she'd already recovered enough to go on. "I couldn't see that well, so I can't say. The captain there, he said he thought it was a few of our strike-force troops running in, taking down a few of them, then getting out of reach."

Magaran said it. "Kul."

Had to be.

The Southern leaders had underestimated how many to send to our back gate. And they hadn't counted on being attacked from behind, least of all by opponents who struck fast, then vanished into the brush. The gate defenders had a hawk's-eye view of that interplay, minute by minute.

"In the end, the enemy retreated. They left their dead and sneaked off into the dark. We're still on guard, But I think we're done here." As she finished her narration, the runner pressed her hand to the rag she'd wrapped around the wound. The bleeding had stopped while she was talking. "Sorry I took so long to get here, sir. There's fighting and fires all through town. No one was on the ropes, either. Had to climb up on my own."

So, she'd come in by the kitchen.

Magaran put down whatever he was eating. Jerky, that time, I think. "What's the situation in the house?"

"The king's house? Uh, sorry, sir, there's Southern forces occupying it." She lifted her arm. "Mostly leaving noncombatants alone. They ignored me, until I came on a group of important-looking guys and one of their bodyguards slashed at me. I dodged the wrong way."

"Important guys?" The room vanished. The sounds of pen on paper, the rasp of breath, the shuffle of boots ceased. I saw the stairway of my home, occupied by foreigners, heard rough voices in that incomprehensible tongue.

Her voice wrapped itself into my vision, as if we stood together, watching the invaders. "I don't know, sir. You get a feeling. Fancier uniforms? Clean ones? These guys weren't—pardon me—drenched in blood like everyone else out there. And hats. They had these hats covered in feathers. Made them look taller."

Leadership. They'd brought their leadership into the king's house. They thought they'd won.

When instead we had them trapped.

The smell of the runner's blood brought me back to the moment, to the murmur of voices in our command center. I clapped my hands together, and the room went silent. "Everyone, we have a development. Runner, I have one more commission for you, before you get yourself stitched up."

She winced. "What, sir?"

"Get to your House leaders. They're right nearby, in the stables." I lifted my hand. "Don't laugh. And it's on your way to the hospital. I need runners to track down Commander Radeo. Your Master Runner will need to choose those who can manage dodging past the fighting. Radeo might be near the training ground, but I haven't had a report from him recently. Tell him this." I waited for her to take on that attentive expression runners have, recording a message. "The Southern leadership is heading for the council chamber. Get men behind you. I want their leaders taken prisoner, not killed." I spoke slowly, enunciated clearly. "Say this: We need a surrender. I'll meet you at the king's house"

She wasted no time, left almost before I'd finished speaking. If she hadn't bled on my desk, I might have thought I'd nodded off and dreamed the whole thing.

33

"YOU'LL 'MEET HIM at the king's house'?" Durse had taken a defensive posture—poised, knees slightly bent, one hand cross-body towards his weapon, the other arm extended for balance … and maybe to block my path to the door. "Can't have you out there, sir. You haven't seen it."

I brushed past, muttering low, for his benefit alone. "You were at NeverSnows, weren't you? Can't be worse than that."

He relaxed, once he saw I wasn't headed for the door, but for our scribe's table. That scribbler had been on staff a long time; I hoped he had what I needed. As I approached, he left off the annotations he was making. His wry, attentive look reminded me of Yutek.

"Listen—" I realized I didn't have his name, and forged on without it. "Have you got the Wind River articles of surrender?"

He chuckled, in a fatherly way, as if one of the kids had asked if he knew his letters. "From a century ago?" He caught my expression and laughed again, tapping the side of his head with the end of his pen. "It's a classic, sir. Of course I've got that document."

"How fast can you write it out? Leaving space for us to fill in new names, new signatories? I think the terms are what we need—relinquishment of weapons, immediate withdrawal beyond our borders, surrender of their prisoners—"

"You want the reparations clause?"

I'd nearly forgotten about that one. "No. I can't imagine they'd honor it." A fresh thought struck me. "Add in a clause about disbanding and repatriating the army of light."

"Ah, glad I asked. Right, then. Ten minutes? Won't be elegant, but it'll be clean-written." He set to smoothing out a fresh sheet, choosing a large page, one that might have served for map-drawing. His brow creased as he sharpened his pen. "Is army of light a formal name? Or a description?"

He was expecting me to call it formal, like the King's Guard. What would Calestinise think, if I let it go down in the histories as a real military force? Their "army" was nothing but an instrument of war terror. And the Southerners didn't think of our kids as fellow soldiers—they were merely tools. "It's a description," I told the scribe. "Put the words down in plain form; make them acknowledge those are our people."

His frown was thoughtful, not disapproving; it reminded me that he was a father, too. I added, "My son's out there, trying to save other kids from that so-called army."

I thought he might reply, but he waved me off, his pen already scratching over the paper. "If you'll give me a bit of air, sir, I don't work as fast otherwise."

What would Yutek have thought of me, letting scribes and bodyguards order me around?

While I'd been arranging paperwork, Durse had reorganized his guys. Two of them backed him up at the front door, while the other three had taken positions at the rear exit.

Magaran left his favorite post—the snacks table—adjusting his sword belt and snugging his jacket. Behind him, his fellow seniors were belting up. "So," he said. "What's your objective, Corren? You've given us ten minutes to formulate a plan."

"Isn't it obvious, Master Commander? Get to the king's house, reinforce—or stand in for—Radeo's guys. No guarantee he'll get the word, or have troops to call on who aren't already in a fight. I want an official surrender in hand before this mess goes on any longer." I counted heads: myself, Magaran, the six bodyguards, three junior officers and Magaran's four seniors—the scribe would have recorded their names. Who would I take with me?

When I spread a blank map sheet on the table, one of the juniors, the guy I'd thought might have wanted to leave, said, "I can sketch out routes from here to the king's house." He had a pen flying over that paper before I could respond. So—a nervous young officer, but one with a good visual memory.

Durse left his front-door team to add notes on the patterns he'd seen from the roof. "The forces are in motion, as you might expect, but the action's mostly clear of the structures—nobody's stupid enough to let themselves get trapped against a wall."

Magaran suggested a wall-hugging route. "Likely that's how the runner made her way here. And we should be two troops, not one. Draw less attention."

I could see where he was heading and it made my nerves run hot. "We don't all need to go. I just need my guys."

"Beg to differ, Corren. Sir." He rubbed at his chin as he worked out an argument. "We leave anybody here, they're vulnerable. The tide turns out there, someone will try these doors—and this is no stronghold." He jabbed his thumb towards the front entry. "That door's got nothing but a lock a kid could kick through, and there's no impediments on the supposedly secret door back there. Besides, you said it yourself: Radeo will be short-handed or worse. We've got reinforcements here. Excepting our documentarian."

Without pausing his pen, the scribe called out, "You aren't leaving me behind, sir. You'll need it annotated and updated properly on the scene."

One consequence of my reorganization of the Guard—nobody's too low in rank to be left out of strategic planning. The scribe had a point: we'd need him on the spot. I waved over the rest of my bodyguards. "Let's do this right. We're two troops, then—Durse, you sort out our people between yourself and Magaran. Master Commander, be prepared to cover for me if I'm late or don't make it."

The juniors laid out multiple and separate routes, which the seniors criticized and improved upon. The scribe used the extra time to draft an outline of the terms on a second copy, to carry himself while I took the completed one. Durse and Magaran argued about whether to split their troops, but decided each was best working with their familiar team, which gave Magaran's crew our junior officers, one of them our map-maker. We didn't have time for discussion. Everyone checked arms, secured loose clothing, tied back their hair.

The night air welcomed us as we slipped into the back alley, wished each other luck, and moved out. Each step I took carved weight from my shoulders. This last operation would determine the conclusion of the battle—no, of the war that had begun at NeverSnows. I'd trained for the kingship since childhood; soon enough, I would hand it off to a peacetime king.

I avoided thinking about what might follow if our margins slipped us into failure.

The sounds from the plaza grew as we approached, blended to a dark, grumbling roar punctuated by bright clashes of steel striking steel. The sword at my side had been made in my true-father's workshop, by the northerner who'd taken over the business. The sweet hiss as I slid it from its scabbard tied me to my fathers—both of them, Orkast and Yutek. I drew my knife—the one Orkast found beyond a thin patch—and followed Durse's lead.

On the ground, the wall-hugging routes proved impractical. Sure, a path would be clear for a moment or two—an agile runner could follow such a route, even a succession of single individuals, but not a troop in formation. There simply wasn't enough room between the swirling mob and the bricks.

Durse abandoned the idea in seconds. "We'll go direct!" he shouted over his shoulder. "Hold firm!" We set ourselves in arrow formation, with Durse at point, me just behind and offset to his left, where he could keep an eye on me. "Advance!"

We were a spear, cutting through the melee. Torchlight cast moving shapes across the pavement, flowing over the fallen like the shadows of condors. Aside from maintaining footing on the blood-spattered pavement, the greatest challenge was distinguishing friend from foe in the murk and noise. As Magaran—and my first true enemy, Yutek-en—had taught, I watched the weapons, not the faces. Jeskan swords are symmetrical, straight-edged on both sides; the Southerners used curved blades designed to slash on their leading edges.

We were only passing through, but we cut down our fair share as we went. At a thick clot of conflict about halfway across the plaza, Durse took us to a halt and set us to crescent formation, so we could demolish a gang of Southerners who had a cluster of our own surrounded. It was almost like the old days, taking down brigands with my Six. I hadn't realized it, but the time I'd spent with Durse and his men had attuned us to one another. We didn't need detailed orders; a formation cue gave us all the direction we needed. I fell into my old rhythms—observe, wait for an attack, dodge, strike, move on. I'd always been one to let the enemy strike first. It's how you see their weaknesses—and they always make mistakes.

As we approached the king's house, the proportion of enemy to friend shifted in their favor. The spare glances I could send towards the king's house revealed no remarkable turmoil there—no sign of Radeo. "Tighten up!" Durse shouted, and we compressed our formation, plunged forward. I switched my blade to my left hand, for better reach as we passed through the conflict, dealing our share of death, but not stopping.

Focused so hard on the swirl of blades and knives around us, I almost tripped when we hit the steps. Durse caught my arm and shoved me into the center of the formation. "Star!" he ordered. The men closed in, cutting me out of the action. I started to shout an objection, but we were climbing the stairs at a run. Besides, the higher we climbed, the less action there was to miss. One of the guys stumbled, and I braced him. Somebody dropped their knife and I pulled out my spare and gave it to him. We were a troop in action. Every man contributed.

My job was to make it to the surrender. Durse's job was to keep me from getting killed.

Since our runner had passed this way, the Southern leaders had brought in an occupying force. Now, those invaders had to defend their prize from its true owners. The hallways and stairs I'd galloped up and down so easily all my life demanded a slow march, won step by step. One of Durse's men took a crippling stroke and fell aside. I marked the hall, the turn, the doorway, so I could send help when I could. Durse didn't complain when I filled the empty place in our formation. There wasn't time.

At the council chamber doors, a double row of enemy soldiers barred the way, two of them wearing those tall feathery hats the runner had described—Arnim's runner had talked about those, reporting on the first engagement at the Narrows. The hat-wearers shouted at the others, and their soldiers plunged into action. At the onslaught—there were at least a dozen of them, rested and ready for us—our formation frayed. We didn't have room to maneuver in the space between the steps and the doors. One of my guards took a wrong step and tumbled backwards down the stairs.

Two of the enemy soldiers pursued him as he rolled and regained his stance on the landing.

Their long, narrow swords swept at him—he blocked one with his knife, his sword sliding down the stairs behind him. Suddenly, the second attacker's sword fell to the stones as if it wanted to try stair-sliding, too, while its owner screamed and fell thrashing like a speared fish.

"Yield to the hand of the Empire!" A deep voice belled through the hall, the words barely recognizable through a heavy accent.

Disinclined to yield to anybody, I continued fending off a wiry guy with a grim, determined face—but as we dodged each other's blows, a thick-bodied arrow flung itself between us and buried its head in the back of another Southern soldier. The way he shrieked reminded me of something out of a story … *the screams of the dying …*

A moment later, my opponent staggered backwards, pressing an arm to his side. He dropped to the ground, clenching his teeth as if screaming would be more humiliating than dying. With a quick thrust, I gave him that death.

I parried a slash from another curved, blood-spattered sword, and tried to ignore the next arrow skittering across the floor.

From below, another voice, a familiar one, filled the air. "Lay down your arms before the King's Guard of Jeska!" At that moment, I realized why the arrows seemed odd—the hafts wore the pitch coating of fire-arrows. Who but Radeo would bring archers indoors? I had barely a glimpse, from the corner of my eye, but a silhouette on the landing below had my fake cousin's height and build.

I sliced a gash across the chest of a man who thought he could match me and shoved him out of the way. That left me facing one of the tall-hatters. He lifted his sword, a long, vicious blade with rivulets of Jeskan blood running down it. I repeated Radeo's order, using my knife to point at his weapon, "Put that—" then at the floor "—down!" I steadied my honest Jeskan blade in the direction of his worthless Southern heart. "Or die."

He lifted the sword further, to hold it vertical, until it nearly touched the feathers on his hat. Then he lowered himself to one knee, and slowly set the sword in front of him. He called out an order in his own tongue, in the deep voice I'd heard a minute earlier. The rest of his men obeyed. Only then did I hear my heart pounding in my ears, feel the screaming ache in my calves from running the stairs. With the tail of Errem's jacket, I mopped at the sweat running down my face, then dredged a cloth to clean my blade while I stood over the foreign captain.

Durse and his men gathered up the surrendered weapons as Radeo and his troop—a single bowman and a collection of what might have been makers' apprentices—made their way up the stairs. "Glad you could make it to the party, Cousin," he greeted me. "Sorry we weren't at the front door when you arrived." Beyond him, at the far end of the hallway, I thought I spotted Magaran's troop making their way towards us.

I gestured to the tight-closed council room doors. "Shall we?"

"After you, sir."

The doors swung wide. Durse and his men took their now-familiar positions as I strode into my council chamber. Radeo and his archer flanked the doorway. Within, a half-dozen enemy commanders clustered together. Not one raised a weapon.

So. They had that much intelligence.

I strode past as if they were a clutch of councilmen, and took the king's chair, one of the few times I ever sat in the thing. "I'm here to officiate over your surrender," I announced. "Any of you know how to talk Jeskan?"

A round-bodied man emerged from behind the leaders. He had tiny feet—did they make this poor guy march all the way from the heart of the Empire down south? He raised a hand that matched the feet—delicate, not suitable for swinging any kind of weapon. "Me, I talk your talk," he said. He pointed out two of the leaders. "Them, they too. But not rest."

I studied their stoic faces, undoubtedly scheming behind those dark eyes for a way to overturn this situation. As I pulled the folded surrender documents from my jacket, I recognized one—he'd been at the Lakeside Shamans' House, hadn't he? Did he recognize me?

It didn't seem so. At least, he didn't gasp and cry out, "You! The man who came and pretended to be a yokel!"

I unfolded the paper and stood up. I always hated chairs.

"Let's get started."

PART IV

MANAGE CLOSURE TO MINIMIZE LOSSES

34

I NSTEAD OF BORING YOU with paperwork, let me walk you back a few years, to the first military engagement of this long war: NeverSnows. My troop and I were eight untried guardsmen and one green lieutenant with no idea what we were walking into that day. We served under a captain with almost as much experience as I had, under a commander who'd never led more than a hundred men. The orders came down from senior commanders—Magaran, for us—to the field commander, to our captain, to me. None of us soldiers knew our strategic objectives—or what to do when things went wrong.

As they did.

The Battle of NeverSnows began in the cool predawn, accompanied by birdsong. For endless hours, a thousand Jeskans and a thousand outsiders hacked at each other: dodging, slashing, fighting our way to aid comrades, charging into combat with blood in our eyes and fury in our hearts. By mid-afternoon, it was over. Our commanders rode up and down the field, shouting the stand-down order and barely controlling their blood-shy ponies. Buzzards and condors patiently rode the simmering-hot air overhead. We soldiers marched down the field, sorting our dead from theirs, while the mercenaries (as, at the time, we thought they were) fell back, then fled into the trackless chaparral, towards Lakeside. Magaran dispatched pursuers to ensure the defeated forces continued their retreat. Hour on hour, scouts reported back. The enemy soldiers dispersed, continued their flight, and vanished.

While the Southerners carried home their hard-won intel on Jeska's force strength, fighting style, and capabilities, we troopers scoured the field, built the pyres that would cleanse our land of the invaders, and tended to our wounded.

At sunset, Magaran ordered everyone down to the creek that winds through HandOverHand on its way to Heart River. We were supposed to wash, but when I put my hands into the water, the lowering light and the reflection of the reddened clouds turned the whole stream to blood. I snatched my hands out of it, shook the droplets off. I might have been one of the ones screaming at nothing, there along the riverbank.

I don't remember.

Keev—no, it was Andus, it couldn't have been Keev—caught my elbow and pulled me back from the water. "Hey, Boss," he said— it was the first time anyone called me *Boss*— "Kul's getting a fire going."

By nightfall, we crouched around our campfire while the evening wind from the mountains carried the bonfire smoke away from us. I assume we ate. There's always someone in a troop makes sure there's food. I don't remember, though. The six of us—no, seven, when will I learn to count?—sat a little apart from the rest. Voices drifted from other circles, but none of us spoke.

We watched the flames in silence, remembering the ones we'd lost, the ones we'd killed, the ones we'd saved, the ones who'd tried to kill us.

I woke at shift change to the sentry's catlike footsteps brushing past like leaves pushed by the wind. He met his reliever and they exchanged fragments of news, the latest orders, in low, gruff voices. In a jumble of arms and legs and snores, my troop huddled against the chill of the night sky, tangled close, like runners at home.

I imagined my brother dodging in and out of the moonlight, on his way to the king with a report from our commander, and from there to the companionship of his House. Staring up at the moon-dimmed stars, I thought about everything we'd done wrong, the errors that had left so many of our comrades to wait for the condors. I resolved to protect these men of mine, even if it meant going against what I'd been taught, the one-way chain of command, a hierarchy that thought nothing of leaving a troop to flounder in the midst of chaos, with no orders, no authority, only their bodies to throw on the enemy's blades.

We won the Battle of NeverSnows, but only just, and we lost too many in the doing of it. We needed change. I would make it happen.

Sure, I was only a lieutenant, but someday I might be king.

35

TECHNICALLY, THE MOMENT the Southern officer laid down his weapons and ordered his men to disarm, I was out of a job. Legally, it was over when their commanders scrawled illegible signatures on the surrender document.

In reality, the ending of that last battle took nearly as long as the conduct of it. I try not to think about how many died after the surrender.

In the old, old days, we'd have executed their commanders and shown the bodies as proof to the men that had followed them. How that ever worked, I don't know. I suspect it didn't, as what would be more effective, to make a force of men-at-arms rise up one last time, than the sight of their treasured leaders as fire-ready corpses?

Instead, we conducted a parade of our prisoners. We gave them an easy choice: order your people to stand down, or suffer consequences. We left it to their vicious imaginations—the types of minds that created the army of light—to imagine what *consequences* might consist of.

Blazing torches surrounding our party caught everyone's attention. Radeo led, flanked by the makeshift troop he'd led into the council chamber—they deserved it, as builders of our secret fire-weapons. Beside Radeo marched the seniormost of the Southern commanders, his silly tall hat bobbing and swirling its feathers under the torchlight.

We became a blade of fire and light cutting through the fatal clash of shadows and steel. At first, the enemy soldiers cheered at our approach, believing their masters had come to announce victory. When the two commanders—Radeo and his opposite— called out orders to stand down, with our people so clearly in control, a wave of silence spread through the Southern forces and cheers rose up from our own fighters.

I placed myself in the guard unit with Durse and his men, conspicuously surrounding the rest of the enemy leaders. Durse fussed at my decision, so I told him, "Where do you want me? Out in front or in the formation?" He allowed as the second would be safer. The guys were unanimous in thinking we should have saved time and killed these black-hearted Southerners. I let them argue that position nice and loud, where our companions could hear, with two of them understanding every word.

In our wake, Magaran and his oldster troop fanned out to carry the news to our people—families in hiding at the barracks, the doctors in the hospital, the guildmasters in the stables. I'd tasked them with rounding up able-bodied volunteers to assist the troops as the surrender proceeded.

After the plaza, we had the challenge of convincing the forces outside the gate to lay down arms. They'd gone back to hammering the re-secured gate with their cobbled-together battering ram. We took our charges up to the wall-walk. On the stairs, I ended up climbing side-by-side with the Southerner I'd seen in Lakeside. About halfway up, he happened to glance my way. I was holding a torch high, to be sure of a good view of our footing. "The idiot!" he burst out.

I shifted the torch around as if to see him better, succeeding in sending a gout of smoke into his face. "Oh! The shaman's lackey! Hey, guys," I called over my shoulder, "it's that loser I told you about, from *Frogtown*."

I laughed, and they laughed with me. "Frogtown?" my nearest bodyguard replied. "I thought you was makin' that up, sir."

"No, no, it's true. Plus, did I tell ya? Those Lakesiders eat frogs. Did they make ya eat frogs, lackey?"

The Southerner grimaced, but kept silent. I jabbed my torch in his direction, making him jig aside, ram his shoulder against the wall. He grunted, but didn't lash out.

"I haven't forgot what your pals did to my kid, lackey," I told him. "Nor has my boy. He's out there, right now, in the fight. I find him hurt or worse, you'll be taking a deep dive off this wall."

From behind came a modification to my threat. "On accident, right?"

"Ya, right. On accident." Laughing felt good, chased away a fraction of the ache in my chest that came from thinking about Calestinise.

Once we reached the wall-walk, the games ended. At the top of the steps, I passed off the torch. Errem was waiting. "Your Majesty, we've got a difficult situation here."

I waved off his formalities even as a group of the younger guardsmen nearby started up a chant of *Corren, Corren, Corren.*

We conferred with Radeo about the situation in town. I'd already approved sending selected troops into the city, to support those Andus had assigned to stay behind as harriers. I'd hoped by now, with darkness fallen, that things would have calmed down, but far from it. Lit by the ongoing fires, we had a live battle in progress, from the fortress to the palisade, possibly beyond.

Shouted orders from the wall wouldn't carry through the din on the ground.

"I've one idea," Errem said. "It'll get their attention."

He'd scrounged up a collection of fire-boms—a few late deliveries, a few that had been dropped and rolled under ledges or gear-bags. A crew of his best tossers would light their boms, wait as long as they dared, then throw them more or less at the same time, to detonate over the heads of the combatants below. Tricky, dangerous, but what else did we have?

I'm not sure what we'd have done if they'd failed. As it was, we had less than a minute of stunned silence below. Radeo shoved the enemy commander to the fore, and torches to either side made it so everyone below could see that fancy headdress and distinctive uniform. His order went out, in that thick, tongue-bending language of theirs. Those in range of his voice obeyed instantly and relayed the command to their comrades further down the hill. For once, the discipline the Southerners instilled in their combined forces served our need.

As he'd done in the plaza, Radeo followed up with orders to our troops below. Not many were in view, but we could trust those who heard would spread the news. Nothing beats a victory to energize the troops.

Slowly, the disengagement spread down the hill … only to stall in the face of a new turmoil boiling at the edge of the fading conflict.

Radeo caught on to it first. "The army of light isn't standing down."

"My son's out there," I reminded him. As if he needed reminding.

The Lakesider kids had been trained under duress to attack any supposed traitors. The surrendering adults had betrayed the cause. Now, they faced the wrath of their minions: an army freed of command.

"We'll need a few troops trained in police action," Errem suggested. "More than breaking up a fight at a pub, but—"

"This isn't exactly a rough night at the inn," I growled. *Where is Calestinise in that mob?*

Radeo advanced on the enemy leader. "I have a better idea."

It didn't seem to me that throwing a body over the wall was going to help, but he'd seen these kids in action. Maybe that's what it would take.

Instead, he dragged the man out of sight of the throng below "Give me your uniform," he ordered. "I'll lead that rabble away." His voice had a weariness I recognized, from that night beside the fire, after he and Harad rescued Calestinise from the training camp.

The man in the silly hat massaged his wrist and glared, but I thought I recognized more confusion than anger in his stare.

"Hey, Frogtown Lackey," I called out. "Tell your boss to hand over his outfit."

The one I'd been toying with on the climb up the stairs muttered an opinion into his superior's ear. The man gestured something sharply negative and the lackey smirked in my direction.

Radeo waggled his fingers. "It's your people I'm going to save." Then he rattled off a string of words I couldn't understand, but I recognized their flavor—Hashtek. Always one more surprise with that man. He told me, "I said his people were dying out there, that I could save them."

Their official translator, the round-bodied fellow with the tiny feet, plucked at the sleeve of his recalcitrant boss, and spouted words that seemed to add weight—or accuracy—to what Radeo had said. At last, the foreigner lifted off his fancy headgear and peeled off his jacket. Then he gestured to his minions—including the Frogtown lackey, who frowned reluctance but also removed his uniform shirt and silly hat. The translator gathered the gear and handed it off to Radeo. "Save people ours," he said. "Make big show. Make safe fast please."

Minutes later, I stood at the inner gate, ringed by my protectors, as Radeo shoved the outer gate open. Silhouetted by the glare of the burning town, the headdress with its dangling feathers and coiled beads made him a spectral figure out of an old myth. Suddenly, the costume made sense—a form of intimidation, not vanity.

The old soldier waded into the sea of subdued attackers, a troop of similarly-disguised Jeskans at his back. They dodged past the battering ram lying in the dust, then formed up and began to run through the mob, aiming for the kids at the back.

I snagged the shoulder of the runner at my side. "Go! Now!" He raced through the gap and spun to the north, following a tight alley that would dump him out on the market road.

Radeo shouted as he ran. "Army of light! To me! To me!" He continued with a shout in Hashtek, presumably with the same message. He soon reached the northbound turn-off, near the swirling shapes that we'd guessed were the kids attacking Southerners. Waving his sword high, he caught beams of orange from the flames overhead and repeated his rallying cries. Youthful bodies surged towards him, roaring like distant rapids. Any adults in the way either dodged to safety or fell under their advance. A smattering of adult

Southerners retrieved their weapons and also followed Radeo in his charge to nowhere.

As planned, he headed towards the evacuated market district. Half the troopers he'd brought with him fell back, to become a wall between Radeo's new followers and the rest of the enemy forces. The rest took up position on the heels of his charge.

The runner I'd dispatched carried a message for the last few northside defenders: *Open the gate—and be prepared to close it on Radeo's order.* The plan hinged on leading the kids outside the town, then locking them out, at least until morning. If any strayed on their course or seemed to realize what was happening, Radeo's troopers were ordered to herd them back into line. The kids' training would help save them.

Once the last shadowy shapes vanished down the market road, Errem's men pushed the outer gate fully open and our troops poured out to complete the disarming of our enemies and take stock of the dead and wounded on both sides. One unit of troops had orders to proceed directly to the gap at the palisade, and, if possible, fashion a closure to last the night and then stand guard there.

We had enough to deal with, inside the city and the fortress. Anyone left outside could howl at the moon and wait for dawn.

36

DRAMIN TURNED UP while my crew and I were watching our troops process the surrendering soldiers outside the gates. He would have been hard at work triaging casualties within the fortress. We walked together back through the gates, dodging workers hauling bodies.

"How bad is it?" I asked him. "Are the doctors managing? Do they need more supplies, or more space to work in? Can they make use of unskilled hands? There's all the citizens to call on."

"Ya, and I'm sure everyone will be glad to help." He took me by the arm and drew me beyond the inner gate, into the shadow of the wall. "That's not why I'm here."

"Sure, right, you'll need to run triage on the ones out there." I waved towards the gate. My gut twisted, fresh images of the fallen clear in my mind. "I warn you, Dramin, there's kids out there, and wounds you'd rather not see—that no one's seen before."

I couldn't see his face, let alone read his expression, but his hand tightened on my arm. He shrugged off the bodyguard who tried to interfere. "Still not why I've come. You should have had a runner already, but you left command. He couldn't find you." His tone was accusatory—*what did you think you were doing?*

"We had a situation—a chance I couldn't ignore. A lot's happened, Dramin. I know it looks like chaos, but it's over man, it's over. We've won."

He jerked at my arm. "Listen, Corren. It's about Heyliannin."

In the moment, I was glad of Dramin's grip. Relieved he couldn't see my face in that shadow. I couldn't feel my lips moving. I couldn't visualize her face. "How did she die?"

His other hand dropped on my shoulder, then slid down my arm. "No, no, that's not it. Pay attention, Corren. She's missing. That's all. Missing."

The shouts and clatter behind me faded to silence, as if walls enclosed us. Events of the past few hours jumbled together in my mind. "She's at the hospital—no, wait, you were going to take her to save Andus."

If my bodyguards had been able to see clearly, the next moments might have gone badly. Dramin shook me, hard, an angry man shaking sense into a fool. "She couldn't have saved Andus. I couldn't take her there, Corren. Not after I'd seen her at the hospital. You should have told me!"

"Told you what?" I used Errem's phrase. "Say it straight."

"She has syncope."

"And I definitely know what that is." The one time someone tells me the truth, they use a word I don't know. If the dark hadn't blinded me, I might have pulled a knife on him. I was tired. Probably hungry.

He inhaled, then blew out a long breath. The night air carried from him a stink of blood, sweat, and burned flesh. "She can't see blood and stay upright, Corren. She said you knew. Why send her to that duty?"

It's a wonder I could stay upright, with my guts tangling themselves. "I forgot. She wanted to be useful. Where did you send her instead?"

"Send? Heyliannin? You don't tell that woman where to go." He'd released my arm by then. Imagining him arguing with my wife eased the agony in my chest. "She rounded up her guards and left. She might have said something about Stevvin and the other kid."

"Affram."

"Ya, Affram. You get kids' names well enough, Boss."

If he was done calling me by name, then it was true. Heyliannin was all right, but somewhere unexpected. One thing I knew for certain about that woman: she was a survivor. "When was this?"

I had to listen to him breathe for a minute. "About when we first started getting serious casualties. About the time Andus— About the time I came round to talk to you in command."

"That's hours ago." I didn't care if he could hear the anger in my voice. It burned in my throat.

"Sorry, Boss. I sent someone to check up on her. They found her guards, frantic. She'd slipped them."

"My fault, that." For taking Radeo and Harad as my own, sticking her with new guys and men who hadn't spent enough time with her. "When?"

"As I said, about that same time. Where would you guess she was going, really? In retrospect, she's not the type to coddle boys who can take care of themselves."

I closed my eyes against the lights of distant fires. "She'd have come to me," I said. "But she didn't." If she'd gone to command, she wouldn't be missing. She'd have spent the past few hours annoyed, angry, sitting in a closed room being ignored by me and my crew … then fighting my orders to go back to the hospital when I'd cleared the room. An idea boiled up from the pain in my chest. "She's with Andus."

He made a strange, sighing noise. "Corren …"

So he was back at trying to comfort me. "Dramin, listen. She talks to people. She would have heard the news. She'd go there. She knows …" *how I feel about you guys. Better than I do.* "And now—she might not know the fighting's done. She'd be keeping safe." I thought back to those few minutes, before Dramin turned up in command. "Durse."

"Yessir?" Which shadow was speaking?

"You heard the message about Andus first. You know where he is." I debated making him lead me there.

"Ya." The nearest shadow bowed his head and shuffled his feet. "Yessir."

He didn't say more, though I knew he wanted to. I knew myself, though. I couldn't put myself in that place, not even for

Heyliannin. And if I went to her, she'd need me, wouldn't she? And I still had a duty to discharge, one that couldn't wait.

"Sir?"

How long was I wandering in my own head? "Go. Fetch my wife. Take the troop. Leave someone to guard his body. You might need to drag her to the apartment. She might … fight you." *She might not be rational*, I wanted to tell them. *She might be as crazy as those kids out there, if she wasn't able to help him.* I recognized the hope in the back of my mind, but I knew it for what it was—a fantasy no better than a shaman's promise. If Andus were alive, we'd have had word of that.

"No, sir. We can't leave you unguarded." He sounded like Harad, like Kul, like Errem.

It's time for them to stop looking after me. "Yes, you can. It's over, Durse. We're done here." I swept a bow to the shadowy forms facing me. "Guys, thanks, you're getting one last task from me. Dramin, you've got a lot of casualties to assess out there."

"Boss—" Strangely, the alarm in his voice lightened my mood.

"Not anymore, Dramin. You were there when I made that agreement with Adestinian. The defense of Jeskaryan's done. I'm going to the elders, now."

I shook off their hands and put my fingers to the hilt of my blade, that I'd put to work for only that one dangerous expedition across the plaza and up the stairs of my house. My former home. They stepped aside, saluted. I gave that back to them.

The summer night wrapped itself over my shoulders and drew out all the pain as I walked alone, at last, slipping from shadow to shadow like a boy sneaking out to watch the stars roll over the sky.

37

WHEN I ARRIVED at what had been our commanders' briefing room, Tymon was already with the elders. The old ladies slouched around the conference table as if they'd been planning the next campaign. One by one, they passed their eyes over me, then looked away.

Maledestine stood from the spot that was usually mine and drummed her fingers on the shaft of her whacking-officials staff. "You took your time." None of the rest of them told her to shut up, so I figured it was unanimous.

I couldn't blame them.

Tymon left Adestinian's side and dodged around the abandoned chairs to meet me. "You're here. I was worried about you." Then he did that thing I'd been afraid Dramin had been about to do—my brother swung those endless arms of his around me and forced me close in a suffocating, sweaty hug. I let him do it. He would need something to get him through finding out what postwar job I'd arranged for him.

"You can stop crying now, Corren," he whispered in my ear.

"I'm not—"

But I was. Eldennian used to take me somewhere private, when the weather reminded me of NeverSnows. She had ways of shutting down those memories.

I shrugged him off and wiped my face with my jacket sleeve. Errem's jacket. *Will he want this back? Could I ever get it clean?* Every bone in my spine complained, but I stood to attention in front of the elders, delivered a proper salute. *By the time I'm through with this, they'll have found Heyliannin, she'll be on her way back to the apartment.*

To the room that wasn't ours anymore.

Adestinian raised her eyebrows at the salute, while the woman next to her hesitantly crossed a hand to her shoulder in an amateurish version of the gesture.

Maledestine seemed to have promoted herself to Chief Elder. "Explain yourself, Corren."

Her superior reached over and snapped her fingers in Maledestine's face. "Enough."

I reached for a chair. "May I sit?"

I counted three nods and two frowns.

I've always hated chairs, but my legs wouldn't hold me up any longer. I eased down to that hard wooden seat as if my bones were made of glass.

"Seems you got the news early," I began. I filled them in on the events of the past hours—the surrender of the enemy leaders, the calming parade within the fortress, the quandary of the mob outside the gate, and Radeo's solution to the army of light. I left out details. They didn't need to hear about my wife, about Andus, but I tried to help them see the flame-lit turmoil in the streets, hear the furious roar of the children's army, taste the acrid smoke of burning pitch as boms hurtled overhead. Even grim Maledestine leaned her stick against the wall and shifted her gaze to the table in front of her, as if she'd decided to devote her remaining years to the study of wood grain.

"So. Ladies." Adestinian waited until they'd all given their attention. "Is it settled, then?"

Their replies came as grunts and murmurs that apparently satisfied their leader.

"Corren, have you changes in your recommendation? Will you appeal your removal?"

There was something in her expression I couldn't read. What was she trying to tell me? I'd said I'd resign, but I recoiled at the idea of being *removed*. My gut didn't have any answers for me. "No, no changes. But I have a request, ma'am."

Her dark eyes fixed on mine. "What request might that be?"

"That you put aside those charges. They were fabrications, I'm sure you see it by now. I know I said I'd pretend, to save face on your side, but—" I had to stop and wipe off my face again. Words I hadn't known were in me fought their way out. "I've paid enough. Most of my friends are dead. My foster-son is missing, probably dead. It's more than my losses—we've seen so many fall today. I can't go up in front of those who've survived and claim to be a traitor. I can't tell them they were betrayed by a man they trusted with their lives, who spent the lives of *their* friends, of *their* children."

I'm not sure where the energy came from, but my voice became strong, filled the room like a speech. I slipped my knife out, laid it on the table, and spun it. The weaving of light over the moving steel kept my eyes from those faces and their uninterpretable expressions. "I can't tell that lie, Elders. I'm sorry, but I'd rather climb up the hill and kill myself over Yutek's bones." I set my finger on the table such that the knife would catch against it and stop, pointing to my heart. It made a tiny cut, and the blood dripped on the table, made dark ripples on the woodgrain. Two of the old ladies made soft choking sounds in their throats. "I'll step down. But let me go in peace, without a false stain on my history."

They began to argue. I didn't have the energy to listen to them. It was hard enough to stand, sheathe my knife, and walk to the door.

Tymon jumped up and followed me, his face a mass of confusion. "You're going? Now?"

I wasn't the only one who needed to be told things straight. "I've resigned, Tymon. The commanders have the mopping-up in order. Don't worry, you'll be fine."

"I'll be *fine*?" Did he think one hug, one moment of comfort, had resolved everything between us?

"You're taking over from me, Tymon. They're going to start the process of investing you tomorrow. Probably install you right after." I looked past him to the elders, still saying bad and partially-good things about me. "You'll be king, just like I always wanted."

You'd have thought I'd punched a hole in him.

"No." His eyes had the sheen of panic to them. It reminded me too much of that night, when he came to me for help, to get him to the runners and away from Yutek-en.

"Yes." I put a hand on his shoulder. He was shaking. *Don't take this so hard, brother.* "You'll do great. Train up Stevvin and Affram right, and maybe you can retire early, too."

"Train who?"

I tugged him closer, made a bad job of giving him a hug. "I'm dead on my feet, Tymon. I told Yutek to pick you, and now I get to be right."

"But you won't, will you?" He'd lowered his voice, but couldn't control the pitch. Or the sense.

"Won't what, brother? Be right? Of course I'm right. I do the right thing." My favorite saying didn't seem to be calming him.

"No, Corren, don't go up there. You wouldn't let me, so why should you?" His voice wandered up and down like a mockingbird testing out a new call.

What's all this?

Oh. I remembered that look on his face, when I threw him out of the house at Lakeside. I'd warned him not to kill himself over it, that I'd burn his body like a brigand's if he did. Is that what sent him to the shamans?

I pulled back and smacked his cheek with the flat of my hand. The noise made the elders look at us, so I spread a smile across my face. "I'm not going up the hill to lie down with Yutek's bones, Tymon. I'm going to bed. To sleep." I leaned in close, risking another hug. "Stay a while, listen to the elders. They'll argue, but they'll grant what I asked. They're your bosses, Tymon, but you don't need to be scared of them. Say what you need. Be direct."

Several times, on my way back to the king's house, I wondered if it wouldn't be better to curl up in a corner, like a dog. Of course, that made no sense at all, but playing with the idea kept me moving until my boots hit the stone steps. I may have been sleeping on my feet, because I don't remember climbing upstairs, navigating the hallways, or greeting the staff tasked with cleaning the blood off the floors. In one moment, a chill breeze dragged at my stained sleeve; in the next, the rough fabric of a drape rasped across my palm, and a woman's voice came at me out of the darkness.

"Corren, is it you? Is it over?"

• • •

She wanted to talk; that woman could talk forever. On our last journey together, she told me she'd spent a year after an injury unable to talk at all. It must have driven her crazy. Was that why we'd got her to spill her secrets so fast, me and Arnim? Was it not our clever maneuvers, but her own need to tell somebody? Somebody who could keep her secrets?

That night, even though I wanted to hear her story, I couldn't stay awake, and she spared me the nightmare of dozing in and out of a monologue.

It wasn't the best of sleep. I kept waking into dreams. I woke as a child, curled up at Tymon's back, counting the new marks there—scattered burns, a few fresh torturing cuts, the bruise at his neck from whoever had held him down that time. "I'll get him, Tymon," I whispered.

I woke enfolded by our huddle at NeverSnows, and the sentries changed shifts and named the numbers of our dead. Were there even that many people in the world?

I woke in that cave-like space, up on the Wall, with Orkast's mantle spread on the soil-dusted granite. Asdyel's voice hissed my name.

I woke to Eldennian stroking my forehead and murmuring, "It's a dream, Corren, it's all over, all over and done with now."

Or it might have been Heyliannin.

In one dream, I imagined waking from a worse one, the shadows of my shout echoing back to me from the honest walls of Yutek's room. A ghost glided into our bedchamber, a spirit formed of the smells of battle: blood, vomit, piss. It made a rhythmic guttering, hissing sound as it advanced, the sound a ghost would make, if a ghost breathed. "Hey, Dad," it whispered. "Hey, Dad, you awake?"

The memory of Calestinise's voice sent me down into another dream of weeping.

38

EVEN A SICK BRAIN like mine can only come up with so many nightmares. I think there were a few hours I didn't dream at all, before light from the outer room stole in and ate the darkness. I fell into a perfectly ordinary bad dream, in which the king (except the king wasn't Yutek, but one of the old kings from the histories) had sent me to defeat a monstrous bear that was terrorizing a village. I entered the bear's den, to find the beast had settled down to hibernate. It lay on its back, monstrous paws with bladelike claws flopped over its chest, like a puppy begging for attention. Its massive jaws gaped … and it snored—it snored like thunder in the mountains, like a landslide filling a canyon, like …

Heyliannin sleeping on her back.

I gave her a shove, and she rolled over. I looked up at the ceiling and realized I hadn't looked at the stars last night. I'd meant to, on my walk, but I kept getting distracted. Some kid had sneaked out to watch the action and got cut off from her escape route, so I led her down to the practice yard, where most of the market families were. A runner who wasn't from Jeskaryan stopped me to ask directions to the Shamans' House, so I had to figure out if he meant the building in town or the waste disposal area—and then convince him he really didn't want to go into town, not yet, that the shamans would be in the manure pits, definitely, it wasn't a joke. I tripped over a sack that had been dropped at the edge of a walkway, to find it was a wounded man, a Southerner who couldn't even understand me when I said I wasn't going to kill him. I had to trek halfway to the hospital to find a free medic and lead her back to the injured guy.

So the elders had been right to be pissed off at me.

Speaking of which, I needed the privy.

Heyliannin beat me to the closet in the corner. On my way to take my turn, I asked her, "Would it break your priyyam drectiff to share a better way to get piss out of an indoor privy than making a servant carry a stinking pot down three flights of stairs?"

"It's complicated," she said.

The room was still chilly, so I pulled the blanket over me when I came back.

She wrinkled her nose. "You never changed last night."

"Never mind. We'll burn these bedclothes. Explain to me what's complicated about privies?"

She played along. "First, you need to invent *plumming*. Then you need a … No, that word sounds like something else … Let's say, a water closet."

"Hmm."

So for a little while, we pushed the shadows back by designing a system for moving water out of the hills and into people's houses. She was right. It's complicated. I wondered if we'd be able to build such a project in my lifetime.

The light grew stronger. People might start checking up on us soon. Her eyes had shadows under them, proving she'd not slept much better than I had.

I waved off the next invention she was proposing. "So what happened last night? Why'd you ditch your guards in the middle of a war? You seem all right, but are you?"

"Are *you* all right?"

"I'm great. I'm retired."

"What—"

"Go ahead and talk, Heyliannin." I rolled to face her, propped my head on my hand. She studied my eyes in that way she had, trying to figure me out when I couldn't figure myself out. "I can manage, wife of mine. I think it's important stuff you need to tell, that I need to hear before this day gets any older."

She blew through closed lips, puffing out her cheeks. "We heard about— about the accident, I mean." She paused, measuring my reaction.

"I know. You don't have to jump around it."

She blinked slowly, distracting me with the way her dark lashes cast shadows. In the moment, her smile seemed natural enough. "Just because I fainted a couple of times, they kicked me out of the hospital crew. I figured I'd go help you with paperwork or something. Who knew you were the biggest draw in town?"

She and her guards ended up in the queue outside the command center, where the kid scribes were taking notes and my spares were screening new arrivals. One of her men had gone to the head of the line, to convince somebody that the king's wife shouldn't be made to wait. A frantic-looking citizen appeared from nowhere, but was moved up the line quickly. He bobbed apologetically at everyone he passed, saying, "Sorry, big news. The commander's fallen." Heyliannin asked which commander, and he spilled the detail, though he shouldn't have. You can't blame a pony-keeper for not knowing runners' rules.

The door had closed tight after he was taken in to see me. That left a crowd of anxious gossips outside, comparing notes. Everyone knew Andus had been running the campaign in the town. Somebody knew that meant the wall defense. What had taken the commander? An enemy arrow? Did Southern forces scale the wall? Had anyone heard of an incursion? Did they have ladders? No one in town had a ladder that big.

Heyliannin, the accountant, put two and two together and decided that, to an ordinary citizen, "fallen" didn't necessarily mean "killed in battle." Bad riders fall off ponies, drunks fall off chairs, and a man running around on a wall-walk might very well fall off it.

She played a game with her bodyguards, sending them up and down the line for "more information." The moment she had them distracted, she faded into the shadows.

"I knew they wouldn't let me go. I had the notion maybe Asdyel could do something for him. I know—"

"I had the same idea. I told Dramin to send you, but he didn't do it." A shadow of yesterday's gut-ache curled up in my innards, readying itself.

She slid her hand across the mattress, to lie on top of mine, the one that wasn't busy keeping my head from falling off. "It wasn't the same idea, Corren. Asdyel isn't magic; you know that. He can't fix broken bones and crushed organs." She stopped, studied my face again, and eased up on the details. "But I thought we could make it easier, if he was—" Her fingers tightened around mine. "Do you understand?"

"The beast could take up a fever, but not cure a disease." The weight of the mantle on my skinny kid shoulders, hallucinations evaporating before my eyes, my father's fingers easing the tangles from my sweaty hair. I'd never told her about that time with Asdyel, though. Why not?

"Right. He cured my infection, but he couldn't have saved the baby." It had done more than cure her; it had healed her.

"It made you well, though, Ta-ma. How? It's a flappy creature that can't even walk." I sat up, suddenly worried about where that beast—person?—was. *There*. Draped over the back of a chair. The sight took me back to that room, Orkast's terror when I described my hallucinations. I shivered as I'd done then, wracked by fever. "Can it hear me? Does it get insulted? Does it remember?" *And how much, and in what way?*

"Yes, probably he knows what you're saying. But no, he's hard to insult. I don't think they have the concept of pride. He doesn't like lies. That's the closest you could come to angering him." She tugged at my hand. "Shut up and listen, why don't you. And sit up. I don't want you falling asleep in the middle of it."

Like a proper husband, I followed her orders. She went on, and the regret coiled inside me slowly dissipated. As Errem had explained, as Dramin had concluded but not told me, Andus could not survive such a fall. That didn't mean the impact killed him. He had a terribly long time to wait for death.

"Dramin would have gone, himself, taken care of it," I told her.

"I prefer my way, Asdyel's way."

"Which is?"

"Complicated." Again I found myself being measured in her eyes.

"Like water closets?" She acted as if Jeskans were stupid, because we didn't have the tools and capabilities of her so-called advanced world. Her scrood-up world. "Try me."

Instead of answering, she turned away from me, then tipped her head and pulled her hair off the back of her neck. "You see that?"

"You mean your scar? How did you get that? When I shoved you off that rock? Or did the snake-men do it?"

"It's not what it seems. It's … a connection." She fended off the question I was about to ask. "Asdyel's people, they have a thing, an organ. It's …" She closed her eyes, to think without taking my stare, and drew a snaky shape in the air between us. "It's part of their nervous system, but it looks sort of like a rope—or a tongue. Long and skinny, formed of millions of strands of special *tishoos*, it's alive, it's part of them, and they use it to communicate by … by physical connection." She opened her eyes and watched my reaction.

I said the first thing I thought. "So, like sex? Their brains do sex?" I wondered, watching her eyes crinkle, if two people could connect their brains, during sex, or any other time, wouldn't that be … useful?

For instance, right then, I was having a serious, reasonable thought, but she looked like she might be about to hit me. "No. What an idea!" I didn't need a physical connection to hear her thinking, *Have you forgotten what we're talking about?*

I replied to her thought, not her words. "No, I know. Go on."

"All you really need to know is this: Asdyel can reach into another living thing's body, connect with them. He kept me alive, when we had nothing to live on in the mountains but the sunlight he absorbed. He cured me, the day before yesterday, by filtering bad stuff out of my blood, adding good stuff his own body can make."

"And Andus?"

"We could help with his pain." She took hold of my hand again. "When I got there, a few people were hanging around, soldiers and citizens." At the sight of someone they took to be a shaman, everyone deferred to Heyliannin. Maybe in the dark they couldn't tell she was a woman. They told her the commander was dead, and they were waiting for someone to tell them what to do with the body. She sent them away.

"He wasn't dead. Not yet. Asdyel sent in strands, felt for his mind. Don't imagine they could communicate. That takes time and practice, and we didn't have either. But he was in there, and he was in pain. So we talked, me and Asdyel, and we figured a way he could share something to take off the worst of the pain."

Then you sat there and watched him die? I knew better than to say that out loud. She watched my face and read my thoughts.

"Yes, we sat there and helped him die. It didn't take all that long, Corren. I didn't even faint." Her hands trembled. When she blinked, fat tears ran down her face. "Please, tell me I did the right thing."

My throat felt like I'd swallowed nutshells. "Ya, you did fine. Likely in his mind he was waiting for Karthi." I needed to turn the topic before I heard what I was saying. "But if it didn't take long, why were you missing for hours?"

"Because those shamans came through, the ones that opened the gate, for the trap. After that, they hung around, watching the action. I stayed in the shadows, invisible. I couldn't be sure how they'd treat me, carrying a mantle and all."

Did she expect me to miss the important thing? "Shamans opened the gate? You're sure?"

"What? Yes. Of course."

"Don't give me 'of course.' Give me details." I couldn't conduct an interview snuggled in bed, so I flung the blanket off my shoulders and got up. Suddenly, the stink of the uniform I'd worn for the past day-plus filled my head. I coughed and started pulling off my shirt. I needed to get changed, get back to the elders.

Heyliannin crouched on the bed, watching with wide eyes. It reminded me of that day in Lakeside, with Tymon. Only this time she had a nightdress on. "There were four shamans, two with mantles, two without."

"Apprentices. You couldn't have run to command? Told us what was happening?" The laces weren't working for me, so I left them and dragged on my pants—the ones with bloodstains all over them.

She held up both hands in her *wait, wait* gesture. "But wasn't it part of your plan? To trap part of their army inside? I told you—

the only thing that wasn't clear was whether you were taking advantage of their move or if they were cooperating with you."

"Neither! We had no idea." Though I might have suspected.

She waved her arms, trying to show things in motion. "But … but … right after the gates opened, letting those enemy soldiers in, your guys made that big explosion, and a troop jumped out of nowhere to close the gate. It seemed so obvious. You're telling me it was a coincidence?"

I closed my eyes, to better imagine her description. The timing would have been close, with Errem as quick to action as he was. It might well have seemed like a strategy, to a civilian. This late, what information could be useful? Somebody needed to hear this news. Who did I report to now? Magaran? Adestinian?

I rubbed the itch out of my eyes. "Do you know which shamans?" A terrible notion rippled through my imaginings … apprentices. Tymon walked in with the shamans. Was it a coincidence? "Tell me my brother wasn't one of them."

"Tymon wasn't there. I couldn't see their faces, but I could recognize voices. And Asdyel might—"

"Your magic demon might what?" I couldn't be submitting evidence from her creature.

"I think he'd recognize the … mantles. And he's not magic."

"The point is, it can't testify to the elders."

"I can. I will."

The clean clothes I rummaged out of the nearest trunk didn't go together, but they were civilian and they weren't bloodstained. It would have to do. "That's good. Get dressed. Let's go."

39

I LEFT HEYLIANNIN to put together her own costume for the first day of my retirement. The sitting room had an odd stillness. I hadn't realized how much I'd gotten used to bodyguards hanging around all the time.

Even so, the room wasn't empty. A hulking figure sat at my desk, his back to the bedchamber, messing around with whatever I'd left there. At the rustle of the drape, the invader lumbered to his feet and turned to face me.

Lucky I didn't have a knife in my hand.

"Ya took yer own sweet time gettin' outta bed, Boss." Kul stepped to one side and gestured to the desktop, empty of papers for once but now crowded with plates and bowls. "I was about to quit waitin' on ya and let ya breakfast on my leavings."

I let my mouth do the talking, given my brain couldn't believe what I was seeing. "That's fine, you can have it all, I have to go talk to the elders."

"Radeo said not to let ya outta here without breakfast." He sidled a little way towards the door, ready to block my path. Kul can be a hard man to get around, and not only because of his size. "Besides, ain't ya wantin' my report?'

I couldn't breathe. "I think I'm having an attack heart."

A warm pressure at my back pushed me further into the room. Behind me, Heyliannin laughed gently. "Then you'd better sit down until it goes away. You can eat something and then go yell at people."

"Who's to yell at, Boss?"

"Everybody. The shamans, mostly." I dropped into my seat and began to peel an egg. My mouth filled with saliva. *When did I last eat something?*

"The shamans opened the gate," Heyliannin explained, while I stuffed eggs and bread into my face. "I thought it was a strategy, but it wasn't."

"Why would letting the enemy inside be a strategy?" Kul asked, shoving his share onto a plate. Kul gets a big share.

"The thing with the *fierkrakkas*, that the guys on the wall did, right after, it was so coordinated, it felt intentional."

Kul shrugged and handed her a plate with not quite so much on it. "We was kinda busy on the north side, then."

I picked up a handful of little plums and leaned back. "You should be reporting to Magaran now, not me, but I want to know."

He gave me a tight, clean summary of his adopted unit's movements in pursuit of the enemy contingent, and the autonomous-troop tactics that weakened the attack on our vulnerable north gate. At that approach to the city, a more moderate slope helped the Hashtek archers, while the fire-arrows from our side had less of a flight advantage. Early on, Kul had tipped off his troopers to do what they could to whittle away at the Southerners, keep them off-balance. The task wasn't easy, and the risks were high.

"We've too many lying out there in the north fields, Boss." Kul wasn't one to hold back on emotions, but his eyes were dry. Maybe he'd done his crying already. "I was gonna stay with 'em, after, get the fires going, but Radeo put me on kid duty, ya know."

Kid duty? "The army of light?"

"Oh, that, ya, that was something, Boss. Ya shoulda seen 'em, they was pouring outta that gap like water through a broken dam.

Then the gate slammed shut, and they doused the fires up top, and everything went dark. Ya shoulda heard 'em howl." The underage warriors couldn't do much damage. Kul and his men hammered away at the adults until they started slinking off the field. Apparently, about half the kid soldiers followed them, but it wasn't clear whether anybody of any age knew where they were going, in the dark, through croplands and brush lands, led astray by irrigation ditches and game trails. Moonlight's fine when you're on a road you know. Not so much in open country that isn't your own.

Heyliannin sat through the story without saying a word, but I had the eerie feeling she was talking to Asdyel the whole time. She'd pulled on the cape before we left our room and didn't take it off when she sat down. I wasn't sure if she reminded me of my father or Fennic, Master Shaman of Jeska, that snake.

The door slammed open and someone called out, "Got more food like ya said."

Heyliannin leapt to her feet, the cape flapping as if it was trying to lift her into the air. She screamed and ran across the room, the black cloud fluttering behind her. "Calestinise!"

The cup in my hand fell from my numb fingers, struck the edge of the table, and shattered into a million pieces. When I stood up, I jammed a bunch of shards into my feet, but I didn't care.

"Whatcha so excited for?" Kul complained. "Told ya I had the kid."

My wife and son were by then locked in an embrace that would have been weird if you didn't know them, the two sobbing out loud like it was our worst fears come true, not one of our least-likely hopes. Calestinise's eyes shone at me over Heyliannin's shoulder—he'd gotten tall that summer.

"Hey, Dad," he said. "You know you cry in your sleep? When did that start?"

I may well have been crying then, too, but nobody was watching, not with Kul behind me and the two of them gone back to hugs and all that. I got the sleeve of my clean shirt a little messy before I turned around and sat down to finish my breakfast.

•   •   •

The elders barely had time for my report, or rather, Heyliannin's. They had decisions to make as to what to do with the Southern commanders, while at the same time planning their installation ceremony for Tymon. Given we had nothing but Heyliannin's word to go on, the best I could accomplish was getting the four shamans she (or rather, Asdyel) identified onto a cart bound for the barracks at Koresh. Adestinian took advantage of my standing in front of her for five minutes to demand that I continue working at government business for a few days. So much for retirement.

I had to admit, she made sense. Tymon would be fine once things settled down, but not now. Radeo, Magaran, and Errem had more than they could handle, dealing with the usual aftermath, and more. Scouring the battlefield for survivors and casualties meant house-to-house searches, even while crews were still putting out fires. A number of Southern soldiers failed to retreat after the last of the fighting ended. They formed a camp at the bottom of the hill, and I took the job of walking down there and telling them to go home. A large contingent refused to leave until their leaders were released—another argument for killing off the leadership. One group formed up into marching units, but then turned around and asked for guides to get them to the border. Do they not teach navigation down south?

A surprising number refused outright, declaring their intent to settle in Jeska. That was unexpected. Then again, what did I tell you before? Everybody wants to live in Jeska. I was against it, but the elders pointed out how many good strong, smart people we'd laid out on the battlefield. The asylum-seekers had to be vetted, and I made a fuss about having that done by the military, but to my surprise the old ladies agreed. We would have to find places to put these unlikely immigrants, and ways to keep track of them, because it's one thing to pick up a new language, but another thing to learn how to behave in completely new ways. So … I delegated their citizenship training to the matriarchy. *Make sure these newcomers learn from the start who's in charge in their new country.*

Day by day, I worked for the moment I could move out of the king's apartment, get myself to a town with no shamans in it, and start a new life. I didn't dare ask if Heyliannin planned to go with me, or, if not, what she planned. Calestinise allowed as how he'd go pretty much anywhere she wanted. Didn't see much of Tymon, but he had a lot of memorizing to do for the ceremonies, not to mention sitting through hours of advice and demands from his new bosses.

Everyone kept me busy enough I didn't have to think too often about Andus, whose bones are up on the king's hill, where mine will never be. I didn't need to imagine Karthi's last moments. A mind-numbed trooper wandered in during the setting of the bonfires and told us in far too much detail. A bundle of fire-arrows had tipped over into their lighting-fire. They'd begun to smoke, just barely, as Karthi rushed to pull them free of the flames. Those trickster demons, the arrows, waited for the instant when he held the sticks ready to hurl them safely aside. Before he could release them, the arrows burst in rapid succession. I'd seen enough of the injuries wreaked by those weapons that I couldn't avoid imagining his final hours.

That was the worst of it: the fire-arrows killed, but not instantly, the way a well-placed bolt from a skilled archer can take a man down in one strike.

I could imagine Harad to my heart's content, because nobody at all knows what happened to him. There weren't too many unrecognizable Jeskan bodies, and none of those matched Harad's height and shape. I like to think he set down his gear and left, got himself somewhere nobody would ask him to take up arms against children. Maybe he's up north somewhere, pulling fish out of a river for a living.

The kids he fought—the members of the army of light who fell between HandOverHand and Jeskaryan—we let lie alongside the city's defenders. They weren't invaders or criminals; they were victims of the war who were forced into what they did. The survivors of that army? A lot of them eventually bounced back to normal—you'd never know what had been done to them, what they did. Especially the younger ones. Others, you could tell even in those early days, would be living tortured lives for a long time. How do you go back to your family after what they thought was a summer at your cousin's farm and tell them you murdered kids, burned their bodies, beat up a bunch of little kids, and tried to hand your country over to a foreign power?

40

THE ELDERS COULDN'T have picked a better day for Tymon's investiture and installation as king. The sky cracked open to a blue so deep you'd have thought we were up in the mountains. An early-autumn rainfall that night had swept the air clean and scrubbed the bloodstains off the pavement. By midday, everything had dried off, the temperature stayed reasonable, and the platforms and ceremonial pieces were in place, ready to go.

Tymon enjoyed the investiture ceremony—at least up to the moment when I seared the king's mark into the thick flesh at the base of his thumb. The standing around naked part—he took that in good fun, even tried to chat up the old ladies as they did their meticulous inspections. Being a runner, he had no trouble memorizing the speeches, and he looked impressive in the fancy robes. A small contingent of young people clustered together near the platform and made *ooh* and *aah* noises at every pause.

In normal times, after the investiture, there'd be an all-night feast, a party that only the strong could survive. This time, we got a reception with little snacks and awkward milling around. It reminded me of the welcome party at Lakeside, but without any excuses to not know everyone's name. I talked Dramin into walking the circuit with us, to keep me from accidentally insulting anybody.

Besides the crowd of citizens, we had the smiths and other makers forming a cluster for shop talk, a gang of upper-tier shopkeepers aiming to make Tymon their customer, the elders themselves, and their retinue of lesser matriarchs. And the shamans.

Fennic took it on himself to approach me. Good thing for him it was a no-weapons party.

He cast his eyes familiarly on my wife, with Orkast's cape flowing over her shoulders, and said, "I see you've found your own way to become part of the community of shamans, Corren. Do you regret now, not joining with us yourself?"

I swirled my cupful of tepid fruit juice and considered how he might look wearing it. "No regrets. Yutek taught me well, Fennic. Power needs to be distributed, or you end up like the Southerners."

I hated that sly smile of his, the one he couldn't control, that said he had a secret plan I wouldn't want to know about. "Is that so?" He sipped his over-fermented drink. The smell of it turned my stomach. "Ma'am? Do you agree? Wouldn't the world run better if the matriarchs managed everything?"

"You're kidding me," she snapped. "The Lakeside accounts were rancid with corruption. Much of it inside the matriarchy. As well you know."

He leaned back and spread his arms wide, pretending to be struck by the force of her words. Wine splashed on the pavement. "Mercy, ma'am. I assure you I know no such thing."

She leaned in, dropped her voice in a way that reminded me of myself. "Where I come from, we make things harder for people like you by splitting up the government. Not the same way you do, but still, as Corren said, power isn't all in one place."

His smarmy grin failed to counter her strength. "How can you possibly make progress without a singular direction, a primary leader? You may dismiss the Hashtek Empire, but they've done great things. Great things."

Dramin reminded us he was there. "Depends on what you mean by greatness, Master Shaman. We have Southerners at our gates begging to become Jeskans."

His lips curled in disdain, Fennic tossed back the rest of his drink. "They're disappointed. They think they're losers, so naturally they think they should punish themselves by staying here." A servant passed with a tray, and the shaman snagged himself a fresh cup. "We can do better in Jeska. And we will. You'll see."

My gut hadn't bothered me for days, but right then it had apparently decided to kill me in front of everybody. I took Heyliannin's arm. "Let's find the boys before the rest of the show gets started. Enjoy your drink, Fennic." *Be glad it isn't poisoned.*

A shadow passed over his face, as if he'd heard my thought. As we walked away, I could have sworn the two capes snarled at each other like argumentative hounds.

Halfway across the plaza, Heyliannin made me slow down. "What's that evil old man planning?"

"Whatever it is, we'll take care of him. I'll take care of him," I promised. I shifted course to find Magaran or Radeo, to warn them something might be up, advise them to keep an eye on the shamans in their little cluster of fake magicians. It was possible they'd gotten hold of weapons or sabotaged the ceremonial platform. Up on that stage, Tymon would be as vulnerable as a target in the practice yard.

My own installation had taken five minutes. A retired elder, parchment-skinned, straight-backed, handed me the book and the ring and the ceremonial talking stick—all lately retrieved from the valuables storage. A grizzled veteran, one of Yutek's own true friends, presented me with a folded paper and explained *This here's the note Yutek left sealed for his successor.* The elders thumped their staffs and Maledestine reminded me, *Just until the fighting's done.*

No speeches. No parties. Then again, no conspiracies.

•　　　•　　　•

When Durse trotted down the steps of the king's house in his sharp, new formal uniform, I knew things were about to get started. I intercepted him on his way to make a final check of the ceremonial platform. I wasn't worried about assassins hiding under the boards, but I couldn't escape the feeling that something would go wrong, that Tymon would get hurt.

249

"We kept you alive, didn't we, sir?" he said, keeping his eyes on his work while he listened to my warnings. "Commander Radeo's lent me the better part of a unit to keep eyes on anyone acting oddly in the crowd."

That sounded good, it was more than I'd expected, but, "Shamans always act oddly."

"Ya, Radeo told us the story." The story of Calestinise and the army of light. "We've got a group of real sharp-eyed guys stationed around your enemies, there, sir."

"You can stop calling me sir."

"Na, can't do that." He crouched to lift the decorative drape that hung from the front edge of the platform. Together, we peered into the undercarriage, well-lit enough by openings on the sides. He counted off the men who'd been stationed under there, just in case. "Anything in particular you'd suggest we watch for? Sir?"

I couldn't help with specifics. Durse had the most-likely tactics covered. What would a shaman consider? How much did they believe in their magical powers? How much was pure fakery? "I'm thinking they'll try a trick, create an illusion that one thing is happening when it's really something else."

"Ah, yessir, that was my thought as well, so I've told the lads to think like sportsmen or pebble-gamers, pay attention to the true patterns, not the distractions." Satisfied with his inspection, Durse led me around to the back of the platform, near the stairs the elders and Tymon would be using. The steps looked rickety to my eye. Could someone have sabotaged them?

"Is there any way we could rearrange the parties, find a place for me up there?" If something happened, I'd have to run through the crowd, then clamber onto the platform, by which time it would be too late.

"Sir, the forms are well-set, very traditional. There's no place for the old king, since, well—"

"Ya, ya, the old king's supposed to be up the hill. I know, I know." My gut wouldn't let the issue go. "There's got to be something I can do."

He looked down at me with that steady, serious gaze I'd nearly gotten used to. "There is, sir. Go out to your position, the one we've arranged, be where your brother expects you to be. The sight of family's the best cure for nerves."

Concerned for Tymon's life, I hadn't been thinking about his nerves, but Durse was right. My brother would find all this off-putting. He was used to long runs alone—and now he was doomed to have a team of men dogging his footsteps forever. His idea of a social gathering involved food, drink, and more than a little close contact—not long speeches, complicated rituals, and lots of formalized bowing and saluting, without much touching. I took my leave of Durse and went to look for my wife.

Heyliannin had roped the two registered fosters and Calestinise into a family-looking group and taken command of our patch of pavement. A half-dozen conspicuous guardsmen pretended to be doing other things while remaining in formation around us. So Durse had been thinking of the old king, while planning the protection of the new one. I exchanged quick salutes with the nearest guardsmen and then ignored them.

I'd had to break it to my wife that Stevvin and Affram were signed to the king, which would now mean they were Tymon's fosters, not mine. Stevvin kept us entertained by proposing various schemes to get out of his contract, each more outlandish than the next. It worried Affram, I could tell. Who would want to be stuck being Tymon's only kid?

When the Master Shaman turned up on the platform, a clutch of his mantled henchmen thumping behind like shaggy ponies, Stevvin had a new idea. "I know. I'll steal a mantle and jump through a thin patch."

Affram punched him.

Good move, kid.

"Cut it out, you two," Heyliannin ordered. "Stevvin, do you really want to go back to shoveling manure?"

The boy rubbed the red mark on his cheekbone. "He coulda broke my nose if he hadn't missed!"

I crouched to study his injury better. "It'll make an impressive bruise if you keep poking at it." I lowered my voice. "If ya really want out, kid, there's ways, but if not, you gotta stop teasing your *brother*."

His eyes were wet with something more than physical pain. "There's ways? Real ways?"

"Sure. Me and Tymon, we had four other foster-brothers. Ya think we murdered 'em all?" *I wanted to, so many times.*

"Oh. All right, then."

The next moment, the boys were back to discussing strategies for that pebble game of theirs, while Stevvin reknotted the bundle of toss-ups bulging in his pocket.

Heyliannin looped her arm into mine. "You'd have been a good father," she said. I couldn't tell if I was supposed to read more into that.

Luckily, Calestinise had to stick his nose into the conversation. "Listen, I didn't mind calling you guys Mom and Dad, but I'm not doing that with Tymon. I ain't signing those papers." I'd had the contract set up, but none of it was executed.

I started to argue with him. Arguing was what we did best. He'd be pretty well-fixed as senior foster. But did that matter? So all I said back at him was, "Fine."

An elbow in my side took my attention back to my wife. "What?"

"Didn't Tymon leave the runners?" She seemed serious, so this wouldn't be one of her your-world-is-backward jokes. "Isn't being married a requirement to be king? Isn't that why you and I are … well, you and me."

I thought for a minute. "My understanding is that retiring doesn't break the bond. He wasn't *divorced*—that has to come from the community, and they do that only when someone does something very wrong. He cashed out, asked not to be assigned more work. He was entitled."

Calestinise started laughing so hard. It's a good thing the refreshments had been taken away or he'd have been spraying food everywhere. "Oh, Mom, you're hilarious. Do you think he hasn't been over at Runners' House every other night since he got back?"

The varied shades of pink on Heyliannin's face could have matched a good sunset.

The shamans had taken their place, and the elders were being helped up the steps, so Heyliannin got to think things through in the privacy of her own head. I kept scanning the crowd for suspicious movements, while in the back of my mind, I was thinking of a new job for the smiths to work on. Stairs are tough for oldsters. Must be something better.

Once the old ladies got settled, Tymon and his escort—my former bodyguards—took the stage. The traditional layout made a triangle—the matriarchs, the shamans, and the king-designate. Ceremonies have to have their symbolism. Everything was planned, rehearsed, traditional.

First, a round of speeches. Neither Adestinian nor Maledestine did the elders' opening speech. The one they designated, a tough creature who must have been a terror in her youth—thick arms, strong back, a wide, powerful stance—delivered a sweet, poetic tribute to the unity of Jeska, our stewardship of the land. Not a dry eye remained. Fennic, too, had picked one of his colleagues for the opener. The chosen one had long streaks of grey in his hair, but moved with the agility of a younger man. He delivered a wandering narrative on the value of fellowship.

In the middle of his talk, a rush of movement off to my left distracted me. By the time my eyes focused on the scene, Durse's crew were hauling away a pair of tough-looking young men. My heart thumped and shadows floated through my vision. My hand fumbled for a knife that wasn't there. One of the guys assigned to us shuffled a little closer to me and said, "Pair of drunks, sir. We've had a lot of that today."

I'd suggested to the elders that the ceremony include a nice speech from the retired king, but they slapped that idea down so flat you couldn't even see its guts. Maybe they'd heard how good I was at speeches.

Tymon stepped forward—and my insides twisted as my eyes flicked over the crowd. He'd tried out this speech with me, the night before. To my ear, it had too many parts where he made fun of himself, but he insisted that was a good way to make people like him. It hadn't made sense to me. Point out your flaws? To impress people?

He only spoke for a few minutes, but from where we stood, at the front of the audience, you could feel the tension easing. Ripples of laughter flowed through the crowd. I couldn't laugh with them—my gut hurt too much—but the boys thumped each other's shoulders and Calestinise nearly smiled.

The ritualistic part came next. Adestinian took charge and recited the lengthy formula speech about the duties of the king with respect to the matriarchy. It takes up four pages in the documentation of the rite, so you can imagine how much fun it was to listen to, with the sun turning the tops of our heads to sizzling plates of stew. Her henchwomen interjected the regular chant of *In service to Jeska, so shall the king* that marked off each section of the speech.

She concluded by taking up her staff and pivoting in place to march to Tymon's position. He performed a practiced bow, and she presented him with the ring that had burned its mark into his flesh a few hours ago. He slipped it onto a finger of the hand without a bandage on it, and gave her another bow.

Once she returned to her spot, a sighing rustle erupted in the audience as everyone shuffled their feet and stretched and accepted the yawns they'd been suppressing. You're supposed to be still during a ritual, and only the smallest of children had broken that rule during the Chief Elder's presentation.

I didn't listen, but I watched Fennic like a wolf stalking a deer as he recited the shaman's rote for the ceremony. I couldn't pick up all his facial expressions, but that smirk of his kept fighting its way onto his lips, and when he glanced over at Tymon, you'd have thought he was a starving man looking at lunch.

Or maybe he hadn't taken the time to eat during the reception, being too busy baiting me.

The oddest moment came when he carried to Tymon the shaman's symbol, the Book of Knowing—a real snore, full of aphorisms that sound wise, but make no sense. The oddity? Instead of matching bows, he and Tymon exchanged hugs. It gave me the creeps, but maybe it was nothing more than that the shamans had taken him in for a while.

For the final stage, the king receives a ceremonial gift from the people. The crowd parted for a cute little procession: a pair of children, thankfully, both the boy and the girl much younger than any of the army of light. They walked side-by-side, each holding one end of an ancient burnwood twig about as long as they were tall. The talking-stick had been replaced many times over Jeska's lifetime, but this one had lasted at least four kings, so it had gained a certain mystical aura. The kids didn't look excited; they looked terrified they'd manage to break the thing. When they reached the front, a pair of guards hoisted them up to the stage.

Tymon met them there, kneeling to accept his final badge of office. He said a few words to the children, and they hugged him, which isn't part of the ritual. Maybe it should be—the audience sighed in unison, *aaaaaaw*. When the soldiers lifted the kids down again, and sent them back down the aisle, the pair giggled and skipped the whole way, and good humor flowed through the crowd like a clean autumn wind.

With the talking stick in his hand, the ring on his finger, and the book tucked under his arm, Tymon stood as close to the edge as he could. I knew every word of his speech. It's a formula I'd memorized years ago. But at the same time, I hardly recognized it. He put warmth into every phrase, made every formal pledge a personal promise. I cried, and I didn't care. I'd been right when I told Yutek he should choose Tymon. I'd been right all along. His voice flowed over us like warm wax, filling in the divisions, covering up the sharp edges, blending us into one. I couldn't tell if I was breathing or not, I was so proud of my brother.

When he finished, and we could all move again, Heyliannin pulled a rag out of somewhere and set to mopping at my face. I made her stop by hugging her. "It's going to be all right," I said. "I knew he could do it."

Adestinian and Fennic joined Tymon at the front of the stage. The elder had a few words of praise to the community for their hard work of the past week. The shaman pretended he was sorry about the sad losses people had suffered. Tymon thanked everyone for their kindness and support.

"It's been a difficult time," he said, and the audience murmured *yes*, and *indeed*, and *so it has*. "As we move forward, we're resolved more than ever to be a unified Jeska, to break down the barriers between us." He got a round of cheers for that. "We're taking a new step today, to bring together the forces that serve our matriarchy: the runners who keep us linked together, the government that protects us from outsiders and manages the business of a nation, and the shamans who tend to our souls and connect us to other worlds."

This wasn't part of the ritual. And he'd already made his thank-you speech.

Corren. The rasp of Asdyel's voice at my shoulder made all the hair on my body stand to attention. *Corren.*

Fennic shrugged and his mantle slipped from his shoulders, a wave of blacks and browns and greys that he cradled in both arms. While at the same time, he still had his cape on.

"He was wearing two of them!" Heyliannin hissed, her voice a weird counterpoint to her creature's. She was right. This whole time, the Master Shaman had been standing there with, not one thick, enormous cape, but with two of them. *Why didn't I notice?* I glanced over at his colleagues. *Yes.* They'd all done it, to create the illusion Fennic wasn't doing anything unusual, nothing tricky.

My wife went into motion before I did, but neither of us were close enough to make a difference. Tymon accepted the mantle, swung it over his shoulders, and bowed his head.

Connection, that's how Heyliannin had described it. The thing that happens when a person blends with a mantle. Not a mystical connection, but a *physical* one, blood and brain, with one unavoidable first step, where the one must invade the other.

I had my hands on the platform edge, the boards pressing lines into my palms, when Tymon made that noise I can't get out of my head. Sharp as a dagger, its tones rising from the guttural night-call of a stag to the rasping scream of a frustrated hawk. It tore its way from my brother's throat like a monster ripping through a thin patch to destroy our world.

By the time I reached him, moments later, he'd collapsed. I caught hold of the cape, to tear it free again, but Heyliannin struck my arm away. "No, no," she sobbed. "It's too late for that. If there's any chance at all, it'll come from the mantle."

A bundle of bony flesh hurled itself into me. I toppled onto my back and gaped up at Fennic, his knee threatening to snap one of my ribs, his face contorted. "This is your fault!" he cried. "All you had to do was say yes! All the years we prepared, to find a boy who could do the job, a father who would give him up, and it went so perfectly. But you threw it all away, you fool!" He hammered blows at me until the guardsmen pulled him off. I didn't even defend myself; I was too far away, remembering too much, while Tymon's fading, shuddering breaths washed over the boards between us.

41

THE WAY HEYLIANNIN PUT IT, the mantle creature tried its best. But Tymon either wasn't ready or wasn't suited to the connection process.

"Not everyone can do it," she told me, sharing my sitting-rock up on the king's hill. "The snake-men, none of them could, not even one. Here, I'd guess the reason shamans usually take a year for training is so they can test things out. Or hide the failures." Her voice came calm and steady, but her eyes seemed to have an infinite supply of tears. "I saw part of a study the snake-men did, on the few survivors they had. They were struck down like Tymon, except that some lived in that state for years and years."

I stared out at the view, the wonderful panorama that had always inspired me. I'd persuaded her to come, so she could see Tymon's future resting place as beautiful, not terrible. It had already been a full day since he'd stopped breathing. Since Asdyel told my wife that my brother had stopped thinking. Stopped hurting. We needed to get his remains up here, send him out to the world, but she needed to understand, first.

She seemed half-undressed, without her mantle. She claimed she'd left it behind because Asdyel wanted to stay with the other one, to comfort it. The two creatures had seemed to work together, to try to help the blank-eyed, drooling body that used to be Tymon.

I needed her to know I knew what I'd done wrong. "It's my fault, because I reclaimed it. I took Asdyel right out of his hands. I thought he was rescuing it for you. But he was training with it, wasn't he?"

She took my hand, and her fingers brushed the scar on my palm. "Don't. You're seeing it wrong. It's a physiological response, like my syncope—and just as unpredictable. It wouldn't matter which mantle he used. It might have been worse. If Asdyel was familiar with him, then maybe he'd have made Tymon live longer. He couldn't have fixed him, any more than he could fix—"

Her silence said *Andus*.

She stood and rubbed the tears from her face. "You have to stop blaming yourself, Corren. He felt prepared. You know Tymon—he'd have put everything he had into the project. He did, right? He even spent all his money on it. He put his trust in the shamans. That was his mistake, not yours."

"When did they get to him, do you think? Before we went to Lakeside? When he went missing, during my investment? After the two of you … after I sent him away?"

I couldn't help noticing how her hand strayed to her belly at the thought. "We can't know for sure. Any of those times, or all of them."

I remembered the look on the Master Shaman's face, after that first trip into the mountains, when I returned with my dead father's cape. I thrust the mantle at Fennic and told him I'd never take it up. At the time, I mistook his desperate fury for professional disappointment. Had they assumed, all those years, that I'd follow my father? Orkast always thought so, didn't he? I never really told him *no*, unless you count a twelve-year-old's dreams of soldiering glory. I knew it wasn't a glorious job by the time I signed my contract, and I'd told my father at the time that I'd outgrown those notions. Had I made it clear I'd grown into adult ideas, a better understanding of what it meant to stand for Jeska?

The Southerners thought they were using the shamans, but it was the other way around. How many kings lived and died while the brotherhood schemed to undermine the matriarchy, to rebuild our nation in the image of their allies? I took myself out of the running at the worst possible moment: Yutek had made it clear I'd succeed him, my reputation was solid—so the Council of Elders would approve my candidacy—and Orkast had died. Perfect timing to bring me into the fold, make me a shaman ready to become king—a commander in chief ready to first, prove his value by defeating the enemy, and then … to defy the matriarchy, reduce the Council of Elders to a committee of powerless old women.

The would-be patriarchs would have had to wait another generation or longer to make their power grab. So they turned to their backup. In retrospect, they'd been kind and generous to my brother all those years, from when we were children. They must have continued to groom him while he and I grew into our own careers … and especially when we spiraled apart. Tymon would serve as a puppet king, but they still needed to get rid of me. They could hope for my death in the war … but Lakeside was primed for the rumor mill. Why not push the elders to do the job of removing me, let them set themselves up for disaster? So long as Fennic's machinations ensured the elders installed the shamans' selected king, the conspirators would achieve their goal.

They'd gambled and lost. The matriarchy was secure.

They'd try again, wouldn't they?

Plain as night, I could see the shamans laying fresh groundwork. With the new weapons I'd unleashed, the next foray from the south might go differently. The cycle had to be stopped.

I let my mind roam around that idea, while I got myself to my feet and stood with my arm around my wife. We watched the distant clouds floating over the southern mountains of the Wall. Those peaks weren't quite as high as the ones up by Koresh, but I figured they'd be almost as impressive, once you got up into those ridges and valleys.

I listened hard, for that voice in my head, the one that always said, *No, Corren*, and *Stop, now*.

The wind shushed over the stones and made the branches in the oaks creak against each other. There were no voices, unless you count Heyliannin's breath catching in her throat.

"I've got something I need to do," I told her. "Let's go down. Have you had enough time? Would you rather stay?"

"No. It's all right. I almost understand. And I have work waiting, as well." She pulled free, probably so she could get her back to me and cry some more, and led the way down the hill.

42

OUR BELONGINGS WERE STACKED in crates and trunks lining the hallway outside the king's apartment. Who knew we had so much stuff? I flipped lids until I found my own things—an old uniform that didn't seem too worn-out, my sword, my favorite knife. There wasn't anybody guarding the door, so I stepped into the apartment to change clothes. It felt as though Yutek had died again, the emptiness in that room echoing the emptiness in my chest. Heyliannin had packed well: Tymon wouldn't have cared about our foster-father's books, his favorite pens, the collection of wood-carvings he'd polish while he was thinking through a problem. So those things had become mine. And this place had become nobody's.

After today, they won't want me back.

I ducked into the hall and rummaged through papers until I found Calestinise's incomplete fosterage contract. I signed it, backdated it, and left it on the desk, weighted down by an ink jar.

As I headed down the stairs and out to the bright day, my vision became clouded, like when I was younger and emotions would overtake me. I listened for the voice that would pull me out of those moments, but nothing came, so instead I made myself look straight into the face of each person I passed. I gave them my best fake smiles and said the names I remembered, which weren't many but enough to get me out of the building without a mistake.

Because Heyliannin couldn't bear it, I needed to go to the hospital, tell them to release the body. Why we took him to our ordinary human doctors, I can't say. Desperation?

Dramin met me at the door and blocked me from entering.

"I'm here to sign the release," I told him, but he didn't move out of my way.

"Arrangements are in progress, Corren," he said. "You don't need to be here. I'll bring you the paperwork."

"Step aside," I ordered. "I have other business as well." His eyes tightened, but he shifted to give me room, and made to follow me. I told him to stay back. This wasn't any of his business.

I needed to see my brother one last time. He lay alone in a narrow room at the end of a windowless corridor. Someone had smoothed out the folds in the ceremonial robe and laid it over him. I didn't touch his body, didn't put my hand to his forehead or press his fingers between mine. I'd already done those things. I needed to listen, to be sure he wouldn't tell me to stop, not this time.

I spent barely five minutes in that cool, dark corner room, listening to the silence. The king's signet still gleamed on Tymon's finger. He wouldn't need it up the hill, so I took the ring back from him.

"All right, then, Tymon," I whispered. "I'll take care of them."

On the way out, I stopped at the registrar's desk and signed the papers she gave me, without reading anything. I passed Dramin at the door but didn't speak to him.

It's a long way from the hospital to the front gate, and it's a good thing I knew my way without looking, because my vision kept getting worse. Whatever was right in front of me, that was plain, clear, something I could focus on. Everything else tunneled away to a fog the same ash grey of a Southern uniform.

They caught me at the gate, Kul's bulk looming into my clear frame of sight.

"Whatcha up to, Boss?" he said.

I looked down at my hand, to be sure I hadn't pulled a knife on him. "Got business in town." My voice sounded as if it came from somewhere outside my body, echoing hollow in my skull.

"Oh, look," he said. "And here's Radeo now, with his young friend Errem."

I wasn't so far gone that I didn't know what they were doing. "Gotta go." I started walking, but something stopped me. I checked my hands again, peered at the band of thick fingers encircling my arm, then looked at Kul. "Let go."

"In a minute, Boss. Dramin had to run get his gear."

Radeo's steady footsteps sounded plain behind me. "Hey, Cousin," he said. "You think you can wrestle with Kul, now?"

I didn't want his jokes, not then. "Of course not. Tell him to let me go."

"Na, don't think so. What's the hurry?"

I couldn't see Errem through the fog in my vision. What would he be thinking? He hadn't seen me this way. Had he? I couldn't recall much from our training days. He knew enough to not say anything, so maybe he did remember.

"Ah, there we go." The grip on my arm vanished, but now there was something new blocking my path.

"Get out of the way, Dramin." A ringing buzz filled my ears with each sound I made.

"First, tell us what this is about." He bent down, got his face where I could see it plain, blinked at me with his doctoring eyes. "Can you do that, Corren?"

I had to move while the fury was working. If I stopped I'd never get this done, what had to be done. I dredged up words from somewhere, forced them out. "Maybe. If we go now, I'll try to tell you."

"Where's Heyliannin?"

"Who?" Names again. Dramin knew my trouble with names. My chest burned with the need to move, the need to make him get out of my way. I checked my hands, and they were empty, but crunched into tight fists.

Dramin ignored my twitching. "Your wife. Where is she?"

What kind of a question was that? Did he think I didn't know where my wife was? "She's at Runners' House. Collecting his things." Tymon tended to save mementos from his travels.

"Let's head out. Where to?"

"Shamans' House."

"Ah. Shall we?" Dramin took up position in front, and Radeo and Errem flanked me, with Kul at the rear, like they were guarding me. In that formation, they could all hear what I said.

I didn't have much energy to spare for talking, but bit by bit, with their help, I gave them the outline. How the shamans had manipulated everything, for years, for decades, to take over the government entirely. If the Southerners had won, likely they'd have left their partners—the shamans—to manage things, but with their style of authority. What could the matriarchy do about it, then? Fight off the military with sharp words and lectures on stewardship? If the Southerners lost, then, again, the shamans would have control, through Tymon.

All because I'd refused the mantle.

"It's not your fault, Cousin," Radeo said.

"No, it's not. I'm not saying that. It's their fault, and nobody's going to make them pay. Nobody's going to stop them from doing it again."

"Nobody but you, sir?" That was Errem.

"Your jacket's in the laundry," I told him. "It's clean. Left it dripping this morning."

"Er, thank you, sir."

That stopped the questions. I expect they were giving each other signals. I kept my eyes focused on Dramin's back, the streets and charred buildings flowing by like an ash-soaked river.

That the city burned didn't mean everything was destroyed. The Runners' House had been spared, though the roof took damage. The Shamans' House stood untouched in a block that was mostly downed timbers and drifting ash. I imagined Southern soldiers beating back the fire, but it could have been the building's position on the hillside. When we got within about ten feet of the entry, I stopped.

"Kul."

"Yessir?"

"How about you grab my arm again?" I knew it would sound weird, but my control was slipping. The pressure of his hand around my arm pulled my mind back. I recalled that afternoon with Harad, on the way to Frogtown, planning an attack on the

Shamans' House there, working through the details. Harad talked me out of it that time. But here as well, there'd be noncombatants in the building, as we saw in Racac's stronghold.

"Radeo, Errem. Do one thing for me. Go in there, get the civilians out. Any citizens who aren't shamans. Prentices, too, if there are any. But hold those, they'll need to be vetted. Like Racac's apprentices."

I couldn't see his nod, but I could hear the snap in his voice. "Yes, of course. I've an idea. Kul, if you three could step aside, out of line of sight from the door."

Errem and Radeo conferred while Kul more or less dragged me aside. He's a smart guy, Kul. It was my knife arm he'd immobilized.

Once the door opened, Radeo's voice rang out. "Urgent demand from the elders, to interview any apprentices here."

A mumble I couldn't parse answered him.

Errem provided the counterpoint. "Not to worry, sir, but there's been an allegation of licensing issues. I'm sure it'll be cleared up by evening. Sorry for the inconvenience. But, yes. This is an *immediate* request from the Council of Elders."

"Demand," Radeo barked. "Mandatory compliance."

Again, Errem softened it. "By your favor, sir."

The door creaked as it opened wide, and they followed the doorkeeper into the building.

"I could have done that," Dramin muttered.

"Ya," Kul said. "But you'd get recognized, same as me."

"We really doing this?"

"You do any fighting recently, Dramin? Heard you'd been spending time chatting up the elders and being pushed around by doctors."

I let them trade barbs over my head. I needed to marshal the shadows that gathered in me, clouding my vision but strengthening my resolve. I wouldn't release the rage until the right time.

I don't know how long it took, except that I had moved on to trying to peel Kul's fingers off my upper arm. Not much of a contest, there, but it kept my hand off my blade. When the pair of them emerged, herding a cluster of short-haired acolytes and a cranky-looking citizen, Kul let go. As I strode past Errem, he gave me a look I couldn't interpret, so I left it at saluting him.

Kul and Dramin were right behind me. I couldn't think of a way to keep them out of it, so I put my back to the door and prepared a speech. Kul had his ready face on, his body relaxed, prepared. Dramin kept opening his mouth and shutting it again, trying to come up with something to say.

Words wouldn't stop them, but a plan might protect them. "This is my job, not yours." Kul rolled his shoulders and started to speak. I forged ahead. "Keep me alive long enough to finish."

"Sure, Boss," Kul said. No hesitation, as if I'd asked him to pass the cider.

Dramin took a moment, scratched his nose, and went one better than Kul. "I'll not promise to stop there, Corren."

It was enough.

The doorkeeper came out irritated, assuming Radeo was back to annoy him. I shoved the door in his face, sent him tumbling to the floor. Out of the edge of my tunnel vision, I saw Kul put out a hand, help him to his feet.

"Ya might take a walk, if yer as clever as ya think." The man moved so fast, I didn't hear his footsteps in flight.

At the first turn, we encountered two shamans leaning against a wall, laughing and arguing over some finer point of shamanistic skullduggery.

Unarmed men are sickeningly easy to kill. These didn't even have the sense to try to run. Taking the first one took a few seconds; a knife to the heart isn't as fast as people imagine. The second one got a sword-slash, much quicker, but extremely messy. Kul kept to his word, did no more than raise a blade to block the belated effort at escape. Dramin became professional, pronounced them dead, then asked, "Where to?"

"Master Shaman's office, first."

No one there. I pulled Dramin into the room. "There'll be evidence here. Find it. I don't want you guys to go down with me."

"You're joking. We're here to do research?"

"This place needs to burn." A fire sparked in my core, a fire made of shadows. I pressed my arm across my chest in a crude parody of a salute, and the blood on my knife glittered like liquid gemstones. "Don't argue with me, Dramin."

He angled his head to see past me, to Kul. Whatever the big man signaled, it satisfied our medic. "If that's what you need, Corren. But where will you be?"

"Meeting hall. It's too quiet. There must be a gathering." I wiped my knife on my sleeve and sheathed it. Shoved the sword back in its scabbard without bothering to clean it. This would be our last time.

We left Dramin pulling out bins, dumping papers.

The meeting hall at Jeskaryan, as I've said, wasn't nearly as grand as the one in Lakeside. More comfortable, though. I recalled a long, low, traditional table ringed by colorful cushions, where my true-father had taken me for celebrations and banquets. Fennic always made a fuss, begged me to show off my reading, acted as if I mattered. If I hadn't been so fixated on joining the Guard, I'd've been flattered; they might have sucked me in the way they did Tymon. As it was, even then the old man's attentions gave me a stomach-ache. He taught me well, to trust my gut.

I flung open the doors, just as I'd done down south, in search of justice for my son, and we marched in. This time, I had Kul at my back and a dark fire in my heart.

Good thing, too.

The shamans weren't alone.

"Them's mine," Kul growled, the moment his eyes fixed on the Southerners lazing along one side of the table. The shamans had laid out a grand feast much like those I remembered. I recognized the man from Lakeside. The others might have been among the leadership. I gave Kul the sign, and he advanced on them, drawing his blade as he moved. They leapt to their feet, fumbling for weapons they didn't have, resorting to table knives and over-dramatized hand-to-hand moves. There were three or four of them, but unarmed men against a bear is a short match.

I didn't watch, no more than the glimpses that came as I worked my own way through the room. A few of the shamans imitated their guests, holding up little knives against my sword. A quick downward slice to remove the hand, then an upward sweep to the most convenient fatal point. I never liked going for a man's throat—and a real soldier will usually at least wrap a leather around his neck—but it was quick. Supposedly relatively painless, but I think that's a myth borne of the fact a man with his throat cut doesn't scream. With the knife-holders, that was the simplest route.

They left a lot of blood on the table.

The ones that tried to run, I'd snag the mantle to stop their flight, then slice their hamstrings, put them on the floor. With the leisure to aim properly, I could get a thrust past the ribs without damaging my blade.

I kept my eye on Fennic. At first, he tried to dodge past Kul, but my man wasn't having that. He shifted weight to one foot, and lashed out a kick that sent the Master Shaman to the wall. The traitor dragged himself to his feet and hobbled in the other direction, but the table blocked his path to the big door, and I blocked his path to the little door, the one to the kitchen where that banquet had come from. I hoped Errem and Radeo had thought to warn off the servants.

Then again, servants have smarts. They'd have cleared out when the screaming started.

To get to Fennic, I had to dispatch the guy with the white stripes in his hair, the one who did the dull speech that began Tymon's death ceremony. That one dodged and jumped with an agility you wouldn't expect from an oldster. His creature must have done something to keep him healthy. Having seen my trick with the mantle, he kept his face towards me and jigged one direction, then another, trying to catch me off guard. Finally, he jumped onto the table, nearly out of my reach. As he turned to run, he put one foot into the puddle of a colleague's blood and went down on his back. Soon enough, his blood mingled with his brother shaman's. I'd had to reach over the table, so it was a rough stroke; he'd take longer to pump red onto the banquet. Maybe as long as he'd taken to spout nothings before his master killed my brother.

A shadow brushed behind me. Fennic.

I whirled and reached for the mantle, catching the edge of the thing, in the same move I'd made when I grabbed Asdyel and tried to take it from Heyliannin, on that blazing-white rock by the shocking blue lake up on the Wall.

Easily as a snake shedding its skin, Fennic released the mantle, and he ran for the kitchen door like a boy aiming to steal a pan of fritters.

I was too eager to get rid of the shaman who moved to block my pursuit. Maybe his feeble bravery excited my battle nerves, but I got my sword lodged in his ribs. He flailed at my leg as I planted a foot on his chest for leverage to wrest the blade free. The withdrawal killed him outright, so that had to be the reward for his courage.

"Go!" Kul called. "I'll settle the laggards!"

There weren't many left by then, but he was right, I needed Fennic most.

The kitchen was empty. The door to the hallway stood open. I took two long strides in that direction, then stopped. The kitchen *seemed* empty. I listened. The noises from the next room were enough to cover the panicked breathing of a man hiding in a cupboard. But did I have time to search everywhere? Then I lifted my eyes to the door that lay flat against the wall, the one beside the washing-up sink. Along the edge of the panel: a band of grey, the shadow of an edge that didn't lie flat.

Did he think he could fit down the sluice? I'd tried it once, as a kid. It was tight, especially for a boy cradling a hot pan of food for his brother. But no, an adult wouldn't escape that way.

I stomped to the hallway door, slammed it shut, then crept silently back across the room. With two fingers, I drew open the plain white sluice panel and jumped to avoid the kitchen knife that Fennic stabbed out with. The tip of it marked a fresh scar for my knife arm, but once he'd extended fully, it took no effort to drive my sword straight under his puny blade. He didn't have time to cry out a challenge, a complaint, a last curse. As if I'd fear a curse from a faker who'd spent my father's life, and my brother's, and mine as well, in a burnt offering to his greed, his treason.

Kul waited in the meeting hall, his arms loaded with mantles, like a coat-keeper at the entry to a winter party. None of the creatures seemed interested in *connecting* with him. Or dared— Heyliannin said they were clever. Together, we walked through the maze of the House, pounding doors, chasing out a few servants hiding in corners. No more shamans.

I found a broom and carried it back to the kitchen, where a banked fire warmed the far corner. The broom made a decent torch. The building contained plenty of objects easy to set alight. Furniture. Clothing. Papers. I wished I'd brought lightning powder. It would have gone quicker. A few additional dead shamans turned up in the front hallway, and I recognized Dramin's surgical style as I collected the mantles.

Dramin waited for us in the street, a pair of overloaded boxes leaning against his boot. He stood at ease, his arms folded, and stared at the roof of the House, where flames from the fires at the back had begun to find their way to freedom.

"Hey!"

I dropped the mantles I carried and raised my sword as I spun to face the challenger.

Heyliannin jumped backwards, jostling the bundle in her arms. A few small items clattered to the stones, and a sheet of parchment fluttered after them.

"What's going on?" she cried.

I lowered my arm. "Nothing." Blood ran down my blade, splashed on the pavement. Droplets skittered across the stones, spattered onto the paper she'd dropped, adding color and a sense of life to Tymon's map, the one Orkast gave him, that led to the thin patch he'd found.

"It's not nothing. Why are you here? What are you doing?" My wife threw her bundle to the ground and stepped over the map. She was so close, my head filled with the green, woodsy scent of the stuff she used in her hair, that reminded me always of the forests above Koresh, where we'd met.

The burning shadows still floated through my vision, clouded her face.

I reached for an answer, found the reason, the only one I ever had.

"I'm doing the right thing."

43

LISTEN.

I've given this a lot of thought, all these nights, staring at the cold sky.

Heyliannin taught me that the worlds the thin patches lead to aren't far away. They aren't distant worlds like the wandering lamps that roam across the sky beneath the stars, betraying their closeness to us. She described them as bubbles that sometimes touch one another, enough to open a passage between them. All the ways our world could be are out there, and many of those ways are stranger than anything you can imagine. Stranger than snake-men. Stranger than her Asdyel. Not much stranger, I'd warrant, but could be I'm wrong.

Some of those bubble worlds aren't that much different from ours; a change pinched them off, spawned a world where the ripples of that change spread wide. I wonder if worlds ever merge together like raindrops.

In her world, it seems they're figuring out how to find thin patches, without the help of mantles. In the snake-man world, they build engines to make what they call transfer points. We're a long way from that, here. I've picked up bits and pieces, listening to your people, while I've waited here. But I can't spend all my time up near the thin patch. Summers, fine. But I've got to earn my keep, one way and another, though Kul and Dramin put aside a little for me now and again, what they can spare.

I look out at the stars in these short summer nights, and watch the flying worlds above, and wonder about the bubble worlds that neighbor us. I've thought long and hard, and I know why it all happened, what made us the way we were.

It was Tymon. It was always Tymon.

I never recognized it, never understood, but I know it now, for certain.

·　　·　　·

I remember every moment of that first day, the day Tymon set my life's course.

The man from up north, the one who'd bought my father's shop, cold stock and tools and the house furnishings besides, had a deep, rumbling voice. The two men clasped arms and then embraced like brothers, before the northerner took the ring of keys from my father's hand and rubbed his big rough palm on my head.

"For luck," he said.

That made my father laugh, but a little sadly, it seems to me, now. He smoothed out my hair again and took me by the hand.

The dust rose up around our feet and glittered in the early-morning sunshine, as if the streets of Jeskaryan were filled with gleaming flecks of gold. I kicked the ground to send more dust flying. Orkast pulled at my hand and told me, "Easy, now, easy there. Don't be dirtying up your clothes, Corren."

I didn't want to stop. I didn't like the big stranger touching my head. I didn't like leaving my house, my room, my bed. The sparkling dust, though, I wanted that. I wanted to fill the world with shining glimmers.

"Here, now," Orkast said. He caught me under the arms and lifted me up, high into the dust cloud I'd made, and I swept my hands through it. With one quick motion, he settled me on his shoulders, where I could see over everybody's heads. We went that way up and up, along the twisting, turning street of the markets, right to the fortress gate. I kept one hand in Orkast's thick black hair, in case I needed something to hold onto, but he strode along, even-paced, never jostling me. I felt like a giant bear, or a condor in flight, or a king.

He took us to a long, low building made of brown clay bricks, with a heavy thatched roof and no windows. He stopped and rapped on the doorpost.

"Are we there?" I asked him.

"Ya," he told me. "Best get you down." He put up his hands to my arms and lifted me down. I kicked at the ground, but it was clean-swept stone, and not a speck of dust rose up.

The door opened, and a woman came out. She was narrow, tight-strung, a tall thin tree standing before the mountain that was Orkast.

"Is this the boy?" she asked him.

"Yes, ma'am," he said, all formal, like when a swordsman came to the shop to place an order.

She crouched down and looked me over. She had cold, hard eyes that reminded me in no way whatever of my mother. Suddenly, she smiled, and the ice in her eyes melted away. "What's your name, boy?" she asked me. Her voice sparkled like the dust in the marketplace.

"Corren, son of Orkast," I told her, putting pride into my voice, the pride of an armorer's son.

"Is that so?" she said.

"Yes, ma'am." I knew how to talk right, to respect the women who run our world. My father had taught me that.

She stood then, and her pretty eyes left mine. Behind her, peering out from the door, was a boy with big, round eyes and tight-braided hair. The woman said something to my father, something about money, and turned. The boy vanished as if he'd never been there.

My father crouched down beside me, and his thick arms went around me. "You be good, Corren," he told me. "Do the right things, my boy."

I said the words, "Yes, Papa," but I had no idea what I was saying. I had no way to understand what was happening.

I made that promise not knowing I'd spend my life keeping it.

She came back out with a bag on her palm, the kind of bag that rich people carry money in. My father took it, and she took my hand and led me into the house. I was so confused, I didn't even turn around to watch my father leave me.

The sparkly-voiced woman kept talking and talking, saying meaningless words—dormitory, discipline, education—while she walked me down a long aisle between two rows of narrow beds, each with an angry-faced boy standing beside it, all of them older than me, one of them nearly as small. As we passed by, she named the boys: Dawat, Fentin, Talvin, Gorton, and … She seemed to have run out of names.

"Find him," she ordered them, like dogs set to chase down a rat.

They leapt into action, moments later dragging the round-eyed boy out from under the bed at the far end, the one with nothing but a folded blanket on it. They hauled him by his wrists and ankles, and it must have hurt, but the boy kept silent. They dropped him at her feet and scurried back to their posts.

"Tymon," she said, pointing to the bed opposite.

He walked to his assigned place, limping a little.

She gave me a push on my back. "Corren, the last is yours."

I shuffled over to that cot, the one with the folded blanket. Was I supposed to go to bed? It was still morning.

"Boys," she said to them all. "Make your new foster-brother feel at home."

She left. The other boys watched, unmoving, until the door had swung tight closed. They waited a minute more, while her footsteps clacked along beyond the wall. I put my hand down on the thin blanket. It was the softest thing I'd ever touched.

"Ssst!" The warning hiss came from the battered boy, Tymon. I turned to face the others just in time.

I'm not sure where they'd gotten those boys. Gorton son of Gorton, whose unimaginative true-father turned out to be a money-grubbing traitor, would have been an upper-class reject, an extra son in a family that didn't need laborers. He could hardly hit anything with his fists. Gorton enjoyed kicking, so he'd wait until an opponent was down.

He never kicked me. Not that day. Not any day after.

One thing's for sure, none of them had ever picked a fight with a smith's son. I'd been carrying hammers since I could walk. My mother'd been sick for a long time, and if I wanted something to eat when my father was working, I had to steal it off a market cart and fight the dogs for it. I knew how to move fast, how to dodge, and I had no sense of my own strength. I'd learn to pull my punches one day, to reserve my fury for when it was most needed, but that day I hit them with everything I had, all my anger, all my despair, all my grief.

It ended with Tymon's hand on my arm, his saying, "You can stop now, Corren."

I was straddling Dawat, the biggest of them, and there was a smear in the blood on his face from the last time I'd hit him. I'm not sure how many times I punched him that first day, but there'd be plenty more in the days to come. Tymon shouldn't have stopped me.

Afterwards, I sat on the edge of that bed, in the place I'd been given, and tried not to drip Dawat's blood on the beautiful, soft blanket. I might have been crying. I don't remember. I was thinking about that door over there, how I might get it open. I could run then, I could run home, to … to … the big stranger with the rough hands. So, no, I'd run to my father, wherever he'd gone. I'd run and run until I found him. I'd run like a runner does, never getting tired, never stopping.

I was about to go and try that door when Tymon came and sat beside me, his body pressed close to mine from hip to shoulder. It was a kind of comfort I'd forgotten how to remember. His long, thin arm settled across my shoulders. "I'm glad you've come, Corren. We're brothers, now," he said. "Don't cry. Everything will be all right, now that we're together."

44

I DON'T KNOW how long we stood there, watching the Shamans' House burn.

Magaran sent a half-dozen men back with Errem and Radeo, a short troop, to pull us away from the conflagration. Heyliannin gathered up the things she'd dropped, Tymon's mementos. As she rolled up the bloodstained map, the thick paper made noises like wind and thunder, and flames reflected in her eyes. Intent on watching Fennic's stronghold descend to ash and charred timbers, I stood where she left me. Dramin loaded papers into the arms of two of the troopers and hefted the rest of his hard-gathered evidence. Kul shared out the mantles we'd gathered, shoving three of the furry beasts into my arms.

"What're ya plannin' on doin' with these, Boss?" he asked, as if talk of the future might deflect me from the present.

"Set them free," I told him, which hardly answered the question, not to anyone outside the secret of the mantles.

Heyliannin caught the exchange. "Yes. Thank you for saving them."

I lifted my eyes from the flames, to follow the billows of smoke rising to the cold stars. "Asdyel will need to tell us which are deserving."

Errem's hand on my shoulder turned me away. "Time to get going, sir. Magaran's waiting in the command center."

People in the street let us pass without comment as we made our way back up the hill. We might have been any family fleeing a fire, clutching the few possessions we'd saved.

•　　•　　•

The Council of Elders declared a tribunal to address my crimes, to take place within the month. There were two findings open to them: that I'd committed criminal murder or that I'd overstepped my duties. I'd hadn't done either of those things, but it wouldn't do for the leaders of our society to conclude that the massacre of a significant fraction of a major House could be justified. I'd either see an end to my life or live out my days resenting that my actions were found to be wrong. I wasn't sure which would be worse.

Heyliannin found the whole business unnerving. Not that the process dragged—apparently, in her world, such a case might take years, even decades, to resolve. Here, however, she was expected to take part. Not only had she been at the Shamans' House, afterwards, but she'd witnessed the shamans opening the gates to the enemy. It troubled her, to think something she said, or the way she said it, might tilt the balance the wrong way.

That I was let alone, free to do what I liked while the matriarchy rolled its stone wheels of justice—that confounded her.

She lit into me one morning, after breakfast, before I'd done mopping up the crumbs I'd scattered on the table. "Why aren't you locked up somewhere?" You'd have thought she wanted rid of me more than Maledestine did.

I folded up the cloth I was using. What was she worried about, now? "It's not like I'm going to go out and murder anyone else."

She slapped out at me, knocking the rag from my hand. Crumbs flew through the air. "Don't say that! Don't say you murdered people." Her voice trembled like ripples in a stream.

I debated whether it was really my job to clean up the mess. "That's the charge, Heyliannin. We can't ignore it. That's why Dramin got that evidence for the elders to study. They need to see that the shamans were behind it all—and were ready to start again. I had to act." I didn't tell her that my bosses would still think I'd overstepped.

She didn't seem to have anything to say, so I stopped lecturing. *When no one's talking*, she'd told me, *look at people and see if you can figure out what they're thinking.* This time, it wasn't too big a challenge. Her face was all scrunched up and her eyes were bubbling tears. She knew, by now, the penalty for murder.

What was I supposed to say? I wanted to say it would be all right, but how could I know that? I held out my arms, she stepped between them, and then we didn't have to say anything for a while.

·　　·　　·

Tymon ended his days as King of Jeska, so his funeral couldn't be what I wanted, a private gathering of family and close friends. There's not much ceremony to a royal funeral, but there are forms to be followed.

The forms don't include inviting criminals.

I clambered to the roof of the command center and sat alone in the thatch, my eyes on the king's hill. The procession wove up from the eastern wall, the sun catching the fluttering ribbons fixed to the ceremonial spears carried by the honor guard. Up close, you'd be able to read the words flowing alongside the shafts, messages painstakingly transcribed there, final thoughts from citizens, officials, friends, relatives. There were so many ribbons—undoubtedly, every one of the husbands, wives, and children of Runners' House had sent one.

I'd enlisted one of my wartime scribes—the kid who'd performed the old yarn about the foolish hunter looking for the mother bear—to get my message included, though I wrote it out myself.

The boy had no sense of privacy and read every word of it. "Are you sure that's what you want to send, sir?" He'd warned me that if he was caught, his father, the senior scribe, would be forced to exclude my ribbon. If anyone read it, they'd know it was me.

"I'd say a lot more, if there was room," I told him. "Please. Do your best to make it happen. Think of your brother. What would you do if they wouldn't let you say goodbye?" Though my eyes prickled, I didn't turn away.

His eyes went wide, then narrow, and he frowned at me as if I'd cut him. He was right. Kids shouldn't need to think of such things. He coiled the ribbon tightly, so the words were partly hidden by the curve of the fabric. "It's fine, sir. It'll be there. Don't worry."

From below, I couldn't see which of those ribbons was mine. I had to trust the kid's word, that it was there.

No, I'm not telling you what I wrote.

•　　　•　　　•

About a week after Tymon's funeral, an unseasonable storm swept in, interfering with travel, so the elders deferred the tribunal for a few more weeks.

The delays gave us more time to work out the problem of the mantles. We had nearly thirty of them. Before, I'd spread them out in the council chamber, but the elders weren't going to put up with that; they were using the space for their own meetings, wrangling over the investigation, the accusations, everything conflated with the old rumors. Nothing quite matches having the people deciding your fate arguing about it right above your bedchamber.

"The mantles need sunlight," my wife told me. "And a safe place at night. And companionship. They're used to people; they may *need* human companionship."

I shook my head. "Isn't that how it all got started? That's what made the shamans think themselves worthy of taking control."

At the time, we were walking the fortress, trying to identify a space where she could harbor the mantles. There'd be more, soon. I'd convinced Magaran to send for the rest of the shamans in Lakeside, but he put out word that *all* shamans were to report to the Council of Elders. I hoped Heyliannin and Asdyel could convince the things to abandon their masters.

A few more shamans might have to be killed, but it wouldn't be me doing it.

Heyliannin interrupted that train of thought, before it went too far. "All I'm asking for is a secure refuge, until I can repatriate them."

"And how do you plan to do that?" She sounded too confident. All this time they'd been in Jeska, popping through thin patches with shamans, and hadn't found a way for themselves.

"I learned a lot about the way thin patches work, from talking to the snake-men. I'll find their home, and take them there." She ignored my skeptical frown. "In the meantime, we need people to take care of them. Don't say no right away, but—I suggest we bring in a few of those apprentices. The ones Radeo's cleared."

By then, we'd reached the gardens, where the kitchen staff mostly cultivated fragile vegetables that didn't travel well. I needed time to think through the idea of hiring ex-apprentices. "How about we build a sort of barn here? They can hide when the gardeners are around."

She clapped her hands. "Yes! We'll build a green house."
"Why?"

Her enthusiasm faded. "Glass. We'd need a lot of glass." She stared up at the clouds, as if the precious stuff that glazed windows formed itself naturally, in the sky. "Is a green house technology?"

I sighed. "You can make your mantles' house whatever color you want. What's special about green?"

She explained about making a box out of windows to keep a space sheltered through the winter but still bright, for plants to grow. Or for mantles to feed on the sun.

I think that piece of technology is going to make a bigger difference in the world than lightning powder, in the long run. So much for her priyyam drectiff.

45

SMEARED IN HEAVY, WET SOIL, I was digging a trench for the foundation of Heyliannin's greenhouse, when someone tapped my shoulder.

A vaguely-familiar toff stood over me, his fine boots polished to a glow that didn't make sense for the rainy season. He bowed at me, the ditch-digger. "Sir," he said. "I'm pleased to say that our mother has agreed to represent you in the tribunal."

"Who?" I squinted at him. Was this one of the failed fosters?

"Tallivansey, keeper of the northeast quarter." As for any land in Jeska, the earth below Jeskaryan is managed and advocated for by the family entrusted to do so. Northeast was a complex sector, bearing the weight of workshops—with the risk of harm to the land below—markets, and homes. So this shiny guy's mother would be one of the preeminent matriarchs of the city.

"You said, 'our mother.' My mother is long dead, and Yutek was a widower when he adopted me."

His lips pursed in that brand of insult that toffs seem to specialize in. "My brother's and mine." He lifted an eyebrow in a gesture I suddenly recognized.

"You're Arnim's brother." One of Yutek-en's friends. The boys who'd taken part when the king's son tortured Tymon.

He pressed a hand to his chest and bowed again. Obsequious snob. He probably couldn't see my skin flushing, what with all the mud.

"I thought I kicked you out," I told him.

Again the bow. "Indeed. Justly so, though I say it myself." Another bow. I was getting tired of looking at the top of his head.

"Cut that out. What does Tallivansey want?" *Get to the point.*

"My mother is much taken by your case, sir. She elevated me from a clerkship under her least-favored assistant, to convey her offer." At least he'd been suffering. Not enough.

"What would that offer constitute?" Lawyers, like doctors, have an irritating habit of assuming everyone understands their arcane, secret-laden jobs.

I leaned on the shovel as he yammered about coordinated investigations, witness studies, and enhanced documentation. He seemed oddly sincere. He kept starting to bow again, stopping himself, then launching into another layer of proffered services. I raised my hand, and he stopped mid-sentence.

"Whose idea was this?"

"Sir?"

"Who suggested that a high-level matriarch might stand for me in this matter?" At my core, I had to admit a measure of relief. No one else had stepped forward. But why? That was still in question.

Again with the bowing. "A person who wishes to see the right prevail, sir."

I scooped up a shovelful of water, mud, and rocks and made as if to toss it at him. "Spill it, man. Was it you?"

His face went several shades darker, but he didn't dodge away. "I've a great deal to make up for, sir, from my misguided youth. Allow me this."

I shifted the shovel-load to the pile, away from my new advocate's son.

My dead enemy's friend.

My dead friend's brother.

"Fine, then. Tell your mother I accept." I looked him in the eyes. Still didn't recognize him. Some people do change, but it doesn't necessarily show. "Convey our gratitude, mine and my household's."

He bowed again, and backed away when I plunged my shovel back into the muck. "She says, sir, to keep in mind you're still king."

That got me to look up. "I am?"

"Yes, sir, as the duty hasn't been transferred, it remains where it lies. It's important to your defense, sir. Please remember it."

"I will. I will." I watched the sweat run down his face. "What's your name?"

He told me. I don't remember it.

$$\bullet \qquad \bullet \qquad \bullet$$

They delayed the tribunal so many times, I began to wonder if the elders had decided to keep me on and were fishing for a reason. Tallivansey huffed out what passed for a laugh with her and drew a hard line through something in her notes. She was a large, imposing woman with a broad face that didn't invite argument. She dressed plainly, as if disguising herself as one of her own sub-assistants, and wore none of the jewelry managers at her level affected. She said she didn't have time for frippery.

Time was her marker for everything.

"Big cases take time. On every side. And you're wasting ours. Repeat that back."

I cleared my throat and recited the latest batch of words she'd come up with that boiled down to: It's the king's job to identify and punish criminals. They were criminals, and they were planning new crimes. It had to be done. I'm the king, so I had to do it.

She had objections to my spending time training Calestinise. "It creates the impression you're not committed to your position as king."

I twirled the ring on my finger—that was one of her demands, that I wear it all the time, to remind everyone. How to explain this to her? "No, it doesn't. Or it shouldn't. It's always been that the king trains his fosters. You never know when a plague will roll through. Or an accident. Or—"

"That reminds me. You should keep your bodyguards."

There, I had the upper hand. "No. I've assigned the crew to the kids because they're more at hazard. Cal can swing a blade, but he's better at persuasion. And the other two … well, I've got them in under-guards, but they're lightweights. I can't risk something happening to any of them. As for me, I've got Kul and Dramin and Radeo. And Errem. Trust me, I'm guarded. Anybody making a try for me would know."

There had been attempts. Should I tell her about them?

She grunted and granted me a bob of her head. "Sometimes, Your Majesty, I forget that the story we're trying to tell is a true one. Very well, then, let's review how we'll work through the line of argument about the accounting irregularities raising suspicions. That's what puts a solid foundation on what followed."

It's because my advocate chose money as her opening salvo that Heyliannin came to be first to bring testimony in the formal proceedings. It took me back to those days down in Lakeside, when she scoured through those old records and screamed like a furious hawk if anyone so much as touched one of her papers. Everyone says accountants are boring.

They never saw my wife in action.

She stepped into the circle of judgment, clutching her sheaf of papers like a bundle of weapons. I suppose they were, to her. She knew who was who, so she mostly faced the council members, seated in relatively fancy chairs hauled up from the cellars. The rest of the circle was occupied by the senior matriarchs—with one chair left empty, given it should have been Tallivansey's. They each had a say (excepting my advocate), but the final judgment would fall to the Council of Elders. They aimed for the appearance of consensus, though when have you ever seen a collection of competitive people ever agree wholly on something?

It's all in the records, so I know you know how it went, but let me give you a little of it.

"I've had copies made for all of you," Heyliannin announced, walking the circle and handing each woman a sheaf of number-riddled paper. "The moment I opened the books in Lakeside, it was clear something was going on. Something being kept secret from the people of Lakeside, from the king in Jeska, and from you, my fellow matriarchs." (Tallivansey had schooled her hard on using that term for herself.)

She walked them through it line by line, and not in a slow, pedantic way. She bounced from one side of the circle to the other, stretching her arms to describe the size of a discrepancy, gesturing to the south when bringing up a name or a household that was part of the Lakeside cash shuffle. Velisennin's name came up more than once. She'd been summoned, but never showed. They say she took her household over the mountains. My guess is she moved south, when news of the defeat reached her. I wanted to see her called to account, but it helped our case that she'd fled.

By the time Heyliannin was done, there wasn't anybody in that circle who didn't believe there had been financial shenanigans going on.

But the money issue didn't seal the fate of the shamans, not on its own.

Maledestine stood up and banged her stick on the stone and said as much. Why that woman had it in for me from the start, I'll never know. Maybe she despised short men. I'm not ugly enough to make someone want to kill me for that.

They put Dramin in the circle next, to attest on his honor and his family's management rights that the documents presented about the inner workings of Shamans' House Jeskaryan were in fact taken directly from that House, by himself, with no changes afterwards and no planning beforehand.

Or, as Maledestine put it, "They could have been there because you put them there, Corren!"

I stood from the little table in the back and asked Tallivansey, "Now?"

She tapped my elbow with her pen. "Now. Remember your lines, *Your Majesty*." She'd schooled me harder than I worked with Calestinise, but, as she put it, she risked my life if she didn't.

I took my turn in the middle of those suspicious eyes. I told them how Fennic kept his records contained, how impossible it would be to slip a falsified document into those files. Then I had one of the clerks haul in the trunk filled with the incriminating documents.

"Let alone this *many* documents, respected Elders and Matriarchs." I ferreted out a handful and copied my wife's move, walking the circle and passing out samples. "You'll see they're written in many hands, but if you look closely, you'll see one hand dominates—Fennic's. I held up one sheet I'd kept hold of, an unrelated letter from Fennic to the Council of Elders, on a social event they were coordinating. "Elders, you've all seen Fennic's hand." I pulled a blank sheet from my pocket and rested it on the closed lid of the trunk. When I snapped my fingers, my favorite scribe dashed into the circle with ink and a pen for me.

He leaned close, whispered, "Good luck, sir."

I put the two sheets side by side and copied out Fennic's brief, unctuous message of goodwill and cooperation. Then I took the two papers and placed them in Maledestine's hands. "Samples of both, ma'am. You'll see they don't match, and that the one matches the proof documents. Also, you may notice, my handwriting isn't good enough to do forgery with."

"You could have hired a scribe for it," the elder growled at me.

"But then it would have been much better-done, wouldn't it? Look how lazy Fennic is with his lettering. None of my scribes would stoop to imitate that."

From outside the circle, the kid scribe called out, "That's right!" and Tallivansey shushed him.

"Also," I added. "You've heard from almost everyone who lives here that I was kind of busy at that time. What with the war. You know." Tallivansey wanted me to sound sure, but humble. It was a tough combination.

Maledestine folded the papers together and crushed them as she passed them off to Adestinian, who ordered me to move on to my next piece of testimony.

"You need to hear what the shamans were doing with that money, and who they were doing it with," I said. "But I can tell you one more thing, that my wife can attest to."

So I told them what Fennic said, on the ceremonial stage, while my brother lay dying beside us: that the shamans planned that day from at least my early childhood, to place a shaman in the kingship and rope the matriarchy into thinking that would be a good idea. I'd ruined his plan, but there was no one to stop him from trying again.

No one but me.

I gestured to Heyliannin to step back into the circle, but Adestinian stood from her chair. "No need to bring her in. I was there. I heard what Fennic said." She resumed her seat and smoothed out the folds in her dress. "I should have taken action on it."

Murmurs flowed around the circle until Adestinian called for silence. "Now, then, Corren. Your witnesses to calumny and treason."

One by one, my men stepped into the ring of eyes. Radeo told of his experience with the army of light camp, the collusion between the shamans and the Southerners. Kul spoke to the evil that flowed from that partnership—the deaths of Jeskan children, the masses of dead Jeskan soldiers, the destruction of our city. Then he yielded the floor to Calestinise.

Tallivansey had her toughest job in training my son on what to say and what not to say. *You're there to support Corren as justified in his actions, not to call out the matriarchy for failing to act*, she told him.

He began by verifying Radeo's testimony, then moved on to the Lakeside confrontation. "My dad said he'd clean out Shamans' House Lakeside, burn it to the ground. He was so angry. I wanted him to do it. I wanted to make them pay. But he listened to Harad. He took the wiser course. With all those army of light soldiers and the Southern officer there, we'd have all got ourselves killed, and then what? They'd have won the war.

"But he didn't lose track of what was going on. The whole time, he knew they were dangerous. Radeo told me—Dad advised you not to bring the shamans into the fortress, but you said they had to come in, like everyone else. Why didn't you listen to him? Think of the people who died because they opened the gates!" His eyes were getting red, his skin flushed, and he stopped himself, caught control.

He'd do all right, as king. That's the first time I knew it, for certain.

"But that doesn't matter now. What matters is, when he knew what had happened, and what would happen again—when he knew you wouldn't be able to order the destruction of a major guild—he did his job. The king recognized the crime, decided the penalty, and exacted it.

"It's no different than a tax rebellion or brigands on the border. It's the king's responsibility to enforce the law, and that's what he did."

The whole thing went on for hours, but you get the sense of it.

It was long after noon when they sent us out and called for food to be brought in. So they weren't going to decide quickly.

We couldn't wait in the king's apartment, so we wandered together down to the practice yard. Stevvin and Affram brought out their practice gear, and we had a bit of sparring. Calestinise surprised me; he'd had very little training, but he made up for it with smarts and a lot of pent-up energy. Kul bragged on him a lot, which made Heyliannin laugh.

It was good to hear her laugh. I drew her into the game, put a sword in her hand, a kids' practice blade, and let her mash her way around the yard for a while. Radeo disappeared, then returned with a gang of people from the kitchens, hauling trays and plates and cutlery.

I'd never thought of having a picnic in the practice yard. We were sweaty and tired, and the food tasted so good. Afterwards, we lazed around and talked about everything except mantles and shamans and money.

A runner came down to the yard around sunset.

"They're ready."

They made it too formal. Why not send a message: ya, you're dead, or na, you're exiled? I wished I had a bucket of cider to slosh down.

Heyliannin wanted to stand in the circle with me, but that's not how it's done. Traditionally, of course, it's because a positive verdict calls for an immediate execution. In modern times, no, but there's that undercurrent.

The Council of Elders stood, Adestinian holding a freshly-scribbled-on paper in one hand. "The matriarchs are excused," she ordered. There followed a scraping of chairs, and the rest of the circle evaporated, the women who'd helped them argue through to their verdict merging into the men and women standing at the back, watching, preparing to disperse the news throughout the city.

"Corren of Jeska," Adestinian announced. I saluted her, and her hand moved at her side as if she might have been tempted to salute back. "You stand accused of multiple murder, arson, exceeding the duties of a guardsman, and overstepping the rule of law."

"I understand." It was what I was supposed to say. Legal proceedings have a lot of nonsensical garbage.

"With the advisement of our peers, and subject to the investigations we have conducted in cooperation with the town representatives, the military leadership, and the shamans who have been willing to provide evidence, we have reached a full and complete verdict."

Full and complete? Isn't that saying the same thing twice? Like I said ...

"Firstly, we find valid the claim put forward that you remain king of Jeska. Under our founding agreements, the nation cannot be without a king, so your retirement became void the moment your successor expired."

Expired? My brother *died*. I guessed I might be crying and rubbed my sleeve over my face, just in case.

"Secondly, we find valid the conclusion that the shamans of Jeskaryan and Lakeside did conspire to make use of the military of a foreign country to destroy our social structure in order to take power in Jeska."

Well. This was looking promising. I wondered if Eldennian would help us get settled in Koresh. If that's where she was, now. She seemed to have cared about Heyliannin, in an older-sisterly way. I thought about Delia, and how long it had been since I'd seen my daughter, and maybe I started crying again.

"Further, we find that the king was obligated to ferret out the traitors who had performed these deeds, document their acts, and conduct proper punishments. As the penalty for treason is death, the actions taken were appropriate in context."

She took a breath and fanned her face with the paper. "As the disposition of both criminals and enemy combatants is the flame, and there was no need to preserve a structure with no legal inhabitants, and further that available combustible materials had already been largely exhausted in disposing of the invaders, we further find burning the House to have been an efficient and effective solution.

"Finally, we have a question for you, Corren of Jeska, which will determine our last finding."

My palms began to sweat. A question. "Ma'am?"

"Will you reconsider your retirement?"

I should have been prepared. Tallivansey had asked me the same question, more than once. I'd figured she was sounding out my attitude, determining whether I'd turn and fight to stay at the last minute. Was that not it? Had she been trying to give me a warning? She would have been in that circle of senior matriarchs, had she not been my representative. She'd have heard hints, remarks, in the course of her life outside my case.

For a moment, I could see it—living out my life as Yutek had done, running the country as had been done for generations. I'd have my kids close, my friends.

But not my wife. No doubt about it—Heyliannin was already making plans, studying that map every time she thought I wasn't looking. I didn't need to be king to gather with my few remaining friends, to remember those we'd lost.

Besides, the times were changing. We didn't need a king who'd make everything the same as before. The tax revolt, the connivance in Lakeside—those were signals we needed change. Not the kind of change the shamans wanted, but still—

Maledestine rapped her staff on the floor. The hollow boom swelled into the silent space. "Your Majesty," she said. "We're waiting." So even she was prepared to acknowledge me again?

I couldn't waver. "I've done what Yutek made me for. And that's over now. So, Elders, Matriarchs, respectfully, no, I won't reconsider. It's time for me to step down."

Adestinian frowned, and the paper in her hand rustled. She looked around her circle, received their nods and hand-signals. "Very well. Per the nation's charter, the kingship must be passed on to a duly recognized heir, whom we hereby identify and invest as Calestinise of Jeska."

"What! You can't just do that!" Calestinise was standing on a chair at the back of the room. He didn't look happy, but I figured he'd be happier when I told him he got to skip the ritual of getting his naked body inspected in public by these old ladies.

Maledestine, anyone could have predicted it, smacked her staff on the floor. "We can do anything we like, young man! Sit down and shut up! You're not king yet."

So that was it. They let me off. Entirely. They *sided* with me.

Tallivansey said, afterwards, "I knew they would."

46

THE MARCH TO KORESH felt like a walk through time. Heyliannin and I traveled with a troop of younger guardsmen, led by a lieutenant who'd served with the Harriers. They were standoffish, nervous around the almost-murderous ex-king, until we camped at the same spot my first troop and I had used. I told them the story about how I'd tried to give a speech and dumped my dinner in the fire by mistake. I didn't tell them about lying under the stars that night, arguing with Tymon and then listening to him snore.

The troop had a mission, and we were part of it, not free to be on our way until it was done.

The Lakeside Master Shaman, his henchmen, and the gate-openers—including two apprentices—had spent the past months under guard in the barracks of the guard station I'd established at Koresh so many years ago. Back then, I'd been worried about an invasion of snake-men, never imagining our true enemies skulked within our own borders. There remained those few mantles to be retrieved and sent to Heyliannin's mantle-farm. Through the winter, in twos and threes and sevens, shamans had trickled into

Jeskaryan to be relieved of their duties. Most yielded to persuasion. The remainder refused and went to the fire.

Heyliannin and I hadn't had to be there; Calestinise's men brought us the mantles afterwards, and my wife's cadre of rebel apprentices coddled the things back to health. These young men affected a new hairstyle to declare themselves, keeping the left side shaved while letting the right grow back. They look ridiculous, but you won't catch me saying so.

This time, I came to Koresh with an assignment from the king, and Heyliannin, too, had a job.

Back in the council chamber in Jeskaryan, Calestinise had leaned over me from his post in Yutek's chair. "I can't trust anyone else with this, Dad. It was Racac and his people who made the army of light. The revolt, the planning, yes, that was Fennic's crew, but what happened in Lakeside was Racac. I leave the apprentices for you and Mom to judge, but the seniors, no. I wish you'd taken care of them when they were here—"

"The elders wouldn't have stood for it, son, you know that. They were half of them ready to burn me at the time."

He rolled his eyes in that way he had. "Ya, ya, I know." Then his face went still, in the new way he'd taken on after the war. "You understand, this is an order. No one's going to come after you this time."

I straightened, gave him a salute. "Yes, sir."

When the guards admitted us to the barracks-turned-to-jayle, I had a flash of memory. That night in the Jeskaryan Shamans' House, Kul and I caught our targets in the middle of a meal. Here, the nine traitors sat around a long, low table. Two leapt to their feet, but Racac spread his arms as if we'd arrived at a banquet in his honor and said, "Welcome." His plate was already full, but he made a show of piling more food onto it, then shoving bread and fruit into his mouth.

At a gesture from me, two of the troopers rounded up the apprentices—one of them standing, the other making himself small at the far end of the table—and took them to Heyliannin. She put a hand on one shoulder of each man and lowered her head— she was talking with Asdyel, while keeping her eyes away from what was coming.

The lieutenant leaned towards me and murmured, "Sure you don't need our help, sir?"

I remembered Kul, lifting his blade to block an escape. "Keep the door, that's all." The room had no windows. That helped.

I slipped the borrowed sword from its scabbard and made a few quick passes. It'd do. The hiss of steel in the air made a smooth counterpoint to the slurping gobble of Racac's display. The rest of the shamans were silent, motionless.

My personal knife came to my hand without my needing to think about it. "By order of the king," I said. "You have been found guilty of treason, calumny, child-stealing, and murder." There was no need to state the penalty.

I began with the quiet ones, saved Racac for last so he could watch the last shreds of his empire fall. Most of them tried to run, despite the obvious lack of escape. I can't fault them for that; it's only natural. I tried to keep the blood flow to a minimum, what with my sensitive wife standing in the room. Knife-work is slow, but then one man had the stupidity to try that trick of fending me off with a table-knife, so that made a mess. Racac stopped his performance when the overspray showered his plate.

Heyliannin sobbed and pushed one of the apprentices away from her. "I'm sorry," she said to him, and to me: "Asdyel says this one's mind is poisoned."

I dropped him before he realized what was happening. That was fair. It hadn't been his fault. I hoped he was a secret Returner, that he'd get another chance. A sudden commotion behind me turned out to be Heyliannin collapsing. The remaining apprentice had tried to catch her, and they both ended on the floor.

Racac laughed and pushed himself up and away from the table. "When you've killed off all the *real* shamans, will you be handing over the rest of men's duties to the women? Will the king be a woman? All the soldiers, too? Will men be nothing but toe-lickers and tea-makers?"

His hands trembled, contradicting his bravado. The smear of plum juice on his face made it look as though he'd been trying to camouflage his skin, to blend in with the blood on the floor and the table.

I wanted to torture him, make him fall on his knees, cower, and beg. But what good would that do? Would it heal the minds of the children he'd cursed for life? Would it bring Tymon back? No, better to end it, to finish my career as I'd begun, following a just order from a rightful king. I gave him the same as Fennic got—a clean thrust to the heart. He went down quickly, and nobody had to listen to him ever again.

47

"I T WAS LIKE THAT, wasn't it, back in Jeskaryan." Heyliannin hadn't said anything all morning, and hadn't talked much since the executions.

"You couldn't help fainting. I'm sorry you had to be there."

We'd stopped partway on a long uphill trek along a steep ridgeline. We had a good view of Koresh, nestling between the slopes below. A streamer of smoke stretched northward, away from the town. So the troop had found a safe place for the fire.

"No," she said. "I meant, in the Shamans' House. Was it like it was yesterday? Like you were digging a ditch or washing windows."

I stared at her. Digging ditches? Then I realized what she was saying. "You were watching? How?" They were still cleaning up the blood when we left.

"I ... watched you, not them. I pretended it was a *moovee*." Which she'd informed me was a type of theater I would "never understand."

"But, why?" She was supposed to be vetting those apprentices. "You had a job there, too, Ta-ma."

She shrugged and the cape shifted on her shoulders. "Asdyel was talking to the other mantles. And I thought I should ... see you at ... work. It was—" Her voice caught on a word, and she took a drink, stalling. "I was far away from the action in Lakeside. And I didn't really see anything in the city, either." She shrugged. "I don't know what I expected, but that wasn't it."

"You were always the one reminding me what I was, Ta-ma." She'd given me that speech, the night before the battle, about not giving up.

It was even harder than usual to read her expression. She waved her hands in the air as if she was trying to catch words to use. "I thought I'd be scared. Or faint. But it was different, being on the outside. Listen—" It was funny hearing her say that, the thing I always say. "Remember when you used to play those games, interrogating people—"

"Like you."

"Yes. *That* was scary. It wasn't as though I thought you were going to ... hurt me. But—"

"That wouldn't have been practical, Ta-ma."

"Let me finish." I watched her eyes for a second, then turned a little away, and looked out over the valley, instead of staring at her while she was trying to talk. I could hear her breathing, though. I could almost hear her heartbeat. "When you guys questioned somebody, it was scary because no one could tell what you were thinking, what you *might* do. That's what scary is, not knowing what comes next.

"It was different yesterday. It was ... elegant. That's not the right word, I know. But you went around that room like a dancer, Corren, from one beat to the next. Even though everyone was moving, you walked through them like a woodcutter clearing a forest—"

I couldn't help it. "That's not how lumbering works."

She grunted. I could imagine her face getting pink. "I know. I'm painting a picture here, Corren, not building a house." She had the weirdest proverbs. "I thought there'd be anger in it, but you were only doing your job. Weren't you? A job I could never do."

She was close enough, I didn't need to look at her to slip my hand onto her shoulder, slide it up to the back of her neck, under her sweat-dampened hair. She was trembling. I thought back to the start of this conversation. "You asked about Shamans' House." Her neck tensed as her head tipped in a nod. "That was different, Ta-ma. It might have looked the same, but it wasn't. I used my anger, then. I had to. For Tymon." There was an ache in my chest, like an attack heart coming on. I pressed my free hand against my ribs, as if that could make the pain go away. "They killed him. If he hadn't died, they would have used him to kill Jeska."

I was losing track of my words. My voice felt strange. It seemed to descend from the top of my head, as if my own words were rain, not language. "If the shamans had succeeded, if they'd made Tymon their puppet king, I'd have had to kill him. It would have been my *job*."

I tried to breathe, but I couldn't do more than gasp. It was like I was choking to death, standing on a shady mountainside, watching the cloud-shadows flow over the land. Heyliannin moved in close, wrapped her smooth, strong arms around me, and rested her cheek on the hand I was holding to my chest. Her warmth eased through, and the pain faded, but I was still breathing strangely, in gulps and rasping exhalations.

"It's all right," she said. "You're allowed to cry for him, now, Corren."

"Ya?"

She lifted up her face, but she didn't try to kiss me. "Ya," she said, which she never did. "You can do that, now."

We couldn't stand wrapped around each other for long. We sat for a while, side-by-side on a long, grey-marbled boulder, until she decided I was done crying.

"I'm glad I watched yesterday, even though I fainted in the end."

She'd pronounced sentence on that apprentice; she probably thought it was her fault. "You couldn't help it."

"If Asdyel and I hadn't been there, though, you'd have had to kill the other guy, right?"

Would she take this the wrong way? Would it make her feel more at fault to understand it better? "We would have had to interrogate them, the regular way. The wrong one could have got off. Shamans are trained liars." Did she get it? That she—and her creature—had tried him, found him guilty. That his death was on him, not her. Not me.

"Well, that's over now." She resealed her waterskin and hung it back on her belt.

I hurried to copy her. Like Tymon, she wasn't one to wait once she started moving. "What do you mean?"

"Aren't any shamans." She started walking before I could say anything clever about her being the last shaman in Jeska. She hated being called a shaman. *I don't pretend to do magic*, she'd say.

Yet there we were, heading out to the middle of nowhere so she could jump through a thin patch.

•　　　•　　　•

We talked the whole rest of the way. More private talk, mostly. She went on about her home, her family, people she hoped to see, ones she thought might help with her project. She claimed she'd learned from the snake-men more than her own people knew about thin patches.

"And they're not *snake-men*," she said. "The ones I know are *Korlovians*."

Apparently, these Korlovs had proven that not all worlds touched all the other ones. They'd encountered mantles too, but things didn't go so well, because *connection* didn't work.

"So, I'm guessing that's how they got here. I figure they must have gone through that first gateway to Korlo and then from there to here."

"How? When?"

The confidence faded from her voice. "I didn't see all the records, so I don't know how. And if they'd come through up in the mountains here, what then?" She stopped, and dust puffed up around her boots. "Listen, I'm not sure about a lot of this. I wish the Korlovians hadn't bailed on this place. But I know enough, and I know people in my world who can help me get back there. Somehow."

More than that was bothering me. "I asked *when* that happened. Korlo."

"Oh. Sorry. About ten years ago." She adjusted the straps on her pack and started hiking again.

How was I going to tell her? *Tell it straight*, Errem whispered in my mind. "They can't have come that way. Mantles have been here much longer than ten years."

She stopped again, turned around. "What do you mean?"

"I first met Asdyel, heard him speak, thirty years ago, Ta-ma. They've been here longer than that. At least two generations. Maybe longer."

She frowned and her eyes crinkled down tight. I thought she might cry. She sucked in a long, ragged breath and blew it out slowly. "I promised Asdyel I'd get them home."

"Doesn't he know how they got here? I thought he'd show you the way, and you'd come back with help for the rest of them."

"No. He knows that somebody *sent* them here. And not from their home, from somewhere else. They don't think the way we do; I ... got an impression. It felt familiar, and I assumed it was the Korlovians. It made sense." She sniffed. "It'll be more complicated, but it's a network. We know it connects. I'll find a way through the maze."

"Can your people make thin patches, like the Korlovs do?"

"Well, maybe. I hope so. If I understood right, they detect microscopic thin patches and make them big, so there's more chances than you get with natural ones. It's not easy. Takes huge machinery, lots of energy." She waved her arms to indicate something monstrously large and made a growling sound. I remembered the roar of the snake-men's thin patch, the way it shook the air, made you think eagles were diving at you.

Imagining it made my head hurt. "You should have brought the Master Smith with you."

"You sure you don't want to come?" She'd never asked directly, only hinted, as if fishing for how I might respond. I figured that meant she didn't want me along. This time, she roved to, "You're really retired now, you can do whatever you want."

What did she expect me to say to that? "You need someone here, to run your errands, be sure the mantles are taken care of. And there's the boys, too." She could have ordered me to follow her, but after all that time, she still didn't realize her position as head of our household. I gave her a hint. "You can't be ordering *Calestinise* around, now."

She let the moment go by. "I wonder how I'll explain to my family that I married a prince, and I've got three kids now, and one of them is a king."

So she was already thinking of how it would be, returning home, making up stories to entertain her old friends, her parents. It wouldn't help to be there in person, her scarred, murderous, less-than-handsome prince. I was about to make a joke along those lines, when she called out, "There it is!"

The tattered shreds of my attempts to bind us closer fluttered away in the mountain wind.

She ran ahead, to an outpouring of gravel in a cleft leading up to the next windswept saddle. A half-day ago, we'd marched past the lake where me met, and now we'd climbed higher than any of my Six had explored that day. Maybe she was getting light-headed from the elevation. There was nothing to see but rocks, scraggly plants, and a trickle of water fed by one of those year-round snow fields hanging from the northeasterly flank of the mountain.

I trudged to her side. "Let's find a spot out of the wind, lower down, and set up camp. You need to eat." I dragged the map out and compared it to our position. "Look, we've gone off course. We're supposed to be well south of here, lower down, and nearer the lake. No wonder I can't catch my breath."

She snapped her fingers under my nose, to get my eyes off the map. "Corren, the thin patch is right here. Let's go." She took hold of my arm and walked forward several steps, towards the messy pile of rocks, then stopped so suddenly I nearly stepped on her foot. "Wait, you need to duck."

What was she playing at? "Why?" We stood in a treeless wasteland.

She tugged at my elbow. "Humor me. Lean down."

"Aha." I figured she wanted to *kiss*. I'd almost gotten used to the practice. I leaned, watching for the moment she'd usually close her eyes.

Instead, the instant I got my face level with hers, she stepped backward, pulling me with her.

And then we were falling. Or something like falling. Where was the cliff? How hadn't I seen it? I wondered what would happen if I threw up, as my stomach threatened to do ...

Until we weren't falling, but walking again, on soft grass, not rocks. A smoothed slope led uphill to what might be a ledge. Heyliannin was already on the move again, striding through the grass. "Come on, let's make sure."

I followed, but looked around me at the same time. The mountains were gone. Or—not that—*my* mountains were gone. In place of them: other mountains, similar in some respects, but different in others. Mostly, these were smaller, tamer, not as sharp-edged. Older? Or younger? What did anybody know about the lives of mountains? Heyliannin seemed to think our worlds were hardly different except for the people in them.

She was wrong. If whole mountain ranges were different, then there was more to it than social structures and legal systems.

Ignoring the vastly-changed landscape, Heyliannin climbed rapidly and made the ledge first. That surface had been paved over in a smoothed, blackened layer of rock. The shelf curved around the mountainside, vanishing from sight in both directions. I wondered how far it went and why they'd do such a thing in an uninhabited area. She told me it went—I'm sure she was having me on—hundreds of miles, and that it was a road, like the one we followed to Koresh, only better. She pointed a little way ahead, to something resembling an oversized road marker. It blared something in giant white letters on a green background. "Look. Miner's Campground."

I started to follow her, but she stopped me with a hand to my chest. "Leave this to me. You stay out of sight." She slipped the mantle off her shoulders and handed it to me while she doffed her pack as well, then spread the creature over her pack. "There. I don't look too weird, now, do I?"

"You look fine to me." I focused on the sign. "What if the miners give you trouble?"

"There aren't any miners. It's a place-name for a campsite. Where my people camped, when I was here before."

She seemed certain she knew the place. But was she making another error, like about where the mantles came from? "How can you be sure this is the place? Look—you said this would be barely different from my world. Can't you see?" I swept my arm out to the view. "The mountains are completely different. This place is too different from where we came from."

I could see her wavering, and pushed a little harder. "You have to stay safe, Ta-ma. Don't take chances."

I'd gone too far. She flicked her hair over her shoulders and stood straight. "I'm not taking chances. This is fine. Trust me, Corren. You're the one scary thing here."

I fingered the hilt of my sword. "Something goes wrong, you'd better scream loud."

That made her laugh, which didn't make me feel any better. There I stood, hiding behind trees and bushes, guarding our packs, while she vanished down an offshoot of the paved roadway.

I was about to march down there and fetch her back when she finally emerged, running. I drew my sword and looked for pursuers. "What's wrong?"

She slapped my sword-arm down. "Nothing. I'm in a hurry. They're going to give me a ride."

"Who? A ride where?" That old gut-ache of mine announced itself. I'd thought we'd spend a day or two together, before she stepped through her thin patch. But here we were, both of us, on the wrong side of it.

"There's a nice family, stopped for a picnic. I told them my ride hadn't shown up, and asked if they could call me an *oober*—a ride, but they said they'd take me down the hill. They're on their way home anyhow."

"What about the scary guy with the sword?"

"I told them I needed to run and get my gear from my campsite. Let's leave my pack here. We'll walk you through the thin patch. Then I'll run back. They're still eating. They said they'd wait." She flung the cape over her shoulders and started down the slope.

I had a vision of her tripping over a rock and falling, and I jogged after her. Halfway down, she stopped and raced back up to dredge in her bag. She ran back down even faster than the first time. "Here. You keep this." She thrust a bundle into my hands.

The tayablett. Wrapped in its soft, protective cover.

I held it out to her. "You need this, don't you? There's notes, information the snake-men gave you."

She winced. "*Korlovians*, husband-of-mine. There's nothing I need that I didn't memorize years ago, Corren. I didn't expect the tayablett to last this long. Keep it for me, oh-kayy?"

All that dumped into my head at once kept me confused enough I didn't get too sick the second time through the thin patch. So she wasn't casting me off. Calling me *husband* meant she intended to come back. Didn't it?

I breathed in the bitter air of our own, true mountains, the Wall that divided us from the mysterious redlands. The tayablett felt like a block of ice in my hands, heavy, fragile, maybe dangerous. "What about your priyyam drectiff?"

"That river's been crossed, Corren. Don't you think?"

"Ya, ya." I crouched to tuck the thing into my own pack, shifting around a few items to get it settled. I had a feeling she'd judge me badly if I didn't keep it safe while she was gone.

"Isn't it a stroke of luck?" She beamed at me, and the sun setting over my shoulder made her skin glow. "If we'd followed Tymon's map the way he drew it, we'd never have found our way." She reached for me, and I gave her the good-bye she wanted, and didn't make any jokes about kissing, like I normally would.

Then it was my turn, and I pulled her in close and pressed my face into her hair, to remember the smell of her, the way her heart beat in time with mine. We were a patch of warmth in the cold, as the sun slipped towards the horizon.

She stepped back. "I'd better go."

The mantle swirled around her knees as she spun around and faced the thin patch alone.

In two steps, she became a shadow. In three, she was gone.

PART V

REMEMBER WHERE YOU STAND

48

S O, YOU SEE HOW IT WAS. All I'd needed to do, to keep her with me, would have been to keep to the map, never stray from the path. Neither of us would ever have known.

I'd never have had to tell this story.

But then again …

Listen.

There's another world, isn't there? One where none of what I've told here happened.

If you think about it, you might wonder if you've come to the right world, if you're talking to the man you think I am. With the tiniest of errors in your thin-patch traveling machine, you could find yourself in a place that looks the same, with the same land shapes, same kinds of people and animals, even many of the same individuals.

Ask yourself that question, when you think about my story.

Which tale is truer? The one I've just told, or the one I'd rather tell, the one nobody remembers?

•   •   •

In the unremembered world I'm thinking of, on the day Orkast sold me off, the battered boy didn't comfort me. He saw my anger and respected it. He kept to his place and let me be. Later, I crept down the row of cots, worked the latch free and ran to my father. Orkast had already paid his apprenticeship fees, but he made up the funds by selling me instead to the northern smith who'd bought his shop. Once I'd worked off the debt, I signed up for the Guard.

You'd have to jump through a lot of thin patches to find a world where I didn't become a guardsman.

In that world, I retired early. I made it up to captain, but Orkast was right—a man needs to make a life after soldiering. My wife runs the Inn at the Crossroads, up in Heart's Bend, where eventually everyone passes through. I'm at her beck and call nine days out of seven.

One fine summer day, in our place's public room, my Six are gathered—no, why not, make it my Eight, with Keev and Shellon acting out the tale of how they stood back-to-back at NeverSnows and cut down more mercenaries than even Kul. Any minute now, they'll be standing on the table.

I dodge thrusting arms and duck under the ghosts of remembered blades. They make a game of interfering as I slide plates onto the table and refill their mugs. Eldennian will be after me to have them quiet down, but I'll let them go on until she catches my elbow and pulls me to the office behind the bar and reminds me who gives the orders in this place.

Our girl Delia walks in on us and howls to wait for evening why don't we and aren't we too old for all that, before she snatches her apron off the wall and heads out to keep the bar.

When I get back to work myself, Delia's leaning over the bar telling jokes to that rabble-rouser from up north, the one who's always after our governor to hold back a share of the taxes and spend the money on a home for runaway kids. Calestinise had been one of those, on account of how they treat a girl-looking boy up north, so that gives him a reason, but does he need to be so noisy about his politics right here in my bar?

The Eight have settled down to eat the meal they ordered. They lean back, make satisfied noises, and compare notes on families and work. There's a moment they all go silent at once, which makes me look up from wiping down tables.

An odd-looking woman's at the door. Odd in two ways, one that she looks ill or has a skin condition that keeps her out of the sun. The other oddity is she's wearing a shaman's cape. Could be she's a woman-looking man, but it doesn't seem so, given she's wearing women's clothes, the drabbest grey stuff you ever saw, but none of it hiding her woman-ness.

Women can't be shamans. Can they?

Then again, we're an inn and public house, and anyone's a customer until they make themselves a problem. I give her my best table, one with a view out to the wide plaza in front of the Governor's House, and a bit far from Calestinise, so she needn't be distracted by his politicking.

"If you don't mind my asking," I say, while Delia draws a tall cider for our new guest. "you're a shaman, aren't you?"

She makes a weird gesture, holding her hand flat and waggling it side to side. "More or less. Don't hold much with the mumbling and dancing, but, yes, I travel, I do." She seems to be waiting for me to react to that near-heresy.

I choose to jab her thoughts a little. "You walk through the thin patches?"

She draws in a quick breath and looks straight into my eyes, a forceful, demanding stare. "What do you know of such things?"

"My father was a shaman, a long time ago." She seems to accept that, and I hurry to the bar to collect her drink and a plate of fried frog-legs. "On the house," I tell her. "Just in from Lakeside. They're the latest thing."

She gives them a try, but sends the plate over to my friends in the corner. Should have guessed from the clothes she'd be a northerner, with pedestrian tastes. I choose from the menu for her, something less adventurous—ironical, I suppose, a shaman preferring mundane fare.

She doesn't seem inclined to move on, and I've worked enough today, so I pull up a chair and make friends. Seems she's a new assignee at the tiny Shamans' House of Heart's Bend. Never hurts to have a friend in the brotherhood. Or is it a sisterhood now?

I was always good at an interrogation. After another drink, well, a few drinks, and a few remarks from my old friends, and a swat with a towel from Eldennian, I work the shaman's story out of her.

She's not from the north, no, she's from the other side of a thin patch. She met one of our shamans there. He helped her out, she says, brought her through the thin patch to our world, to keep her safe from some hazard. He was planning to go for help, because he was worried the danger might follow them through the thin patch, put all of our country at risk. But suddenly, unexpectedly, he died. There she was, alone in a strange world, with nothing but a shaman's mantle and no idea how to use it.

She found her way to civilization after a long time of wandering in the mountains—all this happened somewhere up on the Wall, where the redlanders are someday going to attack us from. Or not. It's only ever been rumors.

She had to learn our language, start her life over, and fight to keep hold of the mantle, when everyone told her she couldn't have it.

All this time, though, she's been looking for two things: the way home to her own world, and the man the shaman was going to go see, to protect this world from hers. She wandered so much, she has no idea where that thin patch is, the one she came through. The shaman had told her his son would bring defenders, because his son was a soldier, and he had gone on at length as to how much she'd like his son.

Word by word, as the story falls from her lips, the drink I've taken in dissipates to nothingness, my head rings with clarity.

"You'd have thought he was trying to arrange a marriage," she laughs. "Imagine! Me? Married?"

My tongue feels like it belongs in someone else's head. I'm saying words, but not sure what they mean. "Do you remember the shaman's name?"

"He never told me." She does remember him, though, the way you remember a person you've thought about a lot. She describes him in deep detail—his big, sharp-edged nose, like mine, his muscular arms, the way he smiled more on one side than the other, because he didn't want to show off the tooth that got chipped when a piece he was working fragmented under his hammer. I let her ramble on, building up a picture of my father, the widowed armorer who sold off all he had to become a shaman and maybe find his dead wife somewhere on the Other Side.

Instead, seems he thought he'd found a wife for his abandoned son.

"His name was Orkast," I tell her. If she remembers him that well, she deserves to know.

"What?" She looks up abruptly, sloshing her drink. "What did you say?"

"You're talking about my father, Orkast. He went out looking for thin patches one time, and never came home. No one ever knew what happened."

"Your father?"

"Yes, Orkast of the Shamans' House in Jeskaryan."

"You're him? You're Corrryn?" It stirs something in me, the way she imitates the burr in my father's voice, the rough flavor of the way he said my name. I can't seem to answer, though. Whatever controls my mouth isn't working right now. I feel as though someone's splashed soup on my face, so I get up and find a towel. Then I figure out what's going on, and I go find Eldennian, so there'll be someone to tell me when I've done crying.

The shaman's still there when I come back. She's not drinking fast, but steady, waiting out the day, maybe waiting for me. I can't tell. I stop by to collect the glasses she's done with and to tell her, "Thank you."

I've passed off another load of dirty dishes to the lad in the kitchen, the one I call Stevvin for no good reason—as it's not his name, it just suits him—when the door thumps open.

A tall, stiff military type steps through. He's not in uniform, but like knows like. Maybe he's retired. He scans the room, then goes back out. A moment later, the toff he's been set to bodyguard comes in. I've seen it before—those rich men who need a sense of security but still want to mingle with the lower classes.

My shaman friend has the best table, but I'm not moving her for some toff. I offer my second-best table as the ideal spot, but he can tell I'm putting him on. He has his eyes on the shaman the whole time I'm taking his order: cider—light—and a plate of crunchy frog.

I forget the sauce for the side dish, but he doesn't complain about the delay when most of his kind would make a fuss. Maybe I've misjudged. There's something about this guy—a warmth, a depth you don't normally see with the high-born. He's around my age, no youngster, but not old yet. Not like I am, in this world.

He has the long, lean form that would have made him a good runner, but you can also see the lines of hardship on him. A rough childhood, I'd guess, cruelties borne and survived, to win to adulthood working a job with a lot of responsibility. As a guardsman, I've spent time around such men, the ones who take governing seriously, who make the work of a guardsman worthwhile.

I can tell the shaman is watching him back.

He can see it, too. He gets up and turns to call out an order to me, where I'm standing at the bar.

Calestinise, the cheapskate, who's been nursing that one drink this whole time, looks at him and falls off his stool. It makes a horrific clatter, and the toff bursts into laughter. It's not mocking laughter. It's delighted, happy, as if what he'd come for today was to find one thing to take his mind off something troubling, and an earnest do-gooder falling off a chair did the trick.

That gets everyone else laughing, because everyone knows Calestinise, and we all know that falling off anything is about the least likely thing for him to do. I'm expecting him to be insulted—he can get obnoxious, then, but he's not angry this time. He's … I can't tell what. When I reach to help him back to his feet, he pulls me close, so I can't avoid seeing for the thousandth time his incongruously charming features. "It's the king!" he hisses in my ear.

"What is?"

"The guy. The one talking with your lady shaman."

Talking with? Yes, he's settling down across the table from the woman who took up my father's cause, who fulfilled the mission Orkast gave her, even though it took years and years.

"Him? Our king? How would you know him?"

"Seen him. I told you. Went down and spoke at the council, about my project, looking for money." He had done that, I remember. Nothing scares this crazy man when he's on a mission.

"You're sure." I'm still scrunched up close to Calestinise. It feels ridiculous, but we're whispering so soft I'd never hear him otherwise.

The two of them sit there a long time, talking. Their eyes meet in that way I've seen a lot of eyes meet, here in this tavern, a way that sells us out of rooms sometimes. I'm wondering what kind of story this is going to make.

My friends will attest it's true, that this really happened.

He's come among us, to be our friend for this little while, our own good king, Tymon of Jeska.

ABOUT THE AUTHOR

Vanessa MacLaren-Wray writes science fiction and fantasy about people—human and otherwise—trying to communicate and form attachments in a complex universe. She's the author of the Patchwork Universe series, including *All That Was Asked*, *Shadows of Insurrection*, and *Flames of Attrition*, as well as the prequel story "The True Son." She's also a member of the Truck Stop at the Center of the Galaxy consortium, with "Coke Machine" and *The Smugglers*. Her short fiction has appeared with Dragon Gems and in the award-winning anthology *Fault Zone: Reverse*.

As an engineer, she has analyzed electric power systems, studied climate-safe technology, and written extensively on energy issues. She feels lucky to live in farm country, where fields of strawberries and artichokes hold the developers at bay. When not arguing with her cats, she works on new stories and her email journal *Messages from the Oort Cloud*.

ALSO IN THIS SERIES

SHADOWS OF INSURRECTION
BOOK ONE OF THE UNREMEMBERED KING

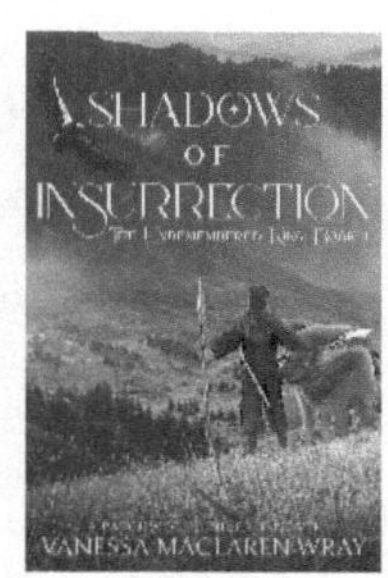

Once in a generation, the matriarchs of Jeska choose a new king to manage the government and command the Guard. But this is an unsettled time: rumors of strange incursions, grumbling discontent, and increasing brigandry.

THE TRUE SON
A STORY OF THE UNREMEMBERED KING

As foster-son to the king, Corren is technically a candidate for the kingship, a position filled only at the discretion of the matriarchs of Jeska, but he doesn't want the job.

ALL THAT WAS ASKED
A PATCHWORK UNIVERSE NOVEL

For the wild beast…freedom, even from compassion. For the person … all that is asked.

– from the Physician's Oath

Available from Water Dragon Publishing in
hardcover, trade paperback, and digital editions
waterdragonpublishing.com

ALSO BY THE AUTHOR

COKE MACHINE

FROM THE "TRUCK STOP AT THE CENTER OF THE GALAXY"

Every truck stop needs a coke machine.

PARRISH BLUE

Sallie never expected to discover a world she'd forgotten how to imagine.

THE SMUGGLERS

FROM THE "TRUCK STOP AT THE CENTER OF THE GALAXY"

Attachment is everything.

Available from Water Dragon Publishing in
hardcover, trade paperback, and digital editions
waterdragonpublishing.com

YOU MIGHT ALSO ENJOY

SEEKER
BOOK ONE OF "THE UNWOVEN TAPESTRY"

by Morgan Chalut

Does the need for knowledge balance its burden?

SKY CHASE
BOOK ONE OF "THE FLIGHT OF SHIPS"

by Lauren Massuda

Travel to a vast world of airborne ships and floating islands.

THE DRAGON EATER
BOOK ONE OF THE "THRASSAS CYCLE"

By J. Scott Coatsworth

Raven's a thief who just swallowed a dragon.

Available from Water Dragon Publishing in
hardcover, trade paperback, and digital editions
waterdragonpublishing.com

9 781959 804901